Hired: Mistress

KATHRYN ROSS

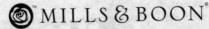

MILLS & BOON

All the characters in this book have no existence outside the imagination of the author, and have no relation whatsoever to anyone bearing the same name or names. They are not even distantly inspired by any individual known or unknown to the author, and all the incidents are pure invention.

First published in Great Britain 2010
Harlequin Mills & Boon Limited,
Eton House, 18-24 Paradise Road, Richmond, Surrey TW9 1SR

HIRED: MISTRESS © by Harlequin Enterprises II B.V./S.à.r.l 2010

Wanted: Mistress and Mother, His Private Mistress and *The Millionaire's Secret Mistress* were first published in Great Britain by Harlequin Mills & Boon Limited in separate, single volumes.

Wanted: Mistress and Mother © The SAL Marinelli Trust Fund 2006
His Private Mistress © Chantelle Shaw 2006
The Millionaire's Secret Mistress © Kathryn Ross 2005

ISBN: 978 0 263 88100 4

05-0410

Printed and bound in Spain
by Litografia Rosés S.A., Barcelona

WANTED: MISTRESS
AND MOTHER

BY
CAROL MARINELLI

Carol Marinelli recently filled in a form where she was asked for her job title and was thrilled, after all these years, to be able to put down her answer as writer. Then it asked what Carol did for relaxation and after chewing her pen for a moment Carol put down the truth – writing. The third question asked – What are your hobbies? Well, not wanting to look obsessed or, worse still, boring, she crossed the fingers on her free hand and answered swimming and tennis, but, given that the chlorine in the pool does terrible things to her highlights and the closest she's got to a tennis racket in the last couple of years is watching the Australian Open – I'm sure you can guess the real answer!

Don't miss Carol Marinelli's exciting new novel,
Knight on the Children's Ward, **available in**
June 2010 from Mills & Boon® Medical™.

CHAPTER ONE

INAPPROPRIATE.

It was the first word that sprang to mind as dark, clearly irritated eyes swung round to face her, black eyes that stared down at Matilda, scrutinising her face unashamedly, making her acutely aware of her—for once—expertly made-up face. The vivid pink lipstick the beautician had insisted on to add a splash of colour to her newly straightened ash blonde hair and porcelain complexion seemed to suddenly render her mouth immovable, as, rather than slowing down to assist, the man she had asked for directions had instead, after a brief angry glance, picked up speed and carried on walking.

Inappropriate, because generally when you stopped someone to ask for directions, especially in a hospital, you expected to be greeted with a courteous nod or smile, for the person to actually slow down, instead of striding ahead and glaring back at you with an angry question of their own.

'Where?'

Even though he uttered just a single word, the thick, clipped accent told Matilda that English wasn't this man's first language. Matilda's annoyance at this response was doused a touch. Perhaps he was in the hospital to visit a sick relative, had just flown in to Australia from… In that split second her mind worked rapidly, trying to place him—his appearance was Mediterranean, Spanish or Greek perhaps, or maybe…

'Where is it you want to go?' he barked, finally deigning to slow down a fraction, the few extra words allowing Matilda to place his strong accent—he was Italian!

'I wanted to know how to find the function room,' she said slowly, repeating the question she had already asked, berating her luck that the only person walking through the maze of the hospital administration corridors spoke little English. That the tall, imposing man she had had to resort to for directions was blatantly annoyed at the intrusion. 'I'm trying to get there for the opening of the hospital garden. I'm supposed to be there in…' She glanced down at her watch and let out a sigh of exasperation. 'Actually, I was supposed to be there five minutes ago.'

'*Merda!*' As he glanced at his watch the curse that escaped his lips, though in Italian, wasn't, Matilda assumed, particularly complimentary, and abruptly stepping back she gave a wide-eyed look, before turning smartly on her heel and heading off to find her own way. He'd made it exceptionally clear that her request for assistance had been intrusive but now he was being downright rude. She certainly wasn't going to stand around and wait for the translation—she'd find the blessed function room on her own!

'I'm sorry.' He caught up with her in two long strides,

CAROL MARINELLI 9

but Matilda marched on, this angry package of testosterone the very last thing she needed this morning.

'No, I'm sorry to have disturbed you,' Matilda called back over her shoulder, pushing the button—any button—on the lift and hoping to get the hell out of there. 'You're clearly busy.'

'I was cursing myself, not you.' He gave a tiny grimace, shrugged very wide shoulders in apology, which sweetened the explanation somewhat, and Matilda made a mental correction. His English was, in fact, excellent. It was just his accent that was incredibly strong—deep and heavy, and, Matilda reluctantly noted, incredibly sensual. 'I too am supposed to be at the garden opening, I completely forgot that they'd moved the time forward. My secretary has decided to take maternity leave.'

'How inconsiderate of her!' Matilda murmured under her breath, before stepping inside as the lift slid open.

'Pardon?'

Beating back a blush, Matilda stared fixedly ahead, unfortunately having to wait for him to press the button, as she was still none the wiser as to where the function room was.

'I didn't quite catch what you said,' he persisted.

'I didn't say anything,' Matilda lied, wishing the floor would open up and swallow her, or, at the very least, the blessed lift would get moving. There was something daunting about him, something incredibly confronting about his manner, his voice, his eyes, something very *inappropriate*.

There was that word again, only this time it had

nothing to do with his earlier rude response and everything to do with Matilda's as she watched dark, olive-skinned hands punching in the floor number, revealing a flash of an undoubtedly expensive gold watch under heavy white cotton shirt cuffs. The scent of his bitter, tangy aftershave was wafting over towards her in the confined space and stinging into her nostrils as she reluctantly dragged in his supremely male scent. Stealing a sideways glance, for the first time Matilda looked at him properly and pieced together the features she had so far only glimpsed.

He was astonishingly good-looking.

The internal admission jolted her—since her break-up with Edward she hadn't so much as looked at a man—certainly she hadn't looked at a man in *that* way. The day she'd ended their relationship, like bandit screens shooting up at the bank counter, it had been as if her hormones had been switched off. Well, perhaps not off, but even simmering would be an exaggeration—the hormonal pot had been moved to the edge of the tiniest gas ring and was being kept in a state of tepid indifference: utterly jaded and completely immune.

Till now!

Never had she seen someone so exquisitely beautiful close up. It was as if some skilled photographer had taken his magic wand and airbrushed the man from the tip of his ebony hair right down to the soft leather of his expensively shod toes. He seemed vaguely familiar—and she tried over and over to place that swarthy, good-looking face, sure that she must have seen him on the

TV screen because, if she'd witnessed him in the flesh, Matilda knew she would have remembered the occasion.

God, it was hot.

Fiddling with the neckline of her blouse, Matilda dragged her eyes away and willed the lift to move faster, only realising she'd been holding her breath when thankfully the doors slid open and she released it in a grateful sigh, as in a surprisingly gentlemanly move he stepped aside, gesturing for her to go first. But Matilda wished he'd been as rude on the fourth floor as he had been on the ground, wished, as she teetered along the carpeted floor of the administration wing in unfamiliar high heels, that she was walking behind instead of ahead of this menacing stranger, positive, absolutely positive that those black eyes were assessing her from a male perspective, excruciatingly aware of his eyes burning into her shoulders. She could almost feel the heat emanating from them as they dragged lower down to the rather too short second half of her smart, terribly new charcoal suit. And if legs could have blushed, then Matilda's were glowing as she felt his burning gaze on calves that were encased in the sheerest of stockings.

'Oh!' Staring at the notice-board, she bristled as he hovered over her shoulder, reading with growing indignation the words beneath the hastily drawn black arrow. 'The opening's been moved to the rooftop.'

'Which makes more sense,' he drawled, raising a curious, perfectly arched eyebrow at her obvious annoyance, before following the arrow to a different set of lifts. 'Given that it is the rooftop garden that's being officially opened today and not the function room.'

'Yes, but…' Swallowing her words, Matilda followed him along the corridor. The fact she'd been arguing for the last month for the speeches to be held in the garden and not in some bland function room had nothing to do with this man. Admin had decided that a brief champagne reception and speeches would be held here, followed by a smooth transition to the rooftop where Hugh Keller, CEO, would cut the ribbon.

The logistics of bundling more than a hundred people, in varying degrees of health, into a couple of lifts hadn't appeared to faze anyone except Matilda—until now.

But her irritation was short-lived, replaced almost immediately by the same flutter of nerves that had assailed her only moments before, her palms moist as she clenched her fingers into a fist, chewing nervously on her bottom lip as the lift doors again pinged open.

She didn't want to go in.

Didn't want that disquieting, claustrophobic feeling to assail her again. She almost turned and ran, her mind whirring for excuses—a quick dash to the loo perhaps, a phone call she simply had to make—but an impatient foot was tapping, fingers pressing the hold button, and given that she was already horribly late, Matilda had no choice.

Inadeguato.

As she stepped in hesitantly beside him, the word taunted him.

Inadeguato—to be feeling like this, to be *thinking* like this.

Dante could almost smell the arousal in the air as the doors closed and the lift jolted upwards. But it wasn't just her heady, feminine fragrance that reached him as he stood there, more the presence of her, the… He struggled for a word to describe his feelings for this delectable stranger, but even with two languages at his disposal, an attempt to sum up what he felt in a single word utterly failed him.

She was divine.

That was a start at least—pale blonde hair was sleeked back from an elfin face, vivid green eyes were surrounded by thick eyelashes and that awful lipstick she'd been wearing only moments ago had been nibbled away now—revealing dark, full red lips, lips that were almost too plump for her delicate face, and Dante found himself wondering if she'd had some work done on herself, for not a single line marred her pale features, her delicate, slightly snubbed nose absolutely in proportion to her petite features. She was certainly a woman who took care of herself. Her eyes were heavily made up, her hair fragranced and glossy—clearly the sort of woman who spent a lot of time in the beauty parlour. Perhaps a few jabs of collagen had plumped those delicious lips to kissable proportions, maybe a few units of Botox had smoothed the lines on her forehead, Dante thought as he found himself scrutinising her face more closely than he had a woman's in a long time.

A very long time.

He knew that it was wrong to be staring, *inadeguato* to be feeling this stir of lust for a woman he had never met, a woman whose name he didn't even know.

A woman who wasn't his wife.

The lift shuddered, and he saw her brow squiggle into

a frown, white teeth working her lips as the lift shuddered to a halt, and Dante's Botox theory went sailing out of the absent window!

'We're stuck!' Startled eyes turned to him as the lift jolted and shuddered to a halt, nervous fingers reaching urgently for the panel of buttons, but Dante was too quick for her, his hand closing around hers, pulling her finger back from hitting the panic button.

She felt as if she'd been branded—senses that had been on high alert since she'd first seen him screeched into overdrive, her own internal panic button ringing loudly now as his flesh closed around hers, the impact of his touch sending her into a spin, the dry, hot sensation of his fingers tightening around hers alarming her way more than the jolting lift.

'We are not stuck. This lift sometimes sticks here… see!' His fingers loosened from hers and as the lift shuddered back into life, for the first time Matilda noticed the gold band around his ring finger and it both disappointed and reassured her. The simple ring told her that this raw, testosterone-laden package of masculinity was already well and truly spoken for and suddenly Matilda felt foolish, not just for her rather pathetic reaction to the lift halting but for the intense feelings he had so easily evoked. She gave an apologetic grimace.

'Sorry. I'm just anxious to get there!'

'You seem tense.'

'Because I *am* tense,' Matilda admitted. The knowledge that he was married allowed her to let down her guard a touch now, sure in her own mind she had completely misread things, that the explosive reaction to him hadn't been in the least bit mutual, almost convincing herself that it was nerves about the opening that had set her on such a knife edge. Realising the ambiguity of her statement, Matilda elaborated. 'I hate this type of thing—' she started, but he jumped in, actually nodding in agreement.

'Me, too,' he said. 'There are maybe a hundred places I have to be this morning and instead I will be standing in some *stupido* garden on the top of a hospital roof, telling people how happy I am to be there…'

'*Stupid*?' Matilda's eyes narrowed at his response, anger bristling in her as he, albeit unwittingly, derided the months of painstaking work she had put into the garden they were heading up to. 'You think the garden is stupid?' Appalled, she swung around to confront him, realising he probably didn't know that she was the designer of the garden. But that wasn't the point—he had no idea who he was talking to, had spouted his arrogant opinion with no thought to who might hear it, no thought at all. But Dante was saved from her stinging response by the lift doors opening.

'Don't worry. Hopefully it won't take too long and we can quickly be out of there.' He rolled his eyes, probably expecting a sympathetic response, probably expecting a smooth departure from this meaningless, fleeting meeting, but Matilda was running behind him, tapping him smartly on the shoulder.

'Have you any idea the amount of work that goes into creating a garden like this?'

'No,' he answered rudely. 'But I know down to the last cent what it cost and, frankly, I can think of many more important things the hospital could have spent its money on.'

They were walking quickly, too quickly really for Matilda, but rage spurred her to keep up with him. 'People will get a lot of pleasure from this garden—sick people,' she added for effect, but clearly unmoved he just shrugged.

'Maybe,' he admitted, 'but if I were ill, I'd far rather that the latest equipment was monitoring me than have the knowledge that a garden was awaiting, if I ever made it up there.'

'You're missing the point…'

'I didn't realise there was one,' he frowned. 'I'm merely expressing an opinion and, given that it's mostly my money that paid for this "reflective garden", I happen to think I am entitled to one.'

'Your money?'

'My firm's.' He nodded, revealing little but at least allowing Matilda to discount the movie-star theory! 'Initially I was opposed when I heard what the hospital intended spending the donation on, but then some novice put in such a ridiculously low tender, I decided to let it go ahead. No doubt the landscape firm is now declaring bankruptcy, but at the end of the day the hospital has its garden and I appear a man of the people.' All this was said in superior tones with a thick accent so that Matilda was a second or two behind the conversation, blinking angrily as each word was deciphered and finally hit its mark. 'Never look a gift pony in the mouth.'

'Horse,' she retorted as she followed this impossible, obnoxious man up the disabled ramp that she had had installed to replace the three concrete steps and opened the small door that led onto the rooftop. 'The saying is never look a gift horse…' Her words petered out, the anger that fizzed inside, the nerves that had assailed her all morning fading as she stepped outside.

Outside into what she, Matilda Hamilton, had created.

The barren, concrete landscape of the hospital roof had become available when the helipad had been relocated to the newly built emergency department the previous year. The hospital had advertised in the newspaper, inviting tenders to transform the nondescript area into a retreat for patients, staff and relatives. A landscape designer by trade, most of her work to that point had been courtesy of her fiancé, Edward—a prominent real estate agent whose wealthy clients were only too happy to part with generous sums of money in order to bolster their properties prior to sale, or to transform Nana's neglected garden into a small oasis prior to an executor's auction. But as their relationship had steadily deteriorated, Matilda's desire to make it on her own had steadily increased. Despite Edwards's negativity and scorn, she'd registered a business name and duly made an appointment to take measurements of the rooftop and start her plans. Though she hadn't expected to make it past the first round, the second she had stepped onto the roof, excitement had taken over. It was as if she could *see* how it should be, could envision this dry, bland area transformed—endless potted trees supplying wind breaks and shade decorated with fairy lights to make it magical at night, cobbled paths where patients could meander and find their own space for reflection, mosaic tables filled with colour, messages of hope and inspiration adorning them like the stained-glass windows of a church where families could sit and share a coffee.

And water features!

Matilda's signature pieces were definitely in the plural—the gentle sound of running water audible at every turn, blocking out the hum of traffic or nearby people to enable peace or a private conversation. Hugh Keller had listened as she'd painted her vision with words, her hands flailing like windmills as she'd invited him into her mind's eye, described in minute detail the image she could so clearly see—a centre piece of water jets, shooting from the ground at various, random intervals, catching the sun and the colour from the garden—a centre piece where the elderly could sit and watch and children could play. And now that vision was finally a reality. In just a few moments' time, when Hugh cut the ribbon, the water features would be turned on and the garden declared open for all to enjoy!

'Matilda!' From all angles her name was being called and Matilda was glad for her momentary popularity—glad for the excuse to slip away from the man she'd walked in with. Not that he'd notice, Matilda thought, accepting congratulations and a welcome glass of champagne, but cross with herself that on this, perhaps the most important day of her life, a day when she should be making contacts, focusing on her achievement, instead she was recalling the brief encounter that had literally left her breathless, her mind drifting from the vitally important to the completely irrelevant.

He'd been nothing but rude, Matilda reminded herself firmly, smiling as Hugh waved through the crowd and made his way over towards her.

Very rude, Matilda reiterated to herself—good-looking he may be, impossibly sexy even, but he was obnoxious and—

'Hi, Hugh.' Matilda kissed the elderly gentleman on the cheek and dragged her mind back to the important event that was taking place. She listened intently as Hugh briefed her on the order of the speeches and part she would take in the day's events, but somewhere between Hugh reminding her to thank the mayor and the various sponsors Matilda's mind wandered, along with her eyes—coming to rest on that haughty profile that had both inflamed and enraged her since the moment of impact. Watching a man who stood a foot above a dignified crowd, engaged in conversation yet somehow remaining aloof, somehow standing apart from the rest.

And maybe he sensed he was being watched, perhaps it was her longing that made him turn around, but suddenly he was looking at her, making her feel just as he had a few moments ago in the lift, plunging her back to sample again those giddy, confusing sensations he somehow triggered. Suddenly her ability to concentrate on what Hugh was saying was reduced to ADHD proportions, the chatter in the garden fading into a distant hum as he blatantly held her gaze, just stared directly back at her as with cheeks darkening she boldly did the same. Although the sensible part of her mind was telling her to terminate things, to tear her eyes away, turn her back on him, halt this here and now, somehow she switched her internal remote to mute, somehow she tuned out the warnings and focused instead on the delicious picture.

'Once things calm down, hopefully we can discuss it.' Someone inadvertently knocking her elbow had Matilda snapping back to attention, but way too late to even attempt a recovery, Matilda realised as Hugh gave her a concerned look. 'Are you OK?'

'I'm so sorry, Hugh.' Reaching for her mental remote control, Matilda raised the volume, glanced at the gold band on the stranger's ring finger and, pointedly turning her back, flashed a genuinely apologetic smile. 'I really am. I completely missed that last bit of what you said. I'm a bundle of nerves at the moment, checking out that everything's looking OK…'

'Everything's looking wonderful, Matilda,' Hugh soothed, making her feel even guiltier! 'You've done an amazing job. I can't believe the transformation—just a bare old helipad and rooftop and now it's this oasis. Everyone who's been up here, from porters to consultants, has raved about it. I'm just glad it's finally going to be open for the people who really deserve to enjoy it: the patients and relatives.'

'Me, too.' Matilda smiled. 'So, what was it you wanted to discuss, Hugh?'

'A job.' Hugh smiled. 'Though I hear you're rather in demand these days.'

'Only thanks to you,' Matilda admitted. 'What sort of job?'

But it was Hugh who was distracted now, smiling at the mayor who was making his way towards them.

'Perhaps we could talk after the speeches—when things have calmed down a bit.'

'Of course.' Matilda nodded. 'I'll look forward to it!' More than Hugh knew. The thought of giving a speech— of facing this crowd, no matter how friendly—had filled her with dread for weeks now. The *business* side of running a business was really not her forte, but she'd done her best to look the part: had been to the beautician's and had her hair and make-up done—her hair today was neatly put up instead of thrown into a ponytail, expensive foundation replacing the usual slick of sun block and mascara. And the shorts, T-shirts and beloved Blundstone boots, which were her usual fare, had been replaced with a snappy little suit and painfully high heels. As the dreaded speeches started, Matilda stood with mounting heart rate and a very fixed smile, listening in suicidal despair as all her carefully thought-out lines and supposedly random thoughts were one by one used by the speakers that came before her. Tossing the little cards she had so carefully prepared into her—*new*—handbag, Matilda took to the microphone, smile firmly in place as Hugh adjusted it to her rather small height and the PA system shrieked in protest. Staring back at the mixture of curious and bored faces, only one really captured her, and she awaited his reaction—wondered how he would respond when he realised who he had insulted. But he wasn't even looking—his attention held by some ravishing brunette who was blatantly flirting with him. Flicking her eyes away, Matilda embarked on the first speech in her adult life, carefully thanking the people Hugh had mentioned before taking a deep breath and dragging in the heady fragrance of springtime and, as she always did, drawing strength from it.

'When I first met Hugh to discuss the garden, it was very clear that the hospital wanted a place that would provide respite,' Matilda started. 'A place where people could come and find if not peace then somewhere where they could gather their thoughts or even just take a breath that didn't smell of hospitals.' A few knowing nods from the crowd told her she was on the right track. 'With the help of many, many people, I think we've been able to provide that. Hospitals can be stressful places, not just for the patients and relatives but for the staff also, and my aim when I took on this job was to create an area void of signs and directions and overhead loud-speakers, a place where people could forget for a little while all that was going on beneath them, and hopefully that's been achieved.'

There were probably a million and one other things she could have said, no doubt someone else who needed to be thanked, but glancing out beyond the crowd, seeing the garden that had lived only in her mind's eye alive and vibrant, Matilda decided it was time to let Mother Nature speak for herself, to wrap up the speeches and let the crowd explore the haven she had tried so hard to create. She summed up with one heartfelt word.

'Enjoy!'

As Hugh cut the ribbon and the water jets danced into life, thin ribbons of water leaping into the air and catching the sunlight, Matilda felt a surge of pride at the oohs of the crowd and the excited shrieks of the children, doing just as she had intended: getting thoroughly wet and laughing as they did so. Only there was one child that didn't join in with the giggling and running, one little toddler who stood perfectly still, staring transfixed at the jets of water with huge solemn eyes, blonde curls framing her face. For some reason Matilda found herself staring, found herself almost willing the little girl to run and dance with the others, to see expression in that little frozen face.

'It's pretty, isn't it?' Crouching down beside her, Matilda held one of her hands out, breaking the stream of one of the jets, the cool water running through her fingers. 'You can touch it,' Matilda said, watching as slowly, almost fearfully a little fat hand joined Matilda's. A glimmer of a smile shivered on the little girl's lips, those solemn eyes glittering now as she joined in with the simple pleasure. As she saw Hugh coming over, Matilda found herself strangely reluctant to leave the child, sure that with just another few moments she could have had her running and dancing with the rest of the children.

'My granddaughter, Alex,' Hugh introduced them, crouching down also, but his presence went unnoted by Alex, her attention focused on the water running through her hands. 'She seems to like you.'

'She's adorable.' Matilda smiled, but it wavered on her lips, questions starting to form in her mind as the little girl still just stood there, not moving, not acknowledging the other children or her grandfather, just utterly, utterly lost in her own little world. 'How old is she?'

'Two,' Hugh said standing up, and pulling out a handkerchief, dabbing at his forehead for a moment.

'Are you OK,' Matilda checked, concerned at the slightly grey tinge to his face.

'I'll be fine,' Hugh replied. 'I've just been a bit off colour recently. She's two,' he continued, clearly wanting to change the subject. 'It was as actually Alex that I was hoping to talk to you about.'

'I thought it was a job…' Her voice trailed off, both of their gazes drifting towards the little girl, still standing there motionless. But her face was lit up with a huge smile, utterly entranced at the sight before her though still she didn't join in, she still stood apart, and with a stab of regret Matilda almost guessed what was coming next.

'She's been having some problems,' Hugh said, his voice thick with emotion. 'She was involved in a car accident over a year ago and though initially she appeared unharmed, gradually she's regressed, just re-treated really. She has the most appalling tantrums and outbursts followed by days of silence—the doctors are starting to say that she may be autistic. My wife Katrina and I are frantic…'

'Naturally.' Matilda gave a sympathetic smile, gen-uinely sorry to hear all Hugh was going through. He was a kind, gentle, friendly man, and even though they'd chatted at length over the last few months, he'd never given so much of a hint as to the problems in his personal life. But, then again, Matilda thought with a sigh, neither had she.

'I told my son-in-law last night that my wife and I would like to do this for Alex as a gift. There's a small gated area at the back of his property that I'm sure would be perfect for something like this—not on such a grand scale, of course, just somewhere that doesn't have rocks and walls and a pool…'

'Somewhere safe,' Matilda volunteered.

'Exactly.' Hugh gave a relieved nod. 'Somewhere she can't fall and hurt herself, somewhere she can run around unhindered or just sit and look at something beautiful. Look, I know you're booked up solidly for the next few months, but if one of the jobs gets cancelled could you bear me in mind? I hate to put pressure on you, Matilda, but I saw the joy in the children's faces when they saw the garden today. And if it can help Alex…' His voice trailed off and Matilda knew he wasn't attempting to gain her sympathy, Hugh would never do that. 'My son-in-law thinks that it's just a waste of time, that it isn't gong to help a bit, but at the very least Alex would have a garden that's safe and gives her some pleasure. I'm sure I'll be able to talk him around. At the end of the day he adores Alex—he'd do anything to help her.'

Matilda didn't know what to say—her diary was fill to burst with smart mews townhouses all wanting the inevitable low-maintenance, high-impact garden—but here was the man who had given her the head start, given her this opportunity. And more importantly, Matilda thought, her eyes lingering on Alex, here was a little girl who deserved all the help she could get. Her mind was working overtime—she could almost see the lazy couple of weeks' holiday she'd had planned before plunging into her next job slipping away out of her grasp as she took a deep breath and gave a small smile.

'Hugh, I'd need to get some details and then I'd need to actually see the site before I commit, but I have a couple of weeks off before I start on my next job, and I'm on pretty good terms with a few people. If I called in a few favours maybe I could do it for you. Where does Alex live?'

'Mount Eliza.' Hugh saw her give a small grimace. It had nothing to do with the location—Mount Eliza was a stunning, exclusive location overlooking Port Phillip Bay—but the distance from the city meant that it would cut down Matilda's working day considerably. 'It was their holiday residence before the accident, but since then… Look, would it make it easier if you stayed there? There's plenty of room.'

'I don't think I'd be able to do it otherwise,' Matilda admitted. 'I'll have workers arriving at the crack of dawn and I'm going to need to be there to meet them and show them what I need done.'

'It won't be a problem,' Hugh assured her, and after a moment of deep thought Matilda gave a small nod and then followed it up with a more definite one.

'I'd be happy to do it.'

'You mean it?'

'Of course.' Matilda smiled more widely now, Hugh's obvious delight making her spur-of-the-moment choice easily the right one.

'I feel awful that you won't even get a break.'

'That's what being in business is all about apparently.' Matilda shrugged her shoulders. 'Anyway, I'm sure lean times will come—it won't stay spring for ever and anyway it mightn't be such a big job. I'd be glad to do it, Hugh, but I do need a few more details from you, and you need to get your son-in-law's permission—I can't go digging up his land and planting things if he doesn't want me there in the first place. Now, I need to know the size of the land, any existing structures…' Matilda gave in as yet another group was making its way over, and Hugh's secretary tapped him on the arm to take an important phone call.

'It's impossible to discuss it here.' Hugh gave an apologetic smile. 'And it's probably inappropriate. You should be enjoying the celebrations—perhaps we could do it over dinner tonight. I'll see if my son-in-law can come along—I'm sure once he hears first hand about it he'll be more enthusiastic. Actually, there he is—I'll go and run it by him now.'

'Good idea,' Matilda agreed, crouching down again to play with Alex, her head turning to where Hugh was waving. But the smile died on her face as again she found herself staring at the man who had taken up so much of her mental energy today—watching as he walked around the water feature, a frown on his face as he watched her interact with his daughter.

'Dante!' Clearly not picking up on the tension, Hugh called him over, but Dante didn't acknowledge either of them, his haughty expression only softening when Matilda stepped back, his features softer now as he eyed his daughter. Matilda felt a curious lump swell in her throat as, with infinite tenderness, he knelt down beside Alex, something welling within as he spoke gently to his daughter.

'I'll have a word with Dante and make a booking for

tonight, then,' Hugh checked hopefully—too pleased to notice Matilda's stunned expression. The most she could manage was the briefest of nods as realisation started to dawn.

She'd barely managed two minutes in the lift with him and now she was about to be his house guest!

He's a husband and father, Matilda reminded herself firmly, calming herself down a touch, almost convincing herself she'd imagined the undercurrents that had sizzled between them.

And even if she hadn't misread things, even if there was an attraction between them, he was a married man and she wouldn't forget it for a single moment!

CHAPTER TWO

SHE didn't want to do this.

Walking towards the restaurant, Matilda was tempted to turn on her stiletto heels and run. She *hated* with a passion the formalities that preceded a garden make-over, looking at plans, talking figures, time-frames—and the fact she hadn't even seen the garden made this meeting a complete time-waster. But, Matilda was quickly realizing, this type of thing was becoming more and more frequent. As her business took off, gone were the days where she rolled up on a doorstep in her beloved Blundstone boots, accepted a coffee if she was lucky enough to be offered one and drew a comprehensive sketch of her plans for the owners, along with a quote for her services—only to spend the next few days chewing her nails and wondering if they'd call, worrying if perhaps she'd charged too much or, worse, seriously underquoted and would have to make up the difference herself.

Now her initial meetings took place in people's offices or restaurants, and even if she *was* lucky enough to be invited into their homes, Matilda had quickly learnt that her new clientele expected a smart, efficient professional for that first important encounter.

But it wasn't just the formalities that were causing butterflies this evening. Ducking into the shadowy retreat of a large pillar beside the restaurant, Matilda stopped for a moment, rummaged in her bag and pulled out a small mirror. She touched up her lipstick and fiddled with her hair for a second, acknowledging the *real* reason for anxiety tonight.

Facing Dante.

Even his name made her stomach ball into a knot of tension. She'd wanted him to remain nameless—for that brief, scorching but utterly one-sided encounter to be left at that—to somehow push him to the back of her mind and completely forget about him.

And now she was going to be working for him!

Maybe this dinner was *exactly* what she needed, Matilda consoled herself, peeling herself from the pillar ready to walk the short distance that remained to the restaurant. Maybe a night in his arrogant, obnoxious, pompous company would purge whatever it was that had coursed through her system since she'd laid eyes on him, and anyway, Matilda reassured herself, Hugh was going to be there, too.

An impressive silver car pulling up at the restaurant caught Matilda's attention and as the driver walked around and opened the rear door in a feat of self-preservation she found herself stepping back into the shadows, watching as the dignified figure of Dante stepped out—she had utterly no desire to enter the restaurant with him and attempt small talk until she had the reassuring company of Hugh.

He really was stunning, Matilda sighed, feeling slightly voyeuristic as she watched him walk. Clearly she wasn't the only one who thought so. From the second he'd stepped out of the car, heads had turned, a few people halting their progress to watch as if it were some celebrity arriving on the red carpet. But just as the driver was about to close the car door, just as the doorman greeted him, a piercing shriek emanating from the car had every head turning.

Especially Dante's.

Even from here she could see the tension etched in his face as he walked back towards the car, from where an anxious young woman appeared, holding the furious, livid, rigid body of his daughter. Grateful for the shadows, Matilda watched with something akin to horror as, oblivious to the gathering crowd, he took the terrified child from the woman and attempted to soothe her, holding her angry, unyielding body against his, talking to her in low, soothing tones, capturing her tiny wrists as she attempted to gouge him, her little teeth like those of a feral animal. Matilda had never seen such anger, never witnessed such a paroxysm of rage, could scarcely comprehend that it could come from someone so small.

'That child needs a good smack, if you ask me,' an elderly lady volunteered, even though no one had asked her. Matilda had to swallow down a smart reply, surprising herself at her own anger over such a thoughtless comment—tempted now to step out from the shadows and offer her support, to see if there was anything she could do to help. But almost as soon as it had started it was over. The fight that had fuelled Alex left her, her little body almost slumping in defeat, the shrieks replaced by quiet, shuddering sobs, which were so pain-filled they were almost harder to bear. After a moment more of tender comfort, with a final nod Dante handed her back to the woman, his taut, strained face taking in every detail as the duo headed for the car, before, without deigning to give the crowd a glance, he headed into the restaurant.

Pushing open the door, though shaken from what she had just witnessed, Matilda attempted assurance as her eyes worked the restaurant, her smile ready for Hugh, but as the waiter took her name and guided her towards the table, she was again tempted to turn tail and run.

It was definitely a table for two—but instead of the teddy bear proportions of Hugh, instead of his beaming red face smiling to greet her, she was met by the austere face of Dante, his tall muscular frame standing as she approached, his face expressionless as she crossed the room. If Matilda hadn't witnessed it herself, she'd never have believed what he'd just been through, for nothing in his stance indicated the hellish encounter of only moments before.

In her peripheral vision she was aware of heads turning, but definitely not towards her, could hear flickers of conversation as she walked towards him.

'Is he famous…?'

'He looks familiar…'

He looked familiar because he was perfection—a man that normally glowered from the centre of the glossiest of glossy magazines, a man who should be dressed in nothing more than a ten-thousand-dollar watch or in the driver's seat of a luxury convertible.

He certainly wasn't the type of man that Matilda was used to dining with…

And certainly not alone.

Please, Matilda silently begged, please, let a waiter appear, breathlessly dragging a table over, and preferably, another waiter, too, to hastily turn those two table settings into three. Please, please, let it not be how it looked.

'Matilda.' His manners were perfect, waiting till she was seated before sitting down himself, patiently waiting as she gave her drink order to the waiter. She was pathetically grateful that she'd chosen to walk to the restaurant—no mean feat in her fabulous new shoes, but there was no chance of a punctual taxi this time on a Friday evening, and by the time she'd parked she could have been here anyway.

Good choice.

Good, because she could now order a gin and tonic, and hopefully douse some of the rowdier butterflies that were dancing in her stomach

'Hugh sends his apologies.' Dante gave her a very on-off smile as Matilda frowned. The Hugh she knew would be the last person to have bailed—no matter how important the diversion. After all, he'd practically begged her to do the garden.

'He had a headache after the opening. He didn't look well, so I walked him back to his office where he had…' Dante snapped his fingers, clearly trying to locate his word of choice. 'He had a small turn,' he said finally, as Matilda's expression changed from a frown to one of horror.

'Oh, my goodness…'

'He's OK,' Dante said quickly. 'His blood pressure has been very high for the past few months, the doctors have had him on several different combinations of tablets to try to lower it, but it would seem the one they'd recently given him has brought it down too low— that's why he had a small collapse. Luckily we were in the hospital when it happened—all I had to do was pick up the phone.'

'You're not a doctor, then.'

Dante gave a slightly startled look. 'Heavens, no. What on earth gave you that impression?'

'I don't know,' Matilda shrugged. 'You seemed to know your way around the hospital…'

'I've spent rather too much time there,' Dante said, and Matilda could only assume he was talking about Alex. But he revealed absolutely nothing, promptly diverting the subject from himself back to Hugh. 'He's resting at home now, but naturally he wasn't well enough to come out. Hugh feels terrible to have let you down after you were kind enough to accommodate him at such short notice. I tried many times to contact you on your mobile…'

'My phone isn't on,' Matilda said, flustered. 'I never thought to check.'

Fool, Matilda raged to herself. He'd been frantically trying to cancel, to put her off, and because her blessed phone hadn't been turned on, Dante had been forced to show up and babysit her when he hadn't even wanted her to do the garden in the first place, when clearly he wanted to be at home with his daughter.

Taking a grateful sip of her drink, Matilda eyed the proffered menu, her face burning in uncomfortable embarrassment, utterly aware that here with her was the last place Dante either wanted or needed to be tonight.

'I've agreed to the garden.' Dante broke the difficult silence. 'Hugh said that I had to see you to give my consent. Do I need to sign anything?'

'It isn't a child custody battle.' Matilda looked up and for the first time since she'd joined him at the table actually managed to look him in the eye. 'I don't need your written consent or anything. I just wanted to be sure that you were happy for me to work on your garden.'

'It's not a problem,' Dante said, which was a long way from happy.

'I have brought along the plans for you to look at— I've highlighted the area Hugh discussed with you.' Glancing up, Dante nodded to the waiter who had approached, giving him permission to speak.

'Are you ready to order, sir?'

The waiter hovered as Dante turned to Matilda, but she shook her head.

'Could you give us a minute?' Dante asked and the waiter melted away. Clearly assuming she was out of her depth, he proceeded to walk her through the menu. 'I will be having my usual gnocchi, but I hear that the Tasmanian salmon is excellent here—it's wild—'

'I'm sure it's divine,' Matilda interrupted. 'I do know

how to read a menu, Dante. And there's really no need
to go through the charade of a meal…'

'Charade?'

Matilda resisted rolling her eyes.

'The pretence,' she explained, but Dante interrupted her.

'I do know how to speak English, Matilda.' He
flashed her a tight smile. 'Why do you call it a charade?'

'Because we both know that you don't want the
garden, that you've probably only agreed because
Hugh's unwell…' He opened his mouth to interrupt but
Matilda spoke on. 'You tried to contact me to cancel.
I'm sorry, I never thought to check my phone. So why
don't I save up both an uncomfortable evening? We can
drink up, I'll take the plans and ring tomorrow to arrange
a convenient time to come and look at your property.
There's really no need to make a meal out of it—if
you'll excuse the pun.'

'The pun?'

'The pun.' Matilda bristled then rolled her eyes. 'It's
a saying—let's not make a meal out of things, as in let's
not make a big deal out of it, but given that we were
about to *have* a meal…'

'You made a pun.'

God, why was the English language so complicated at times?

'I did.' Matilda smiled brightly, but it didn't reach her
eyes.

'So you don't want to eat?'

'I don't want to waste your time.' Matilda swallowed
hard, not sure whether to broach the subject that was undoubtedly on both their minds. 'I saw you arrive…'

Taking a gulp of her drink, Matilda waited, waited for his face to colour a touch, for him to admit to the problem he had clearly faced by being here, but again Dante revealed nothing, just left her to stew a moment longer in a very uncomfortable silence. 'Alex seemed very…upset; so I'm sure that dinner is the last thing you need tonight.'

'Alex is often upset,' Dante responded in a matter-of-fact voice, which did nothing to reassure her. 'And given it is already after eight and I haven't stopped all day, dinner is exactly what I need now.' He snapped his fingers for the waiter and barked his short order. 'My usual.'

'Certainly, and, madam…?'

Matilda faltered, desperate to go yet wanting to stay all the same.

'*Madam*?' Dante smiled tightly, making her feel like one.

'The salmon for me. *Please*,' she added pointedly as the waiter took her menu. Then, remembering that as uncomfortable as she might feel, this was, in fact, a business dinner, Matilda attempted an apology. 'I'm sorry if I was rude before,' she said once the waiter had left. 'It's just I got the impression from Hugh that this meeting tonight was the last thing you wanted.'

'Funny, that.' Dante took a long sip of his drink before continuing, 'I got the same impression from Hugh, too…' He smiled at her obvious confusion.

'Why would you think that?' Matilda asked.

'Hugh gave me strict orders not to upset you.' He flashed a very bewitching grin and Matilda found herself smiling back, not so much in response to his smile, more at the mental picture of *anyone* giving this man strict orders about anything. 'He told me that you were booked up months ahead, and that you'd agree to come in and do this job during your annual leave.'

'Yes…' Matilda admitted, 'but—'

'He also told me that you were doing this as a favour because he'd backed your tender, that you felt obliged—'

'Not all obligations are bad,' Matilda broke in, rather more forcibly this time. 'I *did* agree to work on your garden during my holiday and, yes, I *did* feel a certain obligation to Hugh because of the faith he showed in my proposal for the hospital garden, but I can assure you that I was more than happy to do the work.'

'Happy?' Dante gave a disbelieving smile.

'Yes, happy.' Matilda nodded. 'I happen to like my work, Dante. I just want to make sure that you're fine with me being there.'

'I'm fine with it.' Dante gave a short nod.

'Because Hugh's sick?'

'Does it really matter?'

Matilda thought for a moment before answering. 'It does to me,' she said finally. 'And whether it's ego or neurosis, I'd like to think that when I pour my heart and soul into a job at least my efforts will be appreciated. If you and your wife are only doing this to pacify Hugh, then you're doing it for the wrong reasons. To make it effective, I'm going to need a lot of input as to your daughter's likes and dislikes. It needs to be a reflection of her and I'd like to think that it's going to be a place the whole family can enjoy.'

'Fair enough.' Dante gave a tight shrug. 'I admit I do not believe that a garden, however special, can help my daughter, but I am willing to give it a try—I've tried everything else after all…'

'I clearly explained to Hugh that this garden isn't going to be a magical cure for your daughter's problems—it might bring her some peace, some respite, a safe place that could help soothe her…'

'If that were the case…' Dante said slowly and for the first time since she had met him his voice wasn't superior or scathing but distant. Matilda felt a shiver run through her as she heard the pain behind his carefully chosen words. 'It would be more than worth it.'

'Look.' Her voice was softer now. 'Why don't I take the plans and have a look? Then maybe on Sunday I could speak with your wife about Alex…'

'My wife is dead.'

He didn't elaborate, didn't soften it with anything. His voice was clipped and measured, his expression devoid of emotion as he explained his situation, the pain she had witnessed just a second before when he'd spoken about his daughter gone now, as if a safety switch had been pushed, emotion switched off, plunging his features into unreadable darkness as she faltered an apology.

'I had no idea,' Matilda breathed. 'I'm so very sorry.'

He didn't shake his head, didn't wave his hand and say that she couldn't have known… just let her stew in her own embarrassment as their food arrived, raining salt and pepper on his gnocchi until Matilda could take it no more. Excusing herself, she fled to the loo and leaned over the basin, screwing her eyes closed as she relived the conversation.

'Damn, damn damn!' Cursing herself, she relived every insensitive word she'd uttered, then peeped her eyes open and closed them again as a loo flushed and she was forced to fiddle with her lipstick as a fellow diner gave her a curious glace as she washed her hands. Alone again, Matilda stared at her glittering eyes and flushed reflection in the massive gilt-edged mirror and willed her heart to slow down.

She'd apologise again, Matilda decided. She'd march straight out of the bathroom and say that she was sorry. No, she'd leave well alone—after all, she'd done nothing wrong. Of course she'd assumed his wife was alive. He had a child, he wore his wedding ring. She had nothing to apologise for.

So why had she fled? Why didn't she want to go back out there?

'Everything OK?' Dante checked as she slid back into her seat.

'Everything's fine,' Matilda attempted, then gave up on her false bravado and let out a long-held sigh. 'I'm just not very good at this type of thing.'

'What type of thing?'

'Business dinners.' Matilda gave a tight smile. 'Though I should be, given the number that I've been to.'

'I thought that your business was new.'

'It is.' Matilda nodded, taking a drink of her wine before elaborating. 'But my ex-fiancé was a real estate agent…'

'Ouch,' Dante said, and Matilda felt a rather disloyal smile to Edward twitch on her lips.

'He was very good,' Matilda said defensively. 'Incredibly good, actually. He has a real eye for what's needed to make a house sell well. It's thanks to Edward that I got started. If he was selling a deceased estate often it would be neglected, the gardens especially, and I'd come in…'

'And add several zeros to the asking price!' Dante said with a very dry edge, taking the positive spin out of Matilda's speech. She gave a rather glum nod.

'But it wasn't like that at first.'

Dante gave a tight smile. 'It never is.'

'So what do you do?' Matilda asked, chasing her rice with a fork as Dante shredded his bread and dipped it in a side dish of oil and balsamic vinegar, wishing as she always did when she was out that she'd had what he'd had!

'I'm a barrister. My specialty is criminal defence.' Matilda's fork frozen over her fish spoke volumes. 'Ouch!' he offered, when Matilda didn't say anything.

'Double ouch.' Matilda gave a small, tight smile as reality struck. 'Now you come to mention it, I think I know your name…' Matilda took another slug of wine as newspaper reports flashed into her mind, as a lazy Sunday afternoon spent reading the colour supplements a few months ago took on an entirely new meaning. 'Dante Costello—you defended that guy who—'

'Probably,' Dante shrugged.

'But—'

'I defend the indefensible.' Dante was unmoved by her obvious discomfort. 'And I usually win.'

'And I suppose your donation to the hospital was an attempt to soften your rather brutal image.'

'You suppose correctly.' Dante nodded, only this time

his arrogance didn't annoy her—in fact, his rather brutal honesty was surprisingly refreshing. 'I try to give back, sometimes with good intentions.' He gave another, rather elaborate, shrug. 'Other times because…'

'Because?' Matilda pushed, and Dante actually laughed.

'Exactly as you put it, Matilda, I attempt to soften my rather brutal image.' She liked the way he said her name. Somehow with his deep Italian voice, he made it sound beautiful, made a name that had until now always made her cringe sound somehow exotic. But more than that it was the first time she'd seen him laugh and the effect was amazing, seeing his bland, unfathomable face soften a touch, glimpsing his humour, a tiny peek at the man behind the man.

They ate in more amicable silence now, the mood more relaxed, and Matilda finally addressed the issue that they were, after all, there for.

'It would help if you could tell me a bit about Alex— her likes and dislikes.'

'She loves water,' Dante said without hesitation. 'She also…' He broke off with a shake of his head. 'It's nothing you can put in a garden.'

'Tell me,' Matilda said eagerly.

'Flour,' Dante said. 'She plays with dough and flour…'

'The textures are soothing,' Matilda said and watched as Dante blinked in surprise. 'I found that out when I was researching for the hospital garden. A lot of autistic children…' She winced at her insensitivity, recalled that it was only a tentative diagnosis and one that the family didn't want to hear. 'I'm so—'

'Please, don't apologise again,' Dante broke in with a distinct dry edge to his voice. 'It's becoming rather repetitive. Anyway,' he said as Matilda struggled for a suitable response, 'it is I who should apologise to you: I embarrassed you earlier when I told you about my wife. You can probably gather that I'm not very good at telling people. I tend to be blunt.' He gave a very taut smile and Matilda offered a rather watery one back, reluctant to say anything in the hope her silence might allow him to elaborate. For the first time since she'd met him, her instincts were right. She watched as he swallowed, watched as those dark eyes frowned over the table towards her, and she knew in that second that he was weighing her up, deciding whether or not to go on. Her hand convulsed around her knife and fork, scared to move, scared to do anything that might dissuade him, might break this fragile moment, not even blinking until Dante gave a short, almost imperceptible nod and spoke on.

'Fifteen months ago, I had a normal, healthy daughter. She was almost walking, she smiled she blew kisses, she waved, she was even starting to talk, and then she and my wife were involved in a car accident. Alex was strapped in her baby seat. It took two hours to extricate my wife and daughter from the car…' Matilda felt a shiver go through her as he delivered his speech and in that moment she understood him, understood the mask he wore, because he was speaking as he must work, discarding the pain, the brutal facts, the horrors that must surely haunt him. And stating mere facts—hellish, gut-wrenching facts that were delivered in perhaps the only way he could: the detached voice of a newsreader. 'Jasmine was unconscious, pronounced dead on arrival at hospital.' He took a sip of his drink, probably, Matilda guessed, to take a break from the emotive tale, rather than to moisten his lips. But other than that he appeared unmoved, and she could only hazard a guess at the torture he had been through, the sheer force of willpower and rigid self-control that enabled him to deliver this speech so dispassionately. 'At first Alex, apart from a few minor injures, appeared to have miraculously escaped relatively unscathed. She was kept in hospital for a couple of nights with bruising and for observation but she seemed fine…'

Dante frowned, his eyes narrowing as he looked across to where Matilda sat, but even though he was looking directly at her, Matilda knew he couldn't see her, that instead he was surveying a painful moment in time, and she sat patient and still as Dante took a moment to continue. 'But, saying that, I guess at the time I wasn't really paying much attention…' His voice trailed off again and this time Matilda did speak, took up this very fragile thread, wanting so very much to hear more, to know this man just a touch better.

'You must have had a lot on your mind,' Matilda volunteered gently, and after a beat of hesitation Dante nodded.

'I often wonder if I failed to notice something. I was just so grateful that Alex seemed OK and she really did appear to be, but a couple of months later—it was the twenty-second of September—she started screaming…' He registered Matilda's frown and gave a small wistful smile. 'I remember the date because it would have been Jasmine's birthday. They were all difficult days, but that one in particular was…' He didn't elaborate, he didn't need to. 'I was getting ready to go to the cemetery, and it was as if Alex knew. When I say she was screaming, it wasn't a usual tantrum, she was *hysterio*, deranged. It took hours to calm her. We called a doctor, and he said she was picking up on my grief, that she would be fine, but even as he spoke, even as I tried to believe him, I knew this was not normal, that something was wrong. Unfortunately I was right.'

'It carried on?'

Dante nodded.

'Worse each time, terrible, unmitigated outbursts of rage, and there's no consoling her, but worse, far worse, is the withdrawal afterwards, her utter detachment. I spoke to endless doctors, Hugh was concerned, Katrina in denial…'

'Denial?'

'She refuses to admit there is a problem. So do I too at times, but I could not pretend things were OK and Katrina was starting to get…' he stopped himself then, took a sip of his drink before continuing. 'After a few months I took Alex home to Italy—I thought a change of environment might help. And, of course, it did help to have my family around me, but Hugh and Katrina were devastated,' Dante continued. 'They'd lost their daughter and now it seemed to them that I was taking away their granddaughter. But I had no choice and for a while Alex improved, but then suddenly, from nowhere, it all started again.'

'So you came back?'

'For now.' Dante shrugged. 'I am back in Australia to try and sort things out and make my decision. I have a major trial coming up in a week's time so I am still working, but I am not taking on any new cases. You see now why it seemed pointless to renovate the garden when I do not know if Alex will even be here to enjoy it. But I think that Hugh and Katrina are hoping if they can do something—*anything*—to improve things, there is more chance that I will stay.'

'And is there?' Matilda asked, surprised at how much his answer mattered to her. 'Is there a chance you might stay?'

'My family is in Italy,' Dante pointed out. 'I have two brothers and three sisters, all living near Rome. Alex would have her *nona*, *nono* and endless cousins to play with, I would have more family support, instead of relying on Katrina and Hugh, but…' He halted the conversation then, leaving her wanting to know more, wanting a deeper glimpse of him. Wondering what it was that kept him here, what it was that made him stay. But the subject was clearly closed. 'It cannot be about me,' Dante said instead, giving a tight shrug, and there was a finality to his words as he effectively ended the discussion. But Matilda, wanting more, attempted to carry it on.

'What about your work?'

'I am lucky.' He gave a dry smile. 'There is always someone getting into trouble, either here or in Italy— and being bilingual is a huge advantage. I can work in either country.'

'Doesn't it bother you?' Matilda asked, knowing that she was crossing a line, knowing the polite thing to do would be to leave well alone, but her curiosity was piqued, her delectable salmon forgotten, barely registering as the waiter filled her wine glass. 'Defending those sorts of people, I mean.'

'I believe in innocent until proven guilty.'

'So do I,' Matilda said, staring into that brooding emotionless face and wondering what, if anything, moved him. She'd never met anyone so confident in their own skin, so incredibly not out to impress. He clearly didn't give a damn what people thought of him; he completely dispensed with the usual social niceties and yet somehow he managed to wear it, somehow it worked. 'But you can't sit there and tell me that that guy who killed—'

'That guy,' Dante broke in, 'was proved innocent in a court of law.'

'I know.' Matilda nodded but it changed midway, her head shaking, incredulity sinking in. She certainly wasn't a legal eagle, but you'd have to live in a cupboard not to know about some of the cases Dante Costello handled. They were *Big*, in italics and with a capital B. And even *if* that man she had read about really had been innocent, surely some of the people Dante had defended really were guilty. His job was so far removed from hers as to be unfathomable, and bewildered, she stared back at him. 'Do you ever regret winning?'

'No.' Firmly he shook his head.

'Never?' Matilda asked, watching his lips tighten a touch, watching his eyes darken from dusk to midnight.

'Never,' Dante replied, his single word unequivocal. She felt a shiver, could almost see him in his robes and wig, could almost see that inscrutable face remaining unmoved, could see that full mouth curving into a sneer as he shredded seemingly irrefutable evidence. And anyone, everyone, would have left it there, would have conceded the argument, yet Matilda didn't, green eyes crashing into his, jade waves rolling onto unmovable black granite.

'I don't believe you.'

'Then you don't know what you're talking about.'

'I know I don't,' Matilda admitted. 'Yet I still don't believe you.'

And that should have been it. She should have got on with her meal, he should have resumed eating, made polite small talk to fill the appalling gap, but instead he pushed her now. As she reached for her fork he reached deep inside, his words stilling her, his hand seemingly clutching her heart. 'You've been proud of everything you've done.'

'Not everything,' Matilda tentatively admitted. 'But there's certainly nothing big league. Anyway, what's that got to do with it?'

'It has everything to do with it,' Dante said assuredly. 'We all have our dark secrets, we all have things that, given our time again, we would have done differently. The difference between Mr or Ms Average and my clients is that their personal lives, their most intimate regrets are up for public scrutiny. Words uttered in anger are played back to haunt them, a moment of reckless-ness a couple of years back suddenly relived for everyone to hear. It can be enough to cloud the most objective jury.'

'But surely, if they've done nothing wrong,' Matilda protested, 'they have nothing to fear.'

'Not if I do my job correctly,' Dante said. 'But not everyone's as good as me.' Matilda blinked at his lack of modesty, but Dante made no apology. 'I *have* to believe that my clients are innocent.'

She should have left it there, Matilda knew that, knew she had no chance against him, but she refused to be a pushover and refused to be swayed from her stance. She wasn't in the witness box after all, just an adult having an interesting conversation. There was no need to be intimidated. Taking a breath, she gave him a very tight smile. 'Even if they're clearly not?'

'Ah, Matilda.' He flashed her an equally false smile. 'You shouldn't believe all you read in the newspapers.'

'I don't,' Matilda flared. 'I'm just saying that there's no smoke without fire...' She winced at the cliché and began to make a more eloquent argument, but Dante got there first.

'There are no moments in your life that you'd dread coming out in court?'

'Of course not!'

'None at all?'

'None,' Matilda flushed. 'I certainly haven't done anything illegal, well, not really.'

'Not really?' Nothing in his expression changed, bar a tiny rise of one eyebrow.

'I thought we were here to talk about your garden,' she flared, but Dante just smiled.

'You were the one who questioned me about my work,' Dante pointed out. 'It's not my fault if you don't like the answer. So, come on, tell me, what did you do?'

'I've told you,' Matilda insisted. 'I've done *nothing* wrong. I'm sorry if you find that disappointing or boring.'

'I'm *never* disappointed,' Dante said, his eyes burning into her, staring at her so directly it made her squirm. 'And I know for a fact that you have your secret shame—everyone does.'

'OK,' Matilda breathed in indignation. 'But if you're expecting some dark, sordid story then you're going to be sorely disappointed. It's just a tiny, tiny thing that happened when I was a kid.'

'Clearly not that tiny,' Dante said, 'if you can still blush just thinking about it.'

'I'm not blushing,' Matilda flared, but she knew it was useless, could feel the sting of heat on her cheeks. But it wasn't the past that was making her blush, it was the present, the here and now, the presence of him, the feel of his eyes on her, the intimacy of revelation—any revelation.

'Tell me,' Dante said softly, dangerously, and it sounded like a dare. 'Tell me what happened.'

'I stole some chocolate when I was on school camp,' Matilda admitted. 'Everyone did,' she went on almost immediately.

'And you thought that you'd look an idiot if you didn't play along?'

'Something like that,' Matilda murmured, blushing furiously now, but with the shame and fear she had felt at the time, reliving again the pressure she had felt at that tender age to just blend in. She was surprised at the emotion such a distant memory could evoke.

'So, instead of standing up for yourself, you just went right along with it, even though you knew it was wrong.'

'I guess.'

'And that's the sum total of your depraved past?' Dante checked.

'That's it.' Matilda nodded. 'Sorry if I disappointed you.'

'You didn't.' Dante shook his head. 'I find you can learn a lot about a person if you listen to their childhood memories. Our responses don't change that much…'

'Rubbish,' Matilda scoffed. 'I was ten years old. If something like that happened now—'

'You'd do exactly the same,' Dante broke in. 'I'm not saying that you'd steal a bar of chocolate rather than draw attention to yourself, but you certainly don't like confrontation, do you?'

Shocked at his insight, all she could do was stare back at him.

'In fact,' Dante continued, 'you'd walk to the end of the earth to avoid it, steal a chocolate bar if it meant you could blend in, stay in a bad relationship to avoid a row…' As she opened her mouth to deny it, Dante spoke over her. 'Or, let's take tonight for an example, you ran to the toilet the moment you thought you had upset me.'

'Not quite that very moment.' Matilda rolled her eyes and gave a watery smile, realising she was beaten. 'I lasted two at least. But does anyone actually like confrontation?'

'I do,' Dante said. 'It's the best part of my job, making people confront their hidden truths.' He gave her the benefit of a very bewitching smile, which momentarily knocked her off guard. 'Though I guess if that's the worst you can come up with, you really would have no problem with being cross-examined.'

'I'd have no worries at all,' Matilda said confidently.

'You clearly know your own mind.'

'I do.' Matilda smiled back, happy things were under control.

'Then may I?'

'Excuse me?'

'Just for the sake of curiosity.' His smile was still in place. 'May I ask you some questions?'

'We're supposed to be talking about your garden.'

He handed her a rolled-up wad of paper. 'There are the plans, you can do whatever you wish—so that takes care of that.'

'But why?' Matilda asked.

'I enjoy convincing people.' Dante shrugged. 'And I believe you are far from convinced. All you have to do is answer some questions honestly.'

The dessert menu was being offered to her and Matilda hesitated before taking it. She had the plans, and clearly Dante was in no mood to discuss foliage or water features, so the sensible thing would be to decline. She'd eaten her main course, she'd stayed to be polite, there was absolutely no reason to prolong things, no reason at all—except for the fact that she wanted to stay.

Wanted to prolong this evening.

With a tiny shiver Matilda accepted the truth.

She wanted to play his dangerous game.

'They do a divine white chocolate and macadamia nut mousse,' Dante prompted, 'with hot raspberry sauce.'

'Sounds wonderful,' Matilda said, and as the waiter slipped silently away, her glittering eyes met Dante's. A frisson of excitement ran down her spine as she faced him, as this encounter moved onto another level, and not for the first time today she wondered what it was about Dante Costello that moved her so.

CHAPTER THREE

'YOU will answer me honestly?'

His smile had gone now, his deep, liquid voice low, and despite the full restaurant, despite the background noise of their fellow diners, it was as if they were the only two in the room.

His black eyes were working her face, appraising her, and she could almost imagine him walking towards her across the courtroom, circling her slowly, choosing the best method of attack. Fear did the strangest thing to Matilda, her lips twitching into a nervous smile as he again asked his question. 'You swear to answer me honestly.'

'I'm not on trial.' Matilda gave a tiny nervous laugh, but he remained unmoved.

'If we're going to play, we play by the rules.'

'Fine.' Matilda nodded. 'But I really think you're—'

'We've all got secrets,' Dante broke in softly. 'There's a dark side to every single one of us, and splash it on a headline, layer it with innuendo and suddenly we're all as guilty as hell. Take your ex—'

'Edward's got nothing to do—'

'Location, location, location.' He flashed a malevolent smile as Matilda's hand tightened convulsively around her glass. 'Just one more business dinner, just one more client to impress. Just one more garden to renovate and then, maybe then you'll get his attention. Maybe one day—'

'I don't need this,' Matilda said through gritted teeth. 'I've no idea what you're trying to get at, but can you please leave Edward out of this?'

'Still too raw?' He leant back in his chair, merciless eyes awaiting her response.

'No,' Matilda said tersely, leaning back into her own chair, *forcing* her tense shoulders to lower, *forcing* a smile onto her face. 'Absolutely not. Edward and I finished a couple of months ago. I'm completely over it.'

'Who ended it?'

'I did,' Matilda answered, but with renewed confidence now. She *had* been the one who had ended it, and that surely would thwart him, would rule out his image of a broken-hearted female who would go to any lengths to avoid confrontation.

'Why?' Dante asked bluntly, but Matilda gave a firm shake of her head.

'I'm not prepared to answer that,' she retorted coolly. 'I had my reasons. And in case you're wondering, no, there wasn't anyone else involved.' Confident she'd ended this line of questioning, sure he would try another tack, Matilda felt the fluttering butterflies in her stomach still a touch and her breathing slow down as she awaited his next question, determined to answer him with cool ease.

'Did you ever wish him dead?'

'What?' Appalled, she confronted him with her eyes—stunned that he would even ask such a thing. 'Of course not.'

'Are you honestly stating that you never once said that you wished that he was dead?'

'You're either mad…' Matilda let out an incredulous laugh '…or way too used to dealing with mad people! *Of course* I never said that I wished that he…' Her voice faltered for just a fraction of second, a flash of forgotten conversation pinging into consciousness, and like a cobra he struck.

'I'm calling your friend as a witness next—and I can assure you that her version of that night is completely different to yours…'

'What night?' Matilda scorned.

'*That* night,' Dante answered with absolute conviction, and Matilda felt her throat tighten as he spoke on. 'In fact, your friend clearly recalls a conversation where you expressed a strong wish that Edward was dead.' Dante's words were so measured, so assured, so absolutely spot on that for a tiny second she almost believed him. For a flash of time she almost expected to look over her shoulder and see Judy sitting at the other table, as if she had stumbled into some macabre reality TV show, where all her secrets, all her failings were about to be exposed.

Stop it, Matilda scolded herself, reining in her overreaction. Dante knew nothing about her. He was a skilled interrogator, that was all, used to finding people's Achilles' heels, and she wasn't going to let him. She damn well wasn't going to give him the satisfaction of breaking her.

'I still don't know what night you're talking about!'

'Then let me refresh your memory. I'm referring to the night you said that you wished Edward was dead.' And he didn't even make it sound like an assumption, his features so immovable it was as if he'd surely been in the room that night, as if he'd actually witnessed her raw tears, had heard every word she'd sobbed that night, as if somehow he was privy to her soul. 'And you did say that, didn't you, Matilda?'

To deny it would be an outright lie. Suddenly she wasn't sitting in a restaurant any more. Instead, she was back to where it had all ended two months ago, could feel the brutal slap of Edward's words as surely as if she were hearing them for the first time.

Maybe if you weren't so damn frigid, I wouldn't have to look at other women to get my kicks.

He'd taunted her, humiliated her, shamed her for her lack of sexual prowess, demeaned her with words so vicious, so brutal that by the time she'd run from his house, by the time she'd arrived at Judy's home, she'd believed each and every word. Believed that their relationship had been in trouble because of her failings, believed that if only she'd been prettier, sexier, funnier, he wouldn't have had to flirt so much, wouldn't have needed to humiliate her quite so badly. And somehow Dante knew it, too.

'You did say it, didn't you?' It was Dante's voice dragging her out of her own private hell.

'I just said it,' Matilda breathed, she could feel the blood draining out of her face. 'It was just one of those stupid things you say when you're angry.'

'And you were very angry, weren't you?'

'No,' Matilda refuted. 'I was upset and annoyed but angry is probably overstretching things.'

He swirled his wine around in the glass and Matilda's eyes darted towards it, watching the pale fluid whirl around the bottom, grateful for the distraction, grateful for something to focus on other than those dark, piercing eyes.

'So you were only upset and annoyed, yet you admit you wished him dead!'

'OK,' Matilda snapped, her head spinning as the barrage continued. 'I was angry, furious, in fact. So would anyone have been if they'd been told…' She choked her words down, refusing to drag up that shame and certainly not prepared to reveal it to Dante. Dragging in air, she halted her tirade, tried to remember to think before she spoke, to regain some of the control she'd so easily lost. 'Yes, I said that I wished he was dead, but there's a big difference between saying something and actually seeing it through.' She felt dizzy, almost sick with the emotions he'd so easily conjured up, like some wicked magician pulling out her past, her secrets, clandestine feelings exposed, and she didn't want it to continue, didn't want to partake in this a moment longer.

'Can we stop this now?' Her voice was high and slightly breathless, a trickle of moisture running between her breasts as she eyed this savage man, wondering how the hell he knew, how he had known so readily what buttons to push to reduce her to this.

'Any time you like.' Dante smiled, his voice so soft it was almost a caress, but it did nothing to soothe her. 'After all, it's just a game!'

The dessert was divine, the sweet sugary mousse contrasting with the sharp raspberry sauce, but Matilda was too shaken to really enjoy it, her long dessert spoon unusually lethargic as she attempted just to get through it.

'Is your dessert OK?'

'It's fine,' Matilda said, then gave in, putting her spoon down. 'Actually, I'm really not that hungry. I think I'll go home now…'

'I'm sorry if I destroyed your appetite.'

God, he had a nerve!

'No, you're not.' Matilda looked across the table at him and said it again. 'No, Dante, you're not. In fact I think that was exactly what you set out to do.' Reaching for her bag, Matilda stood up and picked up the roll of plans.

'I'll be at your house on Sunday afternoon. I'll look at the plans tomorrow but until I see the garden I really won't know what I'm going to do.'

'We've all said it.' Dante's smile bordered on the compassionate as she stood up to leave, and he didn't bother to elaborate—they both knew what he was referring to. 'And as you pointed out, there's a big difference between saying it and following it through. I was just proving a point.'

'Consider it proven,' Matilda replied with a very tight smile. 'Goodnight, Dante.'

Of course it took if not for ever then a good couple of minutes for the waiter to locate her jacket, giving Dante plenty of time to catch up with her. Rather than talk to him, she took a small after-dinner mint from the bowl on the desk, concentrating on unwrapping the thin gold foil as she prayed for the waiter to hurry up, popping the bitter chocolate into her mouth and biting into the sweet peppermint centre, then flushing as she sensed Dante watching her.

She'd said she wasn't hungry just two minutes ago—well, just because he was so damned controlled, it didn't mean that she had to be. What would a calculating man like Dante know about want rather than need? The man was utterly devoid of emotion, Matilda decided angrily. He probably peeled open his chest and pulled out his batteries at night, put them on charge ready to attack his next victim. Consoling herself that she could make a quick escape while he settled the bill, almost defiantly she took another chocolate, pathetically grateful when the waiter appeared with her jacket and helped her into it. She stepped outside into the night and closed her eyes as the cool night air hit her flaming cheeks.

'How far do you have to go?'

She heard Dante's footsteps as he came along behind her, recognised his heavily accented voice as he uttered the first syllable, his scent hitting her before he drew her aside, yet she'd known he was close long before, almost sensed his approach before he'd made himself known.

'How did you…?' She didn't finish her question, didn't want to be drawn into another conversation with him. She just marched swiftly on, her stilettos making a tinny sound as she clipped along the concrete pavement.

'I eat regularly there. They send my account out once a month or so and my secretary deals with it.'

The one who'd dared to allow herself to get pregnant, Matilda wanted to point out, but chose not to, clutching the plans tighter under her arm and walking swiftly on.

'Would you like a lift home?'

'I have an apartment over the bridge.' Matilda pointed to the a high-rise block on the other side of the river. 'It's just a five-minute walk.'

'Then I'll join you,' Dante said. 'You shouldn't be walking alone across the bridge at this time of night.'

'Really,' Matilda flustered, 'there's absolutely no need—it's just a hop and a skip.'

'I'd rather *walk* if you don't mind,' Dante said, his face completely deadpan, but his dry humour didn't even raise a smile from Matilda. Frankly, she'd rather take the chance of walking across the bridge alone than with the evil troll beside her.

'I have an apartment near here also,' Dante said, nodding backwards from whence they'd come, but despite the proximity to hers, Matilda was quite sure any city apartment Dante owned wouldn't compare to her second-floor shoebox!

'I didn't somehow envisage you as having an apartment,' Dante mused, and Matilda blinked, surprised he *envisaged* her at all. 'I thought, given your work you would have a home with a garden.'

'That's the plan, actually,' Matilda admitted. 'I've just put it up for sale. I never really liked it.'

'So why did you buy it?'

'It was too good an opportunity to miss. And location-wise, for work it's brilliant.' She gave a low groan at the sound of her own voice. 'Can you tell I spent the last couple of years dating a real estate agent?' Matilda asked, glancing over to him and surprised to see that he was actually smiling.

'At least you didn't mention the stunning views and the abundance of natural light!'

'Only because I'm on the second floor,' Matilda quipped, amazed after the tension of only a few moments ago to find herself actually smiling back. 'I guess the drive from Mount Eliza to the city each day would be a bit much,' Matilda ventured, but again she got things wrong.

'I don't generally drive to work, I use a helicopter.'

'Of course you do,' Matilda sighed, rolling her eyes.

'It is not my helicopter.' She could hear the teasing note in his voice. 'More like a taxi service. I would rather spend that hour or two at home than in the car. When we bought the place it was meant more as weekender, or retreat, but since the accident I have tried not to move Alex too much. It is better, I think that she is near the beach with lots of space rather than the city. A luxury high rise apartment isn't exactly stimulating for a small child.'

Why did he always make her feel small?

'I use the apartment a lot, though. I tend to stay there if I am involved in a difficult trial.'

'I guess it would be quieter.'

'A bit,' Dante admitted. 'I tend to get very absorbed in my cases. By the time they go to trial there is not much space left for anything else. But it is not just for that reason.' They were walking quickly, too quickly for Matilda, who almost had to run to keep up with him, but she certainly wasn't going to ask him to slow down. The sooner they got to her apartment block the sooner she could breathe again. 'The press can be merciless at times. I prefer to keep it away from my family.'

They were safely over the bridge now, walking along the dark embankment on the other side of the river.

'This is me,' Matilda said as they neared her apartment block, and she rummaged in her bag for her keys. 'I'll be fine now.'

'I'm sure that you would be,' Dante said, 'but you are my dinner guest and for that reason I will see you safely home.'

Why did he have to display manners now? Matilda wondered. He'd been nothing but rude since they'd met—it was a bit late for chivalry. But she was too drained to argue, just gave a resigned shrug, let herself into the entrance hall and headed for the stairwell, glad that she lived on the second floor and therefore wouldn't have to squeeze into a lift with him again.

'Home!' Matilda said with false brightness.

'Do you always take the stairs?'

'Always,' Matilda lied. 'It's good exercise.' They were at her front door now. 'Thank you for this evening. It's been, er…pleasant.'

'Really?' Dante raised a quizzical eyebrow. 'I'm not sure that I believe you.'

'I was actually attempting to be polite,' Matilda responded, 'as you were by seeing me to my door.' She was standing there, staring at him, willing him to just go, reluctant somehow to turn her back on him, not scared exactly, but on heightened alert as still he just stood there. Surely he didn't expect her to ask him in for coffee?

Surely!

How the hell was she going to spend a fortnight in

his company when one evening left her a gibbering wreck? She *had* to get a grip, had to bring things back to a safer footing, had to let him know that it was strictly business, pretend that he didn't intimidate her, pretend that he didn't move her so.

'Thank you for bringing the plans, Dante. I'm looking forward to working on your garden.' She offered her hand. Direct, businesslike, Matilda decided, that was how she'd be—a snappy end to a business dinner. But as his hand took hers, instantly she regretted it.

It was only the second time they had made physical contact. As his hand tightened around hers she was brutally reminded of that fact, despite the hours that had passed, despite a dinner shared and the emotions he had evoked, it was only the second time they had touched. And the result was as explosive as the first time, and many times more lethal. She could feel the heat of his flesh searing into hers, as his large hand coiled around hers, the pad of his index finger resting on her slender wrist, her radial pulse hammering against it. And this time the feel of his gold wedding band did nothing to soothe her, just reminded her of the depths of him, the pain that must surely exist behind those indecipherable eyes. Never had she found a person so difficult to read, never had she revealed so much of herself to someone and found out so very little in return.

But she wanted to know more.

'You interest me, Matilda.' It was such a curious thing to say, such a hazy, ambiguous statement, and her eyes involuntarily jerked to his like a reflex action, held by his gaze, stunned, startled, yet curiously reluctant to move, a heightened sexual awareness permeating her.

'I thought perhaps I bored you.'

'Oh, no.' Slowly he shook his head and she started back, mesmerised, his sensuous but brutal features utterly captivating. 'Why would you think such a thing?'

'I just…' Matilda's voice trailed off. She didn't know what to say because she didn't know the answer, didn't know if it was her destroyed self-confidence that made her vulnerable or the man who was staring at her now, the man who was pinning her to the wall with his eyes.

'He really hurt you, didn't he?' It was as if he were staring into her very soul, not asking her but telling her how she felt. 'He ground you down and down until you didn't even know who you were any more, didn't even know what it was that you wanted.'

How did he know? How could he read her so easily—was she that predictable? Was her pain, her self-doubt so visible? But Dante hadn't finished with his insights, hadn't finished peeling away the layers, exposing her raw, bruised core, and she wanted again to halt him, wanted to stop him from going further— wanted that mouth that was just inches from hers be silent, to kiss her…

'And then, when he'd taken every last drop from you, he tossed you aside…'

She shook her head in denial, relieved that he'd got one thing wrong. 'I was the one who ended it,' Matilda reminded him, but it didn't sway him for a second.

'You just got there first.' Dante delivered his knockout blow. 'It was already over.'

He was right, of course, it had been over. She could still feel the bleak loneliness that had filled her that night and for many nights before the final one. The in-difference had been so much more painful that the rows that had preceded it. She could still feel the raw shame of Edward's intimate rejections.

'I'm fine without him.'

'Better than fine,' Dante said softly, and she held her breath as that cruel, sensual mouth moved in towards hers. She still didn't know what he was thinking. Lust rippled between them, yet his expression was com-pletely unreadable. The same quiver of excitement that had gripped her in the restaurant shivered through her now, but with dangerous sexual undertones, and it was inevitable they would kiss. Matilda acknowledged it then. The foreplay she had so vehemently denied was taking place had started hours ago, long, long before they'd even reached the garden.

He gave her time to move away, ample time to halt things, to stop this now, and she should have.

Normally she would have.

Her mind flitted briefly to her recent attempts at dating where she'd dreaded this moment, had avoided it or gone along with a kiss for the sad sake of it, to prove to herself that she was desirable perhaps.

But there was no question here of merely going along with this kiss for the sake of it—logic, common sense, self-preservation told her that to end *this* night with a kiss was a foolish move, that for the sake of her sanity she should surely halt this now. But her body told her otherwise, every nerve prickling to delicious attention, drawn like a magnet to his beauty, anticipating the taste of him, the feel of him in a heady rush of need, of want.

His mouth brushed her cheek, sweeping along her cheekbone till she could feel his breath warm on the shell of her ear then moving back, back to her waiting lips, slowly, deliberately until only a whisper separated them, till his mouth was so close to hers that she was giddy with expectation, filled with want—deep, burning want that she'd never yet experienced, a want that suffused her, a want she had never, even in the most intimate moments, experienced, and he hadn't even kissed her. Her breath was coming in short, unyielding gasps, his chest so close to hers that if she breathed any deeper their bodies would touch. She was torn between want and dread, her body longing to arch towards his, her nipples stretching like buds to the sun, his hand still on the wall behind her head, and all she wanted was his touch.

As if in answer, his mouth found hers, the weight of his body pushing her down, his lips obliterating thought, reason, question, his masterful touch the only thought she could process, his tongue, stroking hers so deeply so intimately it was as if he were touching her deep inside, his skin dragging hers as his mouth moved against her, the sweet, decadent taste of him, the heady masculine scent of him stroking her awake from deep hibernation, awareness fizzing in where there had been none.

His power overwhelmed her, the strength of his arms around her slender body, the hard weight of his thighs as he pinned her to the wall and a vague peripheral awareness of a warm hand creeping along the length of her spinal column then sliding around her rib cage as his mouth worked ever on. A low needy sigh built as it slid around, his palm capturing the weight of her breast, the warmth of his skin through the sheer fabric of her dress had her curling into him, needy, wanton, desperate, swelling at his touch, her breasts engorging, shamefully reciprocating as the pad of his thumb teased her jutting nipple. So many sensations, so many responses, his tongue capturing hers in his lips, sucking on the swollen tip, his body pinning her in delicious confinement, his masculinity capturing her, overwhelming her. Yet she was hardly an unwilling participant—fingers coiling in his jet hair, pulling his face to hers as her body pressed against him, his touch unleashing her passion, her desire, flaming it to dangerous heat, a heat so intense there was no escape, and neither did she want one. His kiss was everything a kiss should be, everything she'd missed.

Till now.

And just as she dived into complete oblivion, just as she would have given anything, anything for this moment to continue, for him to douse the fire within her, he wrenched his head away, an expression she couldn't read in his eyes as he looked coolly down at her.

'I should go.'

Words failing her, Matilda couldn't even nod, embarrassment creeping in now. He could have taken her there and then—with one crook of his manicured finger she would have led him inside, would have made love to him, would have let him make love to her. What was it with this man? Emotionally he troubled her, terrified her even, yet still she was drawn to him, physically couldn't resist him. She had never felt such compulsion, a macabre addiction almost, and she hadn't even know him a day.

'I will see you on Sunday.' His voice was completely

normal and his hands were still on her trembling body. She stared back at him, unable to fathom that he could appear so unmoved, that he was still standing after what they'd just shared. Blindly she nodded, her hair tumbling down around her face, eyes frowning as Dante reached into his suit pocket and pulled out a handful of chocolate mints, the same ones she had surreptitiously taken at the restaurant.

'I took these at the restaurant for you…' Taking her hand, he filled it with the sweet chocolate delicacies. She could feel them soft and melting through the foil as he closed her fingers around them. 'I know you wanted to do the same!'

An incredulous smile broke onto her lips at the gesture, a tiny glimmer that maybe things were OK, that the attraction really was mutual, that Dante didn't think any less of her because of what had just taken place. 'You stole them?' Matilda gave a tiny half-laugh, recalling their earlier conversation.

'Oh, no.' He shook his head and doused any fledgling hope with one cruel sentence, cheapened and humiliated her with his strange euphemism. 'Why would I steal them when, after all, they were there for the taking?'

CHAPTER FOUR

WHAT she had been expecting, Matilda wasn't sure—
an austere, formal residence, surrounded by an overgrown wilderness, or a barren landscape perhaps—but
with directions on the passenger seat beside her she'd
found the exclusive street fairly easily and had caught
her breath as she'd turned into it, The heavenly view of
Port Phillip Bay stretched out for ever before her.
Chewing on her lip as she drove, the sight of the opulent,
vast houses of the truly rich forced her to slow down as
she marvelled at the architecture and stunning gardens,
tempted to whip out her faithful notepad and jot down
some notes and deciding that soon she would do just
that. The thought of long evenings with nothing to do
but avoid Dante was made suddenly easier. She could
walk along the beach with her pad, even wander down
to one of the many cafés she had passed as she'd driven
through the village—there was no need to be alone with
him, no need at all.

Unless she wanted to be.

Pulling into the kerb, Matilda raked a hand through
her hair, tempted, even at the eleventh hour, to execute

a hasty U-turn and head for the safety of home. Since she'd awoken on Saturday after a restless sleep, she'd been in a state of high anxiety, especially when she'd opened the newspaper and read with renewed interest about the sensational trial that was about to hit the Melbourne courts and realising that it wasn't just her that was captivated by Dante Costello. Apart from the salacious details of the upcoming trial, a whole article had been devoted solely to Dante, and the theatre that this apparently brilliant man created, from his scathing tongue and maverick ways in the courtroom to the chameleon existence he'd had since the premature death of his beloved wife, his abrupt departure from the social scene, his almost reclusive existence, occasionally fractured by the transient presence of a beautiful woman—anodynes, Matilda had guessed, that offered a temporary relief. And though it had hurt like hell to read it, Matilda had devoured it, gleaning little, understanding less. The face that had stared back at her from the newspaper pages had been as distant and as unapproachable as the man she had first met and nothing, *nothing* like the Dante who had held her in his arms, who had kissed her to within an inch of her life, who had so easily awoken the woman within—the real Dante she was sure she'd glimpsed.

Matilda had known that the sensible thing to do would be to ring Hugh and tell him she couldn't do the work after all—that something else had come up. Hell, she had even dialled his number a few times, but at the last minute had always hung up, torn between want and loathing, outrage and desire, telling herself that it wouldn't be fair to let Hugh down, and sometimes almost managing to believe it. As honourable as it sounded, loyalty to Hugh had nothing to do with her being there today. Dante totally captivated her—since the second she'd laid eyes on him he was *all* she thought about.

All she thought about, replaying their conversations over and over, jolting each and every time she recalled some of his sharper statements, wondering how the hell he managed to get away with it, how she hadn't slapped his arrogant cheek. And yet somehow there had been a softer side and it was that that intrigued her. Despite his brutality she'd glimpsed something else—tiny flickers of beauty, like flowers in a desert—his dry humour, the stunning effect of his occasional smile on her, the undeniable tenderness reserved exclusively for his daughter. And, yes, Matilda acknowledged that the raw, simmering passion that had been in his kiss had left her hungry for more,

'Careful.' Matilda said the word out loud, repeated it over and over in her mind as she slipped the car into first gear and slowly pulled out into the street, driving a couple of kilometres further with her heart in her mouth as she braced herself to face him again, her hand shaking slightly as she turned into his driveway and pressed the intercom, watching unblinking as huge metal gates slid open and she glimpsed for the first time Dante's stunning home.

The drive was as uncompromising and as rigid as its owner, lined with cypress trees drawing the eye along its vast, straight length to the huge, Mediterranean-looking residence—vast white rendered walls that made the sky look bluer somehow, massive floor-to-ceiling windows that would drench the home in light and let in every inch of the stunning view. She inched her way along, momentarily forgetting her nerves, instead absorbing the beauty. The harsh lines of the house were softened at the entrance by climbers—wisteria, acres of it, ambled across the front of the property, heavy lilac flowers hanging like bunches of grapes, intermingled with jasmine, its creamy white petals like dotted stars, the more delicate foliage competing with the harsh wooden branches of the wisteria. The effect, quite simply, was divine.

'Welcome!' Hugh pulled open the car door for her and Matilda stepped out onto the white paved driveway, pathetically grateful to see him—not quite ready to face Dante alone. 'Matilda, this is my wife Katrina.' He introduced a tall, elegant woman who stepped forward and shook her hand, her greeting the antithesis of Hugh's warm one. Cool blue eyes blatantly stared Matilda up and down, taking in the pale blue cotton shift dress and casual sandals she was wearing and clearly not liking what she saw. 'You're nothing like I was expecting. I expected…' she gave a shrill laugh… 'I don't know. You don't look like a gardener!'

'She's a designer, Katrina,' Hugh said with a slight edge.

'I'm very hands-on, though,' Matilda said. 'I like to see the work through from beginning to end.'

'Marvellous,' Katrina smiled, but somehow her face remained cold. 'Come—let me introduce you to Dante…'

Matilda was about to say that she'd already met

him, but decided against it, as clearly both Hugh and Dante had omitted to mention the dinner to Katrina. She wasn't sure what to make of Katrina. She was stunning-looking, her posture was straight, her long hair, though dashed with grey, was still an amazing shade of strawberry blonde, and though she had to be around fifty, there was barely a line on her smooth face. But there was a frostiness about her that unsettled Matilda.

The interior of the house was just as impressive as the exterior. Hugh held open the front door then headed off to Matilda's car to retrieve her bags and the two women stepped inside and walked along the jarrah-floored hallways, Matilda's sandals echoing on the solid wood as she took in the soft white sofas and dark wooden furnishings, huge mirrors opening up the already vast space, reflecting the ocean at every turn so that wherever you looked the waves seemed to beckon. Or Jasmine smiled down at you! An inordinate number of photos of Dante's late wife adorned the walls, her gorgeous face captured from every angle, and Matilda felt a quiet discomfort as she gazed around, her cheeks flaming as she recalled the stinging kiss of Dante.

'My daughter.' Katrina's eyes followed Matilda's and they paused for a moment as they admired her tragic beauty. 'I had this photo blown up and framed just last week—it's good for Alex to be able to see her and I know it gives Dante a lot of comfort.'

'It must…' Matilda stumbled. 'She really was very beautiful.'

'And clever,' Katrina added. 'She had it all, brains

and beauty. She was amazing, a wonderful mother and wife. None of us will ever get over her loss.'

'I can't even begin to imagine…' Despite the cool breeze from the air-conditioner, despite the high ceilings and vastness of the place, Matilda felt incredibly hot and uncomfortable. Despite her earlier misgivings, she was very keen to meet Dante now—even his savage personality was preferable to the discomfort she felt with Katrina.

'Dante especially,' Katrina continued, and Matilda was positive, despite her soft words and pensive smile, that there was a warning note to her voice, an icy message emanating from her cool blue eyes. 'I've never seen a man so broken with grief. He just adored her, *adored* her,' Katrina reiterated. 'Do you know, the day she died he sent flowers to her office. It was a Saturday but she had to pop into work and get some files. She took Alex with her—that was the sort of woman she was. Anyway, Dante must have rung every florist in Melbourne. He wanted to send her some jasmine, her namesake, but it was winter, of course, so it was impossible to find, but Dante being Dante he managed to organise it—he'd have moved heaven and earth for her.'

It was actually a relief to get into the kitchen. After Katrina's onslaught it was actually a relief to confront the man she'd been so nervous of meeting again. But as she stepped inside it was as if she was seeing him for the very first time. The man she remembered bore little witness to the one she saw now. Everything about him seemed less formal. Of course, she hadn't expected him to greet her in a suit—it was Sunday after all—but somehow she'd never envisaged him in jeans and a T-shirt, or, if she had, it would have been in dark, starched denim and a crisp white designer label T-shirt, not the faded, scruffy jeans that encased him, not the untucked, unironed white T-shirt that he was wearing. And she certainly hadn't pictured him at a massive wooden table, kneading bread, with his daughter, Alex's eyes staring ahead as she rhythmically worked the dough.

'Dante, Alexandra,' Katrina called. 'Matilda has arrived.'

Only one pair of eyes looked up. Alexandra carried on kneading the dough and any thought of witnessing Dante's softer side was instantly quashed as his black eyes briefly met hers.

'Good afternoon.'

His greeting was also his dismissal.

His attention turning immediately back to his daughter, picking up a large shaker and sprinkling the dough with more flour as the little girl worked on.

'Good afternoon.' Matilda forced a smile to no one in particular. 'You're making bread…'

'No.' Dante stood up, dusted his floured hands on his jeans 'We are kneading dough and playing with flour.'

'Oh!'

'We've been kneading dough and playing with flour since lunchtime, actually!'

Another 'oh' was on the tip of her tongue, but Matilda held it back, grateful when Katrina took over this most awkward of conversations.

'It's one of Alex's pastimes,' Katrina explained as

Hugh came back in. 'She was upset after lunch—you know what children can be like.' Dante gave a tight smile as Katrina dismissed the slightly weary note to his voice. Something told Matilda that whatever had eventuated had been rather more than the usual childhood tantrum. 'Hugh, why don't you go and take Matilda around the garden?' Katrina said. 'It seems a shame to break things up when Dante and Alex are having such fun.'

'Hugh's supposed to be resting,' Dante pointed out. '*I'll* take Matilda around.'

'Fine,' Katrina said, though clearly it was anything but! 'Then I'll go and check that everything's in order in the summerhouse for Matilda.'

'The summerhouse?' Dante frowned. 'I had the guest room made up for her. Janet prepared it this morning.'

'Well, it won't kill Janet to prepare the summerhouse! She's the housekeeper,' Katrina explained to a completely bemused Matilda. 'I can help her set it up. It will be far nicer for Matilda. She can have some privacy and it might unsettle Alex, having a stranger in the house—no offence meant, Matilda.'

'None taken.' Matilda thought her face might crack with the effort of smiling. 'It really doesn't matter a scrap where I stay. I'm going to be working long hours, I just need somewhere to sleep and eat…'

'There's a lovely little kitchenette in the summerhouse. I'll have some bacon and eggs and bread put in, that type of thing—you'll be very comfortable.'

'It's your fault.' Dante broke the appalling silence as they stepped outside.

'What is?' Matilda blinked.

'That you've been banished.' He gave her a glimmer of a dry smile. 'You're too good-looking for Katrina.'

'Oh!' A tiny nervous giggle escaped her lips, embarrassed by what he had said but relieved all the same that he had acknowledged the problem. 'I don't think she likes me very much.'

'She'd have been hoping for a ruddy-faced, gum-chewing, crop-haired gardener. I have the ugliest staff in the world—all hand-picked by Katrina.' Startled by his coarseness, Matilda actually laughed as they walked, amazed to find herself relaxing a touch in his presence.

'Yesterday's newspapers can't have helped matters much,' she ventured, referring to the string of women he'd dated since his wife's death, but Dante just shrugged.

'Ships that pass in the night even Katrina can live with.'

The callousness of his words had Matilda literally stopping in her tracks for a moment, waiting for him to soften it with a smile, to tell her he was joking, but Dante strode on, forcing Matilda to catch him up, and try to continue the conversation. 'Do your in-laws live here with you?'

'God, no.' Dante shuddered. 'They live a few kilometres away. But we're interviewing for a new nanny at the moment—preferably one over sixty with a wooden leg if Katrina has her way. That's why she's around so much. Like it or not at the moment I do need her help with Alex, but if I decide to stay here in Australia...' He stopped talking then, just simply stopped in mid-sentence with no apology or explanation, clearly deciding he had said enough. Silence descended again as they walked on the manicured lawn past a massive pool, surrounded by a clear Perspex wall. Matilda gazed at the pool longingly.

'Use it any time,' Dante offered.

'Thanks,' Matilda replied, knowing full well she wouldn't. The thought of undressing, of wearing nothing more than a bikini around Dante not exactly soothing.

'This is the garden,' Dante said as they came to a gate. 'It's in a real mess, very neglected, overgrown with blackberries and bracken, I've been meaning to get it cleared, but my gardener is getting old. It takes all his time just to keep up with the regular work, let alone this. Oh, and one other thing…' His hand paused on the gate. 'The bill is to come to me.'

'Hugh employed me,' Matilda pointed out.

'Hugh does not need to pay for my renovations—you will send the bill to me, Matilda.'

But she didn't want to send the bill to him—and it had nothing to do with money. Financially it made not a scrap of difference to Matilda who picked up the bill. Instead, it was the disturbing thought of being answerable somehow to Dante, of him employing her, that made Matilda strangely nervous.

'Do you need an advance?'

'An advance?' Instantly, she regretted her words. Her mind had been utterly elsewhere and now she sounded stupid.

'An advance of money,' Dante not too patiently explained. 'To pay the subcontractors. I don't know what arrangement you had with Hugh—'

'*Have* with Hugh,' Matilda corrected, watching as Dante's face darkened. Clearly he was not used to being defied, but even though an advance would be wonderful now, even though she had a hundred and one people that would need to be paid, and very soon, she damn well wasn't going to give in to him, absolutely refused to let him dictate his terms to her. 'My business is with Hugh. If you want to settle up with him, that's your choice.'

Surprisingly he didn't argue, but as he pushed open the gate she could tell he was far from pleased, but, refusing to back down, refusing to even look at him, she stepped into the garden and as she did all thoughts of money and who was the boss faded in an instant. Despite Dante's gloomy predictions, all she could see was beauty—the sleeping princess that lay beneath the overgrown bracken and thorns.

Dante's manicured gardens were wonderful, but, for Matilda, nothing could beat the raw natural beauty of a neglected garden, a blank canvas for her to work on. It was about the size of a suburban block of land, the centrepiece a massive willow, more than a hundred years in the making, one lifetime simply not enough to produce its full majesty. But that was part of the beauty of her work. A new garden was a mere a sketch on the canvas—the colour, the depth was added over the years, seeds sown that would flourish later, shrubs, trees that would develop, blossom and grow long, long after the cheque had been paid and her tools cleared away.

'Vistas.' It was the first thing that came to mind and she said it out loud, registering his frown. 'Lots of walkways all coming from the willow, lined with hedges and each one leading to a different view, a special area for Alex…'

'You can do something with it?'

She didn't answer, just gave a distracted nod as she pictured the bosky paths, a water feature at the end of one, a sand pit at the end of the other, and…

'A castle,' Matilda breathed. 'An enchanted castle, like a fairy-tale. I know someone who makes the most beautiful cubby houses…' Her voice trailed off as she stared down at the ground, her sandals scuffing the earth. 'We'll use turf for now, but I'll plant lots of different things so that each path will be different—clover for one, daisies for another, buttercups…'

'Will you be able to do it in the time-frame?'

Matilda nodded. 'Less perhaps. I'll know more tomorrow once it's cleared. I've got some people coming at six. There'll be a lot of noise, but only tomorrow…'

'That's fine. Katrina has already said she will take Alex out or to her place during the day. You'll have the place to yourself…' He paused and Matilda wondered if he was going to raise the money issue again, but instead it was a rather more difficult subject he brought up. 'I'm sorry she made you feel uncomfortable.'

'She didn't,' Matilda attempted, then gave in as he raised a questioning eyebrow. 'OK, she did make me feel a bit uncomfortable, but it's fine.'

'I'll take you and show you the summerhouse. But you don't have to cook for yourself, you're very welcome to come over for—'

'I'll be fine,' Matilda interrupted. 'In fact, it's probably better that I stay there…' Blowing her fringe skyward, Matilda attempted the impossible but, ever direct, Dante beat her to it.

'After what happened on Friday?' He checked and despite a deep blush Matilda gave a wry smile.

'I don't think Katrina would approve somehow if she knew. She doesn't even know that we had dinner, let alone…'

'It's none of Katrina's business,' Dante pointed out, but Matilda shook her head.

'Oh, but she thinks it is.'

'Matilda.' His black eyes were boring into her, and she could only admire his boldness that he could actually look at her, unlike she, herself, who gave in after once glance, choosing instead to stare at her toes as he spoke. 'I will tell you what I told Katrina. I have no interest in a relationship—any relationship. For now I grieve for what I have lost: a wife and the happiness of my daughter.' Still she looked down, swallowing down the questions that were on the tip of her tongue. But either he could read her mind or he had used this speech many times before, because he answered each and every one of them with painful, brutal honesty, his silken, thick accent doing nothing to sweeten the bitterness of the message.

'I like women—I like beautiful women,' he drawled, wrapping the knife that stabbed her in velvet as he plunged it in. 'And as you would have seen in the paper yesterday, sometimes I keep their company, but there is always concurrence, always there is an understanding that it can go nowhere. If I misled you on Friday, I apologise.'

'You didn't mislead me.' Matilda croaked the words out then instantly regretted them. In that split second she understood what Dante was offering her, what this emotionally abstinent man was telling her—that she could have him for a short while, could share his bed, but not his heart. And all Matilda knew was that she couldn't do it, couldn't share his bed knowing she must walk away, that deadening his pain would only exacerbate hers. His hand reached out towards her, his fingers cupping her chin, lifting her face to his. Yet she still refused to look at him, knew that if her eyes met his then she'd be lost.

'You didn't mislead me, Dante, because it was just a kiss.' Somehow she kept her voice even; somehow she managed to keep her cheeks from flaming as she lied through her teeth. 'A kiss to end the evening. I certainly had no intention of taking things further, either then or now.' She knew she hadn't convinced him and from the slight narrowing of his eyes knew that he didn't believe her. Taking a breath, she elaborated, determined to set the tone, and the boundaries in order to survive the next couple of weeks. She didn't want to be one of Dante's ships that passed in the night. 'Since Edward and I broke up, I've been on a few dates, had a few kisses, but…' Matilda gave a nervous shrug. 'You know the saying: you have to kiss a lot of frogs…' From his slightly startled look clearly he didn't know it. 'One kiss was enough for me, Dante.'

'I see.' He gave a tight smile. 'I think.'

'It won't be happening again,' Matilda affirmed, hoping that if she said it enough she might even believe it herself.

'I just wanted to clear things up.'

'Good.' Matilda forced a bright smile, relieved this torture was almost over. 'I'm glad that you did.'

'And I'm sorry that you did not enjoy the kiss.' His words wiped the smile from her face, his eyes boring into her. She couldn't be sure, but Matilda was positive he was teasing her, that he knew she was lying and, of course, she was. It had been the most breathtaking kiss of her life, her whole body was burning now just at the mere memory, but it was imperative Dante didn't know. He'd made it clear he wasn't interested in anything more than the most casual of casual flings, and that was the last thing she needed now—especially with a man like Dante. There was nothing casual about him, nothing casual about the feelings he evoked, and if she played with this particular fire, Matilda knew she'd end up seriously burnt. 'Because I thought that—'

'Could you show me where I'm staying, please?' Matilda snapped, following Dante's lead and refusing to be drawn somewhere she didn't want to go. She turned abruptly to go, but in her haste to escape she forgot about the blackberries. Her leg caught on a branch, the thorn ripping into her bare calf, a yelp of pain escaping her lips.

'Careful.' Dante's reflexes were like lightning. He pulled back the branch and held her elbow as Matilda stepped back and instinctively inspected the damage, tears of pain and embarrassment filling her eyes at the vivid red gash.

'I'm fine,' she breathed.

'You're bleeding.'

'It's just a scratch. If you can just show me where I'm staying…' she said. She almost shouted it this time she so badly wanted out of there, wanted some privacy from his knowing eyes, but Dante was pulling out a neatly folded hanky and running it under the garden tap, before returning and dropping to his knees.

'Please.' Matilda was practically begging now, near to tears, not with pain but with embarrassment and want, the thought of him touching her exquisitely unbearable. But Dante wasn't listening. One hand cupped her calf, the other pressed the cool silk into her stinging cut, and it was as soothing as it was disturbing—the ultimate pleasure-pain principle as his hands tended her, calming and arousing. Matilda bit so hard on her lip she thought she might draw blood there, too, her whole body tense, standing rigid as he pressed the handkerchief harder, her stomach a knot of nervous anticipation as she felt his breath against her thigh.

'I'll just press for a minute and stop the bleeding, then I'll take you over to the summerhouse…' Strange that his voice was completely normal, that his body was completely relaxed, while hers was spinning in wild orbit, stirred with naked lust, shameful, inappropriate thoughts filling her mind as he tended her. She couldn't believe her own thought process as she stood there, gazing down. His fingers were pushed into her calf as the cool silk pressed on her warm skin, his breath on her leg as he spoke. And how she wanted to feel that delicious mouth again, but on her thigh this time, almost willing with her eyes for his fingers to creep higher, to quell the pulse that was leaping between her legs, to calm the heat with his cool, cool hand. 'I think there's a first-aid box…'

'I'll be OK.' She shivered the words out.

'Of course you will, it's just a cut, but…' His voice faded as he looked up at her, his eyes fixing on hers. And she stared back, trapped like a deer in the headlights, knowing he could feel it now, could see her treacherous arousal, could smell her excitement, *knew* that she had lied when she had said she didn't want him.

The silence fizzed between them as he continued to stare, and for that moment the choice was entirely his— reason, logic, had gone the second he'd touched her. If Dante pulled her down now, they both knew that she wouldn't even attempt to resist…

'Matilda…' His voice was thick with lust, his eyes blatantly desiring her. Thank God he spoke, thank God he broke the spell, gave her that tiny moment to stab at self-preservation and pull back her leg. Her face flaming she turned around, denied absolutely what was taking place, turning and heading for the gate, practically wrenching it open, just desperate for some space, some distance, a chance to think before her body betrayed her again.

There for the taking.

Those were the words he'd taunted her with on Friday night and those were the words that taunted her now as he led her over to the summerhouse and briefly showed her around.

As the door closed on Dante, not even looking at her surroundings, Matilda sank onto the bed and buried her face in her hands, cringing with shame, as sure as she could be that Dante had witnessed her arousal, had sensed her desire.

What was wrong with her? She wasn't even, according to Edward, supposed to like sex, yet here she was acting like some hormone-laden teenage girl with a king-sized crush, contemplating an affair with a man who wanted nothing more than her body.

And *how* she was contemplating! Despite her attempts at indifference, despite her brave words before, she wanted him. But unlike Dante, it wasn't just bed she wanted but the prelude to it and the postscript afterwards, the parts of him he wasn't prepared to give.

For the first time she took in her surroundings. The summerhouse was certainly comfortable—in fact, it was gorgeous. A cedar attic-shaped building, tucked away at the rear of the property, no doubt it had once been a rather impressive shed, but it had been lovingly refurbished, the attention to detail quite amazing. A small kitchenette as you entered, and to the left a small *en suite* with a shower, the rest of the floor space taken up by a large bed and a television and CDs. Janet, the rather prim housekeeper, came over with her bags and filled up the fridge with produce, explaining that the previous owners had used it as a bed and breakfast, but since the Costellos had owned it, for the most part it had remained empty.

'Mr Costello wanted to know if you'll be joining him for dinner,' Janet said, once she had stocked up the fridge with enough food to feed a small army. 'It's served at seven-thirty once young Alex is in bed, except for Tuesdays and Thursdays. I have my bible class on those nights…'

'No,' Matilda quickly answered, then softened her rather snappy response with a smile. 'I mean, tell him, no, thank you,' she added.

'I'll bring your dinner over to you,' Janet offered, but Matilda stood firm.

'There's really no need. I'll just have a sandwich or something, or go out to one of the cafés.'

'As you wish.' Janet shrugged as she headed out the door. 'But if you need anything, just ring through.'

Alone, Matilda changed into her working clothes— a pair of faded denim shorts that had seen better days and a flimsy T-shirt, topping the rather unflattering ensemble off with a pair of socks and her workboots. She poked her tongue out at her reflection in the mirror—at least Katrina would be pleased! Grateful for the diversion of the garden to take her mind off Dante, she turned on her mobile, winced at the rather full message bank, then promptly chose to ignore it, instead ringing the various people she would be needing, firming up a time with Declan to bring his bob-cat and confirming the large number of skips she had ordered to be delivered at Dante's in the morning. Then she headed off to the garden armed with a notebook and tape measure, ready to turn her vision into the plans that would become a reality. She lost herself for hours, as she always did when a project engrossed her, only downing tools and heading for the summerhouse when the last fingers of light had faded, hot, thirsty and exhausted, ready for a long, cool drink, followed by a long cool shower…

But not a cold one!

Yelping in alarm, Matilda fiddled with the taps, but to no avail, realising with a sinking heart that no amount of wishful thinking was going to change things: the hot-water system really wasn't working. Grabbing a towel,

Matilda wrapped it around her and sat shivering on the bed, trying and failing to decide what on earth to do. If she had been here for a couple of weeks to type up notes or fix some accounts then somehow she'd have struggled through, but even if her business cards screamed the words 'landscape designer,' at the end of the day gardening was a dirty job—filthy at times. And a fortnight of black nails and grit in her hair wasn't a prospect Matilda relished. Of course, the obvious thing to do would be to ring Janet and explain the situation but, then, there was nothing *obvious* about this situation—the absolute last place she wanted to be was crossing Dante's manicured lawn clutching her toiletry bag! Eyeing the kettle, Matilda rolled her eyes, the irony of her situation hitting home as she filled the tiny sink and swished a bar of soap around to make bubbles—here she was in a multi-million dollar home, and washing like a pauper!

CHAPTER FIVE

GOD, it was hot.

Matilda filled up her water bottle from the tap and surveyed the barren scene.

The morning had been crisp—par for the course in Melbourne. Used to the elements, she'd layered her clothing—gallons of sunscreen, followed by boots and shorts, a crop top, a T-shirt, a long-sleeved top, a jumper and a hat. Up at the crack of dawn, she'd greeted the workers and given her directions. Money wasn't the problem, time was, so a small army had been hired for the messy job of clearing the site. They all worked well, the skips filling quickly. As the day warmed up the jumper was the first to go, followed an hour or so later by her cotton top, and as each layer of clothing came off Matilda, so too did the garden start to emerge—until finally, long since down to her crop top, the late afternoon sun burning into her shoulders, Matilda surveyed her exhausting day's work. The subcontractors had finally gone, the skips noisily driven away, leaving the site bare and muddy apart from the gorgeous willow. At last she had her blank canvas!

Gulping on her water bottle, Matilda walked around the site, checking the fence, pleased to see that it was in good order. All it needed was a few minor repairs and a spraypaint but there was nothing that could be done this evening—she was too tired anyway. All Matilda wanted to do now was pack up her things and head for her temporary home. Actually, all Matilda wanted to do was *leave* her things and head for home, but mindful of safety she reluctantly headed over to the pile of equipment. She splashed some water from her bottle onto her face and decided more desperate measures were needed. Taking off her hat, she filled it and sloshed it onto her head, closing her eyes in blessed relief as the water ran down her face and onto her shoulders. Feeling the sting of cold on her reddened face and catching her breath, Matilda delighted in a shiver for a moment, before the sun caught up.

'Matilda.' The familiar voice made her jump. She'd been so sure she was alone, but here she was, soaked to the skin at her own doing, face smeared with mud, squinting into the low sunlight at the forebidding outline of Dante. 'I startled you. I'm sorry to barge in.'

'Not at all!' She shook her head and tried to look not remotely startled. 'It's your garden after all—I was just packing up.' Brutally aware of the mess she looked and with two nipples sticking out of her soaking top, thanks to the halflitre of water she'd just poured over herself, Matilda busied herself clearing up her tools as Dante came over.

'I thought I'd bring Alex to see the garden before she went to bed.' He was carrying her, which was just as well. It was rather more a demolition site than a garden at the moment. Dante picked his way around the edge and let Alex down on the one grassed area left—under the willow tree. It was only patchily grassed, but at least it was clean and dry—and given that the little girl was dressed in her nighty and had clearly had her bedtime bath, it was just as well. Matilda gave up in pretending to look at her tools and watched him as he came over. He was wearing shorts and runners—and no socks, which just accentuated the lean, muscular length of his brown calves. His whole body seemed incredibly toned, actually—and Matilda momentary wondered how. He didn't seem the type for a gym and he spent an immoderate time at the office.

'Hi, Alex.' Matilda smiled at the little girl, not remotely fazed by the lack of her response, just enchanted by her beauty. 'I know it looks a terrible mess now, but in a few days it will look wonderful.'

Alex didn't even appear to be looking—her eyes stared fixedly ahead. A little rigid figure, she stood quite still as Matilda chatted happily to her, explaining what was going to happen over the next few days, pointing out where the water features would be, the sand pit and the enchanted castle.

'You've got a lot done today,' Dante observed. 'What happens now?'

'The boring stuff,' Matilda answered. 'I've got the plumber and electrician coming tomorrow and then the concreters, but once all that's out the way, hopefully it will start to take shape a bit.' And though she longed to ask about his day, longed to extend the conversation just a touch longer, deliberately she held back, determined that it must be Dante who came to her now—she'd already been embarrassed enough. But the silence was excruciating as they stood there, and it was actually a relief when Dante headed over to his daughter and went to pick her up.

'Time for bed, little lady.' Something twisted inside Matilda at the tenderness in his voice, the strong gentle arms that lowered to lift his daughter. But Alex resisted, letting out a furious squeal that pierced the quiet early evening air, arching her back, her little hands curling into fists. Matilda's eyes widened at the fury that erupted in the little girl, stunned to witness the change in this silent, still, child. But clearly used to this kind of response, Dante was way too quick for Alex, gently but firmly taking her wrists and guiding her hands to her sides.

'No!' he said firmly. 'No hitting.'

With a mixture of tenderness and strength he picked Alex up, clasping her furious, resisting body to his chest, utterly ignoring the shrill screams, just holding her ever tighter. Finally she seemed to calm, the screams, the fury abating until finally Dante smiled wryly as he caught Matilda's shocked eyes. 'Believe it or not, I think you just received a compliment. Normally I don't have to even ask to bring her in from the garden. Perhaps she is going to like it after all.'

Two compliments even! Matilda thought to herself. Was Dante actually saying he liked her plans as well?

'I'll take her inside and get her to bed.' Matilda gazed at the little girl, now resting in her father's arms. Not a trace of the angry outburst of only moments before remained, her dark eyes staring blankly across the wilderness of the garden. 'Are you finishing up?'

'Soon.' Matilda nodded. 'I'm just going to pack my things.'

'You're welcome to come over for dinner…'

'No, thanks!' Matilda said, and she didn't offer an explanation, didn't elaborate at all, just turned her back and started to pack up her things.

'It's no trouble,' Dante pushed, but still she didn't turn around, determined not to give him the satisfaction of drawing her in just to reject her again, just to change his mind or hurt her with cruel words. 'I just warm the meal up tonight. Janet has her Alcoholics Anonymous meetings on Mondays and Thursdays.'

'But she said she had…' Matilda swung around then snapped her mouth closed, furious with herself for responding.

'Everyone has their secrets, remember.' Dante shrugged then gave her the benefit of a very wicked smile. 'Come,' he offered again.

'No,' Matilda countered. This time she didn't even bother to be polite, just turned her back on him and started to sort out her things, only letting out the breath she had been holding when, after the longest time, she heard the click of the gate closing. Alex didn't just have her father's eyes, Matilda realised, she had his personality, too. They shared the same dark, lonely existence, cruelly, capriciously striking out at anyone they assumed was getting too close, yet somehow drawing them in all the same, somehow managing to be forgiven.

* * *

A cold shower mightn't be so bad, Matilda attempted to convince herself as she gingerly held her fingers under the jets. All day she'd been boiling, all day she'd longed to cool down—but the trouble with her line of work was that there was absolutely no chance of a quick dart in the shower. Her hair was stiff with dust, her fingers black from the soil, her skin almost as dark as Dante's.

Biting down on her lip, Matilda dived into the shower, yelping as the icy water hit her. Forcing herself to put her head under, she frantically rubbed in shampoo, praying that in a moment she'd acclimatise, that the freezing water might actually merely be cool after a couple of minutes' more torture. Only it wasn't. Her misery lasted long after she'd turned the beastly taps off and wrapped a towel around her, her poorly rinsed hair causing a river of stinging of water to hit her eyes. Shivering and cursing like the navvy Katrina had hoped for, Matilda groped for the door handle, wrenching it open and storming head first into a wall of flesh.

'When were you going to tell me?' Dante demanded. 'I could hear you screaming…'

Matilda stood in shook. 'Are you spying on me?' She felt embarrassed and enraged. Her bloodshot, stinging eyes focused on the walkie-talkie he was holding in his hand.

'It's a child monitor,' he explained with infinite patience, as if she were some sort of mentally unhinged person he was talking down from the roof. But she could see the tiny twitch on his lips, knew that inside he was laughing at her, her misery, her embarrassment increasing as he carried on talking. 'Janet left a note, telling me about the water. I just read it, so will you, please, collect your belongings so that I can help you bring your things over.'

'There's really no need for that,' Matilda insisted, feeling horribly exposed and vulnerable and also somewhat deflated that even standing before him, her body drenched, clearly naked under a towel, she didn't move him at all. 'I've got a plumber coming tomorrow…'

'Matilda.' He gave a weary sigh. 'My daughter is asleep in the house alone so could you, please, just…?' He faltered for just a fraction of a second, telling her in that fraction of time that she had been wrong—that Dante was very aware of her near-nakedness. She clutched the towel tighter around her, scuffed the floor with her dripping foot as immediately he continued. 'Get dressed, Matilda,' he said gruffly. 'I'll come back for your things later.'

Which really didn't leave her much choice.

CHAPTER SIX

It was a very shy, rather humble Matilda that joined Dante at the heavy wooden table that was the centre-piece of his impressive al fresco area, the beastly child monitor blinking at her on the table as she approached, her face darkening to purple as she realised she'd practically accused the man of stalking her. She braced herself for a few harsh words Dante-style but instead he poured an indecent amount of wine into her glass then pushed it across the table to her.

'Is red OK?'

'Marvellous,' Matilda lied, taking a tentative sip, surprised to find that this particular red actually was OK, warming her from the inside out. Holding the massive glass in her pale hand, she stared at the dark liquid, anything rather than look at him, and started a touch when the intercom crackled loudly.

'Static,' Dante explained, pressing a button. 'Someone down the road mowing their lawn or drying their hair. I just change the channel, see.'

'Oh.'

'You don't have any experience with children, do you?'

'None,' Matilda answered. 'I mean, none at all. Well apart from my friend, Sally…'

'She has a baby?'

'No.' Matilda gave a pale smile. 'But she's thought that she might be pregnant a couple of times.'

He actually laughed, and it sounded glorious, a deep rich sound, his white teeth flashing. Matilda was amazed after her exquisite discomfort of only a moment ago to find herself actually laughing, too, her pleasure increasing as Dante gave a little bit more, actually revealed a piece of himself, only not with the impassive voice he had used before but with genuine warmth and emotion, his face softer somehow, his voice warmer as this inaccessible man let her in a touch, allowed her to glimpse another dimension to his complex nature.

'Until Alex was born, apart from on television, I don't think I'd ever seen a newborn.' He frowned, as if examining that thought for the first time. 'No, I'm sure I hadn't. My mother was the youngest of seven children. All my cousins were older and I, too, was the youngest—very spoiled!'

'I can imagine.' Matilda rolled her eyes, but her smile remained as Dante continued.

'Then this tiny person appeared and suddenly I am supposed to know.' He spread his hands expressively, but words clearly failed him.

'I'd be terrified,' Matilda admitted.

'I was,' Dante stated. 'Still am, most of the time.'

Her smile faded, seeing him now not as the man that moved her but as the single father he was, trying yet knowing she was failing to fathom the enormity of the task that had been so squarely placed on his shoulders.

'It must be hard.'

'It is.' Dante nodded and didn't sweeten it with the usual superlatives that generally followed such a state-ment, didn't smile and eagerly nod that it was more than worth it, or the best thing he'd ever done in his life. He just stared back at her for the longest time, before continuing, 'I have a big trial starting next week, but once that it is out of the way, I need to make a decision.'

'Whether to move back to Italy?'

Dante nodded. 'Every doctor I have consulted tells me that Alex needs a routine, that she needs a solid home base—at the moment I am having trouble provid-ing that. Katrina is only too willing to help, but…' He hesitated and took a long sip of his drink. Matilda held her breath, willing him to continue, to glean a little more insight into the problems he faced. 'She wants to keep Jasmine alive, doesn't want anything that might detract from her daughter's memory, which is under-standable, of course, only sometimes…'

'It's a bit much?' Matilda tentatively offered, relieved when he didn't frown back at her, relieved that maybe she understood just a little of what he was feeling.

'Much too much,' Dante agreed, then terminated the conversation, standing up and gesturing. 'I will show you the guest room, it's already made up—then we can eat.'

'I might just grab a sandwich or something when I get my things,' Matilda started, but Dante just ignored her, leading her through the house and upstairs, gesturing for her to be quiet as they tiptoed past Alex's room, before coming to a large door at the end of the hallway.

Clearly Dante's idea of a guest room differed from Matilda's somewhat—her version was a spare room with a bed and possibly an ironing board for good measure. But Dante's guests were clearly used to better. As he pushed open the door and she stepped inside, Matilda realised just how far she'd been relegated by Katrina. Till then the summerhouse had been more than OK, but it wasn't a patch on this! A massive king-sized bed made up with crisp white linen was the focus point of the fabulously spacious room, but rather than being pushed against the wall and sensibly facing a door, as most of the population would have done, instead it stood proudly in the middle, staring directly out of one of the massive windows Matilda had till now only glimpsed from the outside, offering a panoramic view of the bay. Matilda thought she must have died and gone to heaven—ruing every last minute she'd spent struggling on in the summerhouse when she could have been here!

'I won't sleep,' Matilda sighed dreamily, wandering over to the window and pressing her face against the glass, like a child staring into a toy-shop Christmas display. 'I'll spend the whole night watching the water and then I'll be too exhausted to do your garden. It's just divine…'

'And,' Dante said with a teasing dramatic note to his voice that Matilda had never heard before, 'it has running water.'

'You're kidding.' Matilda played along, liking the change in him, the funnier, more relaxed side of him she was slowly starting to witness.

'Not just that, but *hot* running water.' Dante smiled, sliding open the *en suite* door as Matilda reluctantly peeled herself away from the view and padded over. 'See for yourself.'

The smile was wiped off her face as she stepped inside. Fabulous it might be but she couldn't possibly use it, her frantic eyes scanning the equally massive window for even a chink of a blind or curtain.

'No one can see.' Dante rolled his eyes at her expression.

'Apart from every passing sailor and the nightly ferry load on its way to Tasmania!' Matilda gulped.

'The windows are treated, I mean tinted,' Dante simultaneously explained and corrected himself. Even a couple of hours ago she'd have felt stupid or gauche, but his smile seemed genuine enough at least that Matilda was able to smile back. 'I promise that no one will see you.'

'Good.'

'Now that we've taken care of that, can we eat?'

This time she didn't even bother to argue.

Wandering back along the hallway, Dante put his fingers to his lips and pushed open Alex's door to check on his daughter. Matilda stood there as he crept inside. The little girl was lying with one skinny leg sticking out of between the bars of her cot, her tiny, angelic face relaxed in sleep. Matilda felt her heart go out to this beautiful child who had been through so, so much, a lump building in her throat as Dante slowly moved her leg back in then retrieved a sheet that had fallen from the cot and with supreme tenderness tucked it around Alex, gently stroking her shoulder as she stirred slightly.

But Matilda wasn't watching Alex any more. Instead, she was watching Dante, a sting of tears in her eyes as she glimpsed again his tenderness, slotted in another piece of the puzzle that enthralled her.

When he wasn't being superior or scathing he was actually incredibly nice.

Incredibly nice, Matilda thought a little later as Dante carried two steaming plates into the lounge room and they shared a casual dinner. And whether it was the wine or the mood, conversation came incredibly easily, so much so that when Matilda made a brief reference to her recent break-up, she didn't jump as if she'd been burnt when Dante asked what had gone wrong. She just gave a thoughtful shrug and pondered a moment before answering.

'I honestly don't know,' Matilda finally admitted. 'I don't really know when the problems started. For ages we were really happy. Edward's career was taking off, we were looking at houses and then all of a sudden we seemed to be arguing over everything. Nothing I did was ever right, from the way I dressed to the friends I had. It was as if nothing I did could make him happy.'

'So everything was perfect and then out of the blue arguments started?' Dante gave her a rather disbelieving frown as she nodded. 'It doesn't happen like that, Matilda,' Dante said. 'There is no such thing as perfect. There must have been something that irked, a warning that all was not OK—there always is.'

'How do you know?' Matilda asked, 'I mean how do you know all these things?'

'It's my job to know how people's minds work,'

Dante responded, but then softened it with a hint of personal insight. 'I was in a relationship too, Matilda. I do know that they are not all perfect!'

According to everyone, *his* had been, but Matilda didn't say it, not wanting to break the moment, liking this less reticent Dante she was seeing, actually enjoying talking to him. 'I supposed he always flirted when we were out and it annoyed me,' Matilda admitted. 'We'd go to business dinners and I didn't like the way he was with some of the women. I don't think I'm a jealous person, but if he was like that when I was there…' Her voice trailed off, embarrassed now at having said so much, but Dante just nodded, leaning back on the sofa. His stance was so incredibly nonjudgmental, inexplicably she wanted to continue, actually wanted to tell him how Edward had made her feel, wanted Dante to hear this and hoping maybe in return she'd hear about him, too. 'He wasn't cheating. But I wondered in years to come…'

'Probably.' Dante shrugged. 'No doubt when you'd just had a baby, or your work was busy and you were too tired to focus enough on him, not quite at your goal weight.' He must have registered her frown, her mouth opening then holding back a question that, despite the nature of this personal conversation, wasn't one she had any right to ask, but Dante answered it anyway. 'No, Matilda, I didn't have an affair, if that's what you are thinking. I like beautiful women as much as any man and, yes, at various times in our relationship Jasmine and I faced all of the things I've outlined, but I can truthfully say it would never have entered my head to look at another woman in that way. I wanted to fix our problems, Matilda, not add to them.'

And it was so refreshing to hear it, a completely different perspective, her doubts about opening up to him quashed now as she saw the last painful months through different eyes.

'In the end he spent so much time at work there really wasn't much room for anything else…'

'*Anything* else?' Dante asked, painfully direct, and Matilda took a gulp of her drink then nodded.

'You know, for months I've been going over and over it, wondering if I was just imagining things, if Edward was right, that it was my fault he couldn't…' She snapped her mouth closed. In an unguarded moment she'd revealed way, way more than she'd intended and she halted the conversation there, hoping that Dante would take the cue and do the same, but he was way too sharp.

'What was your fault?'

'Nothing.' Matilda's voice was high. 'Wasn't what I told you reason enough to end things?'

'Of course.'

Silence hung in the air. As understanding as Dante might have been, he certainly couldn't help her with the rest. There was no way she could go there, the words that had been said agony to repeat even to herself. It was none of his damn business anyway.

'You know, people like Edward normally don't respond too well to their own failings—they'd rather make you feel like shit than even consider that they had a problem.' His voice was deep and unusually gentle, and though she couldn't bring herself to look at him she could feel his eyes on her. His insight floored her. She felt transparent, as if somehow he had seen into the deepest, darkest part of her and somehow shed light on it, somehow pried open the lid on her shame. And it was madness, sheer madness that she wanted to open it up more, to let out the pain that was curled up inside there…to share it with Dante.

'He said that it was my fault…' Matilda gagged on the words, screwed her eyes closed, as somehow she told him, told him what she hadn't been able to tell even some of her closest friends. 'That maybe if I was more interesting, made a bit more effort, that he wouldn't look at other women, that he wouldn't have…' She couldn't go there, couldn't tell him everything, she could feel the icy chill of perspiration between her breasts, could feel her neck and her face darkening in the shame of the harsh, cruel words that had been uttered.

'I would imagine that it's incredibly difficult to be amazing in bed when you've been ignored all evening!' Her closed eyes snapped open, her mouth gaping as Dante, as direct as ever, got straight to the point. 'I would think it would be impossible, in fact, to give completely of yourself when you're wondering who he's really holding—whether it's the woman in his arms or the one you caught him chatting to at the bar earlier.'

And she hadn't anticipated crying, but as his words tore through her only then did she truly acknowledge the pain, the pain that had been there for so long now, the bitter aftermath that had lingered long after she'd moved out and moved on with her life. But they were quiet tears, no sobs, no real outward display of emotion other than the salty rivers that ran down her smeared cheeks, stinging her reddened face as Dante gently spoke on, almost hitting the mark but not quite. She'd revealed so much to him, but her ultimate shame was still locked inside.

'It was him with the problem, not you.' His accent was thick.

'He said the same thing—the other way around, of course.' Matilda sniffed. 'I guess it's a matter of opinion who's right! I spent the last few months trying to get back what we'd once had, trying to make it work, but in the end…' She shook her head, unwilling now to go on, the last painful rows still too raw for shared introspection. Thankfully Dante sensed it, offering her another drink from the bottle they'd practically finished, but Matilda declined. 'What about you?'

'Me?' Dante frowned.

'What about your relationship?' Matilda ventured.

'What about it?'

'You said that it wasn't perfect…'

'No.' Dante shook his head.

'You did,' Matilda insisted.

'I said that I knew that they were not *all* perfect—it doesn't mean I was referring to mine.'

Matilda knew he was lying and she also knew that he was closing the subject, yet she refused to leave it there. She'd revealed so much of herself, had felt close to a man for the first time in ages and didn't want it to end like this, didn't want Dante to shut her out all over again.

'You said that you wanted to fix your problems, Dante,' Matilda quoted softly. 'What were they?'

'Does it matter now?' Dante asked, swilling the wine around his glass and refusing to look at her. 'As you said, there are always two sides—is it fair to give mine when Jasmine isn't here to give hers?'

'I think so,' Matilda breathed, chewing on her bottom lip. And even if her voice was tentative, she reeled at her boldness, laid her heart on the line a little bit more, bracing herself for pain as she did so. 'If you want to get close to someone then you have to give a bit of yourself—even the bad bits.'

'And you want to get close?'

He did look at her this time, and she stared back transfixed, a tiny nervous nod affirming her want. 'Tell me about you, how you're feeling…'

'Which part of hell do you want to visit?'

She didn't flinch, didn't say anything, just stared back, watching as slowly he placed his glass on the table. His elbows on his knees, he raked a hand through his hair and so palpable was his pain Matilda was sure if she lifted her hand she'd be able to reach out and touch it. She held her breath as finally he looked up and stared at her for the longest time before speaking.

'Always there is…' He didn't get to start, let alone finish. A piercing scream from the intercom made them both jump. He picked up the intercom, which had been placed on the coffee table, and stood up. 'I have to go to her and then I think I'll head to bed, I've got a pile of paperwork to read. 'Night, Matilda.'

'Let me help with her…'

'She doesn't like strangers.' The shutters were up, his

black eyes dismissing her, the fragile closeness they had so nearly created evaporating in that instant.

'Dante…' Matilda called, but he wasn't listening, her words falling on his departing back as he closed the door behind him. 'Don't make me one.'

CHAPTER SEVEN

PREDICTABLY, Katrina had a plumber screeching up the
driveway within seconds of Dante's chopper lifting off
the smooth lawn, and Matilda could almost envisage her
bags being moved yet again, but quietly hoped for a
miracle. And it wasn't all about Dante. Waking up to the
most glorious sunrise, stretching like a lazy cat in the
scrummy bed, as superficial as it might be, Matilda was
terribly reluctant to leave her very nice surroundings.

'White ants!' Katrina almost choked on her Earl Grey
as the plumber she had summoned popped his head
around the kitchen door and Matilda smothered a smile
as she loaded a tray with coffee to take out to the workers
for their break. 'Well, surely you can replace the water
system and then we'll get the place treated once...' She
managed to stop herself from saying it, but the unspoken
words hung in the air and Matilda took great interest in
filling up the sugar bowl as Katrina paused and then,
rather more carefully, spoke on. 'Just sort out the water,
please. It doesn't all have to be done today.'

'Can't do, I'm afraid,' he said cheerfully. 'The wall's

not stable enough to hold a new system. The place needs to be treated and then some of the walls will have to be replaced—it's going to be a big job.'

It wasn't the only big job the next couple of days unearthed.

Katrina practically moved into Dante's, appearing long before he went to work and staying well into the night when Dante finally got home—not that Matilda really noticed. All her energies were taken up with the garden—her efficient start to the job but a distant memory as problems compounded problems. The glorious willow tree had roots that weren't quite as wondrous, thwarting Matilda's carefully lain plans at each and every turn. And a rather unproductive day followed by a floodlit late night were spent with the plumber and electrician, trying to find a suitable spot to lay the pipes for the water features. Then, just when that was taken care of, Matilda awoke to the news that, despite her inspection, the white ants had migrated from the summerhouse to the rear wall of the fence, which would set things back yet another day while it was ripped out and replaced. More skips delivered, more delays ensuing, and by the time she dragged herself back to the house, all Matilda could manage was a warmed-up meal and a very weary goodnight as, drooping with exhaustion, she headed off for bed.

Still as the week drew to a close, if not order then at least a semblance of control had been restored. Finally the pipes were laid, the electricity was on and the garden that had till now merely lived in her mind could actually start to emerge.

'I think we must have a mole on steroids,' Dante quipped, eyeing the mounds of earth that littered the area, and his easy humour bought the first smile in a long time to Matilda's tense face as he wandered in with Alex late one evening to check on the progress. 'I hear things haven't gone exactly to plan.'

'On the contrary,' Matilda replied. 'Things have gone exactly to plan—there's always a disaster waiting to happen with this kind of work. But I think we're finally under control.'

'Will you be joining us for dinner?'

'Us?' Matilda checked, because Alex was clearly ready for bed.

'Katrina and Hugh have come over—I should give Janet the numbers.'

'No, thanks.' Matilda shook her head but didn't elaborate, didn't make up an excuse or reason.

'I'm sorry I haven't been over.' Dante switched Alex to his other hip. 'My trial preparation has taken up a lot of time, things have been busy—'

'Tell me about it,' Matilda said, rolling her eyes.

'I'm sure that I'd bore you to death,' Dante responded, completely missing the point. But somehow the language barrier actually worked in their favour for once, the tiny misunderstanding opening a door, pushing the stilted, polite conversation way beyond the intentions of either participant. 'Are you really interested?'

'Very,' Matilda responded. 'Completely unqualified, of course, but terribly interested.'

'But you know that I cannot discuss it with you.'

'I know,' Matilda answered. 'I mean, at the end of the

day, the barrister mulling over his case with the gardener…'

'I cannot discuss it with *anyone*,' Dante broke in, and she watched as his eyes closed in shuttered regret, felt again the weight of responsibility that rode on his broad shoulders and ached to soothe him.

'I know,' Matilda said softly, then gave him a little spontaneous nudge. 'Well, I don't *know* exactly, but I have got pay TV.' She smiled at his frown. 'I've paced the courtroom floor with the best of them, and from what I've gleaned you're allowed to talk in general terms.'

'You're crazy.' Dante laughed, his palpable tension momentarily lifting, but the shrill of his mobile broke the moment. Matilda watched as he juggled his daughter and flicked out his mobile, watched the vivid concentration on his face, the turn of his back telling her that this call was important. She reacted as anyone would have, held out her arms and offered to take his daughter, lifting the little girl into her arms, hardly registering the surprise on Dante's face as he barked his orders into the phone.

'She went to you!'

A full fifteen minutes had passed. Fifteen minutes of Dante talking into the phone as Matilda at first held Alex but when she got a bit heavy, Matilda put her down, gathering the few exhausted, remaining daisies from under the willow, slitting the stalks with her thumb and making if not a daisy chain then at least a few links—chatting away to an uncommunicative Alex. But the little girl did appear to be watching at least and now Dante was kneeling down with them, staring open-mouthed at what Matilda considered was really a very normal scene.

'Sorry?' Matilda was trying to wrestle a very limp stalk into a very thin one.

'Alex actually went to you.' Dante's voice had a slightly incredulous note as he watched Alex take the small chain of daisies Matilda was offering.

'I'm really not that scary, Dante.' Matilda smiled.

'You don't understand. Alex doesn't go to anyone. You saw what she was like the other day when it was *me* trying to pick her up.'

'Maybe she's ready to start trusting a little again…' Matilda looked over at Dante and spoke over the little blonde head that was between them. Even though it was Alex she was talking about, they knew her words were meant for both. 'Maybe now she's done it once, it will be easier the next time.' For an age she stared at him, for an age he stared back, then his hands hovered towards his daughter, ready to pick her up and head for the house, ready to walk away yet again. But Matilda's voice halted him. 'Let her play for a few minutes. She's enjoying the flowers.' She was, her little fingers stroking the petals, concentration etched on her face, and for all the world she looked like any other little girl lost in a daydream. 'Talk to me, Dante,' Matilda said. 'You might surprise yourself and find that it helps.'

'I don't think so.'

'I do,' Matilda said firmly, watching as his gaze drifted to Alex, and finally after the longest time he spoke.

'Remember when we talked at the restaurant?' She could hear him choosing his words carefully. 'You asked if I ever regret winning and I said no?' Matilda nodded. 'I lied.'

'I know,' Matilda answered.

'Not professionally, of course.' Dante pondered, his accent a little more pronounced as his mind clearly wandered elsewhere. 'I always walk into a courtroom wanting to win, I wouldn't be there otherwise, but, yes, sometimes there is a feeling of…' He snapped his fingers in impatience as he tried to find the right word.

'Regret?' Matilda offered, and Dante shook his head.

'Unease,' he said. 'A sense of unease that I do my job so well.'

'There would have to be,' Matilda said carefully, knowing she couldn't push things, knowing she had to listen to the little information he was prepared to give.

'There is another side, too, though…' His eyes found and held hers and Matilda knew that what he was about to tell her was important. 'There are certain cases that matter more. Matter because…' He didn't continue, couldn't perhaps, so Matilda did it for him.

'Because if you won there would be no unease?' She watched the bob of his Adam's apple as he swallowed, knew she had guessed correctly, that Dante was telling her, as best he could, that the man he was defending was innocent and that this case, perhaps, mattered more than most.

'You'll win,' Matilda said assuredly, and Dante let out a tired sigh and gave a rather resigned smile, pulling himself up to go, clearly wondering why he'd bothered talking to her if that was the best she could come up with! 'You will—you always do,' Matilda said with absolute conviction. 'Your client couldn't have better representation.'

'Matilda,' Dante said with dry superiority, 'we're *not* talking about my client and, anyway, you have absolutely no idea what you're talking about.'

'Oh, but I do.' Her green eyes caught his as he reached out for his daughter.

'You know nothing about law,' Dante needlessly pointed out. 'You know nothing about—'

'Perhaps,' Matilda interrupted. 'But you've already told me what you're capable of, already told me that you can do it even if you don't believe…' She paused for a moment, remembering the rules, remembering that she had to keep it general. 'If I were in trouble, I mean.' She gave a cheeky grin. 'Suppose I *had* been caught taking those chocolates and assuming I could afford you…' She gave a tiny roll eye as her fantasy took on even more bizarre proportions. 'I'd want to walk into court with the best.'

'Am I the best for him, though?' He raked a hand through his jet hair and it was Dante who forgot to keep things general.

'Absolutely,' Matilda whispered. 'I'd want the best I could afford, Dante, but having you believe in me would mean a thousand times more. Think of what you've already achieved then imagine what you're capable of when you actually believe in someone.' A frown marred his brow, but it wasn't one of tension, more realization, and Matilda knew that she'd got through to him, knew that somehow she'd reassured him, maybe helped a little even. 'You're going to be fine,' Matilda said again, and this time he didn't bite back, this time he didn't shoot her down with some superior remark, just gave her a gentle nod of thanks.

'Time for bed, Alex,' Matilda said, holding her arms out to the little girl, and even though Alex didn't hold out her own arms, she didn't resist when Matilda picked her up and wandered with Dante to the gate.

'She likes you,' Dante said as he took a sleepy Alex from Matilda.

'I'm very easy to like,' Matilda answered.

'Very easy,' Dante said, only, unlike before, Matilda knew there were no double meanings or cruel euphemisms to mull over. As he walked away the echo of his words brought a warm glow to her tired, aching body.

Quite simply it was the nicest thing he'd ever said.

CHAPTER EIGHT

'I'M SORRY to have disturbed you.'

'It's fine.' Matilda attempted, struggling to sit up, slightly disorientated and extremely embarrassed that Dante had found her in the middle of the day, hot and filthy in nothing more than the skimpiest of shorts and a crop top, lying on a blanket with her eyes closed. Absolutely the *last* person she was expecting to see at this hour, he was dressed in his inevitable dark suit, but there was a slightly more relaxed stance to him. He held a brown paper bag in one hand and he didn't look in his usual rush—his usually perfectly knotted tie was loosened, the top button of his shirt undone. But his dark eyes were shielded with sunglasses making his closed expression even more unreadable if that were possible.

'You've done a lot.'

'It's getting there.' Matilda nodded. 'And if I keep going at full speed, I could still be done by early next week.'

He didn't say a word, he didn't have to. Just a tiny questioning lift of his eyebrow from behind his dark glasses was enough for Matilda.

'I am allowed to take a break,' Matilda retorted.

'I didn't say anything!'

'You might not have *said* it but I certainly *heard* it. I am allowed to take a break, Dante. For your information, I've been working since first light this morning—apart from a coffee at ten I haven't stopped.'

'You don't have to justify yourself to me.'

'No, I don't.' Matilda agreed.

'How you organise your time is entirely your business. It's just…' His voice faded for a moment, a hint of a very unusual smile dusting across his face. 'I think I must be in the wrong job. "Flat out" for me is back-to-back meetings, endless phone calls, figures, whereas the twice I've seen you work, you're either taking an impromptu shower with a water bottle or dozing under a tree.' She opened her mouth to set him straight, but Dante spoke over her. 'I am not criticising you, I can see for myself the hours of work you have done. For once I was not even being sarcastic—I really was thinking back there when I saw you that I am in the wrong job!'

'You are.' Matilda smiled, the wind taken out of her sails by his niceness. 'And for the record, I wasn't dozing.'

'Matilda, don't try and tell me that you weren't asleep. You didn't even hear me come over. You were lying on your back with your eyes closed.'

'I was meditating,' Matilda said and seeing the disbelieving look on his face she elaborated further. 'I did hear you come over, I just…' It was Matilda's voice fading now, wondering how she could explain to him that in her deeply relaxed state she had somehow discounted the information.

'Just what?'

'I didn't hold onto the thought.'

'You've lost me.' He shook his head as if to clear it. 'You're really telling me that you weren't asleep!'

'That's right—I often meditate when I'm working, that's where I get my best ideas. You should try it,' she added.

'I have enough trouble getting to sleep at one in the morning, let alone in the middle of the day.'

'My point exactly,' Matilda said triumphantly. 'I've already told you that I wasn't asleep. You're very quick to throw scorn, but sometimes the best way to find the answer to a question is to stop looking for it.'

'Perhaps.' Dante gave a dismissive shrug. 'But for now I'll stick with the usual methods. I actually came to see if you wanted some lunch.' Before she could shake her head, before she could come up with an excuse as to why she didn't want to go over and eat with Katrina, Dante held out the paper bag he was holding. 'I bought some rolls from the deli.'

'The deli?'

'Why does that surprise you?'

'I don't know,' Matilda admitted, her neck starting to ache from staring up, feeling at a distinct disadvantage as Dante hovered over her. Wiggling over, she patted the blanket for him to sit beside her. 'It just does. How come you're home?'

'I live here,' Dante quipped, but he *did* sit down beside her, pulling the rolls out of the bag and offering one to her. 'I've spent the entire morning trying to read an important, complicated document relating to the case and haven't got past the second page. My new secretary cannot distinguish between urgent and urgent yet.'

'I don't understand.'

'Invariably anyone who wants to speak with me says that it is urgent—but she puts them all through, then I get waylaid. I decided to follow your business methods, they seem to be working for you.'

'What method?' Matilda gasped. 'I didn't know I had one!'

'Turning the phone off and disappearing. Katrina is out with Alex today. I thought there was more chance of actually getting some work done if I just came home, but first I must have some lunch.'

'I didn't hear the chopper!'

'I drove,' Dante said, 'and it was nice.' They ate in amicable silence until Dante spoiled it, his words almost causing her to choke on her chicken and avocado roll. 'I was thinking about you.'

'Me?'

'And how much I enjoy talking to you.' He took off his dark glasses and smiled a lazy smile, utterly comfortable in his own skin as Matilda squirmed inside hers, wriggling her bare feet in the moss and staring at her toes. 'And you're right, it's nice to take a moment to relax.'

Relaxed certainly wasn't how Matilda would describe herself now. He was so close that if she moved her leg an inch they'd be touching, if his face came a fraction closer she knew they'd be kissing. Desire coursed through her as it had when she'd cut herself, only this time Dante didn't seem to be pulling back, this time he was facing her head on. It was Matilda who turned abruptly away, terrified he'd read the naked lust in her eyes. She took a long drink from her water bottle then, blowing her fringe skywards and trying to keep her voice normal, determined not to make a fool of herself again, to be absolutely sure she wasn't misreading things, she said, 'You should try meditating if you want to be relaxed.'

'It wouldn't work,' Dante dismissed.

'It won't if that's your attitude…' She could feel the atmosphere sizzling between them, knew that if she said what was on her mind then she'd be crossing a line, playing the most dangerous of dangerous games. 'Try it,' she breathed, her eyes daring him to join her. 'Why don't you lie back and try it now?'

'Now?' Dante checked, a dangerous warning glint in his eyes, which she heeded, but it only excited her more.

'Now,' Matilda affirmed. 'Just lie back.'

'Then what?' Dante's impatient voice demanded instruction as, impossibly tense, he lay back.

'You close your eyes and just breathe,' Matilda said, her head turning to face him, her own breath catching in her throat as she gazed at his strong profile. She'd been right with her very first assessment of Dante. He was astonishingly beautiful—his eyes were closed and black, surprisingly long lashes spiked downwards onto indigo smudges of exhaustion. His nose was chiselled straight, so straight and so absolutely in proportion to the rest of his features she could almost imagine some LA cosmetic surgeon downing his tools in protest as he surveyed the landscape of Dante Costello's flawless face.

Flawless.

A perfectionist might point out that he hadn't shaved, but the stubble that ghosted his strong jaw, merely accentuated things: a shiver of masculinity stirring beneath the surface; a glimpse of what he might look like in the intimate dawn of morning. His full mouth was the only softening feature, but even that was set in grim tension as he lay there.

'You have to relax,' Matilda said, her words a contradiction because her whole body lay rigid beside him, her own breath coming in short, irregular bursts. Even her words were stilted, coming in short breathy sentences as they struggled through her vocal cords. 'Use your stomach muscles and breathe in through your nose and out through your mouth.'

'What?' One eye peeped open.

'Abdominal breathing,' she explained, but from the two vertical lines appearing over the bridge of his nose Matilda knew she was talking to the hopelessly unconverted.

'You don't move your chest,' Matilda explained. 'Remember when Alex was a baby and you watched her sleep?'

The frown faded a touch, a small smile lifting one edge of his mouth.

'Babies know how to relax,' Matilda said. 'They instinctively *know* how to breathe properly.'

'Like this?' Dante asked, dragging in air, and Matilda watched as he struggled with the concept. His stomach was moving but so too was his chest.

'Almost. Look, I'll help you. Just push against my hand.' Sitting up slightly, she instinctively moved to correct him. She'd shown this to numerous friends, knew how to show him simply, but her movements were hesitant, her hand tentative as it reached out towards him, hovered over the flat plane of his stomach, knowing, *knowing* where this could lead, wanting to pull back, to end this dangerous game, but curiously excited to start, to touch him, to feel him…

Her hand still hovered over his stomach but it was just too much, too intimate, and instead she placed her other hand on his chest, feeling the warmth of his skin through his shirt, feeing the breath still in him. Her fingers ached, literally ached to move his loosened tie, to creep between the buttons and feel his skin against hers. But she pushed away that thought, concentrated instead on keeping her voice even as she delivered her instructions. 'My hand shouldn't move. Breathe in through your nose, using your stomach, and then out through your mouth—here.' It seemed more appropriate now to touch his stomach than when the initial contact had been made, and she gently brushed her hand along on his stomach, felt the heavy leather of his belt, the coolness of his buckle and the silk of his trousers. Her whole body rippled with a lust she had never experienced—never thought she could experience—and she herself had engineered it because she wanted to be closer to him. More than that she didn't know, just knew she couldn't take a minute more of the crazy feelings that had been going on. 'Push against my hand,' Matilda said, 'and then hold your breath before letting out it. And just let your mind wander.'

For a second, two perhaps, he did. She felt him relax a touch beneath her, but it was fleeting, resistance rushing back in, his hand pushing hers away, Dante turning now to face her.

'Show me,' he said.

'I don't want to.' Matilda shook her head, knew she was incapable of going back to that tranquil place with Dante so close, but he was insistent. 'If it's so easy to do, prove it.'

Lying on her back Matilda closed her eyes, willed herself calm, trying to force herself to relax. But she could feel the tension in her hands and she drew on her reserves, dragged in the fragrant air, holding it, holding it and slowly letting it out, could feel his eyes watching her body move. And amazingly it happened. Somehow she did wander to that place she visited so often, but it was a different journey altogether, one she had never taken before. With every breath she sank deeper and yet her desire grew, visualising, willing his hands to touch her, for him to rest his palm on her stomach, fleeting, decadent thoughts that were hers only, her limbs heavy against the damp grass, the erotic thought of him near her stomach tightening with the anticipation of a touch that might never come.

His breath on her face caught her unawares. Her mind hadn't ever been so attuned to her body. She had been so sure his eyes had been there, the shiver of his breath on her cheeks was a shock, but even as her mind processed the sensation it was experiencing a new one— his mouth, pressing lightly on hers, so soft if it hadn't have been him it would surely have been imperceptible, could almost have been put down to imagination for nowhere else did he touch her. The sun blocked out as he hovered over her, her eyes still closed as she bliss-fully attuned to the feel of his lips lightly on hers until it wasn't enough. He was waiting for her bidding, she instinctively knew that. She could smell the bitter orange and bergamot undertones of his cologne, his breath mingling with hers, and after seconds that seemed to drag for ever she gave him her consent with her mouth, pressed her own lips into his.

The greeting was acknowledged by the reward of his cool tongue parting her lips, slipping inside, and that de-licious taste of him, the intimate feel of his mouth inside hers, his tongue languorously capturing hers, playing a slow teasing game, long strokes that made her want more, countered by a tiny feather-light stroke on the tip of her tongue and then a gentle sucking as he dragged her deeper into him. And it was the most erotic of kisses yet the most frustrating, because still nowhere else did he touch her. Only their mouths were touching only their mouths in contact, and she wanted more, her body arching, trying to convey her needs. But he misread them, just kissed her ever on, till she burnt for more, lit-erally ached for more, and only then did he give it, but in a selfish, measured dose.

The hand that she desired, that she anticipated around her waist to pull her towards him, instead lay on the soft inner flesh of her thigh, and the impact was as acute as if he'd struck her with a branding iron. It was her thigh, for heaven's sake, Matilda mentally begged, just a few square inches of flesh, and it wasn't even moving, but it was intimate, it was so damned intimate that it was surely wrong to be lying here beneath him now. She wished his hand would move, but it didn't. Instead, it pressed harder, almost imperceptibly at first but slowly she could feel his fingers digging into the tender flesh. Her breath in his mouth was coming faster now, and just as she went to push him away, to move his hand to safer ground, Dante was the one who stopped. Propped up on his elbow, she could feel him gazing down at her and she lay there vulnerable, reluctant to open her eyes, terrified, excited at the same time, wondering what he would do next.

'How else?' His words confused her, questions inappropriate now, his touch what she needed, not the mind games he played. 'How else did Edward hurt you?'

'I've told you,' Matilda gulped, screwing her eyes closed tighter wishing he would just leave it, and sure he knew she was lying.

'Not all of it,' Dante said, his finger trailing along her arm as she spoke, the nub of his finger lingering on her radial pulse, like some perverse lie detector as he dragged her secrets out. 'Was *that* supposed to be your fault, too?'

'I didn't help,' Matilda croaked, her eyes still screwed closed, unable to look at him as she revealed her shame. 'Edward said that maybe if I dressed up...'

'Would he want you now?' Dante breathed, interrupting her, confusing her again. 'All messed up, in your work clothes?'

'Of course not,' Matilda started, but her voice trailed off, not sure what he was getting at. Her body was still throbbing with desire, an argument starting somewhere deep within, because Dante had wanted her, hadn't he?

Doubt was starting to ping in, her eyes snapping open, terrified that he was laughing at her, dreading being humiliated again. But in one movement he grabbed her wrist, rammed her tense hand between his legs. She pulled back as if she'd been scalded, the strength of his erection shocking her, the feel of him in her hand terrifying. But Dante pulled her hand back, holding it there till the fear abated, till the arousal that had always been there stirred again.

'You make me feel like this, *mi cora.*'

She could feel him growing in her palm, feel a trickle of sweat between her breasts as he swelled harder beneath her touch, a bubble of moisture between her legs as his fingers crept up her T-shirt now, tiny, delicate strokes as he inched up slowly further, and it had gone too far, way, way too far. She murmured her protest, attempted to halt things, but he kissed her harder, captured her protest with his tongue and silenced it. She could feel the fleshy pad of his index finger circling her aching nipple as he held the soft plumpness of her bosom in his palm. Only now did his lips release hers. Any sooner and she would have begged him to stop, would have halted things.

But now she was putty in his skilled hands, pliable, warm, willing to move, to let him do with her what he wanted, and, oh, how he did—kissing the pulse leaping in her throat as she wriggled out of her top. The second her breasts were free, his tongue paid them the attention they deserved, tender attention, kissing the swollen, needy tips in turn, his finger retracing his steps, working downwards now. Her stomach tightened in renewed tension as he slid down the zip of her shorts, but for the first time

since contact he spoke, the liquid deep tones of his voice
not breaking the spell but somehow deepening it.

'Don't hold onto those thoughts, *bella*, just let them
come and go.' Repeating the words she had said to him,
but with entirely different meaning this time. And she
tried, really tried to just relax as his hand cupped her
bottom and lifted her enough to slip off the shorts and
knickers in one. But the movement erased what had been
achieved, embarrassment flooding in as her flesh was
exposed, her knees lifting instinctively and her hand
moving down in a futile attempt to cover herself. Wanting
to hide her body from Dante's gaze. She half expected
his wrist to close around her hand, as Edward's had done,
to roughly demand to return to where he had just been.

'Don't fight,' he ordered, but unlike Edward he was
soothing her with words instead of touch. 'Don't think
about that, just think about this.' His hand hovered over
her stomach until she caught her breath. She wanted the
contact again and he was very gently tracing tiny
endless circles around the little hill of her abdomen as
his lips dusted her cheeks. He was kissing away the
salty tears that were spilling from her eyes with his
other hand around her neck, massaging her hairline, yet
still the hungry swell of him against her told Matilda
how much he desired her. A barrage of sensations that
could have been confusing but instead soothed, the
panic that had momentarily engulfed her waned until
she lay outstretched and acquiescent in his arms, thrumming with anticipation for all that he might yield.

'I'm going to touch you now.'

He was already touching her, his body was pressed

against her, his lips on her face, his erection jutting into her, but she knew what he meant, was grateful for the strange warning, shivering as his hand reached her damp intimate curls and gently stroked them, his lip capturing the nervous swallow in her throat as his fingers crept slowly deeper, the infinitely gentle strokes he had teased her with before almost rough in comparison to the tenderness he displayed now, gently circling, pressing. But what if she couldn't, what if she let him down? She felt herself tense but not in desire, that panic again creeping in as he slid a finger into her tight space, slid it in slowly, taking her dew and then back to where it was needed. His touch firmer, massaging away her fears and replacing them with need, as she quivered at his touch, uncurling under his masterful skill, his palm massaging her swollen mound, over and over, his fingers gliding in and out, patience in every movement. She opened her eyes once, drunk on lust, moaning at the blissful warmth that fired her, and she saw his eyes smiling down at her, not a trace of superiority in them, just desire.

'Matilda.' It was Dante's voice that was breathless now, *his* body pressing harder into hers. She'd been so indulgent in her own pleasure while he'd been so unselfish, but that he could be so aroused from just touching her was all the affirmation she needed. Bold, so bold now, it was Matilda making the move, wrestling with his heavy belt, unzipping him, pushing the silk of his boxers down and staring with animal lust at him, the swollen, angry tip almost explosive. And even if it was the most wanton, outrageous thing she had ever done, even if all there could be was this moment, she needed

it, needed him deep, deep inside her. She wanted his
weight on top of her and it was heaven as Dante pushed
her down, his clothed body squeezing the breath out of
her, strong knees parting her willing thighs. She could
feel him nudging at her entrance and opened her legs a
fraction more to accommodate him. Even before his
heated length stabbed into her, her body was convulsing, her most intimate place wrapping around his,
dragging him deeper with each quivering contraction of
her orgasm as he moved within her.

'More!'

Her eyes opened. Breathless, speechless, she stared
at him as still he moved within her. What did he mean
more? She'd achieved more than she had ever thought
possible—he'd already toppled her to climax.

'Give me more, Matilda.' He was pushing harder and
now so was she. Now he was sliding over her, pressing
her harder into the ground. But her body wanted to still,
to recover from her orgasm, and she'd thought he'd
been close, was sure he'd wanted her as much as she'd
wanted him. For a second the doubts were back, the tiny
dark voices that told her over and over she wasn't quite
good enough, wasn't sexy enough, wasn't woman
enough to please a man.

'Matilda,' Dante gasped. 'Come with me. I can't hold
on—see what you do to me?'

He stared down at her and it was as if Dante was
struggling to stay in control—and her body that had
begged respite, mere moments before, rippled into delighted action as he ambushed her. Her legs wriggled
free, wrapping themselves tightly around his hips,

pulling him fiercely in, her fingers digging into the taut muscle of his buttocks. And she understood, understood then that she'd never truly let go, had merely glanced around the door of the place Dante was taking her to now.

'You're beautiful *bella*.' Over and over he said it. His chin was rough against her tender face, his breathing rapid and irregular, and she felt powerful now, felt his desire, his blatant need for her irrefutable. 'Dante…Dante.' Over and over she said. Pulling his shirt up, her hands ran over his back as her own frenzied mouth searched for comfort, sucking, licking the salty flesh of his chest,

'What you do to me!' Dante rasped. 'You sexy bitch…' His body his words were one unguarded paroxysm now, but so, too, was Matilda. She felt sexy, he *made* her sexy, her body responding to his debauched words, shivering as he spilled his precious nectar and she dragged it from him, convulsing around his length, dragging each delicious drop as if it was her right, as if it was hers to take, her whole body in rigid spasm, clinging to him as still somehow he moved, slower now, giving her all of him until, sated, exhausted, he collapsed on top of her before rolling onto his side, pulling her into his arms and welcoming her, back to a world that was more beautiful for what had taken place.

'You are so beautiful,' Dante drawled, then gave a small cough. 'Matilda, what I said just then…I mean, maybe I went too far…'

'Maybe I needed to hear it.' Matilda smiled. 'In fact, I think it's one of the nicest things anyone's ever said to me.'

He laughed—a real laugh—and it sounded so good. To see him relaxed, smiling, was like glimpsing somehow a different man, and all she knew was that she wanted more of this. He ran his hand over her warm, naked body and she squirmed with pleasure, not embarrassment, couldn't believe she was lying naked in his arms in the middle of the day and feeling only beautiful. 'At least we've answered your question.'

'What question?'

He kissed her very slowly, very tenderly before answering.

'It was Edward's problem, not yours.' He kissed the tip of her nose as his words sank in.

'Or you're just an amazing lover!'

'Oh, that, too.' Dante grinned.

'You know, sometimes people say things in an argument that they don't really mean.'

Matilda gazed up at him. 'Perhaps,' she said softly. 'Or in anger they find the courage to say what's really on their mind.'

The sun must have gone behind a cloud, because suddenly his face darkened, his body that had been so yielding, so in tune with hers stiffening, and Matilda wasn't sure if it was because of what she'd said or because he'd heard it first. The sound of tyres crunching on the gravel had them both jumping like scalded cats, suddenly aware of her lack of attire and Dante's trousers around his knees. She hated the intrusion, wanted so much to see him properly, the glimpse of his tumescence as he hastily pulled his trousers up and tucked himself in nowhere near enough for Matilda.

'Dante!' Katrina's voice pierced the still afternoon. Completely flustered, somehow Matilda managed to dress in record time, zipping up her shorts and almost falling over as she pulled on her boots, until, with her heart pounding, the footsteps drew closer and the gate was pushed open. Matilda did not even look over as Katrina approached and bluntly addressed Dante. 'I saw your car—what on earth are you doing home?'

'Trying to catch up on some reading,' Dante said casually, but it didn't wash with Katrina and after a long pause he elaborated. 'I thought I'd see how the garden was coming along before I shut myself away for the rest of the day. Where's Alex?'

Katrina didn't say anything at first, suspicious eyes swivelling from Dante to Matilda. 'Asleep in the car,' she finally said slowly. 'I was just going to carry her in.'

'I'll come and help,' Dante offered, but Katrina had already gone, walking out of the garden without a backward glance. Matilda stood with her cheeks flaming, her anxious eyes swinging to Dante, hoping for reassurance.

'Do you think she knew?'

'Of course not.' Dante shook his head but a muscle was pounding in his cheek, his hands balled into fists by his sides, and Matilda realised that Katrina's intrusion hadn't just wrecked the intimate moment—it was almost as if she'd erased it completely. 'Why on earth would she think there was anything between us?'

She truly wasn't sure if he was trying to reassure her, or was blatantly degrading her, but Matilda did a double-take, stunned at the change in him. Gone was the man who had so recently held her and in his place was the inaccessible man she had first encountered.

'Because maybe she guessed that we just made love.'

Matilda eyes glittered with tears, willing him to take it back, to perhaps realise the brutality of what he had just said, to offer some sort of apology. But Dante just stood there refusing to take it as she offered him an out from his rancid words. 'Because maybe she's noticed that over the last few days we've become close…'

'No.' His single word hurt her even more, if that were possible, his refusal to soften it cheapening her more than she'd thought possible.

'So what was that all about?' Matilda asked, gesturing to where they had lain, where he'd found her, held her, made love to her, forcing the confrontation, steeling herself to hear the confirmation of her worst fears. 'What just happened there, Dante?'

'Sex.' Black eyes stung her, a warning note in his voice telling her she'd crossed the line. His lips set in a rigid line as she shook her head, refused his take on the history they'd so recently created.

'It was more than that and you know it,' Matilda rasped, shocked by his callousness, reeling from the ferociousness of his sparse summing-up, yet refusing to buy it, because she knew there was more to him, had witnessed the real Dante only moments before, and all she knew was that she wanted him back. 'Dante, please, don't do this…' Matilda attempted, her hand reaching out for his arm, but he recoiled as if she was contaminated, shook her off as if she revolted him.

'Good sex, then,' came the elaboration she had foolishly hoped for, the bile at the back of her throat appropriate as he told her his poisonous truth. And it was

Matilda recoiling now, Matilda putting up the shutters and swearing she'd never let this man near her again.

'No, Dante, it wasn't.' This time she wasn't lying, wasn't denying what she felt. Looking into his cold, hard eyes, she told him the absolute truth. 'Good sex isn't just the act, Dante, it's about how you feel afterwards, and right now, I couldn't feel worse.' She knew he was about to walk off, knew that if she didn't say what was on her mind now then it would fester for ever, had learnt that much at least, so whether he was listening or not she chose to say what she felt. 'I don't know what your problem is, I don't know what it is that drives you to shut out something that could have been so good. Maybe you can justify it by saying that I'm not sophisticated enough to play by your rules, or that I don't hold a candle to your wife, but that's entirely your business. Frankly, I don't care any more.'

His only response was a blink, but she knew that she'd surprised him, knew that even as he shut her out further, right now a little of what she was saying was reaching him. It gave her the impetus to continue, the pain he'd inflicted more than enough to go round. 'I'm more sorry than you'll ever know for having *sex* with you, Dante, but, let's get one thing clear—I might have lost a bit of my pride here, but you just lost one helluva lot more…' It was Matilda who walked off, Matilda who headed to the house and left him standing in the garden. She refused to cry, just called her parting shot over her shoulder. 'You just lost me!'

CHAPTER NINE

HIS callousness, his emotional distancing after the intimacy they'd shared made the most painful of decisions relatively easy, made walking away from Dante about need rather than want. Because sharing his home, glimpsing his life and being shut out over and over was a torture that couldn't be sustained and gave Matilda the momentum to pick up the phone and call on every friend and colleague she could muster with a view to rapidly finishing the task she had committed herself to, and rapidly removing herself from this impossible situation she had allowed herself to fall into.

It was the most exhausting time of her life. Hanging the expense, more than happy to bill him, more than happy to pay for it herself even, Matilda ordered floodlights to enable her to work long into the warm nights, grateful for the soothing diversion of nature, grateful that by the time her aching body fell into bed at night, all she was capable of was rest, taking the respite of a dreamless, exhausted sleep while knowing the pain would surely come later.

* * *

'I can't believe what you've achieved.' Deep into a humid, oppressive Saturday evening, Hugh poured her a glass of champagne Matilda didn't want from the bottle he was holding, having wandered over from the al fresco area where the *family* had eaten a leisurely dinner. He was now staring in astonishment at the garden, which was almost complete, the sleeping beauty truly awoken, the overgrown wilderness a distant memory. In its place was a child's paradise—a maze of soft hedges, each leading to its own exciting end, soft turf underfoot and thousands of tiny fairy-lights adorning the massive willow—twinkling in the dusky light and bidding enchantment. 'What do you think, Katrina?'

'It's very nice.' Katrina's response wasn't exactly effusive, but Matilda couldn't have cared less. The only thing she needed to see her through was the knowledge that in less than twelve hours she'd be out of there, in less than twelve hours she could start to pick up the pieces of her life Dante had so readily shattered. 'Of course,' Katrina added, 'it's Alex's opinion that counts.'

Almost on cue, the gate opened and, as she had over the last couple of days whenever their paths had inadvertently crossed, Matilda didn't even look at Dante. Instead, she focused her attention on Alex, who walked tentatively alongside him, her tiny hand in his. She looked utterly adorable, dressed in cotton pyjamas and cute kitten slippers, newly washed blonde curls framed her pretty face. And as livid and as debased as Matilda felt, momentarily at least, it faded as she watched the little girl's reaction. Watched as her normally vacant eyes blinked in wonder as she actually surveyed the transformation, a smile breaking out on her serious face as Matilda flicked on a switch and the water features danced into life. It was like seeing the sun come out as a tiny gasp of wonder escaped Alex's lips. She moved forward, reached out and ran, *ran* as most children would have, but because it was Alex it was amazing.

'I think she likes it.' She could forgive Hugh's stilted words, because tears were running down his cheeks as he watched his granddaughter run through the water jets, and for that moment in time Matilda decided that the pain she'd endured had been worth it. To see this distant, reclusive child emerge from her shell, even if only for a moment, that her vision, her concept had actually reached this troubled, fractured child caused something good and pure to well deep inside her. Matilda's usual happiness, which had been stifled since Dante's rejection, bubbled to the surface again as she witnessed her work through the eyes of a child.

A child like Alex.

'Look!' Matilda's voice was an excited whisper. She crouched to Alex's level, as she had on the first day, taking her cautious hand as she had back then and beckoning Alex to new wonders as Katrina and Hugh wandered around to explore. 'Look what's here!' Parting the curtain of willow, Matilda led her inside the cool enclosure, the fairy-lights she had so carefully placed lighting the darkness and creating a cool, emerald oasis, an enchanted garden within a garden, a place for Alex to simply just be. But the innocent pleasure of the moment was broken as the leaves parted, as Dante stepped into the magical space and completely broke the spell.

'You could put engravings on the bark.' Matilda's voice was a monotone now as she addressed Dante, talking like a salesperson delivering her pitch. 'Or hang some mirrors and pictures, perhaps put down a blanket and have a crib for her dolls…'

'She loves it,' Dante broke in, the emotion that was usually so absent in his voice rolling in the distance as he sat down on the mossy ground, watching as his daughter stared up at the twinkling lights, her hands held in the air, fingers dancing along with them. 'It is the first time I have seen her happy in a long time.'

'Not so bad for a *stupido* garden?' Matilda said, and if she sounded bitter, she was: bitter for the way he had treated her; bitter for all they had lost. But because Alex was present, Matilda swallowed her resentment down, instead giving Dante the information he would need if the garden she had planted was to flourish. 'I've just got to clean up and attend to a few minor details tomorrow, but I'll be gone by lunchtime.'

'By lunchtime?' There was a tiny start to his voice, a frown creeping across his brow, which Matilda chose to ignore. 'I probably won't catch up with you tomorrow, but I'll write up some instructions for your gardener and run through a few things with you now. Know that the whole garden will improve with time.' Picking at some moss on the ground, Matilda continued, 'Every day you should see some changes. The paths are littered with wild seeds—buttercups, daisies, clover— so you shouldn't mow too often…'

'Matilda?'

'There are no sharp edges.' Ignoring him, she continued, trying to get through her summing-up, knowing this was one job she wouldn't be following up, knowing she was seeing it for the last time. 'And no plants that can hurt, no thorns that could scratch, nothing that might sting—she should be perfectly safe here. This garden is what you make of it—you could pick marigold leaves with Alex to add to your salad at night—'

'Matilda, we need to talk,' he interrupted again, one hand creeping across the ground to capture hers. But she pulled away, determined to see this last bit through with whatever dignity she could muster, yet unable to stop herself from looking at him for what was surely going to be the last time. Her final instructions to him were laced with double meaning, littered with innuendo, and from Dante's tense expression she knew he felt each one.

'No, Dante, *you* need to listen. This garden may look beautiful now, but tomorrow when I've cleaned up and gone, you'll come for another look and see its apparent faults. Tomorrow, in the cold light of day, you'll wonder what the hell you paid all this money for, because the lights won't be on and the bushes will look a bit smaller and sparser than they do tonight. You'll see all the lines where the turf was laid and the sticks holding up the plants and—'

'It will still be beautiful to me,' Dante interrupted. 'Because it's already given me more pleasure than I ever thought possible.' And, yes, he was talking about Alex, because his hands were gesturing to where his daughter sat, but his eyes were holding hers as he spoke and she knew that he was also referring to them. 'Yes, it might just take a bit of getting used to, but I can understand now that in the end it would be worth it…' She stared back at him for the longest time, swallowing hard as he went on. 'That if I nurture it, care for it, tend it…' With each word he tempted her, delivering his veiled apology in a low silken drawl. 'Then it will reward me tenfold.'

'It would have,' Matilda said softly, watching his wince of regret at her refusal to accept it, actually grateful when Katrina and Hugh ducked inside the emerald canopy and broke the painful moment, because whatever Dante was trying to say it was too little, too late—even a garden full of flowers wasn't going to fix this.

'Join us for a drink,' Hugh offered. 'Dante's just about to put Alex to bed…'

'I've got too much to do here.' Matilda smiled as she shook her head. 'But thank you for the offer.'

'I think we might have to stay over.' Katrina pretended to grimace. 'Hugh's had a couple too many champagnes to drive.'

'I've had one,' Hugh said, but Katrina had clearly already made up her mind. Matilda was tempted to tell her that she needn't bother, that Dante didn't need to be guarded on her final night here, but instead she offered her goodnights and headed to the mountain of tools that needed to be sorted.

'You really ought to think about finishing up,' Dante called. 'There's a storm brewing and with all these cables and everything it could be hazardous.'

She didn't even deign a response, grateful when they left, when finally the garden gate closed and she was alone.

* * *

Despite her utter exhaustion, working a sixteen-hour day, when finally Matilda showered and fell into bed, sleep evaded her, the body Dante had awoken then tossed aside twitching with treacherous desire. Lying in the darkness, she gazed out over the bay, watching the dark clouds gathering in the distance, the ominous view matching her mood as she listened to the talking and laughter coming from the garden below. Katrina's grating voice telling tales about the wonderful Jasmine did nothing to soothe her and she wished over and over that she'd managed to avoid Dante tonight.

Reluctantly she replayed his words in her mind. With total recall she remembered the look on his face as he had spoken to her, and she knew that she'd almost forgiven him, that had he touched her, she'd have gone to him.

A whimpering cry carried down the hallway and Matilda listened as Alex called out in her sleep. Her first instinct was to go to the little girl, but she stayed put, knowing that Dante would hear her on the intercom. She waited for the sound of his footsteps on the stairs, but they never came. Alex's cries grew louder and more anguished and Matilda screwed her eyes closed and covered her ears with her hands in an attempt to block them out, knowing that it was none of her business, while praying someone would come soon.

'Mama!'

Alex's terrified little voice had Matilda sitting bolt upright in bed, the jumbled babbles of a child's nightmare tearing at her heartstrings until she could bear it no more. The sensible thing would have been to go downstairs and alert Dante, and she had every intention of doing so, even pulling on a pair of knickers for manners' sake! But as she padded down the hallway in her flimsy, short nightdress, as the screams got louder, instinct kicked in, and pushing open the bedroom door, she called out to Alex in the darkness, gathering the hot, tear-racked body in her arms and attempting to soothe her, trying not to convey her alarm as Alex sobbed harder, her balled fists attempting to slam into Matilda's cheeks.

'Shush, honey,' Matilda soothed, capturing her wrists. Instead of holding her away, she brought a hand up to her face, controlling the movement, stroking her face with Alex's hand as over and over she told her that everything was OK, relief filling her as gradually the child seemed to calm.

'It's OK, Alex.' Over and over she said it, even letting go of Alex's wrist as finally the little girl started to relax, rocking her gently in her arms.

'What happened?'

She'd been so focused on Alex, Matilda hadn't even heard him come in, but as his deep-voiced whisper reached her ears, for Alex's sake she forced herself not to tense, just carried on rocking the child as she spoke.

'She was screaming. I was going to come and get you, but…' Her voice trailed off. How could she tell him that she'd been unable to just walk past? 'I thought you'd hear her on the intercom.'

'It's not working—there's a storm coming so it's picking up interference.' He was standing over her now and she assumed he'd take Alex from her, but she was wrong. Instead, he gazed down at his daughter, his hand stroking her forehead, pushing back the damp blonde curls from her hot, red face. 'She was really upset,' Dante observed, then looked over at Matilda. 'And you managed to calm her.'

'I just cuddled her,' Matilda said, 'as you do, and spoke to her.'

'No one can usually calm her.' Dante blinked. 'No one except me and sometimes Katrina.'

They stood in silence for the longest time, a deep, pensive silence broken only by the fading sobs of Alex, until finally she was quiet, finally she gave in. 'I think she's asleep,' Matilda whispered, gently placing Alex back in her cot, grateful she'd remembered to put on knickers as she lowered the little body.

'It's hot in here,' Date said, his voice not quite steady. As he opened the window a fraction more, the sweet scent of jasmine filled the air. Matilda stepped back as Dante took over tucking the sheets around Alex, tears filling her eyes as he placed a tender kiss on his daughter's cheek until she could bear it no more, the agony of witnessing such an intimate scene more than she could take. Matilda headed out into the hall, wiping the tears with the backs of her hands, cringing as his hand closed around her shoulder, as Dante tried to stop her.

'Matilda…'

'Don't,' Matilda begged, because she knew what was coming, knew he was going to apologise again, and she was terrified she'd relent. 'Just leave me alone, Dante.'

'I cannot do that.' His hand was still on her shoulder but she shook it off, turned her expressive face to his, the anger that had never really abated brimming over again. Aware of Alex, she struggled to keep her voice down.

'Why me?' she whispered angrily, tears spilling down her face as she glared at him. 'Why, when you could have any woman you wanted, did you have to pick on me?' Her hoarse whisper trailed off as she heard Hugh and Katrina at the foot of the stairs. Horrified, she stared at him, excruciatingly aware of her lack of attire, knowing how it would appear and not up to the confrontation.

His reflexes were like lightning. His hand closed around hers and in one movement he opened a door, practically pulling her inside, but she was plunged from desperation to hell. The mocking sight of his bedroom twisted the knife further, if that were possible, and she let him have it, her fists balling like Alex's, pushing against his chest as she choked the words out. 'You knew what this would do to me. You knew how much this would hurt me in the end. So why did you even start it, why, when you could have anyone, did you have to pick on me?'

'Shh,' Dante warned, the voices on the other side of the door growing nearer, but Matilda was past caring now.

'Why,' she said nastily, 'are you worried what Katrina will say?' She never got to finish. Both his hands were holding hers so he silenced her in the only way he could, his mouth pressing on hers, pushing her furious body against the door as she resisted with every fibre of her being, clamping her mouth closed, trying not to even breathe because she didn't want to taste him, smell him, didn't want to taste what she could never have again.

''Night, Dante…'

A million miles away on the other side of the door Katrina called to him. Warning her with his eyes, he moved his mouth away, his breath hot on her cheeks, his mouth ready to claim hers again if she made a single move.

''Night, Katrina.'

And shame licked the edges then, shame trickling in as he stared down at her till the moment had passed, till Hugh and Katrina were safely out of earshot and Dante told her a necessary home truth.

'I do not have to answer to Katrina, but I do respect her, Matilda. She is the mother of my wife and the grandmother of my child. I will not flaunt a relationship in front of her without fair warning.'

'What relationship?' Matilda sneered, but her face was scarlet, knowing that in this instance he was right. 'Sex with no strings isn't enough for me, Dante.' Which was such a contrary thing to say when her whole body was screaming for him, her nipples like stinging thistles against her nightdress, her body trembling with desire, awoken again by the one-sided kiss.

'It isn't enough for me either,' Dante said softly. 'At least not since you came along.' His hands had loosened their grip but his eyes were pinning her now, and she stared back, stunned, sure she must have somehow misheard. She dropped her eyes, didn't want to look at him when surely he would break her heart again, but his hand cupped her chin, capturing her, ensuring that she remained looking at him, his fingers softly holding her, his thumb catching tears as they tumbled down her cheeks. 'A lady who asks me for directions, a lady who steps into a elevator and into my life. It was I who wanted to see you again. Hugh told me to cancel that dinner, it was I was who insisted that we go ahead…' Utterly bemused, drenched in hope, she blinked back at him, struggled to focus as she shifted the murky kaleidoscope of the their brief past into glorious Technicolor. 'I had to kiss you. I convinced myself that when I did it would be over, but no…' It was Dante who appeared confused how, Dante shaking his head as he recalled. 'Like a drug, I need more, we make love and still I tell myself that it is just need that propels me, male needs, that when the garden is finished then so too will we be. I don't want to feel this, Matilda…'

'Why?' Matilda begged. 'Because of Jasmine?'

Pain flickered across his face and for a fragment of time she wished she could retract, take back what she had just said, yet somehow Matilda knew it had to be faced, that they could only glimpse the future if he let her into the past. But Dante shook his head, refuted her allegation almost instantly.

'Alex is the one who has to come first…'

'She will,' Matilda breathed, sure that wasn't the entire issue, sure that, despite his denial, and his apparent openness, still he was holding back. But as he pulled her into his arms, as he obliterated the world with his masterful touch, she let it go, reassured by his words and a glimpse of the future with Dante by her side and utterly sure she had all the time in the world to source his pain.

One hand was circling the back of her neck now, tiny circular motions that were incredibly soothing but at the same time incredibly erotic. She could feel the steady hammer of his heart against her ear, inhale the unique maleness of him as his gentle words reached her, his lips shivering along the hollow of her neck, moving down to the creamy flesh of her shoulder. His teeth nibbled at the spaghetti strap of her nightdress, his tongue cool against her burning skin, eyes closing as, giddy with want, he pulled the delicate garment downwards, sliding it over her breasts. His hands lingered over her hips as, guided by him, she stepped out of it, facing him now with a mixture of nervousness and raw sexuality, naked apart from the palest of pink silk panties. And the low moan of desire that escaped his lips erased for ever the poison-ous roots of self-doubt Edward had so firmly planted, her body fizzing with new hope and desire as he sank to his knees, knowing that to Dante she was beautiful.

His hands were still on her hips but he was kissing her stomach now, deep, throaty kisses that were as faint-making as they were erotic. She could feel his tongue on her skin and it was overwhelming, her tummy tighten-ing in reflex as one hand slipped between her thighs, stroking the pale, tender skin on the inside as his lips moved down. She could feel the heat through the cool silk fabric, his tongue, his lips on her making her weak with want, desperate for him to rip at her panties, to satisfy the desire that was raging in her. She gave tiny gasps in her throat as her fingers knotted together in his hair, as still he teased her more, his teeth grazing the silk, his tongue moistening her more, and even if it was ev-erything she wanted, it still wasn't enough. Realisation hit her that, despite what had taken place in the garden, she'd never seen him naked. Need propelling her, she pulled back a touch, saw the question in his eyes as slowly he stood up. Her fingers, nervous at first, but bolder as desire took over, wrestled with the buttons of his shirt, pushing the sleeves down over his muscular arms. Closing her eyes in giddy want, her pale breasts pressed against his chest. She felt the naked silk of his dark skin against her, skin on skin, as she opened his belt and unzipped his shorts. She held her breath in wonder as Dante now shed the garments that stood between them, and if he'd been beautiful before, he was stunning now.

Never had she seen a more delicious man, his body toned and muscular, his dark, olive skin such a contrast to hers, the ebony of the hair that fanned on his chest tapering down into a delicious, snaky black line that led to the most decadent, delicious male centre. His arousal was terrifying and exciting at the same time, jutting out of silky black hair, proud and angry and alive, and the bed that had looked so daunting was just a tiny breathless step away. As they lay face to face she held him in her hand, marvelling at the strength, the satin softness of the skin that belied the steel beneath it, nervous, tentative at first. But his tiny moans of approval told her she was doing it right. Her other hand was audacious too, cupping his heavy scrotum, holding all of him, and loving it, as his lips found her breasts, suckling on her tender flesh, a tiny gasp catching in her throat as felt him growing stronger, nearer.

'Careful.' His voice was thick with lust as his hand captured her wrist, stopped her just in time, and she was greedy now for her turn, biting down on her bottom lip as he ran the tip of his erection over her panties, could see the tiny silver flash that told her he was near. She almost wept with voracious need as his finger slipped inside the fabric, gently parting her pink, intimate lips, sliding deep inside as still he teased her on the outside, sliding his heat against her till she was frenzied, her neck arching backwards, her whole body rigid, fizzing with want.

And Dante was the same, she knew it, as he tore at the delicate panties, ripped them open and plunged deep inside, her orgasm there to greet him, her intimate vise twitching around him as he entered, thrusting inside her. And yet he made her wait for his, their heated bodies moving together, long, delicious strokes as his moist skin slid over hers, her orgasm fading then rising again as he worked deliciously on, her fingers clutching his taut buttocks, her neck rigid as his tongue, his mouth devoured it, tasting her, relishing her, arousing her all over again. She could feel the tension in him building, his movements faster now, delicious involuntary thrusts as his body dictated the rhythm for both of them, no turning back as he drove them both forward.

He spilled inside her as she came again, crying out his name as he took her higher than she had ever been then held her as she came back down. But if making love with Dante had been exquisite, nothing could rival the feeling of him holding her in his arms, his body spooning into her warm back, the bliss of being held by him, his tender, warm hand on her stomach, his breathing evening out, experiencing the beauty of a bed shared tonight.

And the promise tomorrow could bring.

CHAPTER TEN

'DANTE!'

She barely said it, more breathed the word, her eyes snapping open as the bedroom door opened. A tiny rigid figure was silhouetted in the doorway, staring at the vast bed, and all Matilda knew was that Alex mustn't see her. She wriggled slightly in his arms, pulling her legs down straight, trying to remain inconspicuous yet somehow awaken him. Gently she prodded him, slipping beneath the covers as he came to, feeling like an intruder hiding, chewing on her bottom lip and cringing inside as Dante took in the scene.

'Alex, darling.' She could feel him pull back the covers, groping on the floor for his boxers then stepping out of the bed and crossing the room. 'Did something wake you?'

And because it was Alex, there was no answer to his question. Instead, Matilda listened to his comforting words as he scooped the little girl up and carried her back towards her bedroom. She waited till the coast was clear before wrapping the sheet around her and heading for the *en suite,* pulling on Dante's bathrobe and, despite the oppressive heat of the night, heading back to the bed to sit and shiver on the edge till Dante returned.

'Is she OK?' Worried eyes jerked to his. 'I don't think she saw me. It's so dark in here I'm sure that she couldn't have. I just heard the door open…'

'She's fine,' Dante instantly reassured her. 'I gave her a drink of water and she settled back down. I don't know what's wrong with her tonight…' Sitting down on the bed, he wrapped an arm around her, but she could sense his distraction, knew that he was worried about what Alex might have seen.

'I heard the door open and saw her. I honestly don't think that she saw me. The only reason I could make her out was because the hall light was on. As soon as I heard something, I slipped under the covers.'

'She didn't seem worried,' Dante agreed. 'I think she was just thirsty…' His voice trailed off and Matilda watched as he raked his fingers through his hair, seeing him now not as a lover but as the father he was…

Would always be.

'I'll go back to my room.'

'No.' He shook his head, one hand reaching out and attempting to grab her wrist. But Matilda captured it, holding his strong hand in her gentler one. And as much as she didn't want to go, as much as she knew Dante wanted her to stay, she knew it was right to leave.

'Dante, it's fine. Alex might come back and neither of us is going to relax now. I'll go and sleep in my room. It's better that way. We've got away with it once…'

'You understand?'

'Completely,' Matilda said softly, her free hand capturing his cheek, feeling the scratch of his stubble beneath her fingers. Although she longed to sleep with him, to wake up with him, she knew some things were more important, knew that she had to act unselfishly now. 'You need to be here for Alex,' she whispered, kissing his taut cheek, feeling the tension in his body as she held him for a precious second, knowing he was torn between want and duty, knowing that she could make things easier for him by going.

And it wasn't a small comfort as she slipped into her king-sized single bed, still wrapped in his robe, still warm from his touch, his intimate spill still moist between her legs. It was the most grown-up decision she'd ever made.

It was love.

'Dante!'

Brutally awoken by the piercing shout, Matilda sat up in bed, her mind whirling as chaos broke out. She tried to piece together the events of the night before and failed as the urgent events of today thundered in.

'Where is she?'

Wrapping the tie of Dante's bathrobe around her, Matilda climbed out of bed, her heart hammering at the urgency in Katrina's voice, waiting, *waiting* for Dante to reply. For him to tell her that Alex was in bed with him. Her stomach turned as she opened her bedroom door and saw Dante's pale, anguished face as he ran the length of the hallway, desperation in his voice as he called his daughter's name, terrified, frenzied eyes meeting hers as he explained the appalling situation.

'Alex isn't in her bed. We can't find her.'

Dashing down the hallway, she careered into Dante, his face a mixture of fixed determination and wretched pain.

'The pool!' They both said it at the same time. His worst nightmare eventuating, she followed him, bare feet barely touching the surface, jumping, running, taking the stairs two, three at a time as her mind reasoned. The pool was fenced and gated, Matilda attempted to reason as she ran; Dante was always so careful with his daughter's security there was no way Alex could have got in. As she dashed across the lawn, Dante was miles ahead, naked apart from his boxers, his whole body taut with dread. Finally she reached him, shared in that anguished look at the cool glittering blue surface. But there was little solace to be taken. The glimmering bay twinkled in the sunrise, a vast ocean just metres away and a tiny, fragile child missing.

'Call the police.' Dante's voice was calm but his lips were tight, a muscle hammering in his cheek as his idyllic, bayside view turned again to torture. 'Tell them to alert the coastguard.'

'She was fine last night!' Katrina's brittle voice grated on Matilda's already shot nerves. The police had long since arrived, their radios crackling in the background as officers started the appalling process—interviewing the adults, searching the house and gardens. A frantic race against time ensued. She could hear the whir of helicopter rotors as they swooped along the coastline. As she stared at Dante, who had returned at the police's bidding from a frantic race to the beach to look for his daughter, sand on his damp legs, his proud face utterly shattered, her first instinct was to reach out and hold him, to comfort him, but aware of Katrina and how it would look, she held back. 'I looked in on her as I went to bed…'

'What time was that?' An incredibly young officer asked as another sat writing notes.

'Eleven, twelve perhaps,' Katrina responded. 'Dante had already gone up.'

'So you were the last person to see her?'

'No,' Dante broke in. 'I was the last person to see her.' Matilda held her breath as he carried on talking, wondering if he would reveal what had happened and with a sinking heart knowing that he had to. 'She was distressed when I went up, but she went back to sleep. Katrina would have seen her a few moment after that, but a couple of hours later she came into my room.'

'She'd climbed out of her cot?'

'She's started to do that,' Dante said, raking his fingers through his hair, his whole body in abject pain. She ached to comfort him yet sat completely still as he spoke on. 'She seemed thirsty so I gave her a drink and cuddled her for a moment.'

'Was she upset?'

'No.' Dante shook his head, his face contorting with agonized concentration as he recalled every detail of the last time he had seen his daughter. 'At least, I don't think so.'

'You don't think so?' the policeman pushed, and Matilda could have slapped him for his insensitivity. But Dante was calmer, explaining Alex's problem in a measured voice, but his voice was loaded with pain.

'My daughter has problems—behavioural problems.' Katrina opened her mouth to argue, but Dante stood firm, shaking his head at Katrina, clearly indicating that now wasn't the time for futile denial. 'She doesn't react in the usual way—you never really know what she's thinking. Look, you *have* to tell your colleagues that they could be just a metre away from her, could be calling her name, and she won't answer them, she won't call out…' His voice broke for a second and Matilda watched as he attempted to recover, his eyes closing for an agonising second as he forced himself to continue. 'You have to tell them that.'

The officer nodded to his partner, who left the room to impart the news before he continued with the interview. 'You gave her a drink—then what?'

'I opened the window a fraction more—there are locks on it, so she could never have opened it wide enough to get out. Her room was…' His English momentarily failed him. Dante balled his fists in frustration as he tried to give the police officer each and every piece of information he could. 'Confined,' he attempted. 'With the storm coming and everything…' As if in answer, a crack of thunder sounded and Matilda watched the fear dart in his eyes. The rain started to pelt on the window, each drop ramming home the fact that his baby was out there with the elements

'Anything else?' the officer checked. 'Is there anything else that happened last night that was out of the ordinary? Any strange sounds, phone calls—anything, no matter how irrelevant it might seem, that might have upset your daughter?'

Dante's eyes met Matilda's.

'No.' He shook his head, dragged his eyes away but his expression haunted her. The guilt in his eyes as he bypassed the truth made her know without hesitation what was coming next, that the only person Dante wanted to protect here, and rightly so, was his daughter.

'Officer, may I speak to you outside?'

'About what?' Katrina demanded as the two of them walked out of the room. 'What aren't you telling us, Dante? What happened last night that you can't say in front of me?'

Embarrassed, terrified, Matilda stood there as Katrina answered her own question.

'You tart,' Katrina snarled, and Matilda winced at the venom behind it. 'That's Dante's gown that you're wearing.' Katrina eyed Matilda with utter contempt but didn't leave it there. Her lips were white and rigid with hatred. 'You were in bed with Dante, weren't you? That's why the poor little mite ran off into the night!'

'I truly don't think that she saw me,' Matilda said. 'We were both asleep and she just pushed open the door…'

'And saw a woman who wasn't her mother in her father's bed! Do you realise what you have done, Matilda?' Disgust and fury were etched on Katrina's features and for an appalling moment Matilda thought that Katrina might even hit her. 'Do you have any idea the damage that you've done to my grandchild?'

'Leave it, Katrina.' Dante's voice was weary as he came back into the room, but it had a warning note to it that Katrina failed to heed.

'I most certainly will not leave it.' Furious eyes

swivelled between Dante and Matilda, her face contorted with disgust. 'Did Alex see you?' Her eyes were bulging in her head. 'That little girl walked in and found the pair of you—'

'It wasn't like that,' Matilda said, but Katrina shot her down in a second.

'Shut up!' she screamed. 'Shut the hell up. You have no say here! None at all.'

'Katrina.' Dante crossed the room, his face grey. 'This isn't helping…'

'Of course it isn't helping. How, Dante, did you think sleeping with her was going to help your daughter? How did you think shaming my daughter's memory like that was going to help Alex? But, then, I suppose you didn't even stop to think. I warned you, Dante, warned you to be careful, to keep things well away from Alex, and then some little—'

'I said leave it!' Still he didn't shout, but there was such icy power behind his words that even in full, rage-fuelled flood Katrina's voice trailed off. It was Matilda who stepped in. Running a dry tongue over her lips, she again attempted to calm things down.

'All we can do for now is give the police all the information we have and then look for Alex. Arguing isn't going to help.'

'She's right,' Dante said, addressing Katrina, which momentarily Matilda found strange. But she didn't hold the thought. Her mind was already racing ahead, trying to work out how they could find Alex, where the little girl might be. But as Dante continued talking, Matilda knew that the agony that had pierced her consciousness since awakening had only just begun, because nothing Katrina had said in rage could have hurt her more than the expression on Dante's face as he turned and finally faced her, his expression cold and closed, his eyes not even meeting hers.

'I think you should leave, Matilda…'

'Leave?' She shook her head, her voice incredulous, horrified by what he was saying. 'Don't shut me out now, Dante. Last night you said—'

'Last night you were his whore,' Katrina shouted. 'Last night he said what he had to, to get you to share his bed. Dante loved my daughter.' She was screeching now, almost deranged. 'Jasmine's barely cold in her grave. Did you really think you could fill her space? Did you really think he meant what he said, that he'd besmirch her memory with you?'

'No one's trying to besmirch Jasmine's memory,' Dante said, his face as white as marble as he turned to Katrina.

'No one could!' Katrina yelled. 'Because if you truly loved my daughter then last night can be nothing more than a fling and I know that you loved her. I know that!'

'I did.' Dante halted her tirade. 'I do,' he insisted, his hands spreading in the air in a helpless gesture, utter panic on his face as reality started to sink in. 'But right now all I can think of is Alex. All I know is that my baby is out there…'

'Let me help with the search,' Matilda pleaded, but Dante's back was to her, demanding action from the officer that stood there, picking up the phone and punching in numbers. 'Dante, please…'

'You want to help?' His face was unrecognisable as he finally faced her. 'If you really want to help, Matilda, you will do as I ask and just go home. It will be better.'

'Better for who?' Matilda whispered through chattering teeth, knowing the answer even before it came.

'Better for everyone.'

It took about ten minutes to pack, ten minutes to throw her things into her suitcase and drag it down the stairs, ten minutes to remove herself from Dante's life. The scream inside was a mere breath away, her teeth grinding together with the agony of keeping it all in. She wanted to slap him, to yell at him, confront him, couldn't believe that he'd done it to her again, that she'd been stupid enough to let him fool her, to be beguiled by him over again, but somehow she choked it down, the horror of a child missing overriding everything. She placed her own pain, her utter humiliation on total hold. Wincing against the sting of the rain on her bare arms, she threw her case into the boot, imagining its impact on a little girl dressed in nothing but pyjamas.

'We need a contact number, miss.' The young officer tapped on the steamed-up car window as Matilda started the engine. She scribbled her number on a piece of paper and handed it to him. 'Can I help—with the search I mean?

'Hold on a second, love.' The policeman halted her as his radio crackled into life and Matilda waited, her heart in her mouth at the urgent note in the officer's voice, flashes of conversation reaching her ears.

'They've found her?' Matilda begged.

'I need to tell the child's father first.' He was making

to go but Matilda shot out of the car and ran alongside him as he headed for the house.

'How is she?' Matilda demanded. 'Is she okay?'

'I'm not sure,' the officer reluctantly answered. 'They found her wandering in some dunes. She seems OK but she's not talking. They're taking her to the local hospital…'

'She rarely speaks.' Matilda could feel relief literally flooding her at the seemingly good news. 'Oh, I have to tell Dante…'

'Miss I really think…' Something in his voice stilled her and, despite the police officer's youthful looks, Matilda saw the wisdom in his eyes as he offered some worldly advice for free. 'I think that for now at least you need to leave this family alone. Emotions are already pretty high. Give it a day or two and it will calm down, but I think the best thing you can do now is take Mr Costello's advice and go home.'

CHAPTER ELEVEN

EVERYTHING was hard—even tidying her tiny apartment required a mammoth effort, yet she felt compelled to do it. Despite her fatigue, and utter exhaustion, she needed to somehow clear the decks, to get things in order before she took on the even bigger task of getting on with the rest of her life.

A life without Dante.

Pushing the vacuum around, Matilda wished the noise from the machine could drown out her thoughts, wished she could just switch off her mind, find some peace from the endless conundrums.

Two weeks ago she hadn't even known he'd existed, he hadn't factored into even one facet of her life, and now he consumed her all—every pore, every breath every cell of her. She was drenched with him, possessed by him, yearned for him, but was furious with him, too. A molten river of anger bubbled over the edge of her grief every now and then that Dante would have let her leave without even knowing whether his daughter was alive or dead, assuming that the world ran on the same emotionless clock as he did, where feelings could be turned off like a light switch and the truth distorted enough to conjure up reasonable doubt.

She'd been home four days now. Four days when he hadn't even bothered to pick up the phone and let her know about Alex—surly she deserved that much at least?

For the first couple of nights Matilda had watched him on the nightly TV news, striding out of the court-room without comment. She had scanned the newspa-pers by day for a glimpse of him, trying to read mes-sages that weren't there in the tiny stilted statements that were quoted. But it had become unbearable, seeing him, reading about him yet knowing she couldn't have him, so instead she'd immersed herself in anything she could think of, anything that might turn her mind away from him and give her peace even for a moment. She knew it was useless, knew that she could work till she dropped, could fill her diary with engagements, could go out with friends every night, but she'd never fully escape, that all she could hope was that the agony might abate, might relent just enough to allow her to breathe a little more easily.

Kicking off the vacuum, Matilda gave in and padded towards the wardrobe, as she had done repeatedly for the last four days. She pulled out Dante's dressing-gown, which in her haste she had inadvertently packed, feeling the heavy fabric between her fingers, knowing that the sensible thing to do would be to throw it into the washing machine, to parcel it up and mail it to him. But it was the one task she was putting off, pathetically aware that apart from her bittersweet memories it was the only reminder of Dante she had. Sitting on the edge of the bed, she buried her face in the robe, dragging in his evocative aroma. And it was like feeling it all over again, every breath reinforcing the agony of his rejection, the blistering pain of his denial. A scent that had once been so beautiful was tainted now for ever. In fact, it almost made her feel nauseous now as she revisited the pain, the devastation…

'Alex!'

For the first time in days, Dante left her mind, the name of his daughter shivering out of her lips, but it wasn't a sob. Her tears turned off like a tap, thoughts, impossible, incredulous thoughts pinging in, realisation dawning. She shook her head to clear it, because surely it couldn't be so…surely the thought that had just occurred would be flawed on examination, that Alex's problems couldn't really be that simple. But instead, the more she thought about it the more sense it made, the more she had to share it.

'Hugh.' Her hands were shaking so much after several fruitless attempts to reach Dante that she'd had to dial his number several times. 'I need to speak to Dante. His phone's turned off, but is there any way when the court takes a break—'

'He's not here.' Hugh's voice was so flat, so low, that Matilda had to strain to catch it.

'Can you give me his secretary's number?' Matilda asked, shame and embarrassment pushed aside. Right now she didn't care about Dante's response to her—this was way, way more important.

'Matilda, have you seen the newspaper, the television?' Hugh asked, as her free hand flicked on the remote, wondering what on earth Hugh was going on about. 'The charges were all dropped, the trial finished two days ago…'

'Two days ago?' Matilda's mind raced for comfort but there was none to be had. She couldn't even pretend it was because of the trial, because of work that he hadn't called her. But she dragged herself to the present, forced herself to focus on the reason she needed to talk to him so badly. 'Hugh, I need to speak to him urgently.' Her voice was the most assertive she'd ever heard it. 'Now, can you, please, tell me how I can get hold of him?'

'He's in Italy.' And even though she wanted to have misheard, even though at the eleventh hour she mentally begged for a reprieve, Matilda knew from the utter devastation in Hugh's voice that there wouldn't be one.

Dante really had gone.

'He's asked me not to ring for a few weeks, Matilda. He wants some time to sort things out and I've tried to respect that—not that it matters. I know that his house-keeper won't put me through and I'm pretty sure she wouldn't put…'

He didn't say it, didn't twist the taut knife any further, but they both knew the words that filled the silence that crackled down the telephone line. If he wouldn't even speak to Hugh, what hope was there of Dante speaking to her?

'Hugh.' Matilda's mind was going at a thousand miles an hour. She knew she couldn't tell Hugh what she thought she knew, couldn't build him up just to tear him down, knew she had to tread carefully now. 'Could I ask you to give me his address?'

'I don't know.' She could feel his hesitation, knew that she was asking him to cross a line, but she also knew that Hugh wanted Dante back in Australia more than anything in the world, and if something Matilda said could make that happen then perhaps it was worth a try. 'I guess it wouldn't do any harm to write to him, then it's up to Dante whether or not he reads it.'

Matilda held her breath as she scrabbled for a pen, then closed her eyes in blessed relief as finally, after the longest time, Hugh gave it to her.

'Thanks, Hugh.' Matilda said, clicking off the telephone, and even though it was the biggest, possibly the most reckless decision of her life, amazingly she didn't hesitate. She flicked through the phone book before making her second call of the day, knowing that if she thought about it, tried to rationalise it, she'd never do it.

'I'd like to book a flight to Rome, please.'

'When did you want to go?' Running a shaking hand through her hair, Matilda listened to the efficient voice, could hear the taps on the keyboard as the woman typed in the information. Taking a deep breath, she uttered the most terrifying words of her life.

'I'd like the next available flight, please.'

CHAPTER TWELVE

'I'M SORRY the flight has been overbooked.'

Matilda could barely take it in, just blinked back as the well-groomed woman tapped over and over at her computer. She was scarcely able to believe what she was hearing, that the seat she'd booked and paid for just a few short hours ago had never been available in the first place, that flights were often overbooked and that if she read the fine print on her ticket she'd realise that there was nothing she could do—that she'd just have to wait until the next flight.

'When is the next flight?' Matilda's trembling voice asked, watching the long, immaculately polished nails stroking the keyboards.

'I can get you on tomorrow at eleven a.m.'

She might just as well have said the next millennium, Matilda realised, because her conviction left her then, the conviction that had forced her to pick up the telephone and book her flight, the conviction that had seen her pack at lightning speed, cancel work, persuade her family, hissed out of her like the air in a balloon when the party was over. And it *was* over, Matilda realised.

If ever she'd wanted a sign, this was it—and it wasn't a subtle one. Neon lights flashing over the ground steward's head couldn't have spelt it out clearer.

She'd been stupid to think she could do it, could convince Dante what she felt in her heart was wrong with Alex. Her family, her friends had all poured scorn on the idea, even she herself had when she'd attempted to write down what was screaming so clearly in her mind. That was the reason she had to see Dante face to face, *had* to tell him now, couldn't put it in a letter, couldn't wait for tomorrow, because only now could she really believe it—only now, before her argument was swayed, before she attempted to rationalise what she was sure was true.

Was true because she'd felt it herself.

Had felt it.

'We can offer a refund.'

'I don't want a refund.' Matilda shook her head. 'I have to get this flight.' She heard the words, knew it was her own voice, but even she couldn't believe the strength behind it. 'I have to get this flight because if I don't get on this plane tonight, I know that I'm never going to…'

And she'd watched the airport shows, had watched passengers pleading their cases, shouting their rage, and had winced from the comfort of her sofa, knowing that no matter how loud they shouted, if the flight was full, if the gate was closed, then they might as well just give up now.

'Gate 10.'

'Sorry?' Matilda started, watching as a tag was swiftly

clipped around a rather shabby suitcase before it bumped out of view, watching as those manicured fingers caught the boarding pass from the printer and offered it to her.

'Gate 10,' came the clipped voice. 'Business and first class are boarding now—you'd better step on it.'

And the most infrequent of frequent flyers Matilda might have been, but she wasn't a complete novice either. Her overwrought mind worked overtime as she made it through passport control then dashed along the carpeted floors of Melbourne airport, walked along the long passageway, knowing that the comfort level of the next twenty-four hours was entirely dependent on a single gesture.

Right for Economy.

Left for Business.

'Good evening, Miss Hamilton.' Blond, gorgeous and delightfully gay, the flight attendant greeted her and Matilda held her breath, playing a perverse game of he loves me, he loves me not. He checked her ticket and gestured her to her seat.

'Straight through to your left, first row behind the curtain.'

And it didn't matter if he loved her or he loved her not, Matilda decided, slipping into her huge seat and declining an orange juice but accepting champagne in a glass. It didn't matter that she couldn't really afford the air fare and that if she lived to be a thousand she'd never be able to justify flying to the other side of the world on a hunch. If she'd wanted a sign then she had one. She really was doing the right thing, not for herself, not even for Dante…but for Alex.

* * *

Rome, Matilda decided, had to be the most beautiful city in the world, because jet-lagged, at six a.m. on a cold grey morning and nursing a broken heart, nothing in the world should have been able to lift her spirits, but hurtling through the streets of the Eternal City in a taxi, Matilda was captivated. So captivated that when the hotel receptionist informed her in no uncertain terms that her room wouldn't be ready for a couple more hours, Matilda was happy to leave her rather small suitcase at the hotel and wander the streets, plunged from the boskiness of a late Australian spring to a crisp Italian autumn.

A fascinated bystander, Matilda watched as the Eternal City awoke, the roads noisily filling up, cars, scooters, cycles, the pavements spilling over with beautiful, elegant people, chattering loudly in their lyrical language as they raced confidently past or halted a moment for an impossibly strong coffee. Everyone, except for her, seemed to know their place, know where they were going. Matilda, in contrast, meandered along cobbled streets which were rich with history, yet welcomed the modern—buildings that had stood for centuries housing a treasure trove of modern fashion, glimpsing a part of Dante's world and knowing that he was near. Wondering how to face him, how to approach him, how to let him know that she was there.

Message Sent

Matilda stared at the screen of her much-hated phone and for the first time was actually grateful to have it. Grateful for the ease of rapid contact without speech.

Well, not that rapid, Matilda thought ordering another latté to replace her long since cold one, watching as some fabulous, twenty-first-century Sophia Loren managed to drink, smoke, read and text at the same time. After a few failed attempts she'd managed to get her message across, had told Dante where she was now and where she would be staying later and asking if they could meet for a discussion—snappy, direct and impersonal.

Everything she'd tried and failed to be.

But when her message brought no response, when, looking at her watch, Matilda realised her room would be ready and she pulled out her purse and unpeeled the unfamiliar money, only then did the magnitude of what she had done actually catch up with her. Nerves truly hit as she realised that for all she knew, Dante might not even be in Italy—he could have stopped in Bangkok or Singapore for a break. It had seemed so important to see him at the time, it had never actually dawned on her that Dante might not want to see her, that she could have come all this way only to find out that he didn't even care what she had to say. Maybe she should have made it clear that she'd come to talk about Alex. Perhaps if she texted him again…

'Matilda.'

Thankful that her fingers were still in her purse and not creeping towards her phone, Matilda took the longest time to look up—truly unsure how she felt when she finally stared into the face whose loss she had been mourning. He looked older somehow, his skin a touch paler, the shadows under his eyes like bruises now, as if all the trouble of the past eighteen months had finally caught up with him—nothing like the dashing young barrister who'd walked out of a Melbourne courtroom a few days ago. Clearly he hadn't shaved since then, but instead of looking scruffy it gave him a slightly tortured, artistic look. Matilda decided, as he slid into the seat next to her and consumed her all over again, there was still more than a dash of the old Dante, still that irrefutable sex appeal.

Odd that when there was so much to say, when it was so outlandish that she was actually here, that the silence they sat in for a few moments wasn't particularly uncomfortable. Matilda gathered the images that fluttered in her mind, knowing she would take them out and explore them later. Dante accepted the coffee and plate of *biscotti* from the waiter and pushed them towards her.

'No, thanks.' Matilda shook her head and Dante obviously wasn't hungry either because he pushed the plate away untouched.

'Seems I was wrong about you,' he said finally. 'You're not afraid of confrontation after all.'

'Actually, you were right.' Matilda gave a pale smile. 'I'm not here to confront you, Dante.' She watched as his eyes narrowed. 'Whatever your opinion of me, please, know that I've got a better one of myself, and chasing after a man who clearly doesn't want me has never been my style.'

She watched his face harden, watched his jaw crease as if swallowing some vile taste down before speaking, his voice almost derisive because clearly he thought he knew better than her, clearly he assumed that she was lying. 'So why are you here, then, Matilda? If not about us, why are you here in Rome?'

'I'm here about Alex.' It was obviously the last thing he'd expected her to say because his face flickered in confusion, his eyes frowning as she continued. 'I think I know what's wrong with her. I think I've worked out what causes her to get upset, why she continues...'

'Matilda.' In a supremely Latin gesture he flicked her words away with his hands. 'I have consulted with the top specialists, I have had my daughter examined from head to toe and you, after one week of knowing her, after barely spending—'

'It's jasmine.' The two words stopped him in mid-sentence. His mouth opened to continue, to no doubt tell her she had no idea what she was talking about, but her urgent voice overrode him, her frantic eyes pinning him. Matilda knew if he would only listen to her for a single minute then it had to be a valuable one, that even if he didn't believe her now then maybe tonight, next week, next month, when they were both out of each other's lives for ever, when the pain of this moment had passed, he would recall her words objectively and maybe, maybe they'd make sense.

'The *scent* of jasmine,' Matilda specified, as Dante shook his head. 'That first day she lost her temper, the first day you called for a doctor, you told me you were on your way to the cemetery.'

'So?'

'Did you take flowers?' When he didn't respond she pushed harder, her heart hammering in her chest, because if she'd got this bit mistaken then her whole theory fell apart. But as she spoke Dante blinked a couple of times, his scathing face swinging around in alarm as she asked her next question. 'Did you take some jasmine from the garden?'

'Of course. But—'

'You sent flowers the day Jasmine died, Dante,' she said softly. 'And Katrina told me you'd had every florist in Melbourne trying to find some jasmine. Alex was trapped in a car for two hours with her mother, calling out for her, desperate for reassurance, trapped with that smell…'

'But a scent cannot trigger such a reaction.' Dante shook his head in firm denial, absolutely refusing to believe it could be so simple. But at least he was listening, Matilda consoled herself as she carried on talking, her own conviction growing with each word she uttered, the hunch that had brought her to this point a matter of fact now.

'Alex's trouble started in spring, Dante, when the jasmine was flowering, and when it became too much, when all she got was worse, you took her back to Italy…'

'Things were better for a while,' Dante argued. 'She was fine until…' His hand was over his mouth, his eyes widening as Matilda said it for him.

'Until spring came again. Dante, she didn't run away because she saw us in bed. Alex ran away because you opened the window. It was humid, the scent would have filled the room…'

'She was trying to get away from it?'

'I don't know,' Matilda whispered. 'I don't know what she's thinking. I just know that I'm right, Dante.'

'Suppose that you are.' His eyes were almost defiant.

'What am I supposed to do? I can hardly rid the world of jasmine, ensure she never inhales that scent again…'

'Why do you always have to go to such extremes, Dante? Why does it always have to be black and white to you? Oh, this isn't working so I'll leave the country. She seems nice, so I'll just be mean. Alex reacts to jasmine, so I'd better get rid of it. Just acknowledge it, Dante, and then find out how to work through it. Tell the experts, the doctors…' She gave a helpless shrug, then picked up her purse and put it firmly in her bag— hell, he could buy her a coffee at least.

'You're going?' Dante frowned as she stood.

'That's all I came here to say.'

'That's all?' Dante scorned, clearly not believing a word. 'You could have put that in a letter, rung me.'

'Would you have read it?' Matilda checked. 'Would you have picked up the phone? And even if you had, would you really have believed it without seeing me?'

'Probably not,' Dante admitted.

'Well, there you go,' Matilda said, heading for the door and out into the cool morning. She stilled as he called out to her, his skeptical voice reaching her ears.

'You're asking me to believe you flew to the other side of the world for a child you have seen four maybe five times.'

'I'm not *asking* you to believe anything, Dante.' The lid was off now, rivers of lava spewing over the edges as she turned round and walked smartly back to where he was standing, her pale face livid as she looked angrily up to him. 'I'm *telling* you that I didn't come here to discuss us. Get it into your head, I don't need a grand closing speech from you, there's no jury you have to sum up for here. You walked out without so much as a goodbye and that's a clear enough message even for me. I'm certainly not going to hover on the edges of your emotions, either waiting for permission to enter or to be told again to leave.'

'I told you from the start that there could be no relationship,' Dante said through gritted teeth.

'Well, you were right.' Matilda nodded. 'Because a relationship is about trusting and sharing and giving, and you're incapable of all three.'

'Matilda, I have a child who is sick and getting worse by the day. I was doing you a favour by holding back. How could I ask you to turn your life around for us? It's better this way…'

'Don't you dare!' Matilda roared, startling Dante and everyone in earshot. Even if the Italians were used to uncensored passion, clearly eight-thirty on a weekday morning was a little early for them. But Matilda was operating on a different time clock. It was the middle of the night in her mind as her emotions finally erupted, oblivious of the gathering crowd as finally she let him have it. 'Don't you dare decide what's best for me when you didn't even have the manners to ask. I loved you and you didn't want it. Well, fine, walk away, get on a plane and leave the country, walk out of my life without a goodbye, but don't you dare tell me it's for the best, don't you dare stand there and tell me that you're doing me a favour—when I never asked for one. I flew to the other side of the world because I care about your daughter and in time I'd have loved Alex, too. I'd have loved Alex because she was a part of you, and you *know* that, you *know* that, Dante.' She jabbed a finger into his chest, jabbed the words at him over and over, ramming the truth home to the motionless, rigid man. 'You didn't want my love—that's the bottom line so don't dress it up with excuses. You love Jasmine and you always will.'

'I loved Jasmine—' He started but she turned to walk away because she couldn't bear to look at him. She pushed her way through the little gathered crowd and started to run because she couldn't bear to be close to him and not have him, couldn't be strong for even a second longer. She'd said all she had come to and way, way more, had told him her truth. There was nothing left to give and certainly nothing more to take. She didn't want his crumbs of comfort, didn't want to hear how in another place, another time, maybe they could have made it.

'Matilda.' He caught her wrist but she couldn't take the contact, the shooting awareness that had propelled them on that first day even more acute, even more torturous. She tried to wrench it away, but he gripped it tighter, forced her to turn around and face him. '*Senti,*' he demanded. 'Listen to me!' But she shook her head.

'No, because there's nothing else to say.'

'Please?'

That one word stilled her, the one word she'd never heard him say, because he'd never had to ask politely for anything. Dante had never had to ask anyone for anything because it had all been there for the taking.

Till now.

'Please,' he said again, and she nodded tentatively. She felt his fingers loosen a touch round her wrist, grateful now for the contact as he led her away from the crowded streets and to the Villa Borghese, a green haven in the middle of the city. He led her through the park to a bench where they sat. Silent tears streaming down her face from her outpouring of emotion, she braced herself for the next onslaught of pain, biting on her lip as Dante implored her to listen, no doubt to tell her as he had in the first place why it could never, ever have worked.

'I loved Jasmine…' he said slowly, letting his hands warm hers. She was touching him for the last time, staring down at his long, manicured fingers entwined in hers and even managing a wan smile at the contrast, her hands certainly not her best feature. But it wasn't her short nails or her prolonged misuse of moisturiser that had Matilda frowning. Eyes that were swimming with tears struggled to focus on a gold band that was missing, a wedding band that to this day had always been there. Her confusion grew as Dante continued talking. 'But not like this.'

'Like what?' Matilda croaked, still staring at his naked ring finger.

'Like *this*.' Dante's voice was a hoarse whisper, but she could hear the passion and emotion behind it and something else that drew her eyes to his, recognition greeting her as Dante continued. '*This* love.'

He didn't have to elaborate because she knew exactly what he meant—*this* love that was all-consuming, *this* love that was so overwhelming and intense it could surely only be experienced once in a lifetime. And she glimpsed his hellish guilt then, guessed a little of what was coming next as he pulled her into his arms as if he needed to feel her to go on.

'We were arguing the day she died—we were always arguing.' He paused but she didn't fill it, knew Dante had to tell her his story himself. 'When I met Jasmine she was a career-woman and had absolutely no intention of settling down or starting a family, and that suited me fine. We were good together. I didn't have to explain the hours I put into my work and neither did she. It worked, Matilda, it really worked, until…' She felt him stiffen in her arms, felt him falter and held him just a touch tighter. 'Jasmine found out she was pregnant. We were both stunned. We'd taken precautions, it just wasn't part of the plan, wasn't what either of us wanted, and yet…' He pulled her chin up and she stared up at him, stared as that pain-ravaged face broke into a ghost of smile. 'I was pleased, too, excited. I loved her and she was having my baby, and I thought that would be enough.'

'But it wasn't?' Her voice was muffled by his embrace but Matilda already knew the answer.

'No.'

Or part of it.

'It wasn't enough for Jasmine. We got married quickly and bought this house and for a few months things were OK, but as Jasmine got bigger as the birth came closer, she seemed to resent the impact her pregnancy was having on her career. She was determined to go straight back to work afterwards, to carry on as if nothing had happened, and that is when the arguments started, because our baby was coming, like it or not, and things had to change. I tried to stay quiet, hoped that once the baby came she'd see things differently, but she didn't. She hired a top nanny and was back at work within six weeks, full time. She hardly saw Alex. I understand women work, I understand that, but not to the exclusion of their child, not when you don't need the money. That is when the arguments escalated.'

'People argue Dante…' Matilda tried to comfort him, tried to say the right thing, but knew it was useless. Despite their closeness, she could feel the wall around him, knew the pain behind it and ached to reach him, *ached* for him.

'She felt trapped, I know that,' Dante said, his voice utterly bleak. 'I know that, because so did I. Not that we ever said it, not that either of us had the courage to admit it. The morning of the accident, *again* she was going into the office. It was a Saturday and the nanny was off and *again* she wanted me to have Alex, only this time I said no. No. No. No…' He repeated the word like a torturous mantra. 'No. You are her mother. No, for once you have her. No, I'm going out. I told her it was wrong, that Alex deserved a better mother. I told her so many things terrible things…' She heard the break in his voice and moved to help him.

'Dante, people say terrible things in an argument. You just didn't get the chance to take them back.'

'I tried to—even as I was saying them I wanted it to stop, to put the genie back in the bottle and retract the things I had said. I did not want it to be over, I did not want Alex to come from a broken home. I rang the housekeeper and was told Jasmine had taken Alex to work with her. She wouldn't pick up when I called and I had the florist send flowers over to her office. I told them to write that all I wanted was for her to come home… She never did.'

'Oh, God, Dante…' Matilda knew she was supposed to be strong now, to somehow magic up the right words, but all she could do was cry—for him, for Jasmine and for the stupid mess that was no one's fault, for the pain, for both of them.

'She *was* coming home, Dante,' Matilda said finally, pressing her cheek against his, trying to instil warmth where there was none, her tears mingling with his. 'She got the flowers, she knew you were sorry…'

'Not sorry enough, though.' He closed his eyes in bitter regret, self-loathing distorting his beautiful features. 'Not sorry enough, because I was still angry. The problems were all still there and even if she hadn't died, I know deep down that sooner or later our marriage would have.'

'You don't know that, Dante, because you never got the chance to find out,' Matilda said softly. 'Who knows what would have happened if Jasmine had come home that day? Maybe you would have talked, would have sorted things out…'

'Maybe…' Dante said, but she could tell he didn't believe it, tell that he'd tried and failed to convince himself of the same thing. 'You know what I hate the most? I hate the sympathy, I hate that people think I deserve it.'

'You do deserve it,' Matilda said. 'Just because the two of you were having troubles, it doesn't mean you were bad people.'

'Perhaps,' Dante sighed. 'But I cannot burst Katrina and Hugh's bubble, cannot tell them that their daughter's last months were not happy ones…'

'You don't have to tell them anything.' Matilda shook her head. 'Tell them if you must that Jasmine made you so happy you want to do it all over again.' She cupped his proud face in her hand and forced him to look at her, smiled, not because it was funny but because it was so incredibly easy to help him, so incredibly *right* to lead him away from his pain. 'You did nothing wrong.

'*Nothing*,' she reiterated.

'But suppose that you'd walked into that lift two years ago, Matilda?' Dante asked. 'Suppose, after yet another row, the love of my life had appeared then? I punish Edward for what he did to you and yet…'

'Never.' Matilda shook her head, blew away his self-doubt with her utter conviction. 'You'd never have done that to Jasmine and you know that as much as I do, Dante, because even if the feelings had been there, you'd never have acted on them. My God, you're barely acting on them now, so surely you know that much about yourself.'

And he must have, because finally he nodded.

'Don't beat yourself up with questions you can never answer,' Matilda said softly. 'You and Jasmine did your best—just hold onto the fact that there was enough love to stop either of you walking away. You sent her flowers and asked her to come home and that's exactly what she was doing. The truth is enough to hold onto.'

And she watched as the pain that had been there since she'd first met him literally melted away, dark, troubled eyes glimmering with new-found hope. But it faded into a frown as Matilda's voice suddenly changed from understanding to angry, pulling back her hands and folding her arms, resting her chin on her chest and staring fixedly ahead. 'You're so bloody arrogant, Dante!'

'What the hell did I do now?' Dante asked, stunned at the sudden change in her.

'Sitting there and wondering whether or not you'd have had an affair with me! As if I had absolutely no say in the matter! Well, for your information, Dante Costello, I'd have slapped your damned cheek if you'd so much as laid a finger on me. I'd never get involved with a married man!'

'Unless he was your husband!' Dante said, uncoiling her rigid arms, kissing her face all over in such a heavenly Italian way. 'That was actually a proposal— just in case you were wondering.'

Matilda kissed him back with such passion and depth that if they had been in any city other than Rome, they'd no doubt have been arrested. It was Dante who pulled away, demanding a response from a grumbling Matilda, who wanted his kiss to go on for ever.

'That was actually a yes.' Matilda smiled, happy to go back to being ravished, to being kissed by the most difficult, complicated, beautiful man in the world. 'Just in case you were wondering!'

EPILOGUE

'ARE you OK?'

Standing in the garden—in *Alex's* garden—Matilda hastily wiped the tears from her cheeks as Dante approached, determined that he wouldn't see her cry. Today was surely hard enough for him without her tears making things worse.

'I'm fine,' Matilda answered, forcing a bright smile as she turned around. But watching him walk over, Alex running alongside him, Dante's hand shielding their newborn son's tiny face from the early morning sun with such tenderness, her reserve melted, the tears resuming as he joined her.

'It's OK to be sad,' Dante said softly. 'And you can't argue, because you said it yourself.'

'I did,' Matilda gulped, but as the sound of the removal trucks pulling into the drive reached her, she gave in, letting him hold her as she wept. 'I feel guilty for being upset at leaving when I know how much harder this is for you. I know this is your house…'

'Our house,' Dante corrected, but Matilda shook her head.

'It was yours and Jasmine's first so, please, don't try and tell me that you're not hurting, too.'

'A bit,' Dante admitted, gazing down at Joe, tracing his cheek with his finger, 'but I was giving Joe his bottle, thinking about our new home and Alex was running around, checking her dolls were all in her bag, laughing and talking, and I promise you, Matilda, all I felt was peace. I knew in my heart of hearts that Jasmine was happy for me, was finally able to admit...' He didn't finish but gave a tiny wry smile and attempted to change the subject, but Matilda was having none of it.

'Tell me, Dante,' she urged, because despite all the progress, despite their closeness, sometimes with Dante she had to. 'Please, tell me what you were thinking.'

'That I loved her.' He was watching her closely for her reaction, an apology on the tip of his tongue, but he held it back as she smiled. 'Is it OK to say that to you?'

'It's more than OK, Dante,' came Matilda's heartfelt answer. 'It's exactly how it should be.'

'I know we had our faults, I know that it probably wouldn't have worked, but sometimes when I see Alex laughing now, sometimes when she is being cheeky or funny, I can actually see Jasmine in her and finally I am able to remember the good bits. Finally I know that she is in a peaceful place. I know that she is proud of the choices I have made, and it's all because of you.'

She didn't even attempt to hide her tears, just leant on him as he spoke on.

'It's right to move on, right that we make a new start, with our little family.'

'But just because we're looking to the future, it

doesn't mean we have to shut out the past,' Matilda assured him. 'Even Katrina seems to have come around.'

She had. In the tumultuous weeks that had followed their revelation, it would have been so easy to hate her, but in the end Matilda had seen Katrina for what she was, a mother that was grieving, a mother terrified of the world moving on and leaving her daughter's memories behind. And slowly the tide had turned. Alex's stunning progress, Dante's respect, coupled with Matilda's patience, had won the coldest heart around.

'We need to do this,' Dante affirmed. 'We need to make new memories, build new gardens and look to the future…' He didn't finish, the words knocked from him as a very jealous young lady flung her arms around both of them, eyeing her new brother with blatant disapproval as she demanded to join in the cuddle.

'Together.' Matilda laughed, scooping up Alex, closing her eyes in bliss as the little girl rained kisses on her face. 'We'll do it together.'

HIS PRIVATE MISTRESS

BY
CHANTELLE SHAW

Chantelle Shaw lives on the Kent coast, five minutes from the sea, and does much of her thinking about the characters in her books while walking on the beach. She's been an avid reader from an early age. Her school friends used to hide their books when she visited – but Chantelle would retreat into her own world and still writes stories in her head all the time. Chantelle has been blissfully married to her own tall, dark and very patient hero for over twenty years and has six children. She began to read Mills & Boon® books as a teenager and, throughout the years of being a stay-at-home mum to her brood, found romantic fiction helped her to stay sane! She enjoys reading and writing about strong-willed, feisty women and even stronger-willed, sexy heroes. Chantelle is at her happiest when writing. She is particularly inspired while cooking dinner, which unfortunately results in a lot of culinary disasters! She also loves gardening, walking and eating chocolate (followed by more walking!). Catch up with Chantelle's latest news on her website, www. chantelleshaw.com.

**Don't miss Chantelle Shaw's exciting new novel,
Ruthless Russian, Lost Innocence, available this
month from Mills & Boon® Modern™.**

CHAPTER ONE

'...AND IN A round-up of local news, staff and patients at Greenacres, the specialist spinal injury unit here in Wellworth, had an unexpected visitor yesterday. Formula 1 champion Rafael Santini arrived by helicopter and spent several hours chatting to everyone at the unit before making a substantial donation. Greenacres manager, Jean Collins, said everyone was excited by the visit,' the radio presenter chuckled. 'I bet the ladies were excited, Santini's reputation off the track is as legendary as on it, if you know what I mean! Before you tell us what the weather has in store, Kate, what do you think of Rafe Santini?'

'Oh, a sex god, definitely, Brian. He'd brighten my day, which is more than can be said for the forecast...'

Eden stabbed her finger on the radio control button, cutting off the presenter's irritatingly bright voice, and stared impatiently at the queue of traffic. The roadworks had sprung up as if by magic overnight and she drummed her fingers on the wheel, refusing to admit that her tension had more to do with nerves than the fact that she was late. She shouldn't have had that second glass of wine last night, she conceded when she finally reached the hotel. No doubt it was the reason she had overslept and was responsible for the dull ache across her temples.

Her high heels clicked on the marble tiles of the foyer and a hasty glance in the mirror revealed that she looked cool and elegant in her cream trouser suit, her long blonde hair falling in a thick braid down her back. Her air of composure disguised the fact that her heart was racing. There was no good reason for the sick feeling in the pit of her stomach, she berated herself; it was ridiculous to feel so *nervous*.

Security at the front desk was tight; she should have expected it, and her irritation grew as she scrabbled in her bag for her Press pass, barely able to contain her impatience as the security guard scrutinised it carefully before waving her through. It would be easier to break into Fort Knox, she decided grimly when she was stopped at the door to the conference hall by another security guard.

'You are late,' the guard informed her unnecessarily, in his slow, carefully pronounced English. 'The interview has already begun.'

'I'll slip in quietly,' Eden promised. 'No one will notice.' She prayed she was right; the last thing she wanted to do was draw attention to herself. If the morning had gone to plan she would already be safely ensconced at the back of the room, buried amidst the huddle of other journalists, unnoticed and anonymous.

The conference hall was packed and again she wondered what she had expected. Rafael Santini rarely gave interviews. He had a love-hate relationship with the media, whereby they loved to report his every move and he abhorred their intrusion into his private life. Since his brother Gianni's terrible accident three years ago, and the fevered media speculation that Rafe had been responsible for the crash, his feelings for the paparazzi had developed into an almost pathological hatred. Even now, in his exalted position as Formula 1 World Champion, his statements to the Press had been condensed into a few terse words and Eden wondered what form of persuasion Fabrizzio Santini had used to coerce his eldest son to face the media.

Eden kept her head lowered as she slunk into one of the last empty seats at the back of the hall, and it was only then, when she was well and truly hidden, that she dared to lift her eyes to the stage. She had been mentally preparing for this moment all morning. Hell, who was she kidding? She had been on edge for days, ever since she had known that she was going to see Rafe again. Even so, that first sight of him, the sheer impact of his stunningly handsome face, caused her to inhale sharply, her stomach churning, and she dropped her gaze, needing to reassemble her defences.

Rafael Santini looked bored. His hard features were schooled into a mask of polite interest, the chiselled perfection of his bone structure, the aquiline nose and heavy black brows from beneath which gleamed eyes the colour of polished jet, acting as a magnet for every woman in the room. But even from a distance Eden could read the signs of his impatience. It was there in the rigid set of his jaw, the way he twiddled a pen between his fingers, his smile revealing a flash of white teeth, but not reaching his eyes. As she watched him he stiffened, his body suddenly taut, his dark eyes hooded as he stared across the room in her direction. He couldn't

possibly know she was there, Eden reassured herself as she
sank lower in her seat. Rafe knew she was a journalist and
that she came from Wellworth; it was where they had first
met, after all. Doubtless he would also assume that she
retained her links with the spinal-injury unit that he had just
presented with a generous donation, but he would not expect
her to be at the Press conference, and the air of tension that
emanated from him was just a trick of her imagination.

Hadn't he always been aware of her the moment she
entered a room? the voice in her head insidiously reminded
her. It was a sixth sense they had shared, their consciousness
of each other so acute that even in a crowded room they had
known the exact moment the other was near. It was a memory
long buried and she wished it hadn't surfaced now. She preferred to remember Rafe as a distant, unemotional lover who
had provided great sex but little else. That was one of the
reasons she had decided to end their relationship, if he hadn't
beaten her to it and dumped her so publicly. It was surprising how much it hurt, even after all this time, and the sudden,
stark memory of just how emotional their relationship had
been was an unwelcome intrusion into her well-ordered life.

A woman at the front of the hall asked Rafe to speculate
on his chances of winning Silverstone in two days' time and
he relaxed slightly, his sexy smile causing a cramping pain
in the pit of Eden's stomach.

'I don't speculate,' he answered with the careless arrogance she remembered so well. 'I intend to win. The car is
performing well, and so am I,' he murmured throatily, with
a suggestive wink at the young journalist, who visibly wilted
under the force of his charm. A ripple of laughter ran through

the crowd at his answer. He wasn't known as the Italian Stallion for nothing—stories of his numerous affairs hit the headlines on a regular basis—and Eden gritted her teeth as she reached for her notebook.

A few basic details, information gleaned from questions she would leave the other journalists to ask. Cliff couldn't expect any more, and if he did he was going to be disappointed because no way was she going to try and snatch an exclusive interview with Rafe Santini. Once, she might have been overwhelmed by his seductive Latin charm, like the young journalist who was still looking flushed and starry-eyed, but she was no longer the impressionable girl who had fallen in love with the world's number-one Lothario.

She knew that her old friend, Cliff Harley, the editor of the *Wellworth Gazette*, was hoping for an in-depth account of the life of Formula 1's ultimate hero.

'Come on, Eden, you're the golden girl, the hotshot reporter, renowned for her daring escapades in Africa,' he had cajoled. 'If anyone can get a good story from the Santini racing team Press interview, it's you.'

'Rafe Santini loathes the media,' Eden argued, 'and he's almost certainly not going to grant any exclusive interviews. I imagine he's only agreed to the Press conference to promote the fact that the Santini group have bought out the sports-car manufacturers in Oxford. It's a damage-limitation exercise after the scandals that have hit the Santini team over the last few years.'

'Yeah, but you have the added bonus of knowing Rafe intimately,' Cliff teased with a salacious grin, and Eden blushed. Oh, yes, she had known Rafe intimately, had been so familiar with every inch of his body that even now, four years on, she could picture his broad, olive-skinned chest, the muscled hardness of his thighs and his powerful physique.

'My friendship with Rafe ended a long time ago,' she told Cliff primly, ignoring his smirk at her description of Rafe as her friend. To be fair, Cliff was right; she had never been Rafael Santini's friend. His mistress, yes, his sexual playmate, whom he had picked up and cast aside whenever he felt like it and whom he had seemed to delight in flaunting before the public as his besotted lover, yes. But the intimacy they shared had never run any deeper than that.

'Well, I want a story with a bit of depth,' Cliff told her. 'I want details, I want to know what makes Santini tick, how he feels just before a race. I want a story that exposes the man behind the myth…'

'You want to know who he's sleeping with,' Eden muttered caustically, cutting Cliff off in mid-flow. Five years ago they'd started out together as junior reporters on the *Gazette*, but since then their lives had taken very different paths. Cliff had remained in Wellworth, married his childhood sweetheart and worked his way up to editor, while she had earned a reputation as a fearless and respected foreign correspondent sending back reports from the trouble-torn Ivory Coast. She'd spent the last three years living on her wits and she needed a break, time to recover.

She had promised her parents she would do nothing more energetic than sit in the garden of their cottage, but after a month of inactivity she was climbing the walls and was grateful for Cliff's offer of a job as a reporter for the *Gazette*. 'I won't do sleaze,' she had warned as she headed out of the office. 'One of the lessons I learned from the year I spent with Rafe was what it feels like to have your face plastered across the tabloids and a load of rubbish written about you.'

Frantically, she shut off the unpleasant memories and scribbled down a few more notes about Rafe's intention to continue competing in Formula 1 for the foreseeable future. There had been talk that Fabrizzio Santini was not in the best of health and certainly he had been devastated by the accident that had left his younger son, Gianni, paralysed. It was rumoured that Fabrizzio wanted to hand over the reins of the Santini Corporation to Rafael, but Eden hadn't taken them seriously. Rafe would never give up racing; it was in his blood, the need for speed and excitement, a degree of competitiveness that had put him at the head of his sport for a decade.

Rafe wasn't like other men. There was a wild element to him that saw him take risks that others would have regarded as madness, but which he always managed to pull off successfully. Many aspired to be like him, not least his younger brother, Gianni, but the rivalry between them had grown beyond the bounds of sibling competitiveness and had ultimately led to Gianni's terrible crash.

It was warm in the conference hall and the journalist sitting next to Eden was overweight and sweating profusely as he juggled with his notebook and a plastic beaker of coffee. He dropped his pen and as he leant forwards to retrieve it he sent a stream of scalding liquid into her lap.

'Oh, heck—sorry, love,' he muttered as Eden yelped and half stood, frantically trying to blot the spreading stain with a tissue.

'Yes, the young lady in the corner.' Rafe's agent's voice sounded from the stage, followed by a long silence.

'He means you,' another reporter hissed to Eden and she flushed and quickly sat down.

'I don't have a question,' she muttered, and the reporter sighed impatiently.

'Well, think of one, for Christ's sake, before Santini gets fed up and ends the interview. He's not known for his patience.'

Aware that her continuing silence was attracting curious glances, she took a deep breath. She had no option but to say something, she realised dismally, but her mind had gone blank and she asked the first question that came into her head. 'Mr Santini, does your interest and financial support for the spinal unit in Wellworth stem from the injuries your brother received in his accident at the Hungarian Grand Prix?'

A murmur rustled through the crowd of journalists, more heads turned in her direction and Eden slid lower into her seat, praying that she had disguised her voice sufficiently that Rafe wouldn't recognise her. It was four years, she reminded herself; with any luck he would give a brief answer and move on.

'You've done it now,' the reporter standing close to her groaned. 'Didn't you hear Santini's agent say at the beginning of the Press call that Rafe won't tolerate any questions about his personal life and, in particular, anything about his brother?'

'I came in late,' Eden said, trying to defend herself. 'I didn't know.'

Up on the stage Rafe had leaned towards his companion and the two men were involved in a heated discussion before his agent stared in Eden's direction. 'Mr Santini requests that you repeat the question, but first will you please stand and state your name?'

So much for remaining anonymous, Eden thought grimly as she eyed the side-exit and debated making an escape bid. It was too late; all eyes were on her and she had no choice but to slowly stand up. Even then she clung to the faint hope that he would not recognise her across the distance of the conference hall, but as she glanced towards the stage the room seemed to miraculously empty and there was no one but Rafe.

Dark eyes studied her with insolent appraisal, stripped her layer by layer and left her bare and exposed. She felt as though he had bored into her and captured her soul, and then suddenly his eyes released her from their hold and she shivered at the level of contempt in his gaze.

'Eden Lawrence from the *Wellworth Gazette*,' she said huskily, forcing the words past the lump in her throat. There was no point in lying about her identity now that he had recognised her. 'I wondered if Mr Santini's patronage of Greenacres, the centre that specialises in aiding those with spinal injuries, was because of the accident that left his brother paralysed?' Her head was thumping; she felt her cheeks burn and gripped the back of a chair as she was subjected to another cold, hard stare.

'Mr Santini wishes to point out that he makes donations to many charitable organisations,' Rafe's agent snapped, 'but, as was made clear at the beginning of this interview, he will not answer any questions regarding his personal life.'

Suitably chastened, Eden went to sit down, but was halted by a voice that even now, with the distance of years to protect her, sent a shiver of awareness down her spine.

'Miss Lawrence, I am flattered by your fascination with my private life, and it's true that there are very…personal reasons for my support of the spinal-injury unit, which does such excellent work.'

There was no evading Rafe's gaze, however hard she tried. Her eyes seemed to be drawn to him by a magnetic pull so that she could only stare helplessly at him, but she was aware of the whispered speculation from the other journalists.

'Eden Lawrence—she wrote for one of the big nationals, didn't she? She was caught up in some military coup in Africa a couple of years ago.'

'Yeah, but didn't she have an affair with Santini…?'

She really needed to get out of here, Eden thought desperately, and then suddenly two security guards materialised on either side of her and she faced the utter humiliation of being escorted from the conference hall under the brooding gaze of the one man she had hoped to avoid at all costs.

'Come this way.'

It was a demand rather than a request, and it was easier to go gracefully than cause a scene. What on earth had induced her to come within a ten-mile radius of Rafael Santini? she thought bleakly as she marched alongside the security guards, her head held high, hiding the fact that inside she felt sick with mortification. She should never have listened to Cliff, never have allowed him to persuade her to attend the Press conference when there was even the slightest risk that she would meet Rafe again.

She couldn't blame Cliff, she admitted painfully. She had been unable to resist the chance to see Rafe again after all these years, but if she had been testing her immunity to him, she'd failed miserably.

Coming here today hadn't been a wise move, she acknowledged as she stepped into the hotel foyer and headed for the door. Immediately, one of the security guards put a hand on her arm and she found herself being guided firmly towards the lift.

'Do you mind?' she demanded icily. 'You've done your job and I'd like to leave now.'

'Excuse?' the guard said with a shrug, although she was damned sure he had understood her. But as she tried to pull free she found that she had been cleverly manoeuvred into the lift. 'Signor Santini will see you in his suite.'

'The heck he will!' The elevator door opened as they arrived at the top floor and the guard who had been holding her arm stood aside to usher her out, but Eden refused to budge and she glared at him belligerently. The security guards were big and, if she was honest, intimidating, but she had had plenty of dealings with henchmen and refused to be cowed. 'You can tell Signor Santini I have no wish to see him.'

'Excuse?' The shrug was almost comical, very Mediterranean, and Eden felt her temper flare.

'Tell Signor Santini…'

'Why don't you tell him yourself?'

Eden hadn't noticed the arrival of the other lift, but suddenly Rafe appeared in the corridor, tall, dark and indecently good-looking. Her heart performed a painful summersault in her chest as she caught sight of him, and some basic instinct for self-preservation saw her scrabble for the button to close the lift door. One handcrafted Italian leather shoe pre-

vented its closure, the smile that split his features so reminding her of a wolf about to devour its prey that she actually
backed up against the lift wall.

'Well, well; Eden Lawrence,' he drawled in his strongly
accented English. 'The most surprising things crawl out of the
woodwork!' he added silkily, and she shivered at the bitter
contempt in his voice. An elderly couple was hovering in the
corridor behind him and he smiled warmly at them. 'Out you
come, Eden, you're holding these nice people up,' he
murmured.

He could turn on the charm the way other people could
turn on a light switch, Eden thought grimly as she found that
she had no choice but to step into the corridor, the guards
moving to stand on either side of her.

As soon as Rafe had pressed the button to close the lift
doors she rounded on him. 'You can call off your bully-boys.
It was bad enough that you had me frogmarched out of the
Press conference without them dragging me up here.'

Dark eyes flicked from her to the two guards and he spoke
to them in voluble Italian that was too quick for her to pick out
more than a couple of words. 'You exaggerate, Eden,' he said
when he turned his attention back to her. 'Paolo and Romano
assure me that they treated you with the utmost respect.' His
tone and the sardonic gleam in his eyes told her it was a respect
he believed to be undeserved and she flushed as he opened the
door to his suite. He stood aside to usher her inside but Eden
stood firm and lifted her chin, her indignation palpable.

'I won't come in; I'm not stopping.'

Rafe's black brows lifted quizzically. 'Yet you came to the
hotel especially to see me?'

No change in his supreme self-confidence, Eden thought darkly, although, to be fair, why should there be? Women had thrown themselves at him for as long as he could remember, but she was determined not to make the same mistake twice. 'As arrogant as ever, Rafe,' she remarked coolly, 'but I'm afraid the only reason I came was that Cliff Harley asked me to attend the Press conference and write an article for my old paper.'

'I see,' Rafe murmured dulcetly, and Eden hoped that he didn't. He had always possessed an uncanny knack of being able to read her mind, but she had been younger then and not as skilled at hiding her emotions. 'Now that you're here, at least allow me to offer you a drink. You look,' he paused, his brows raised in sardonic amusement, 'hot, and you seem to have spilt something down your trousers.'

Instantly, Eden felt as though she was burning up. She knew her cheeks must be flaming, and a glance at her cream linen trousers revealed a dark stain that ran halfway down her thigh. 'It's coffee,' she muttered, 'courtesy of the idiot I was sitting next to. If it hadn't been for him pouring boiling liquid into my lap, you would never have known I was in the conference hall.'

'I knew you were there,' Rafe told her shortly as he indicated that she should take a seat on one of the plush leather sofas. 'What would you like—wine, juice, tea?' he added, obviously remembering her fondness for a cup of tea.

'Orange juice will be fine,' Eden replied hastily. Hot tea would take too long to drink when she was desperate to escape, and she certainly couldn't handle Rafe and alcohol—she needed to keep a clear head. 'What do you mean, you knew I was there? How could you possibly have known?'

'I felt your presence,' Rafe answered simply. 'If you hadn't drawn attention to yourself I would have scoured the room until I found you.'

A heavy silence filled the room and Eden stared at the carpet, studying the intricate gold and beige pattern with apparent fascination while she fought to control the frantic thud of her heart. He was so gorgeous and she had been starved of him for so long. Her eyes kept straying to him, tracing the outline of his strong jaw and the hard planes of his face, hovering for an infinitesimal second on the sensual curve of his mouth.

'You should check that the coffee didn't burn your leg,' he told her as he handed her a glass of blessedly cold juice. 'There's a spare robe in the bathroom. You can wear it while I have your trousers laundered.'

'No, it's fine, thanks.' Eden spluttered on her drink at the mere thought of sitting here with Rafe for however long it would take to have her trousers cleaned.

'But if you don't act quickly, your trousers may be ruined.'

'So I'll buy another pair. Leave it, Rafe,' she ordered when he opened his mouth to argue. 'We haven't met for almost four years, and I've no intention of taking my clothes off in the first five minutes.'

'How long do you need—ten minutes, fifteen? I remember a time when you were only too willing to strip off,' he added unforgivably, ignoring her gasp of outrage as he leaned back on the sofa opposite her, his arms outstretched along the back, one ankle hooked over the other thigh in a position of indolent ease.

Photographs did not do him justice, nor did her memories

of him, and the image she had kept locked in her subconscious for the last four years faded to a shadow before his forceful presence. Nothing had prepared her for his raw, provocative sex appeal, a magnetism that reached across the space between them and trapped her in his spell. His mocking taunts instantly catapulted her back in time, so that she glared at him, pushing away the memories.

'That was a long time ago when I was young and naive, although you dispensed with my innocence pretty quickly, didn't you, Rafe?' One look from those smouldering dark eyes and she'd fallen like a skittle, she remembered despairingly. 'I didn't stand a chance against the great Rafael Santini, did I?' she said bitterly, remembering her humiliating eagerness to fall into his arms and bed.

'You were an avid pupil,' Rafe replied coolly, 'so good that you decided to turn your attentions to my brother.' The barely leashed savagery in his voice shook her. The poison was still there, festering, and she felt a sudden stinging sensation behind her eyelids at the unfairness of his accusation.

'That's a lie…'

'I saw you with my own eyes.' Eyes that were now burning like hot coals as he jumped to his feet and glared at her. 'You and Gianni in each other's arms. Are you telling me that what I saw by the pool was an *illusion*?'

Once she had been afraid of his hot temper. Not that she feared he would be violent, never that, but he possessed a cruel tongue and his angry words had flayed her alive.

'I'm not telling you anything,' she replied calmly, refusing to be cowed. 'Why should I waste my breath? You wouldn't listen to me four years ago and I don't suppose you're any more reasonable now.' Four years ago she had been so unsure of herself, so in awe of him, but not anymore. In the space of five minutes he'd tried her, acted as judge and jury and condemned her and she was damned if she would let him see that she was still serving a life sentence.

'*Reasonable!* I caught you half naked in my brother's arms—did you really expect me to be reasonable?' His fury was blistering and directed solely at her, black eyes flashing fire, and Eden felt her own temper flare. She didn't want to be drawn into a slanging match and certainly didn't want to open up old wounds that were still raw even after all this time.

After piercing her with another furious glare, Rafe paced the room, raking his hand through his thick black hair that had the tendency to curl at the nape despite the fact that he kept it cropped uncompromisingly short. She had loved his hair, loved running her fingers through it, holding his head and drawing his mouth down to hers. The memory was so stark it hurt and she bit back a gasp as she tore her eyes from his broad shoulders. She didn't want to remember anything and for the sake of her self-preservation, she needed to get out of his room.

'It was a long time ago,' she murmured, deliberately lowering her voice in an effort to prevent one of Rafe's typical Latin outbursts. 'Time has moved on and so have I.' Not that it felt like it, she thought dismally. Right now she felt as young and immature as she had done when she had met him for the first time five years ago. That first meeting had also taken place in a hotel, but then, far from wanting to avoid him, she had actually shinned up a drainpipe and had clambered through the window of his suite to land in an ungainly heap at his feet.

Despite everything she felt her lips twitch at the memory and Rafe threw her a questioning look.

'Something amuses you?' he queried in his heavily accented English, and Eden swallowed and felt goose-pimples prickle her skin. If anything, his voice was sexier than she remembered, rich and sensuous, licking over her like molten chocolate.

'I was just remembering the first time we met,' she explained huskily. 'Your room was on the second floor and I climbed up to it by hanging on to a drainpipe and some rather unsafe ivy.'

'It was the third floor,' Rafe replied with a slight shudder, 'and I have never forgotten the mental image I had of you lying smashed and broken on the gravel below, had you fallen.'

Eden blinked back the tears that were still threatening to embarrass her. He didn't have to sound as if he had cared, dammit, when she had irrefutable proof that he had never had any feelings for her other than desire. 'I can't imagine what you thought of me,' she muttered, shaking her head as memories crowded back. She had fallen in through the window and been helped to her feet by Rafael Santini, Formula 1 World Champion and the man she had been so eager to meet, but one look into his dark, flashing eyes had rendered her speechless and she had stared up at him, unable to disguise her admiration for his stunning good looks.

He had been twenty-eight and at the peak of physical fitness, which had no doubt helped him win the championship for the third successive year. That, and a competitive spirit that bordered on obsessive, his ruthless determination to win awarding him a hero status that others could only aspire to. His life away from the racetrack was as legendary as his driving skill and hardly a week went by without him featuring in a newspaper or glossy magazine, his love life exposed in minute detail. He had been successful, sophisticated and drop-dead gorgeous and she hadn't stood a chance against his sexy Italian charm.

'I thought you were beautiful.' The softness of Rafe's voice brought her head up and she stared at him, her pulse racing so that she felt breathless and annoyingly disconcerted. 'You were different from any other woman I had met,' he continued, ignoring the expression on her face that told him she was aware of just how different she'd been compared to his usual diet of glamour models, who were an intrinsic part of the Formula 1 scene. 'You were very sweet, very shy and yet utterly determined. You risked your life to climb up to my room, only to inform me that you were not a fan and had only wanted to meet me because of your brother.'

Eden hid her embarrassment with a smile that tilted her wide mouth at the corners, and Rafe's eyes narrowed as he remembered the touch of that mouth beneath his, the taste of her. 'Simon was a devoted fan,' she agreed, 'and I'd promised him I would try and get your autograph, even if I couldn't persuade you to come to the open day of the spinal-injury unit.' Even then, security surrounding the heir to the Santini millions had been tight and the receptionist at the front desk had coldly informed Eden that Signor Santini would see no one, certainly not a junior reporter from the local paper. But the receptionist had been unaware that beneath Eden's meek exterior lurked a will of iron.

'But you did persuade me,' Rafe pointed out and she nodded, recalling her stunned surprise and Simon's excitement when the world's most revered sporting hero had turned up at the open day. It hadn't been a fleeting visit either, Eden remembered. Rafe had stayed all afternoon and spent hours chatting to the children and teenagers who shared a common bond of being confined to a wheelchair. Simon had spoken about Rafe's visit for weeks after and lined his bedroom walls with yet more posters of his hero, pictures that Eden had found herself staring at whenever she had the opportunity.

At sixteen Simon had spent half his life as a paraplegic after he had fallen out of a tree and broken his spine. He might not have been able to walk but he had made up for that by talking, laughing and bringing such joy to everyone he met that Eden's eyes burned at the memory.

'Does Simon still attend the centre?' Rafe asked. 'I gave a donation but I didn't see him at Greenacres.'

'No.' Eden swallowed hard. 'Simon died of heart failure a few months after we…after I…'

'After you cheated on me with my own brother,' Rafe finished bluntly, and the bitterness in his voice shook her. 'It must have been devastating for all of you, particularly your mother; I remember how devoted she was to him.'

Eden nodded. 'Losing Simon was one of the reasons Dad took up the post of pastor at the missionary church in Africa. He thought that going somewhere where he and my mother were so needed would help her come to terms with Simon's death.' She stared at her lap, fighting the rush of tears, and when she looked up she discovered that Rafe was watching her, a curious expression on his face.

'I know how hard it is,' he offered quietly. 'I too have lost a brother.'

Remorse instantly flooded through her at her insensitivity. 'I was so sorry to hear about Gianni. The accident…it was terrible; I felt so bad for both of you.'

'So bad that you didn't even bother to call,' Rafe taunted, and this time there was no mistaking the anger that darkened his eyes to the colour of jet. '*Madre de Dio*, Eden! You had been close to him, yet you couldn't even be bothered to send a card.'

'That's not fair,' Eden whispered. 'I came to the hospital. I flew to Italy as soon as I heard the news about Gianni's crash.'

The hard stare Rafe gave her spoke plainly of his disbelief. 'You're lying. It was in all the papers that Gianni's injuries were so severe that he would never walk again. You of all people must have realised the hell he was in, especially after you'd lived through it with your own brother. You just didn't want to get involved once you'd heard that Gianni had been left paralysed.' The contempt was back, his black eyes cold and hard as he stared at her, and Eden felt sick at the injustice of his accusation.

'I came to the hospital,' she insisted forcibly, leaning forwards in her desperation to have him believe her. 'I met your father and he said…' She broke off, recalling the unpleasant meeting with Fabrizzio Santini, in which he had made his opinion of her as clear as the fact that she was an unwelcome visitor. 'It doesn't matter what he said,' she muttered, 'it's enough to say he persuaded me that my presence at the hospital wouldn't be welcomed by Gianni and especially not by you.'

'My father made no mention of a visit,' Rafe snapped furiously, his tone so disbelieving that she gave up.

'I don't know why Fabrizzio didn't mention my visit, although I imagine he had his own reasons for not doing so.'

'Meaning what?' Rafe growled.

'Meaning that I'm not a liar! I did go to the hospital. I hoped to see you as well as Gianni. I thought you might need someone to talk to,' she added thickly, remembering the fevered media accusations that Rafe had caused the accident that had left his brother paralysed.

'Did you really think I would talk to you after everything that had happened?' Rafe bit out, his face a taut mask, his olive skin stretched over prominent cheekbones. '*Dio!* Apart from anything else, you're a journalist!' From his tone of voice she might as well have been a mass murderer, but the media had snatched on the rumour that he had caused his brother's accident and had written such scurrilous lies about him that she supposed he had good reason to loathe all members of the Press.

'I went to Italy as a friend, not in my professional capacity,' Eden replied steadily, ignoring the pain around her heart. 'But obviously I was mistaken and you didn't need me at all.'

Silence fell, a silence that thrummed with tension, and Eden set down her glass. It was time to leave. She stood and picked up her handbag, her body stiffening as a door at the far end of the room opened and a woman strolled into the lounge.

'Rafe, darling, I thought I heard you. Are you going to be much longer? I've been waiting for you all morning.'

The pout was pure drama, but the woman was stunning,

Eden acknowledged bleakly, and then derided herself for caring. Rafe had always had his pick of the world's most beautiful girls and he picked with a regularity that reinforced his reputation as a stud. Through the doorway she could see an enormous unmade bed, the tangled sheets and the opened champagne bottle standing in the ice bucket indubitable proof that Rafe still didn't need much sleep.

Memories she believed she had ruthlessly erased forced their way into her mind, memories of another time, of endless hotels where she would spend the days sitting around the pool vainly trying to evoke interest in yet another paperback while she waited for Rafe. The nights had been a different matter, Rafe was a skilled and energetic lover and when she had been in his arms, lost in the exquisite pleasure he wrung from her body, she had almost convinced herself that the lonely days and her loss of self-respect were worthwhile.

'Rafe!' The woman's voice had an edge of petulance, her accent unmistakably Scandinavian, and Rafe threw her an impatient glare.

'I'm busy, Misa; leave us, please.'

With a toss of ash-blonde hair, the woman flounced into the bedroom, slamming the door behind her to emphasise her displeasure.

'Don't ask her to go on my account,' Eden murmured coolly. 'I have another appointment. I take it she's your latest Press officer,' she couldn't resist adding, recalling the job description Rafe had once used as a lure for her to join the Santini team. The glorified title had been nothing more than a smokescreen for her real position as his mistress, and evidently nothing had changed.

Briskly, she walked towards the door but as she reached for the handle she found that Rafe had beaten her to it and the brief contact with his hand sent a jolt of electricity through her so that she instantly dropped her arm.

'Have lunch with me?' The invitation seemed to have been dragged from his soul, his expression thunderous, and she wondered why he had asked when they patently had nothing to say to one another. This close, she was aware of the subtle musk of his aftershave. Heat emanated from his body and curled around her, stirring her senses, and her heart thudded painfully in her chest, so loud she was sure he could hear it. His gaze was focused on her mouth, his eyes hooded so that she couldn't read his expression, but she knew with sudden, blinding realisation that he wanted to kiss her.

Her tongue darted out to moisten her suddenly dry lips, and the unconscious gesture caused him to tense, the silence between them thrumming with electricity. For one dizzy, terrifying moment she imagined the feel of his mouth on hers, the shattering force of his kiss, but for the sake of her own self-respect she couldn't go there again and she tore her eyes from his face.

'No, thanks; I told you I have another appointment.'

'Cancel it.' His arrogant assumption that she would do so made her hackles rise and she gave him a scathing look.

'I don't do threesomes,' she snapped, with a pointed glance at the bedroom door. 'Anyways, it's not an appointment exactly—I'm meeting a friend for lunch.'

Rafe's eyebrows rose quizzically. 'Who is he?' he demanded arrogantly, and Eden glared at him.

'I don't know why you assume it has to be a man, but his

name's Neville Monkton, he owns an estate-agency business in Wellworth.'

'Not to mention an enormous pile called Monkton Hall,' Rafe drawled.

'How on earth do you know that?'

'I know a lot of things,' he told her coolly. 'Is that the reason for your interest, Eden—you fancy becoming lady of the manor?' He paused for a heartbeat before murmuring, 'Does he have a brother?'

'I don't know,' she blinked at him dazedly. 'Why?'

His smile chilled her soul and she shivered at the savage bitterness in his eyes. 'I think I should warn him that you like to keep things in the family,' he murmured silkily, and her fury exploded, her hand lifting, but he caught it before it made contact with his cheek. 'You seem to have developed a temper, *cara*, but then you were never the sweet-natured innocent you had me believe, were you?'

'I was a gullible fool, especially where you were concerned, Rafe. I trusted you but you had your own agenda, didn't you? It was in your interests to believe I was involved with Gianni—that's why you refused to listen to me.' She took a shaky breath and opened the door. 'I was young and painfully naive and you walked all over me, but you won't do so again. I've grown up, Rafe, I've seen you for what you really are, and quite frankly, I'm not impressed!'

CHAPTER TWO

RAFE scoured the ballroom, his smile towards the numerous people who sought to catch his attention barely concealing his impatience. Eden hadn't arrived. Maybe she wasn't coming to the after-race party, although his personal assistant had issued an open invitation to everyone at the local Press office. Maybe she deemed an event to celebrate his win at the British Grand Prix beneath her, he thought darkly as he remembered the cool indifference in her voice when she informed him that she found him to be frankly unimpressive!

Never in his life had he felt so insulted. He was no angel—*Dio,* he was the first to admit that—but he was five times Formula 1 World Champion, he spent his life thrilling packed crowds as he hurtled around a circuit. Yet Eden Lawrence was not impressed. She hadn't been referring to his driving skill. In his heart he knew that, but the fact that she was unimpressed by the man, the real Rafael Santini, sat uncomfortably on his shoulders because she knew him better than most.

He didn't know what he had expected her reaction at seeing him again to be, but a healthy dose of gratitude that he was prepared to overlook the past and speak to her wouldn't have come amiss. The trouble was, he hadn't been able to dismiss the past as easily as he'd thought. Her appearance at the Press conference had startled him. Even though he knew she was back in Wellworth working as a journalist on the local paper he hadn't really expected to see her at the hotel and he'd been unprepared, thrown off balance at the sight of her after all this time. He'd forgotten just how beautiful she was, or maybe not forgotten, just tried to bury the memory of her creamy, satin skin, eyes the colour of the sky on a summer's day and that wide, full mouth. Even now he could feel the softness of her lips beneath his, he could taste her, but every time he closed his eyes he could see her kissing Gianni.

'Rafe, do we have to stand here all night?' Misa pouted prettily and glanced at him appealingly from beneath her lashes in a coquettish gesture that left him cold. After three months their relationship had run its course; all that loomed ahead were the tears and tantrums when he ended it, with the gift of a suitable trinket as recompense, he concluded cynically.

'I'm quite happy standing here,' he replied coolly, his gaze skirting to the ballroom entrance once more, 'but obviously you're free to go where you please.'

'I don't know why you decided to hold the party in this dump anyways,' Misa muttered sulkily. 'Where is Wellworth anyways? It doesn't even have any decent shops.'

Aware that she did not have Rafe's attention, she clung to him and threw back her hair so that her breasts almost escaped the tiny scrap of material that masqueraded as a dress, but to no avail. Rafe's gaze was focused on the woman who had just entered the ballroom.

In contrast to Misa's over-exposed charms, Eden looked as chaste as a nun in a simple navy-blue sheath that skimmed her breasts and hips. The long skirt had a discreet split that revealed one slender leg and when she turned Rafe saw that, although the bodice was high-necked at the front, the back was cut away, leaving an expanse of tantalising, silky skin.

Elegant, sophisticated—Eden had grown up, he conceded, and felt a tug of primitive longing in his gut, so intense it was a physical ache. The most responsive, *generous* lover he had ever known, she wore her sensuality like a cloak, and his feet moved of their own accord towards her, pausing when he noticed that idiot estate agent, Neville Monkton, had beaten him to it. Abruptly he swung away and headèd for the group of promotional models who worked for the various sponsors. They at least found him impressive and no way did he want Eden to think he had been waiting for her. If and when he decided to resume their relationship, it would be on his terms, he would be in control, and it was time his rampaging hormones understood that fact.

'Eden, great to see you; you look stunning.'

'Thank you.' Eden smiled as Neville Monkton strolled across the ballroom to greet her. The obvious admiration in his eyes boosted her confidence, which was decidedly shaky. She hadn't wanted to come to the after-race party. She remembered them too well from the year she'd spent with Rafe—but Cliff had pleaded and she hadn't had the heart to refuse him.

'I can't go, not with Jenny about to go into labour any minute,' he'd said. 'A few details about the aftermath of the Grand Prix will round off your article nicely, especially if you can grab an interview with Santini.'

'I can't promise anything,' Eden had muttered, recalling the interview she had already had with Rafael Santini, which was definitely not for public consumption.

The party was exactly as she had expected, the ballroom packed with nubile blondes who made her feel distinctly overdressed. She couldn't see Rafe and had no intention of looking for him; she was through with acting like a lovesick puppy and she smiled warmly at Nev.

'If I'd known you were coming, I'd have offered you a lift,' he said as he led her over to the bar.

'It was a last-minute decision. Jenny was having twinges and Cliff didn't want to leave her. But I didn't drive, I came by taxi.'

'Sensible if you want to have a drink,' Nev agreed, 'but I did bring the car tonight, so I'll give you a lift home.'

Nev was nice, Eden decided as she took a sip of deliciously cold Chardonnay. He was affable and uncomplicated, two of the characteristics she would look for in a man if she ever considered a serious relationship again. She was done with volatile, passionate, sexy Italians. She didn't want a man who would take her to the edge of ecstasy—the inevitable fall was too painful and it had taken her four years to recover.

'It's quite a do,' Nev commented as he eyed the magnificent buffet set out at the far end of the room, 'but I guess Santini can afford it; he must be loaded. Didn't you know him at one time?' he asked curiously and Eden shrugged noncommittally.

'Briefly, a few years ago.'

'What about the brother, Gianni? The news of his death was pretty tragic. They said he couldn't come to terms with being left unable to walk after his accident, and took his own life. Rafe must be gutted, especially as it was rumoured that he caused the accident.'

The fine hairs on the back of her neck prickled and Eden knew with absolute certainty that Rafe was close—she could feel him with every fibre of her body—and for a second she closed her eyes in despair. She didn't want to feel like this, it had taken her a long time to get over him and she wouldn't let one meeting ruin all that hard work.

'I wouldn't believe everything you read in the gutter Press,' she told Nev coolly. 'Rafe wasn't responsible for Gianni's crash; that fact was proved irrefutably.'

'There was an intense rivalry between them though, wasn't there?' Nev pressed. 'I understood they weren't on speaking terms at the time of the accident.'

'They were friends as well as brothers,' Eden said shortly. 'That's all I know.' It was not for her to reveal that alongside the competitive rivalry between the Santini brothers had existed a deep, enduring love that had seen Rafe believe Gianni over her. It was in the past, she reminded herself, fighting the memory of Rafe's furious face and his scathing denouncement of her as a cheap whore who had played him and his brother for fools. She had barely tried to defend herself, too shocked by Gianni's lies to even think straight, and afterwards, on the flight back from Italy, she'd concluded that Rafe had his own reasons for wanting to believe the worst of her. He'd been looking for an excuse to get rid of her.

'Do you fancy something to eat?' Nev asked as he steered her towards the buffet, but one glance at the mountain of food made Eden's stomach churn.

'You go ahead,' she murmured, 'it's too hot in here for me, I'm going out on the terrace for a while.' She swung round and her heart missed a beat as her eyes were drawn to the group standing a little ways off, with Rafe at its epicentre. He was taller than any man in the room but it wasn't just his height and the breadth of his shoulders that drew attention, it was his air of authority, his power and magnificent arrogance. He was the world's number one and it wasn't just his skill on the racetrack that elevated him to hero status. He possessed a charisma that drew people to him, men and women alike, although inevitably it was women who surrounded him now, the usual array of groupies who were fawning over him while he took their attention as his God-given right. He glanced over at that moment, and she flushed at the sardonic amusement in his eyes that told her he was aware of her scrutiny. She swallowed and hastily dropped her gaze as he dipped his head in a silent, mocking greeting, and, dragging her eyes from him, she headed for the door to the terrace.

The night air was cool on Eden's skin, the mingled scent of honeysuckle and roses soothing her until a familiar voice shattered her peace.

'All alone, Eden? Where's your faithful lapdog?'

No man had the right to look so decadently sexy, she thought bleakly as she sought to control her racing pulse. His black silk shirt emphasised the width of his shoulders, the top couple of buttons left unfastened to reveal the gold chain around his neck. He looked every inch the stud he was reputed to be, she decided with a grimace that she convinced herself was of distaste, not jealousy of all the women who had shared his bed. Wealth and magnetic sex appeal combined with stunning looks; Rafe had it all and she very much doubted that he had spent the last four years celibate. He'd been her first and only lover, but to him she had been just another notch on the bedpost. Why, then, did her subconscious cling to the belief that she was his woman, and why did her body instantly react to his presence as if she had been waiting and longing for him all this time?

'If you're referring to Nev, he's inside and he's hardly my lapdog. I don't even know him that well. He's a friend, that's all.'

'Not to mention the owner of Monkton Hall,' Rafe murmured silkily. 'Are you sure you're not aiming to become the lady of the manor, Eden?'

'You've already made that insulting suggestion, but to be honest I really don't see that it has anything to do with you,' Eden snapped, taking a step backwards when she realised how close Rafe was standing. For such a big man he moved with the stealth of a big cat, silent, menacing, waiting to pounce. Looking at him was a mistake, she realised as her breath snagged in her throat. If anything it was even worse than this morning, this awareness of him, this recognition of her soul mate. He was not her soul mate, her mind screamed. One-time bed mate, that was all he had ever been, but out here on the shadowed terrace the moonlight seemed to be mirrored in his eyes, calling her, drawing her back to him.

'So tell me, *cara*,' Rafe murmured, his deliciously husky accent shivering across her skin, 'if you're not back in Wellworth to snag a rich husband, what are you doing? You gained a reputation as a respected journalist with your work in Africa; why settle for a job with the local rag?'

'I need a break,' Eden admitted quietly, her eyes shadowed. 'The last three years have been…hard.' Culminating in the land-mine explosion that had nearly blown away her left leg, although she refused to reveal that snippet of information to Rafe. After he had ended their relationship so savagely she had returned to England, determined to bury herself in her career, and had been lucky enough to find a job as a reporter with a national paper. She'd been young, free and single and life in London should have been fun, but she had missed Rafe with a clawing desperation that seemed to get worse with every passing day, and the regular features about his love life in the tabloids hadn't helped. The trip to Africa to visit her parents had seemed a good way of exorcising him from her mind; she hadn't known that it would change her life.

The poverty she had witnessed had been appalling, even before the military coup that had plunged the area into a violent battleground, and there certainly hadn't been time to think of anything other than basic survival. Afterwards, when some semblance of peace returned, she had stayed on, so moved by the plight of the gentle people she had met that she had been desperate to help them rebuild their shattered lives. Even now, thinking about them hurt, and the realisation that Rafe believed her to be some sort of gold-digger hurt more.

She took a step back, distancing herself from him mentally as well as physically, and Rafe cursed silently, frantically trying to control the violent emotions that surged through him. 'I read your newspaper reports and saw the documentary you made,' he said huskily as he recalled his feeling of helplessness and his fear for her safety. 'How could you have put yourself in such danger that your life was at risk on a daily basis?' His voice was harsh, rasping over her skin, and she could feel the tension in him, could see it in his eyes, which had darkened with an anger that seemed to be directed at himself. 'If you had been with me I would not have allowed you to go.'

Eden gave a brittle laugh. 'You were the one to end our relationship, Rafe.'

'With good reason, namely that you were screwing my brother!' His temper was at simmering point again; she could see it in the rigid line of his jaw, his eyes burning like hot coals in his hard-boned face. 'I couldn't believe it when a year later I saw the news reports you managed to smuggle out of West Africa. What were you trying to do, atone for your sins? A two-timing harlot transformed into Mother Teresa!'

'You bastard.' Eden swung away from him, blinded by sudden tears that she was determined would not fall. She'd cried a river over Rafe Santini but she was over him; he couldn't hurt her again.

Rafe forced himself to uncurl his clenched fists and laid his hands flat on the low wall that ran the length of the terrace, resisting the urge to shake her. Like thousands of others, he had read the reports that had filtered out of the African state, detailing the violent clashes between opposing groups. He had been horrified by the stories of barbarism inflicted on the local tribespeople caught in the midst of the conflict, but more shocking to him had been the realisation that it was Eden who had been trapped in the area, who had actually been taken hostage at one point and who'd risked her life to smuggle out her reports that alerted the outside world to the crisis. His first instinct had been to save her but he didn't have

the right to interfere in her life. He'd ended all involvement
with her when he'd bundled her on the first flight back to
England after finding her in Gianni's arms, and he'd cursed
himself for his weakness as he scanned the television
channels in the hope of seeing her face.

Eden spun round to face him and his heart clenched at the
over-brightness of her eyes. Beneath that air of sophistication
lurked the vulnerability he remembered so well and he fought
the urge to pull her into his arms and hold her close.

'I don't have to stay here and listen to your insults. You
never would listen, would you, Rafe? You were always so
damn sure you were right. But I no longer care what you
think; I've nothing to be ashamed of. I know the truth and so
did Gianni.' She waited for his anger to break over her, for
the caustic words that in the past had tripped so easily from
his tongue. His silence shocked her and the shadows in his
eyes caused a tug of compassion in her chest. Rafe was
hurting. He had loved his brother, and the tragic circumstances of his death must still be an agonising memory.

'What if I was to listen now?' he asked huskily, and for a
second her heart stopped beating. 'It's too late to talk to
Gianni, but you...'

'You're too late for me, too,' Eden replied, hardening her
heart against him although she was breaking up inside. 'Four
years too late. So if you've been attacked by a belated sense
of guilt you'll just have to suffer, and I hope you do.' As she
had, but no more—if Rafe had expected to find the pathetic
pushover she had once been, he was in for a shock. It had
taken a long time to win back her self-respect and she wasn't
about to lose it, however much her heart ached for him.

He tensed, his body so still that he looked as if he had been carved from stone, his eyes hooded and unfathomable, but then suddenly he relaxed and shrugged as if he couldn't give a damn, which most probably he didn't, she conceded bleakly.

'The little kitten has developed into a she-cat—with claws,' he murmured, and she caught the note of amusement in his voice. 'I don't remember you being so argumentative, *cara.*'

'And didn't you take advantage of my insecurity?' she flung at him bitterly. 'You knew I was in awe of you. I couldn't believe that the great Rafael Santini wanted to be with *me*, a dull little innocent from a sleepy English village. You must have loved the fact that I was desperate to keep you happy.'

'I loved the fact that you were desperate for me,' he mocked, and she flinched as he trailed a finger lightly over her cheekbone, down her neck to rest against the pulse that jerked frenetically at the base of her throat. He was so beautiful. She had forgotten the sheer impact of his height and the width of his shoulders, but time had done nothing to erase the memory of that sensual mouth on hers and she shivered, her senses on fire as she caught the exotic scent of his cologne. Frantically, she pulled herself free of his hold.

'So the sex was good. You certainly deserved your reputation as a stud, Rafe, but our relationship was based on nothing more than that.'

His eyes narrowed, glinting dangerously as he drawled, 'Don't knock it, *cara*. Maybe we should give it another go?'

He couldn't be serious, *could he*? The worst of it was she

was tempted; even after all he'd put her through. She must need her head tested, she acknowledged as she sought to put some space between them before she did something utterly stupid like throw herself into his arms. 'Never in this lifetime,' she snapped, and he gave a lazy smile.

It would be satisfying to make her eat her words, to close the gap between them, tilt her chin and plunder the tremulous softness of her mouth. Her resistance would be minimal, he knew it as well as she, but it was the faint edge of desperation in her eyes that had him fight the urge to show her that in some things at least, nothing had changed. The sexual chemistry that existed between them was as fierce as ever.

He missed her, he acknowledged grimly. Despite coming close to hating her, to telling himself that she was a lying, cheating bitch, he still woke every morning in the hour before dawn and reached for her, and the realisation that she was no longer there never failed to hurt.

'Out of interest,' she queried as she paused in the doorway leading to the ballroom, 'what are you doing in Wellworth? The Bembridge is an excellent hotel but there are others as good and a lot closer to Silverstone.'

'You don't think it possible that I came to find you?' he murmured lightly and she gave a harsh laugh.

'Unlikely; according to the last time we met, I'm a two-timing whore. Why on earth would you come looking for me?'

'Maybe I missed you, *cara mia*,' he suggested softly and she steeled herself against the insidious warmth his words evoked.

'It's more likely that you've run out of women to sleep

with, but whatever your reasons, Rafe, I'm not interested. No doubt you'll be leaving Wellworth tomorrow and for all I care you can go to hell. It's where I've been for the last four years.'

Neville Monkton glanced up as she rejoined him in the ballroom, frowning as he noted her white face.

'Are you OK, Eden? I was just about to send out a search party.'

'Sorry…I've got a thumping headache; I think I'll call a cab.'

'Don't be silly; I'll run you home. I'm ready to leave anyways.'

'It's been a good day,' he told her cheerfully as he steered down the narrow lane to her parents' cottage. 'You know the Dower House, at the far end of the village? A couple of property developers bought it a year ago and have completely renovated it. It's been on my letting books for the last two months and I heard today that I've found a tenant.'

Eden smiled faintly and tried to sound interested although her headache was now a throbbing reality. 'Who's renting it—a family? It's certainly big enough.'

Nev shook his head. 'A business consortium have taken it; they'll probably use it as a base for visiting executives, but, to be honest, for the rent they've agreed to, I don't care if they move a circus in. How did the interview with Rafe Santini go?' he asked as he pulled up in front of the cottage. 'You were outside on the terrace with him for a long time; did you get what you wanted?

'I didn't learn anything new,' Eden replied quietly as she climbed out of the car. She wasn't going to reveal to Nev the one vital fact she'd learned tonight. She was still reeling from the shock of discovering that her much-vaulted belief that she was over Rafe was not as assured as she'd hoped. Seeing him again had been devastating; he'd trampled down her carefully erected barricades with frustrating ease and she was going to have her work cut out reassembling them.

CHAPTER THREE

EDEN watched the removal van disappear from sight before she wandered back into the empty cottage. The past couple of days had been spent in a haze of frantic activity as she organised the packing of her parents' furniture and belongings, but now everything was stowed safely on the lorry that was heading for Scotland.

All that remained was for her to pack her own few possessions before she moved into the flat Nev had found for her to rent. While her parents had been house-hunting in Edinburgh, having decided to move nearer to her elderly grandmother, Eden had overseen the sale of their cottage. The new owner's request to take possession at the beginning of July had been a shock, and meant she only had a few days to organise her own move.

The flat was on a new housing estate on the outskirts of the village. It wasn't her first choice, but property in the pretty Oxfordshire village was expensive to rent and taking on a mortgage on her current salary was out of the question. Her only other choice was to relocate to London and look for a better-paid job with one of the national papers. Her reputation as a dedicated and fearless journalist would stand her in good stead, but the three years she'd spent in Africa had left her emotionally and physically drained.

She loved Wellworth. It had been her home for most of her life and she had happy memories of growing up in the vicarage, an idyllic, if rather sheltered childhood that had left her ill-prepared for the world outside—unprepared for Rafe Santini, that was for sure, she brooded as she made a cup of tea. He'd swept into her life like a whirlwind and she had been utterly overwhelmed by his charm. He was different from any other man she had met, although admittedly there hadn't been many, just a couple of fledgling romances while she was at university.

Rafe had surprised and delighted her when he had arrived at the open day of the spinal-injury unit her brother, Simon, attended, and she'd suffered a serious dose of hero worship, but never in her wildest dreams had she expected him to turn up at the vicarage to ask her out to dinner.

Angrily, she searched through the packing boxes for the teapot as memories plagued her. Perhaps it would be a good idea to move away from Wellworth. A fresh start in London, where there were no reminders of Rafe, might be just what she needed. What she didn't need was the vivid mental image of the first time he had made love to her, his gentle sensitivity when he had discovered she was a virgin and his rather endearing smug satisfaction when he told her she was his woman and his alone.

God damn it! Why couldn't he stay in the past instead of haunting her every waking thought and dominating her dreams? She snatched up her mug of tea and stormed out of the kitchen, only to cannon into something hard and solid and intoxicatingly warm.

'Rafe! What on earth are you doing here? How did you get in?' Acute shock added fuel to her temper and she glared at him furiously. It was bad enough that he was inside her head without finding him a few centimetres in front of her.

'The front door was open. You should be more careful, *cara*; anyone could walk in.'

'Anyone just did, although, to be honest, Jack the Ripper would be preferable. Why are you here, Rafe? I assumed you would be on the other side of the world by now.'

The coldness of her voice warned him that, as far as she was concerned, another planet would be too close, and his lips twitched. There was a new feistiness about her that hadn't been there five years ago. She'd been younger then, he reminded himself, sweet-natured and desperately shy. It had taken every ounce of his patience to persuade her into his bed, but she'd been worth the wait. For a brief moment he closed his eyes and pictured the whiteness of her skin, her firm, full breasts with their pink, acutely sensitive peaks that he loved to suckle. His arousal was instant and embarrassingly hard and he crossed his arms over his chest in the hope of drawing her attention away from his jeans, which were suddenly uncomfortably tight.

'The Canadian Grand Prix isn't for another two weeks,' he informed her. 'I thought I might spend some time in Wellworth.'

'I can't think why—it's hardly Monte Carlo. There's nothing for you to get excited about here.'

'You underestimate yourself, *cara*. I find certain elements in Wellworth highly exciting.'

'Oh, for heaven's sake!' Verbal seduction she could do

without. She couldn't imagine why Rafe was here or what he was up to other than playing a game of cat and mouse, but she refused to award him the satisfaction of knowing that he was getting to her, or that her heart was racing like a steam train. She stomped into the living room, uncaring if he followed or not, and settled on the wide windowsill, which had to suffice as a chair now that all the furniture had gone.

'*Dio!* Have you been burgled?' Rafe's face was a picture as his gaze trawled the empty room and hovered on the torn wallpaper that had been behind the sofa. 'No wonder you're interested in the wealthy squire if you have to live like this.'

'My parents have just sold the cottage and I'm about to move into a flat,' Eden snapped, her patience paper-thin. 'I'm not interested in Nev or anyone else. Have you ever heard the expression "once bitten, twice shy"? Believe me, Rafe, you've put me off relationships for life. I'll never trust another man again.' Or hand over her heart with a naive trust that made her weep just thinking about how gullible she had been.

'Trust!' Rafe threw the word at her, a nerve jumping in his cheek as he sought to control the wave of fury that swept through him. 'You dare speak to me of trust when you shattered mine,' he demanded, his accent suddenly very pronounced. 'You ripped my heart out! I gave you everything including my *trust* and you flung it back in my face.'

Gone was the urbane, charming Rafael Santini he portrayed to the world, in his place a fiery, hot-tempered Italian. He was unlike anyone she had ever met and his volatile outbursts had secretly fascinated her, especially when his anger had so often evaporated as quickly as it came, to be replaced with a passion that shook her with its intensity.

'Tell me, Eden, what would you have thought if you had caught me by the poolside, half naked and in the arms of another woman? Add to that the fact that you were kissing my own brother, a man I trusted beyond any other, and what would your reaction have been in similar circumstances?'

'I would have at least listened,' Eden muttered numbly. She'd never looked at it from his point of view and, if she was honest, the sight of him with another woman would have sent her running, desperately seeking sanctuary to lick her wounded pride. But she had always expected the worst, always assumed that he would one day tire of her ordinariness and replace her. She'd never given him cause to doubt her, with Gianni or anyone else. She'd been too hooked on Rafe, and her wide-eyed adoration was a humiliating memory she preferred to forget.

'I did listen,' Rafe stated forcefully, needing to assure himself of that fact as well as her. In all honesty the sight of her slender bikini-clad body in his brother's arms had made him feel so sick he'd barely heard anything other than the splintering of his heart. 'I listened to your silence while Gianni explained how you had made all the running, until he'd been unable to resist you.'

'And you believed him,' Eden said quietly.

'He was my brother,' Rafe roared, black eyes flashing fire as he paced the empty room that seemed claustrophobically small with him in it. 'Why would he lie?'

'I don't know.' No one would, now; Gianni was dead and had taken his reasons for wrecking her relationship with Rafe with him. She couldn't even blame Gianni entirely. The relationship had already been doomed and Rafe must have been searching for a reason to end it—either that or he really had intended to keep her as his mistress after his marriage to the daughter of an Italian aristocrat.

'It's all immaterial now,' she muttered, wondering how he dared to sound so *hurt* when she had been the one who had been betrayed, who'd had her heart broken into so many pieces that she was still trying to superglue it back together. 'I don't know what you hoped to achieve by coming here.'

Rafe took a deep breath and raked his hand through his hair, aware that the meeting wasn't going as planned. 'I came to offer you my forgiveness,' he informed her with a haughtiness that hid his growing realisation that he was on shaky ground.

He sounded like a statesman making a royal proclamation and, even taking into account his strong accent, there was no disguising the arrogance of his tone. Eden set down the mug of rapidly cooling tea before she spilt it, or threw it at his head. He was waiting, silently watching her with an air of expectancy that made her wonder what she was supposed to do now. Fall at his feet in abject gratitude most likely, she decided and was filled with a cold fury that was murderous in its intensity.

'That's big of you,' she murmured coolly when she trusted herself to speak, 'but actually, no, thanks.'

'What do you mean, no, thanks?' His look of outraged perplexity would have been funny if she hadn't been so close to tears. 'I've realised that what we had together was worth fighting for. I'm prepared to overlook what happened with Gianni and give our relationship another chance.'

'Well, you've realised four years too late!' Her gentle,

pacifist parents had taught her that anger solved nothing and for years, Eden had stifled her emotions. During the year she'd spent as Rafe's mistress she'd been far too in awe of him to ever argue with him, but she was a different person now. The sights she'd witnessed in Africa, the poverty and inhumanity inflicted on its people, had released a great well of anger as she argued their cause. She was no longer afraid to express her emotions and right now Rafe was in her direct line of fire.

'I don't need your forgiveness; I've done nothing wrong, so if you're waiting for some sort of apology you'll be waiting till kingdom come. The only person who needs to apologise is you,' she continued, her eyes blazing as she jumped up and glared at him. 'The only conniving, two-timing cheat around here is you,' she flung at him as she stabbed her finger into his chest. 'So now I'd like you to leave. Go back to Mitzy or Misty or whatever your latest "Press officer's" name is and leave me in peace!'

For a few seconds Rafe appeared completely poleaxed. He'd never heard her raise her voice before, let alone scream at him like a banshee, Eden acknowledged grimly. But then his frown lifted and he actually had the audacity to smile as he murmured, 'I have already ended my affair with Misa. You have no reason to be jealous, *cara*.'

Eden inhaled deeply, her chest heaving, although her voice dripped ice. 'I'm sure your *wife* will be very relieved but I really couldn't care less and I'm certainly not jealous. I'd rather sell my soul to the devil than take another chance on you.'

She had to get away from him before she burst into tears or, even more humiliatingly, flung herself against his chest and begged for the second chance he said he was offering. He stared down at her like an avenging angel, his superbly chiselled features so rigid with tension that he could have been sculpted from marble, and she remembered with stark clarity the feel of that sensual mouth on hers. How could she turn down the chance to experience the exquisite mastery of his possession? He was the love of her life; the bleak emptiness of the last four years were proof of that. But he didn't love her, never had, and she wouldn't sacrifice her self-respect for sex again, however good. She was worth more than that.

'What do you mean, my wife? *Madre de Dio!* I don't have a wife,' Rafe ground out, gripping her arm as she tried to push past him.

'So what happened to Valentina de Domenici, the woman you were intending to marry? I know about her, Rafe. I know that a marriage between the two of you had been arranged by your father years before, and that you were planning to keep me tucked away as your mistress after you'd made Valentina your wife. It was a disgusting plan then and four years on it doesn't look any more inviting.' In her desperation to get away she struggled to pull free of his bruising hold. 'Let go, Rafe; you're hurting me.'

'You know nothing,' Rafe snarled furiously. 'What is this nonsense, Eden—some pathetic attempt to shift the blame? It won't work, *cara. Dio!* I used to watch you flirt with Gianni but I never suspected you would lead him on to such an extent that he could no longer fight his desire for you.'

'Rafe, my arm…' Eden pleaded and he glanced down to where his fingers were biting into her flesh before releasing her with a savage oath in his native tongue.

'I should have listened to my father,' he muttered darkly. 'He warned me about you.'

'I bet he did…he never liked me. He thought I wasn't good enough for you.'

'That's a ridiculous thing to say.' Rafe's gaze skittered away and Eden sighed. Why was she even bothering to fight a battle she knew she would lose? In the year that she had spent with Rafe, Fabrizzio Santini had barely acknowledged her presence, and, as she only ever met him at the racetrack, where nerves were stretched and the tension thrumming, his rudeness towards her went unnoticed, by everyone but her. Later, when she had rushed to the hospital after Gianni's accident, Fabrizzio had bluntly informed her that she would not be welcomed by any of the Santini family. She had been Rafe's whore, he told her, and she had served her purpose; Rafe had moved on.

Suddenly she felt bone weary. Her relationship with Rafe had happened a long time ago and, as Fabrizzio had pointed out, Rafe had moved on, life had moved on and the fact that her heart was trapped in a time warp was no one's fault but her own. 'There's no point in rehashing the past,' she said quietly. 'Let's just accept that it was good while it lasted.'

'So good that you have never been able to forget it.' He was so close that she had to tip her head to look into his eyes and to her shame, his burning gaze caused an answering heat to flood through her veins.

'Your arrogance never fails to take my breath away,' she snapped, mortified that her voice sounded so husky and unsure when she had been determined to be cool and controlled.

'Not arrogance; it's the truth, for both of us. I have never forgotten you, or what we had together.'

She would not be lured by the sweet seduction of his words, Eden assured herself, fighting the quiver of response that ran the length of her spine. 'We had sex,' she stated bluntly, watching as his mouth curved into a knowing smile. 'And in the years that we've been apart I'm damn sure you've had sex with hundreds of other women. Do you think I didn't notice the groupies that used to hang around the track, waiting for you to beckon?'

'None were as good as you,' he assured her, his black eyes gleaming with amusement, and something else. 'And as for taking your breath away…'

She had been focusing so hard on his words that for a few seconds she didn't realise his intentions, and he made good use of the time to pull her into his arms, his mouth coming down on hers with a force that rendered her helpless. It was no gentle caress, no subtle persuasion in acknowledgement of the years apart, but a brutal assault on her senses, fierce and hot, demanding a response she was unable to deny.

It was like finding heaven after a very long journey, Eden thought numbly, and she wondered how she had survived this long without him. The stroke of his tongue as he probed between her lips splintered the last vestige of her control and as she opened her mouth she heard him groan with a mixture of triumph and growing hunger. His fingers threaded through her hair, holding her fast, while his other hand roamed the length of her body, down her spine, over her hips and finally up again to the curve of her breast. Eden revelled in his touch and her arms crept up around his neck, but when she felt his fingers slide beneath her T-shirt, she stilled. Patience had never been Rafe's strong point and in the heat of passion he had frequently ignored buttons and fastenings and simply ripped her clothes off. Reality intruded and with it the realisation that she was in Rafe's arms, the one place she had vowed she would never be again.

As if sensing her withdrawal, he lifted his head, his eyes hard and cold, and shame engulfed her as he gripped her wrists and removed her arms from around his neck in a gesture of mocking distaste.

'You always were an easy lay,' he murmured lazily and Eden spun away from him, blinded by tears of rage at her own weakness, her hip bone coming into sharp contact with the windowsill.

'Get out,' she ordered, unable to bring herself to look at him as she ran towards the stairs, 'before I call the police and have you charged with harassment. I don't want or need your forgiveness and, despite your arrogant assumption that you're God's gift to women, I don't want you.'

'Do you want the good news or the bad news?' Nev asked when Eden walked into his estate agency the following morning.

Having spent a sleepless night during which murder and Rafe Santini had featured highly in her thoughts, the last thing she needed was more problems, and she frowned. 'Tell me the worst.'

'The flat on the Cob Tree estate is no longer available to rent.'

'But it was practically agreed,' Eden cried, unable to disguise her panic. 'I've got to be out of the cottage by the weekend.'

'I know,' Nev murmured sympathetically. 'The owners phoned this morning to say they'd received an offer from a buyer that they can't refuse.'

'Oh, God.' Eden rubbed her brow wearily. 'What am I going to do? Cliff said I could move in with him and Jenny if necessary but now the baby has arrived and I don't want to add to their problems.'

'There is one possibility that's cropped up,' Nev told her and she stared at him expectantly.

'You mean a property that I can afford has come onto your books? Is it in Wellworth?'

'Very much so—it's the Dower House, undoubtedly the most attractive property in the village.'

'With a rent to match,' Eden said dismally as hope receded. 'Anyways, I thought you'd already found new tenants.'

'I have, and the business group that has signed the year's lease has asked me to find a housekeeper. I spoke to the chief executive, Hank Molloy,' Nev continued. 'The company he works for is a global organisation and they want the house as a British base for their top executives. Mr Molloy says he's hoping to bring his grandchildren over from Texas at the end of the summer and it'll probably be used at Christmas, but for much of the time the house will be empty. He wants to install a resident housekeeper to keep the place ticking over.'

'But I already have a job on the *Gazette*,' Eden said slowly, 'and I'm a hopeless cook.'

'You wouldn't have to do any cooking, just a bit of laundry, overseeing the cleaning contractors, that sort of thing. It could be the answer to your problems, Eden, not to mention mine. Hank Molloy is an extremely brash American who wants everything done yesterday and when I told him I might have someone suitable in mind he faxed over a contract.'

'So would I be employed by Mr Molloy's company?' Eden queried.

'Yes, but the contract seems fine; the only sticking point I can see is that you'd have to agree to give three months' notice should you want to leave.'

'That's hardly a problem; I'm not going anywhere in a hurry,' Eden murmured drily. 'It sounds too good to be true— I can't help thinking there's a catch.'

'Talk to Mr Molloy yourself,' Nev urged as he punched several digits into his phone and handed it to her. 'Let him reassure you that everything's above board.'

Hank Molloy spoke at the pace of a speeding train but after their conversation Eden felt happier about signing the contract. She felt as though a great weight had been lifted from her shoulders and smiled warmly at Nev. 'You're a star; I don't know how to thank you.'

'For a start you can agree to have dinner with your favourite estate agent,' he teased, and she hesitated for a moment. Nev was a great guy but she wasn't interested and it would be unfair to let him believe they could be anything more than friends. On the other hand it was only dinner, she argued with herself. She'd been so tense since Rafe had turned up to disrupt her emotional stability and she needed something, anything to banish him from her mind.

The Dower House was a listed building that dated back to the eighteenth century. A spacious six-bedroom house set in several acres of Oxfordshire countryside, it had been expertly renovated and refurbished and Eden had fallen in love with it the minute she'd walked through the door. The position of housekeeper was the most incredible piece of luck, she mused as she climbed the central staircase to the pretty guest bedroom she had chosen. She still couldn't help thinking there must be a catch and she wondered when Hank Molloy would visit. She hoped Nev was right and she wouldn't be expected to cook because she was hopeless in the kitchen and could very well find herself out of her new home.

The night was sultry. A thunderstorm had been brewing all day and when she threw open her bedroom window the air was hot and ominously still. The last few days had been tiring, what with packing up her parents' furniture and moving her own possessions into the Dower House, yet she dreaded going to bed. Inactivity gave her time to think and her thoughts turned with relentless inevitability to one man, her fractured dreams haunted by memories of the closeness she and Rafe had once shared. It had been an illusion, she angrily reminded herself. The feeling that he was her other half, the keeper of her soul, had been a figment of her imagination, cruelly shattered the night he'd found her and Gianni by the pool.

Forget him, she told herself. He had doubtless already dismissed her from his mind and was probably on the other side of the world with his Swedish blonde—or her replacement. The emotion in her heart twisted. She reached for the packet of painkillers the hospital had prescribed, her leg was aching— not surprising when it was held together with a series of metal pins. Usually she was able to ignore the dull pain, but tonight she wanted the sanctuary of oblivion and a good night's sleep.

A few hours later she opened her eyes as a brilliant flash lit up the room. The thunder was a low, angry growl that wasn't really loud enough to have woken her and she lay in the darkness, wondering why her skin prickled, her ears straining for the other faint sound she had heard.

An intruder or an overactive imagination? she queried silently, when the definitive thud of the front door closing sounded up the stairs. Sleep was impossible until she'd set her mind to rest but the faint glimmer of light visible from beneath the living-room door caused her heart to pound, and her palms were clammy with sweat as she tiptoed down the stairs. Cursing the fact that she'd left her mobile phone in her bedroom, she acknowledged that her only option was to slip out of the front door and run down the lane to the nearest house for help, but she was in her pyjamas and now it was raining. Suddenly the living-room door swung open and she gasped and grabbed the nearest potential weapon.

'It seems an odd time for flower arranging,' came a familiar husky drawl. 'What on earth are you doing, *cara*?'

'What am *I* doing?' For all of thirty seconds, words failed her as she set the heavy-based vase back on the dresser. She felt incredibly stupid but relief quickly gave way to sheer fury and she glared at Rafe. 'You don't know how close you came to having this vase smashed over your head.'

From her tone Rafe surmised that she wished she'd carried out the planned attack. Her cheeks were flushed, her hair a tumble of gold silk on her shoulders and despite her voluminous pyjamas he was swamped with a mixture of desire and tenderness as he studied her furious face.

'You seem to be making a habit of walking into my home

uninvited,' she snapped. 'How did you get in? Don't tell me
the front door was open because I know I locked it.'

In reply, he dangled his door key in front of her and she
stared at it, her puzzlement obvious. 'Actually, it's my home,'
he corrected mildly and she drew a sharp breath.

'Since when was your name Hank Molloy?'

'Hank is the chief executive of a subsidiary company of
the Santini Corporation who arranged the lease of this house.
I understand you're my housekeeper—welcome on board.'

Sneaky didn't cover it; Machiavellian was nearer the mark.
She'd known there had to be a catch and patently he was it.
He was studying her with indolent amusement, all powerful,
dominant male, his black jeans and leather jacket emphasis-
ing his height and raw sexual magnetism, and it took all her
reserves of willpower to resist his pull.

'I assume you have a good reason for what is almost certainly a fraudulent act—tricking me into signing that
contract,' she qualified, and he gave a slow smile.

'Several.'

'Do you care to explain them?'

'A practical demonstration would be more illuminating.'
He closed the space between them in a heartbeat, his hand
cupping her nape to angle her head so that he could plunder
her mouth at will. Resistance was impossible when her senses
were drugged by the seductive musk of his cologne. The heat
from his body enfolded her, his arms drawing her in against
the solid wall of his chest and she could feel his heart
thudding furiously beneath her fingertips. He kissed her until
her lips were swollen, until she was boneless and totally
pliant in his arms, and only then did he ease back a fraction,

brushing his mouth gently over hers while she clung to him, desperate to prolong the moment before she would have to admit that her defences had crumbled at the first attack.

'Why are you hounding me?' she whispered when he released her and she wrapped her arms defensively around her body. 'What do you want from me?'

The answer was simple but she wasn't ready to hear it, he acknowledged grimly, her air of vulnerability and the tremulous quiver of her lips causing him a momentary attack of conscience. Perhaps he should let her go, walk away and forget the closeness they'd once shared, the *joy*, but he'd tried keeping his distance and four years on she still dogged his every waking thought.

'I'm hardly hounding you, *cara mia*; you're in my house, sleeping in my bed—figuratively speaking, that is,' he added when she looked as though she would explode.

'Do you honestly expect me to believe that my position here as housekeeper is sheer coincidence?' she demanded bitingly, and he shrugged.

'Hell, no; it took a lot of planning and I still couldn't be certain that when your eager estate-agent friend was asked to find a suitable housekeeper at short notice he would appoint you. He might just have easily given the position to his elderly receptionist, and I have to admit I wouldn't have greeted her so enthusiastically.'

His eyes glinted with amusement as he studied her flushed face and she was torn between the desire to hit him and to burst into tears. She'd forgotten how he loved to tease her, forgotten his easy sense of humour and the laughter they'd shared, and she didn't want to remember any of it now.

'I'm sure Gloria will be an excellent replacement,' she told him coolly, 'because I have no intention of staying here with you.' Swiftly, she ran from the room, tore up the stairs to her bedroom and pulled her suitcase from under the bed. She was in the process of piling her clothes into it when he appeared in the doorway, but she ignored him, her movements jerky and uncoordinated as she tried to fasten the zip.

'You know it's raining?' he queried mildly.

'I don't care.' The storm had worked itself up to a crescendo, the rain smashing against the window. 'I'd sooner go out in a hurricane than spend one more minute under the same roof as you.' He was blocking the doorway, an immovable force, but she pushed against his chest anyways, needing to get away from him before she did something stupid like beg him to kiss her again. 'What part of "I don't want to give our relationship another chance" do you not understand?' she shouted, but even that didn't provoke the loss of temper she was expecting.

'This part,' he said softly, and this time his lips were gentle, his kiss so full of tender compassion that the tears behind her eyelids escaped and slid down her cheeks. He had cupped her face with both his hands and stilled fractionally when he felt wetness on his fingers, but he didn't lift his head, just deepened the kiss, coaxing a response she was powerless to deny.

When he'd done she stepped back, her eyes dark with a mixture of desire and confusion. How could one kiss evoke such a stark hunger for more and, God damn it, what had happened to her *pride*? 'Let me go,' she pleaded huskily but he merely smiled.

'I'm the one who's going. I fly to Canada tomorrow and after the Grand Prix I'm returning to Italy and then on to Bahrain. You signed a contract that stipulated you would give three months' notice should you want to leave,' he reminded her. 'At the weekend one of my top executives arrives in Oxford to oversee the takeover of the factory the Santini Corporation recently bought out. Bruno and his wife and four children are looking forward to staying in an English country house, especially as they've been assured that a resident housekeeper will be on hand to assist them.'

His tone was amiable but Eden sensed the steel resolve behind his words and her fingers tightened around the handle of her suitcase. 'Nev will find someone else to look after the Dower House,' she argued. 'I refuse to be manipulated by you, Rafe. You might have been able to boss me around before but the spell's broken; I'm not in awe of you any more and I won't jump to your bidding whenever you click your fingers.'

'But you have nowhere else to go,' he pointed out, his jaw rigid, and she could see he was fighting to control his temper.

'I'll find a flat. If the other one hadn't fallen through at the last minute I wouldn't be here now.' She paused as an incredible thought struck her. 'The flat on the Cob Tree estate—you couldn't have… Tell me you didn't…?' A couple of hundred thousand pounds was loose change to him but surely he hadn't bought the flat to prevent her from renting it?

'It's a nice little investment,' he admitted idly, 'although the location isn't great.'

'You bastard, Rafe, I won't let you do this to me. I don't even know why you're bothering. Is it some misplaced desire to get your own back, to punish me for a sin I didn't commit?'

He towered over her, the hard planes of his face and the rigid stance of his body faintly menacing. He was used to having his own way and hated to be thwarted. 'I believe that what we had, what we could have again, is worth fighting for,' he told her fiercely, 'and I don't care if I have to play dirty to get what I want.'

'Which is what, precisely?'

'You, back in my bed, where you belong.'

For one crazy moment she hovered on a pinnacle of indecision as capitulation beckoned, and then the mist cleared and she shook her head.

'I don't belong to you, Rafe. You set me free a long time ago and I have no intention of coming back.'

CHAPTER FOUR

THE aroma of freshly ground coffee drifting from the kitchen warned Eden that her unwelcome visitor was still in residence. Having vowed that she wouldn't sleep a wink while under the same roof as Rafe, she'd been horrified to find her room bathed in sunshine when she woke up, a disbelieving glance at her watch revealing that it was almost ten o'clock.

'*Buon giorno, cara,*' he greeted idly, lowering his newspaper fractionally to survey her, and Eden closed her eyes as a wave of memories rolled over her. She'd loved the intimacy of sharing breakfast with him in the big, cool kitchen of his villa that nestled on the edge of Lake Como. Despite his fabulous wealth he was a man of simple tastes, simple pleasures. He employed few staff at the villa and more than anything she'd loved the fact that they were able to spend time alone, away from the circus of the Formula 1 scene. Energetic nights followed by lazy days had been a way of life for a few precious weeks and she had treasured the closeness they shared.

How had it fallen apart so spectacularly? she wondered despairingly. How could he have been so taken in by Gianni's lies? The painful answer was that he hadn't trusted her. To him she had been just another in a long line of women who briefly shared his life and bed, and when it came to crunch time, family loyalty, the blood ties that bound him so closely to the Santinis, had won over a relationship that meant little to him.

'I thought you were leaving,' she snapped, desperate to disguise the way her heart flipped at the sight of him sitting at the table, and his brows rose quizzically.

'You were never this grouchy when you used to spend the night in my bed, but sexual frustration is a well-known cause of depression. Want me to cheer you up?' he added unforgivably and she glared at him.

'The only thing that'll cheer me up is the sight of you walking out of the door, with the assurance that you won't be coming back.' She boiled the kettle and reached into a cupboard for the garish green teapot that was shaped like a frog.

'I see you still have a fascination for slimy creatures,' he observed and she stared at him pointedly.

'I wouldn't bank on it, I stopped being fascinated by you a long time ago.'

His low chuckle did strange things to her equilibrium, as did the slow smile that curved his mouth.

'I assure you I'm not slimy, *cara mia*. Touch me and see.' He moved before she had time to react and she gave an indignant yelp as he jerked her onto his lap, her frantic wriggling to escape only ceasing when she discovered the effect it was having on a certain area of his anatomy.

'You're disgusting,' she hissed, temper her only weapon

against the warmth that flooded through her, as she was held captive against his thighs. 'Let me up, Rafe, you've proved your point—you're not in the least bit slimy and neither, actually, are frogs,' she added, desperate to take her mind off the throbbing hardness of his arousal she could feel beneath her bottom. 'They're cute and definitely my favourite animal.'

'Which presumably is why, when everyone else presented me with expensive gifts after winning the world championship for the fourth time, you gave me a green plastic frog that squeaked.'

Rafe watched the soft colour stain her cheeks with an element of satisfaction. When he had first seen her at the Press conference he'd been struck by her new air of sophistication, but this morning, in her faded jeans and cotton T-shirt, her hair a tangle of gold silk around her sleep-flushed face, she looked like the young, innocent Eden who haunted his dreams. She wasn't as sure of herself as she would have him believe, or as immune to the sexual chemistry that fizzed between them.

With a determined effort she slid off his lap, and the fresh, lemony scent of her hair evoked a curious pain in his chest. Indigestion, he told himself derisively as he glanced down at his paper, but the printed page meant nothing and when he looked at her again the pain was still there.

'I guess the plastic frog was a pretty stupid gift,' she muttered, 'but I didn't know what else to buy for a man who had everything.'

He hadn't had the one thing he really wanted, Rafe reflected and he wondered what she would say if he told her he competed in every race with a squeaky amphibian squashed into the pocket of his flame suit.

'When are you going,' she demanded, 'and, more to the point, when is your executive and his family due to arrive? It would be nice to have a bit of notice, something you obviously didn't feel was necessary.'

'I phoned several times yesterday evening to inform you I was on my way to Wellworth,' Rafe told her coolly. 'You must have been busy, or out somewhere.'

His questioning tone irritated her. What right did he have to query her every move? 'I had dinner with Nev,' she informed him sweetly. 'We didn't get back until late.'

'You entertained him here? Not a wise move, *cara*; don't do it again.'

'Excuse me! What right do you have to veto my friends? And I didn't *entertain* Nev in the way you're suggesting, I simply made him a cup of coffee. It seems ridiculous in the light of things now, but I wanted to thank him for giving me the opportunity to live in the Dower House. If I'd known you were involved I wouldn't have bothered.'

'Just make sure you're not tempted to thank him too enthusiastically,' Rafe warned darkly, and her temper caught fire.

'I'll do what I like and you can go to hell,' she bit out, shaking back her hair and glaring at him, her hands on her hips.

'Not in my house, *cara mia*, and not at all if you value your life.'

He was the most arrogant, infuriating man she had ever met and she felt like stamping her foot like a child in the throes of a temper tantrum. 'Fine, I quit. I'll move my stuff out of the house today and you can find another damn housekeeper to run around your executives.'

'You signed a contract.'

'Which wouldn't stand up in court,' she challenged.

He shrugged nonchalantly. 'Possibly not, although I'm prepared to test its legality. More pertinently, word going round that your friend Monkton can't be relied upon to hire suitable staff would be highly damaging to his business. He deals with a lot of exclusive country-house lets, doesn't he?'

'I hate you,' Eden flung at him bitterly when she realised she had run out of retorts. 'You can't stand not having your own way, can you?'

'I pursue what I want with single-minded determination,' he corrected her, 'and I always win. You should know that by now, *cara*.' He folded his newspaper and closed the lid of his briefcase before he spared her a glance, seemingly unmoved by her bristling fury. 'Bruno is due to arrive on Tuesday. He's aware that you work for the newspaper during the day and you're not expected to run around like a skivvy. However, I assume you'll get up earlier in the mornings, and you'll have to tidy yourself up a bit.'

Eden took a deep breath and counted to ten as his gaze roamed her admittedly dishevelled appearance. She'd dressed in a hurry and simply grabbed the first items of clothing on the top of her suitcase. Her jeans were faded and paint-spattered and her T-shirt had shrunk in the wash so that it clung to her body, drawing attention to the fact that she wasn't wearing a bra. The atmosphere in the kitchen was suddenly sizzling with electricity as Rafe focused on her breasts, and to her shame she felt them swell and tighten.

'Are you cold, *cara*?' he queried mockingly and she blushed and folded her arms across her chest in an effort to hide the prominent peaks of her nipples. It didn't help that he was impeccably dressed. His grey suit was superbly tailored, no doubt designer, as were his silk shirt and tie, and today he looked like the powerful head of a global company rather than a racing driver, but of course, now that his father was unwell, he had to fill both roles.

'Let's make a deal. I'll go and change into something more suitable and you'll just…go!'

His laughter followed her up the stairs, and his query, 'When did you develop that sassy tongue?' didn't deserve an answer, although she took a savage satisfaction in slamming her bedroom door.

The house was empty when she went back downstairs and she assured herself she was glad. It was time to look to the future and Rafe didn't feature in hers. She dumped her suitcase in the hall and groaned as she remembered she had left her bedroom window open. Although she had no intention of staying in the Dower House, she didn't want to be held responsible if it were burgled. Besides, she already loved this house and couldn't bear the idea of it being ransacked by intruders.

She'd known that the chance to live here in its gentle splendour was too good to be true, she thought dismally as she took one last look round, but as she was about to lock the French doors that led onto the terrace a movement caught her eye. Rafe was standing by the fish pond, his arms folded across his chest, his stance as arrogant and supremely self-confident as ever until she looked more closely. He was unaware of her presence and she was able to study him, her greedy eyes travelling over him, drinking him in.

He looked older, she realised with a pang. It was four years, after all, and his life on the racing circuit was demanding, both physically and emotionally. She remembered the intense pressure he had been under to win every race. As a young man his father, Fabrizzio, had been a brilliant engineer whose marriage to the daughter of a wealthy car manufacturer had enabled him to develop the exclusive sports cars that had become one of Italy's major exports. Santini had already been a dynamic and successful company, but when Rafe won his first world championship driving the car that had been developed exclusively by his father's company, it rocketed the Santini name to the top of the table alongside other world leaders such as Ferrari and Renault. The pride and fortune of the Santini Corporation, of Italy itself, it seemed, rested on the shoulders of the country's golden boy. Rafe was a national hero but the price of such adulation was high and the idea of failure inconceivable.

It was lonely at the top, he once confided, and she had looked around the packed room at the throng of guests who had come to celebrate another win, and laughed. At the time she had thought he was joking—everyone wanted to be with Rafe, everyone wanted a piece of him, so how on earth could he be lonely? Watching him now, she suddenly understood and with that understanding came remorse and shame, because she had been as guilty as any of demanding her share of him.

Suddenly he looked up and trapped her gaze, but instead of feeling embarrassed that she had been caught staring at him she was shocked at the bleakness in his dark eyes before his lashes fell, concealing his expression.

'Why did you think I was going to marry Valentina?' he asked quietly and Eden shrugged and tore her eyes from him to stare at a patch of daisies.

'Gianni told me.'

'Gianni!' Rafe's head came up and there was no disguising the shock in his eyes. 'I don't believe you.'

'It's the truth,' she insisted. 'The night you found us together by the pool, it wasn't what you thought. Gianni had just explained that an arrangement between the Santini and de Domenici families had been made years before, and you were determined to marry Valentina to please Fabrizzio.'

'I am not my father's puppet,' Rafe bit out furiously, 'and this is the twenty-first century; arranged marriages went out several hundred years ago.'

'Do you deny that you ever discussed marriage to her with Fabrizzio?'

'It was mentioned,' Rafe admitted with a shrug. 'My father would have liked it, it's true, but he knew there was no chance of it happening.'

'But Gianni told me,' Eden cried desperately. This was the first time Rafe had ever really listened to her, but the contemptuous disbelief in his eyes made it hard to go on. 'He said the fact that you seemed to delight in making our affair so very public, the newspaper scoops and the magazine articles about our relationship, was a ploy. You knew that when you appeared to end our affair, it would be headline news that would please Valentina and her family. But if you believed I would have stayed as your mistress after your marriage, you really didn't know me at all.'

Rafe's jaw tightened ominously but his voice was deceptively soft as he queried, 'And Gianni told you this? My brother, who is dead and cannot defend himself? Now, that's what I call convenient.'

'Why would I lie?' Eden demanded angrily. 'Gianni didn't want to tell me, but things hadn't been right between us for weeks. You were cold and distant and I suspected that you'd grown tired of me. I badgered Gianni until he admitted what you were planning and when you found us together he was comforting me, that's all—despite what he said about us having a secret affair.'

'So that's your version of the truth?' he drawled sardonically, and the tiny flicker of hope in her chest drowned in the depths of his scornful expression. 'Is that really the best you can come up with, *cara*?'

'The truth,' Eden stated with deadly calm, 'is that you are a deceitful, two-timing bastard who hoped to increase his social standing by marrying the daughter of an aristocrat whilst having a mistress conveniently tucked away in the background. This is hopeless,' she muttered. 'You made your mind up about me four years ago and you still haven't got the guts to admit you might have been wrong.'

'I *saw* you, and not just that night. You always had your eyes on Gianni, you were always laughing with him.'

'He was the only one of your family who was nice to me,' Eden said, defending herself. 'Your father made it obvious that he despised me and everyone else followed his lead and treated me like I had bubonic plague. I only had eyes for you,' she whispered sadly, and she still had. He was the only man she had ever loved, the reason, if she was honest, why she had spent the last three years living in constant danger. Focusing on her survival had been the only way she could prevent herself from thinking about him and the life they had once shared.

He, on the other hand, had spent the years since they'd parted jetting around the world, spending his time in glamorous locations with equally glamorous women. She was all too aware that he possessed a high sex drive. Add to that his stunning looks and plenty of Latin charm and it was impossible to believe he had spent the time pining for her.

'How you have the nerve to accuse me of cheating on you beats me when not a week goes by without a feature in the tabloids about you and your latest conquest,' she said bitterly, tensing as he walked around the pool towards her.

'I've had other lovers in the last four years, I can't deny it,' he told her with a shrug, and Eden felt a knife skewer her heart at his casual admission. 'As you say, there are plenty of women on the circuit who advertise their availability, and I have never pretended to be a monk,' he went on, ruthlessly ignoring the flare of pain in her eyes. 'But while we were together I was faithful to you. I certainly wasn't eyeing up members of your family.'

She had to get away from him before her composure cracked. Already she could feel the ache of tears behind her eyelids and she spun away, stumbling blindly towards the steps leading to the house.

'The other women, they meant nothing,' Rafe insisted, catching hold of her shoulder and forcing her to turn and face him. 'I used to close my eyes and pretend I was with you.'

'That's sick,' Eden whispered, and watched, wide-eyed, as he lowered his head until his mouth was millimetres from her own.

'It's the truth,' he whispered back before his lips claimed hers in a kiss that drove every other thought but him from her mind.

Her first instinct was to resist, and it was a desperate attempt at self-preservation that had her beating her fists against his shoulders as she fought the insidious warmth that flooded through her. In reply, he merely tightened his grip and hauled her up close against his chest while his hand at her nape angled her head so that there was no escape from his mouth, which seemed intent on taking everything she was so unwilling to give. His tongue traced the outline of her lips and she clamped them shut, refusing him access as his careless admission that he had had other lovers taunted her.

The image of him holding another woman in his arms, of him kissing her, caressing her, making love to her, caused her body to clench in rejection. It was unbearable and she *hated* him but at the same time it was growing harder and harder to fight her response to the mastery of his touch. He knew her so well, too well, even after all this time, and her fists slowly unfurled and crept up around his neck, the feel of silky black hair between her fingers evoking memories of how he had loved her to massage his shoulders after a race. The pressure of his lips increased and suddenly she couldn't fight him any more. Her mouth parted on a little gasp as he slid his hand down to her bottom, forcing her thighs up against the hardness of his, his arousal a potent force that made her realise she wasn't the only one who was spinning out of control.

'I have fantasised about making love to you every night for the past four years,' he admitted huskily when at last he lifted his head, but by then she was beyond any sort of reply.

Her lips were bruised and stinging and as she ran her tongue over them his eyes narrowed and he muttered something in Italian before he swept her into his arms. As he laid her down, the coolness of the grass broke through the sensual haze that surrounded her, but when she struggled to sit up he came down on top of her, the weight of him crushing her into the earth. Overhead, the leaves on the trees formed an intricate lace canopy beyond which she could see the sky, cloudless and an intense blue. The sweet smell of the grass mingled with the scent of his cologne, musky, male and fiercely elemental, and her senses quivered in recognition of the only man who had ever been a part of her. His mouth captured hers again, gentler this time, as if he knew he had breached her defences, but no less passionate, the sweep of his tongue hot and hungry, fanning the flames of her desire.

His fingers moved to the hem of her T-shirt, his eyes darkening as he pushed it up to reveal her breasts. 'The fantasy was never this good,' he repeated thickly, and she trembled, her body on fire as he lowered his head. She arched up to meet him, unable to stifle her groan of pleasure when he stroked his tongue over her taut nipple. The caress was light, teasing her, tormenting her, and she dug her nails into his shoulders until his mouth closed fully around the throbbing peak and he suckled her. A shaft of sensation coiled through her, so intense that she held him tighter and arched her hips as he rocked between her thighs in an erotic simulation of making love to her.

It was only when she felt his hands release the button at the waistband of her jeans, felt him slide the zip down ready to ease the denim over her hips, that reality hit and with it the realisation that if Rafe removed her jeans he would see her scarred leg. What was she *doing*? Was she completely mad? He believed her to be a liar and a cheat. His opinion of her couldn't get any lower, yet she was about to offer him a quickie on the grass before he flew off to the other side of the world.

Feeling the sudden tension that gripped her body, he stilled, watching her with hooded eyes as she frantically sought to push his hands away.

'No, I don't want this,' she told him fiercely, and he gave a harsh laugh as he rolled off her and lay on his back to stare up at the sky.

'So I noticed, *cara*. I wonder if you know what you do want,' he drawled, cold fury in his eyes as he watched her tug her T-shirt down and scramble to her feet.

'Not you, that's for sure.'

'Is that the reason you're running away? I tripped over your suitcase in the hall,' he added, and she blushed.

'I thought you'd already left.'

'And were you waiting until then to sneak off?'

'I wasn't sneaking anywhere,' she snapped. 'You must see that I can't stay here.'

He rolled onto his side, his head supported on his arm as he studied her silently.

'And if I asked you to stay?'

'Give me one good reason why I should.'

'Another chance at a relationship neither of us can dismiss or deny,' he suggested quietly, and she shook her head, refusing to listen to her heart.

'We've been there, discussed that and I refuse to enter a

relationship with a man who doesn't trust me. I have never lied to you,' she stated with such intensity that the hand around his heart squeezed tight.

'Which means that Gianni—my little brother, who I trusted with my life—did,' he murmured, with a depth of emotion in his voice that crucified her. 'I didn't cause his crash,' he said quietly as he slowly got to his feet, and she put her hand on his arm, desperate to comfort him. He looked *crushed*, there was no other word for it, and she ached for him, the lonely years apart and the bitterness suddenly immaterial.

'I know you didn't,' she assured him, but he didn't seem to hear her, lost in his thoughts.

'I loved him, and the intense rivalry between us was never as serious as everyone else believed, or so I thought. At the Hungarian Grand Prix, I realised just how serious it had become. Gianni was desperate to beat me and I could have let him pass, should have done. Instead, he took a stupid risk, hit the bend too fast, and I will never forget watching his car spin off the track.' He walked slowly into the house, his back rigid, and Eden hurried after him. 'That night, sitting in Intensive Care watching him wired up to all those machines, I promised myself that nothing would come between us again, and that I would end the row that had split us.'

'What did you row about?' she whispered, her heart thudding fearfully as she anticipated his reply. 'Was it about me?' His silent nod confirmed the worst and she blinked back her tears. 'No wonder you hate me. Gianni's accident was my fault.'

'Gianni's accident was Gianni's fault,' he told her firmly.

'It's taken me three years to realise that. He took an unnecessary risk and paid the price, but watching him struggle to come to terms with his paralysis was hard. I felt guilty that I had everything and he had nothing. Losing you was a private hell, but it was nothing compared to the torment he was going through, and in the end I couldn't save him. He chose to end his life.'

For the first time Eden understood how agonising the last few years must have been for Rafe. It must have been a shock to find her in Gianni's arms, and perhaps it was understandable that he'd initially believed his brother over her, she admitted honestly. She had been too hurt to try and defend herself, and by the time Rafe's temper had cooled enough for him to maybe listen to her, Gianni had crashed and been left with his terrible injuries. Rafe had been unable to help him. All he could do was give him his support and trust.

'I have to go—my jet's waiting for me,' he muttered as he strode through the house, stopping only to collect his briefcase and slide his arms into his jacket. 'Where will you go? To Neville Monkton?'

'No! There's nothing going on between us. I don't know what I'm going to do,' Eden admitted huskily. She didn't know what to think, how to react to everything he'd told her, but there was no time to discuss things further; he was already heading out the front door.

He slung his case onto the back shelf of the sports car before coiling his long frame behind the wheel. He'd said he had to leave but he seemed to be taking an inordinately long time to get going, and as she watched him fiddle with the controls on the dashboard she had the strange feeling that he was reluctant to start the engine. Eventually it fired, the throaty roar reminding her of the times she'd stood at the trackside while the cars hurtled past at terrifying speeds, and she was gripped with apprehension.

'Rafe!' He was already turning out of the drive, but he must have seen her in the mirror and he hit the brakes before opening the window.

'What's wrong, *cara*?'

He was so gorgeous, his face all hard planes and satiny olive skin, his black hair gleaming in the sunlight, but she focused on his mouth, remembering the sweetness of his kiss.

'Be careful,' she whispered, leaning down so that her face was on level with his, and his slow smile took her breath away.

'I'll promise to be careful if you'll promise to stay.' He gave her no chance to reply, but slid his hand into her hair to pull her against the car, his lips taking possession of hers with a tenderness that brought tears to her eyes. He increased the pressure slightly, coaxing her response, and she closed her eyes and gave in to pure sensation. 'Do we have a deal?'

She was beyond words and could only stare at him, unaware of the wealth of emotions in her eyes, the confusion. There was still a long way to go, he conceded silently, but it was a journey he was determined to take.

CHAPTER FIVE

'ALL things considered, you've made a pretty remarkable recovery,' the surgeon told Eden as he studied the X-rays of her injured leg. 'The metal pins will stay a permanent feature, I'm afraid—they're what's holding the shattered bone together—but it's all knitting together nicely and I see the scars are fading.'

Privately, Eden couldn't see much improvement to the purple welts that ran the length of her shin, but Dr Hillier was so enthusiastic about her recovery that she felt she couldn't complain. The simple truth was that she was lucky to be alive, and having met countless victims of land-mine explosions while she was in Africa, many of whom had lost limbs, she felt a few scars were nothing.

'If you pop behind the screen and put your clothes on, I'll ask the nurse to make an appointment for six months' time.' Dr. Hillier frowned at the noise of raised voices outside the door. 'Sounds like another satisfied National Health customer,' he murmured as the nurse on the reception desk cried, 'You can't just barge in...'

'Now, look here,' Eden heard the eminent surgeon at the

London hospital say firmly. 'Good God! Rafael Santini—what are you doing here?'

Good question, Eden thought as she scrambled frantically into her clothes. A furtive peep from behind the screen had revealed that Rafe was very much here, big and dark and, from the look of it, in a raging temper.

'Eden, where are you? What are you doing?' he demanded as she stepped from behind the screen, and her heart flipped painfully in her chest at the sight of him after two weeks apart.

'Getting dressed,' she told him calmly, and he took a deep breath, his nostrils flaring as his gaze swung from her to the hapless doctor.

'You mean you stripped off in front of *him*?' Rafe was on a roll, black eyes flashing fire, his fists clenched, and Dr Hillier backed up against his desk.

'A nurse was present. It's all quite above board, I assure you,' he murmured nervously.

'Dr. Hillier is the surgeon who operated on my leg,' Eden explained, giving Rafe a fulminating glare. 'I don't know what right you think you've got to storm in here. How did you know where I was, anyways?'

With another furious glance at the surgeon, Rafe followed her out of the consulting room. 'Your estate-agent friend told me you had a hospital appointment. I arrived at the Dower House to find it deserted,' he added accusingly. 'I knew Bruno and his family had already gone back to Milan, but I expected…hoped,' he amended, 'you would be there.'

They were incurring a lot of interest in the small waiting area—hardly surprising, when Rafe seemed to fill the room—and she sighed impatiently.

'Will you keep your voice down? You weren't due back until tomorrow night and even if I'd known you were coming early I couldn't have changed the appointment—it was made ages ago.'

'What's the matter with you?' His dark eyes trawled her from head to toe, oblivious to the curious onlookers.

'What do you mean? Nothing's the matter with me, other than annoyance at you barging into the consulting room. It was rude.'

Rafe muttered something that she suspected was extremely rude, in his native tongue. 'Why are you here, why did you need to see a doctor and what is the matter with your leg?' he asked with exaggerated patience, as if he were speaking to a halfwit.

She'd missed him so much, Eden acknowledged. She'd almost forgotten what it was like to feel this alive, yet five minutes in his company and the blood was zinging in her veins, as amusement and irritation filled her in equal measures. 'I hurt my leg while I was working in Africa,' she explained, but he remained standing in the middle of the room, blocking everyone's path as he waited for more. 'In an accident,' she added, and his frown deepened.

'A car accident?'

'No,' she hesitated briefly before murmuring, 'an explosion. I stepped on a land-mine—well, not completely on it, of course, or I wouldn't be here now, but something triggered it while I was standing a couple of feet away and…and I nearly lost my leg,' she finished quietly. Rafe looked as if he was going to explode himself, but then he suddenly swung round and flung open the door to the consulting room.

'And you say this doctor operated on your leg? I want to see him and I want a full explanation of the injuries you received.'

'Rafe, you can't just walk in there—he's a busy man, and there's an appointment system.' She was already talking to the back of his head and as he shut the door firmly behind him, she glanced helplessly at the nurse on the reception desk. 'I'm sorry, he's awful, isn't he?'

'I think he's rather wonderful,' the superior-looking nurse said with a grin that made her suddenly human. 'He's very dominant, isn't he?'

'You wouldn't believe,' Eden muttered. Without Rafe to entertain them, the small crowd in the waiting room turned their attention expectantly to her, and she hastily shot into the corridor and headed for the drinks machine.

When she returned ten minutes later she found Rafe leaning against the reception desk. The hospital was warm and she felt decidedly hot and bothered, but he looked cool and relaxed, and, in jeans and a black leather jacket, drop-dead gorgeous. The group of nurses around him obviously thought so, too, she noted sourly. He must be the only man capable of flirting with five women simultaneously, but as she approached he straightened up and strolled towards her.

'Ready to go?' he queried.

'I am—are you sure you can tear yourself away?'

His smile took her breath away and before she could recover, he cupped her chin and took her mouth in a deep, languorous kiss that instantly breached her defences. She was in shock, she defended herself as her lips parted beneath the gentle pressure of his. His mouth was warm and soft and infinitely inviting, and her eyelids drifted down as she lost herself in pure sensation.

'Let's go, *cara*. We're causing a scene.'

'Not we—you. I can't believe you did that.'

'Kissed you?' he asked innocently, and she glared at him as she marched along the corridor.

'I can't believe you stormed into Dr Hillier's room, twice! Heaven knows what he thought.'

'He was extremely helpful. He even showed me the X-rays of your leg after I told him I had your permission.'

'But you didn't!' She broke off with an impatient sigh. 'Rafe, why are you here?'

'Why didn't you tell me you'd been hurt?' Suddenly, he was intensely serious, his dark eyes scanning her delicate features as if trying to reassure himself that she was as fully recovered as the doctor had insisted.

Eden shrugged, wishing the husky concern in his voice didn't make her feel so emotional. Her leg was healing well, better than she'd expected, and she didn't need to relive memories of the explosion that still gave her nightmares.

'My welfare has nothing to do with you. You made that clear four years ago.'

Rafe bit back an oath. 'You could have died. The doctor said you lost so much blood it was touch and go for a while.'

'Well, I didn't. I'm here and I'm perfectly all right, so you can stop the sudden bout of concern.'

She was far from *all right*, he thought grimly. The X-rays might prove that her leg was healing, but the mental scars she'd incurred still haunted her. He could see the shadows in her eyes, and, from the brief description the doctor had given him of the explosion and the full extent of the injuries she'd received, he wasn't surprised. He was still fighting the wave of nausea that had swept over him when he pictured her bloodied and battered body, the guilt that he hadn't been there to save her. If he had believed her over Gianni, she would never have gone to Africa in the first place, never been so horrifically injured. But Gianni was his brother, his flesh and blood. Why would he have lied? It didn't make any sense.

'If you're OK, why are you limping?' he demanded as they reached the hospital exit.

'My leg aches a bit today, but it's hardly surprising when it's been prodded and poked all morning. I'll rest it on the train,' she added, and he frowned.

'Naturally I will drive you back to Wellworth. Did you really expect me to just drop you at the station?'

'I didn't expect to see you here at all,' Eden muttered. She could see his car parked on a double yellow line, but as they walked along the busy London street she was aware that they were the subject of speculative glances from every passer-by. It was to be expected, she supposed; he was six feet, four inches of olive-skinned perfection, and he would draw a second look even before it was realised that he was Formula 1's most famous competitor.

'I thought we could do some shopping while we're in town, but maybe it's not a good idea. Your leg is obviously painful.'

'It's fine, but shopping isn't,' she said firmly. 'You attract too much attention, Rafe, and I don't want a jaunt down Oxford Street to be snapped by the paparazzi. They'll say that we're back together again, which we're most definitely not.'

Rafe looked so stunned that she had actually refused him that she had to hide her smile. It had never happened four years ago, but she was determined he wouldn't walk all over her again.

'Is that better?' he demanded imperiously as he pulled a pair of designer shades out of his pocket and shoved them on his nose.

'Oh, yes, completely incognito. Now you look like a member of the Mafia.'

'Are you ashamed to be with me?'

'Of course not,' she denied, 'but I really don't want to go back to the days when I was featured in the tabloids as the latest addition to your stable.'

'No one ever thought of you like that,' he argued fiercely, and she laughed.

'The whole Santini team knew that my job as Press officer was a cover for the fact that I was your mistress, and if they didn't know, your father made sure they understood that I was your whore.'

He came to a halt by his car, retrieved the parking ticket from beneath the windscreen wiper and shoved it into his pocket without even glancing at it. 'I don't know how you can say something like that.'

'Fabrizzio called me it to my face,' she said stubbornly, and he glared at her, raking an impatient hand through his hair.

'I don't believe you. You're lying.'

'Here we go again,' she muttered wearily. 'Same old story. I'm not lying, Rafe. I've never lied to you, about Gianni or your father or anything else, but I'm sick of having to defend myself. Your father despised me. He wanted you to marry your fancy Italian aristocrat. Maybe he even set Gianni up to lie to me about her, I don't know.'

'Why the hell would he do that?' Rafe shouted, and she took a step back, anticipating the scene of all scenes played out on one of the most public thoroughfares in London.

'Because he wanted to split us up?' she suggested, and he threw back his head and let out a harsh laugh.

'Well, he needn't have bothered. You'd already decided that one Santini couldn't keep you satisfied, and were determined to have the pair. We split up because I caught you making love with Gianni.'

She really couldn't take any more. Already, tears were burning behind her eyelids, queuing up to fall, but she'd be damned if she would let him see her cry. 'Fine, you win. Believe what you like, you will anyways, but the reason we split up, Rafe, is that you had no faith in me, in the same way that I have absolutely no faith in you now, or ever will again.'

She started to walk swiftly away from him. Up ahead, a bus had pulled into the kerb and she broke into a run, jumping onto the platform just as it pulled away.

'Where to, love?' The conductor waited imperturbably while she mopped her cheeks with a tissue.

'King's Cross.'

'Not on this bus—you're going the wrong way; this goes to Marble Arch.'

She didn't care if it went to Timbuktu as long as it meant she was out of reach of Rafe, she thought miserably as she handed over her change and stared unseeingly out of the window.

'So where are we going? I thought you didn't want to be seen in public with me.'

Her eyes widened as Rafe slid onto the bench seat next to her. Heaven knew how he had caught the bus—he must have sprinted after it, but she was far from impressed.

'I don't,' she said pointedly, 'so go away.'

'Do you really think I'd let you wander around London, alone and upset?' he queried gently, and she quickly looked away before she drowned in the velvet softness of his eyes.

'I don't know, I haven't seen you for four years. Why are you suddenly acting like you care, especially as you're the reason I'm upset?'

'There's something between us…' he began, and she rounded on him fiercely.

'No, there isn't, Rafe, not any more. You threw it away when you believed everyone including the cat's mother, over me. I don't want to listen to your reasons,' she added when he made to speak. 'I don't want to talk about the past any more.'

'Good, then we can concentrate on the present,' he said coolly, and she swallowed at the determined gleam in his eyes. 'We'll start from the beginning and get to know one another like two ordinary people. Hi, I'm Rafe Santini; I'm a racing driver.'

Every head on the bus turned, and Eden shook her head, absolutely determined that she wouldn't smile.

'You could never be described as ordinary, Rafe,' she murmured as his big hand closed over hers.

'Nor could you, *cara*, nor could you,' he growled huskily.

He was still holding her hand when they got off the bus and wandered across to Hyde Park. She ought to pull free of his grasp and demand that he leave her alone, she thought, but the honest truth was that she wanted to be with him. She wished they could start from scratch as he had suggested, but there was too much mistrust on either side, emotions that were still too raw, and her only possible saviour, who might prove her innocence, had taken his secrets to his grave.

'How did you get on with Bruno and his family?' Rafe asked as they strolled along the edge of the Serpentine, which glistened like a wide silver ribbon beneath the summer sky.

'Great; he and his wife are a lovely couple, and the children are beautiful.'

For two weeks the Dower House had rung with the noisy exuberance of four small children, the cries and gurgling laughter of the utterly adorable baby, but now the Martinellis were on their way back to Italy. She had enjoyed their company, Eden mused. They had filled a void left by Rafe and were so friendly that she'd had little chance to mope, although missing him had been a constant, nagging ache in her chest.

Watching the young family had brought on a severe case of envy when she witnessed the obvious devotion Bruno felt for his wife and children. If things had been different, could that have been her and Rafe? she had wondered wistfully. At twenty-seven, her hormones were kicking in and when she'd held the Martinellis' baby, she had been overcome with longing for a child of her own.

She had no idea whether Rafe wanted children, they'd certainly never discussed the subject four years ago, and the fantasies she'd spun of marriage and a family had been a secret desire she'd never dared to voice. Rafe was a racing driver, she reminded herself impatiently, an international playboy whose first loves were speed and excitement. She couldn't imagine him ever settling down to a life of domestic bliss, and if he really was serious about giving their relationship another chance, she would have to accept that it would be on his terms, following the nomadic lifestyle that life as a Formula 1 driver demanded.

She must need her head tested if she was even considering going back to him, she thought grimly. She'd hated life in the public eye, their affair played out in the tabloids and glossy magazines. She wasn't a supermodel or glamorous actress, and the paparazzi had speculated constantly on who Rafe might decide to replace her with when he tired of her—which, they suggested, he surely must. Four years ago she'd been unsure of herself and her role in his life. How much worse would it be now, when he believed she had cheated on him with his brother? He said he wanted them to have another chance, but it would be impossible when a chasm of suspicion divided them, and she couldn't bear to have her heart broken again. It still hadn't properly recovered from the first time.

Even wearing his sunglasses, or possibly because of them, Rafe was still spectacularly recognisable and was stopped several times by excited fans who requested his autograph.

'I can't help it,' he muttered as she watched him scribble his name on the back of a stunning brunette's T-shirt. 'Formula 1 attracts a lot of interest, nowadays.'

'No, you attract a lot of interest.' It was ridiculous to feel so jealous; she didn't even care any more, she reminded herself irritably.

'This is hopeless, I can't talk to you when you're in this mood.' He glanced along the lake to the little hut that hired out rowing boats. 'Come on, we surely can't be disturbed in the middle of the water, unless you object to the ducks.' He caught hold of her hand and dragged her after him, unmoved by her protests.

'I don't want to go in a boat. Take someone else. Heaven knows you've got enough choice of females who'd give their right arm to be stuck in the middle of the Serpentine with you.'

'*Madre de Dio*! You would try the patience of twenty saints.' He lifted her bodily into the rowing boat, shrugged out of his jacket and threw it at her with barely leashed violence. She'd opened her mouth to continue the argument, but the sight of him in his tight black T-shirt that clung like a second skin to the muscles of his abdomen rendered her speechless. He had an incredible body, she conceded as she tried to look anywhere but his powerful shoulders and the rippling of his biceps as he rowed them into the centre of the lake. Her mouth felt suddenly dry as she pictured him without the T-shirt, remembered the feel of him, skin on skin, his hair-roughened thighs pressing against the softness of hers.

The only man she had ever wanted; would ever want. Her life suddenly stretched ahead as a long and lonely road, but what was the alternative? To pick up the pieces of their affair and enjoy it while it lasted? She'd done it once, lived with the uncertainty that he would end it any day, soon. She didn't think she was strong enough to do it again.

It was surprisingly peaceful on the lake, and hard to believe they were in the middle of London. The noise of the traffic had receded to a distant hum and she tipped her head back and stared up at the sky.

'That's better,' Rafe noted in a satisfied tone. 'Relax, *cara*. It's not good to be so tense.'

'You make me tense,' she admitted with a sigh, and he gave her a wolfish grin.

'You make me tense, too, but I'm not complaining. Maybe we should help each other relax?'

She was powerless to resist when he turned on his seductive Latin charm. His voice curled around her like thick cream and she felt sleepy and supine, yet at the same time agonisingly aware of him. He had removed his sunglasses and she studied his face, his dark eyes beneath heavy black brows, the strong line of his nose and the sensual curve of his mouth. The feel of that mouth used to send her to heaven, she remembered, unable to drag her eyes from him, and he carefully drew the oars across the boat and leaned towards her.

'Do it,' he bade thickly, and she feigned confusion.

'Do what?'

'Kiss me. You know you want to.'

Pride dictated that she should refute the suggestion, but she felt boneless with longing and she had years ahead to work on restoring her pride. She hesitated fractionally, and then moved so that she was kneeling before him on the floor of the boat. She put one hand on his shoulder and drew his head down to hers, her mouth initiating a gentle exploration that speared his soul. He seemed content to let her control the kiss, taking only what she was willing to give, but he felt so good that the breath left her body in a rush as she increased the pressure, her tongue darting out to explore the contours of his lips.

Rafe hung on to his self-control with difficulty. She was

so beautiful, so warm and giving that he had to fight the urge to push her down onto the floor of the boat and make love to her there and then in broad daylight in the middle of a London park. Take it slow, his mind cautioned. One day at a time. There was too much hurt on both sides to rush things. The tentative probing of her tongue shattered that control, and he groaned and wrapped his arms around her, holding her close while the desire to assert his mastery became an overriding need. He deepened the kiss, passion overcoming his restraint, and he plundered the soft sweetness of her lips with a hunger that bordered on desperation.

She looked stunned when at last he released her and she sat back on her seat, her blue eyes dazed as she ran a shaky finger over her lips. Fool, she derided herself. She was falling into his honeyed trap, but dear God, it was the only place she wanted to be.

'How would you like to see the new musical that's just opened at the Palladium?' he asked as they walked back across the park.

'I'd love to, but it's been sold out for months.'

'I have tickets for tonight's performance, preceded by dinner at a particularly good restaurant I know.'

'I'm not dressed for the theatre,' Eden pointed out, and he shrugged.

'So we'll stop off and buy you something.'

'No.' The invitation to the show was too good to miss when it had received such excellent reviews, but that was all she would accept. 'I'll buy myself something to wear or I catch my train back to Wellworth.' Her arms were folded across her chest, her expression mutinous, and Rafe hid a smile. He didn't know where her fierce temper had sprung from—it certainly hadn't been evident during the year they'd spent together—but he possessed a fairly forceful personality, he admitted honestly. Had she been *afraid* of him? Surely not. The idea was all the more disturbing because he couldn't easily dismiss it. Patience wasn't his strong point and it was true he liked to have his own way, but his outbursts of temper, although explosive, were always short-lived. Perhaps he hadn't taken her feelings into account enough, he conceded. He'd been aware that she hated their life in the public eye, the intrusions into their private life by the tabloids. He had never courted the attention of the paparazzi, but he hadn't minded the pictures of the two of them. *Dio*, he'd been proud to show her off, to proclaim to the world that the beautiful little English rose was his woman, and maybe, if he was honest, it had been a way of getting the message across to his father, too.

'There's a problem you hadn't thought of,' Eden said with a frown as she emerged from the department store, clutching a carrier bag. She had dispatched Rafe to wait for her in the car after he had driven her mad by wandering around the shop, ostensibly trying to help. His selection of dresses with minuscule skirts had caused her a pang of despair. He wouldn't be quite so eager to see her in a skirt up to her eyebrows if he knew the state of her leg. 'Where am I going to get changed?' she queried worriedly, and he gave her a bland smile.

'At the hotel I've booked us into. I think of everything, *cara*.'

'Yes, well, you can just un-book us. I'm not sharing a room with you.'

'You really don't trust me, do you?' he murmured, an edge of seriousness in his voice as he deposited her bags in the back of the car, and Eden gave him a thoughtful look.

'No, I don't,' she said quietly. 'You let me down, Rafe, not the other way round, so don't even go there. Once I handed you my trust on a plate, but I won't be so careless again.'

They crawled through the London traffic in taut silence and Eden sighed as she rubbed her temples. Her head ached, her leg was throbbing and all she wanted to do was go home, except home—for now at least—was also Rafe's home, and whichever way she looked there didn't seem to be an escape route.

The hotel was one of London's finest, its opulence breathtaking, and she glanced around the suite they had been shown to with wide eyes. Rafe had stormed straight into the bedroom and she could hear the faint sounds of the shower from the *ensuite*. She could change into her dress in the sitting room, she supposed, but a shower was tempting, and was a safer way of relaxing than anything Rafe could suggest.

She almost turned tail at the sight of the king-sized bed, refusing to admit that she was filled with nervous excitement rather than trepidation at the idea of sharing it with him. The sensible option would be to slip out of the hotel, take a cab to the station and travel back to Wellworth, but she didn't feel sensible, she felt enervated, every nerve ending prickling with a sense of anticipation she couldn't deny, however hard she tried.

Rafe strolled out of the bathroom, a towel hitched around his waist, and her imagination immediately soared into overdrive at the thought of what was hidden beneath the towel. His hair was slicked to his head, droplets of water clinging to the black hairs that covered his chest, and she felt a curious sensation in the pit of her stomach, a need that was savage in its intensity, and darkened her eyes to the colour of cobalt.

'Do you want something, *cara*?' he queried coolly, and she felt her cheeks flame as she dragged her gaze from his glorious body.

'I, um…need to get changed,' she muttered, and his brows rose.

'Your room is at the opposite end of the sitting room, but I'm happy to share if you insist.'

'You could have said,' she snapped furiously, his sardonic smile telling her he was aware that she didn't just feel an idiot, she also felt agonisingly disappointed.

'You're so determined to think the worst of me, there didn't seem much point in wasting my breath, but let me make one thing clear, *cara*. I'm not so desperate that I need to try and trick you into my bed. I want you, sure,' he continued with a nonchalant shrug, as if the idea of making love to her was as important as choosing a sweet from the pick-and-mix counter, 'but I'm not going to take you kicking and screaming, so you can drop the air of maidenly outrage. One other thing,' he added, seeing that she was temporarily struck dumb. 'Stop looking at me like that with those big, hungry blue eyes.'

'Like what?' Eden managed through numb lips, and he gave her an insolent smile.

'Like you want me to throw you down on the bed and remove every last vestige of your clothing. Trail my lips all the way down your body and then spread those milky thighs I remember so well and thrust into you until we both reach the heights of sexual ecstasy.'

'I don't want you to do that,' she denied grittily, and his eyes narrowed. The tension between them was so intense, the imagery his words had evoked so stark, that one of them, surely, would have to crack.

'Which rather proves my point, *cara*,' he drawled softly. 'I still maintain you're a liar.'

CHAPTER SIX

THE dress was a peach-coloured, full-length sheath that emphasised her slender waist. The long skirt hid her legs while the strapless bodice revealed rather more of her full breasts than she was comfortable with. It was an overtly sexy dress and as Eden stood in front of the mirror she bitterly regretted the impulse that had led her to buy it, the secret hope that Rafe would find her attractive, despite the fact that the skirt hid her long limbs that he had always admired.

A sudden, unbidden image filled her mind, of him smoothing sunscreen over her stomach before trailing his hands lower, past the tiny triangle of material that masqueraded as a bikini, and down to her thighs. He was a leg man, he had informed her in his deep, sexy drawl, and she had laughed breathlessly and teased him by wrapping her long, tanned legs around him and holding him prisoner.

What would he make of her injuries? she wondered, and then shook her head impatiently. After his parting shot a couple of hours earlier, she doubted she would ever find out. He was never going to see her scarred leg. She was still smarting from the realisation that he was aware of her growing need for him, a desire that was becoming harder and harder to conceal. For his part, far from wanting to ravish her at the first opportunity, he seemed relaxed to the point of boredom, and his attitude of take it or leave it made her humiliation complete.

It was the reason she had remained locked in her bedroom, but she couldn't remain there forever. Pride—her only ally when her emotional stability seemed to have gone to pieces—dictated that she walk out and face him, and she checked her appearance one last time, sprayed a liberal amount of perfume on her wrists and opened the door.

Rafe swung round from the window, where he had been staring moodily down at the street, and felt his breath snag in his throat. Exquisite was the only word to describe her, and he felt a familiar ache in his loins as he took in the way her dress clung to her curves and her blonde hair was piled in a loose knot on top of her head. Sensual, sexy and right now as nervous as hell, he assessed, noting the way the pulse at the base of her throat was beating erratically. His woman, and despite the past, he was determined to reclaim her, but it wasn't proving quite as simple as he'd arrogantly assumed.

His gentle English rose had developed thorns, he conceded with a rueful smile. He could practically read the danger sign in her mind that warned him to keep away, but fortunately her body was throwing out different signals. The powerful sexual chemistry that had bound them together in the first place still burned. She didn't want to want him; he understood that and sympathised. He didn't enjoy being held at the mercy of his hormones, either, and it was only when he had accepted that desire was one of a multitude of intense emotions he felt for her that he'd been able to relax and bide his time.

'The dress was a good choice,' he said lightly, wanting to put her at her ease. But couldn't help adding huskily, 'You were always the most beautiful woman in the world to me.'

Eden took a shaky breath and closed her mind to the fact that he spent most of his life surrounded by exotic models. 'Thank you,' she replied quietly. 'Had you considered wearing glasses?'

His smile would melt an iceberg, she acknowledged with a sigh. She wanted to remain cool and aloof but it was difficult when he looked at her with such warmth in his dark eyes, and the bitter fury of a few hours ago seemed to have vanished.

'The car will be here in a minute to take us to the theatre. I thought we could eat afterwards, as the show has an early start. Are you happy with that, *cara*?'

She would be happy to stand here looking at him for the rest of the evening, but she could hardly say so. His black dinner suit emphasised the lean hardness of his body, and she wondered rather desperately if she should ask for a drink. A couple of glasses of wine might anaesthetise her reaction to him.

A discreet knock at the door heralded Room Service—champagne on ice with two glasses, and an exquisite bouquet of cream roses. Rafe handed them to her, selecting a single bloom that had been trimmed into a corsage.

'I thought you would like to wear a flower on your dress,' he murmured, his eyes glinting as he surveyed the creamy expanse of her naked shoulders. 'But there doesn't seem to be anywhere to pin it.'

He was too close, too vibrantly, excitingly alive, and

way too much for her to cope with, Eden thought despairingly as she took the flower from his grasp. 'It can go
here, at the front,' she muttered, struggling to slide the pin
into the low-cut bodice of her dress, and he moved closer
still, taking the corsage from her nerveless fingers and at-
taching it so that the rose bud nestled in the valley between
her breasts.

'Lucky flower,' he murmured teasingly, and she gave up
all hope of acting cool. OK, so she fancied him, hungered for
him, if she was honest. She knew it and so did he, and she
would just have to deal with it, but at least while they were
at the theatre she could drop her guard for a few hours and
simply enjoy his company.

The show—a musical starring several internationally
famous actors—was spectacular, and Eden enjoyed every
minute of it. During dinner afterwards, Rafe entertained her
with amusing stories from life on the racing circuit, and she
rediscovered the man she had fallen in love with five years ago.
He was witty and charming and seemed determined to steer
the conversation away from the past, which suited Eden
fine—she didn't want to think of anything but here and now.
Yesterday was filled with disillusionment and pain, and
tomorrow loomed an uncertain spectre, but now she had Rafe's
undivided attention and she intended to make the most of it.

It was late when the limousine drew up outside the restaurant, and she was forced to admit she was glad they were
spending the night at the hotel rather than travelling back to
Wellworth. The soft leather seats of the Mercedes were
inviting, and she closed her eyes for a moment that stretched
to minutes, unaware that her head had settled on Rafe's

shoulder. The voice in her ear was an intrusion, and she blinked as his face came into view, so close that she could see the fine lines at the corners of his eyes. Was this still part of her dream, or was it reality? she wondered. In her dream Rafe had lowered his head, the touch of his mouth as light as thistledown on hers, but had he kissed her or had she imagined it? She ran her tongue over her lips, trying to re-capture the taste of him, and his eyes narrowed, a frown forming on his brow when he watched the way she tried to disguise her limp as she walked up the steps to the hotel entrance.

'You're tired, *cara*, it's been a long day for you. You must be desperate to climb into bed.'

Desperate to climb into his bed more like, a wicked voice in her head prompted, before every thought was banished from her mind as he swung her into his arms.

'Put me down—everyone's looking,' she demanded as she was forced to cling to his shoulders, and his low chuckle re-verberated through his chest.

'The doorman and receptionist hardly make a packed audience. Your leg's hurting—don't even bother to deny it. You could barely walk up the steps. I blame myself,' he said grimly. 'I've overexerted you.'

He hadn't, but a list of the ways he *could* overexert her filled her wayward mind, and she sighed, fighting the urge to run her hand along his jaw and feel the faint stubble already evident, although he had shaved only a few hours before. He cradled her in his arms as the lift whisked them to the top floor and insisted on carrying her along the corridor to their suite, where he deposited her gently on the sofa.

'Do you think you can manage to get undressed?' he queried, his voice laced with concern, and Eden dropped her head as colour flooded her cheeks.

No, I need you to undress me, very slowly, answered the demon who had taken up residence in her head, and she gave herself a mental shake.

'I'll be fine,' she assured him brightly.

'Can I get you a nightcap?' He walked across to the bar and she couldn't drag her eyes from him, watching the way he moved with the lithe grace of an athlete. Now that he had discarded his jacket she could see the powerful muscle definition of his abdomen beneath his silk shirt and she ached to run her hands over him, feel his golden, satin skin beneath her fingertips and the brush of dark chest hair against her palms. He exuded a magnetism, a primitive sexual energy that tore through her barriers, and she closed her eyes for a few seconds, willing her self-control to reassert itself.

She didn't need any more alcohol, that was for sure. The champagne must have gone to her head and was the reason she felt hot and breathless. 'I think I'd better have coffee, strong and black, please. It might clear my head,' she added under her breath, and he gave her an assessing look.

'If you're worried I'm going to jump on you, don't be. I never pounce unless invited.'

He'd already made that clear earlier in the evening, she recalled miserably. It wasn't him she was worried about. He wasn't the one racked by desire and, if there was any pouncing to be done, she had a horrible feeling she would be the culprit.

'Actually, I think I'll just go to bed.' In her desperation to reach the sanctuary of her room, she stumbled and would have fallen but for the strong arms that caught her and lifted her into the air.

'Easy, there's no need to hurry,' he chided softly, but he didn't understand her urgency to break the spell he had cast over her and she wriggled frantically.

'I have to go to bed now,' she told him fiercely.

'Why?' His eyes narrowed as he glanced down at her tense face and misinterpreted the reason for it. 'Surely the pleasant evening we've spent together proves that you have no reason to fear me, that I can restrain myself from ripping your clothes off, so what's the reason for your frantic rush?'

'You are,' she flung at him furiously, overwhelmed by the stark memory of how he had frequently ignored buttons and fastenings and simply torn her clothing from her body in his desperate fervour to possess her. The air between them crackled with electricity, her heart was pounding, and for the life of her she couldn't drag her gaze from his face.

'I see.' His eyes were hooded and unfathomable, his voice so indifferent that she felt like crawling under a stone, but the arms that tightened around her told a different story, and she gasped when he hauled her close, allowing her to feel the rigid proof of his arousal. 'I think we're both suffering from the same ailment,' he murmured as he lowered his head, his mouth hot and hard on hers, denying her the chance to resist, although, God help her, she tried. 'We always communicated better without words, *cara*,' he told her as she opened her mouth to argue and he captured her denial with his tongue.

Instantly, Eden was transported back to a time when his heated outbursts of temper had ended in passion, anger swiftly replaced by desire, and heat flooded through her body, pooling between her thighs. For the sake of her sanity she should fight him, the voice in her head insisted, but as he lifted her into his arms the room spun, and she curled her arms around his neck. He smelled so good, *tasted* so good, she thought as her face was pressed into his neck and she explored the faint stubble on his chin with her tongue.

'Who needs words when we have this?' Rafe whispered as he sank onto the sofa and drew her down to his lap, his mouth trailing a line of kisses along her neck to the valley between her breasts. 'You are so beautiful, *cara mia*, and I have missed you so much.' His lips found hers once again and coaxed them apart so that his tongue could probe between them in an erotic exploration that made her tremble. She was unaware that he had slid the strap of her dress over her shoulder until she felt the cool air on her breast, but before she could murmur a protest he cupped the soft mound in his hand and she closed her eyes as sensation ripped through her. He drew the zip of her dress down so that the bodice fell to her waist, and she held her breath as he lowered his head and took one hard peak into his mouth. Pleasure engulfed her and she arched her back, linking her hands around his neck to hold him to his task of suckling her.

'Your breasts were always incredibly sensitive,' he said thickly as he transferred his attention to her other nipple, but she was beyond speech, beyond conscious thought, and she groaned when his tongue tormented the throbbing peak, her fingers scrabbling with his shirt buttons in her desperation to feel the warmth of his body against hers.

His bronzed skin was beaded with sweat that dampened

the whorls of dark chest hair, and she ran her hands hungrily over him, feeling the thud of his heart beneath her fingertips. Her dress was split to mid-thigh on the side of her uninjured leg, but when she felt his hand slide beneath her skirt she tensed. Instantly, he sensed her withdrawal and his lips sought hers again, stroking over them, slow and sweet, before deepening the kiss so that she was utterly lost, and she sighed her pleasure when she felt his fingers move beyond the lace band at the top of her stocking to settle on the quivering flesh of her inner thigh.

It had been so long, she thought feverishly, her body on fire as she felt him ease his hand beneath her silk thong. All the time she had been working abroad, ordinary emotions like passion and desire had been buried deep in her subconscious, but as Rafe gently caressed her they flooded back and she clung to him, desperate for him to touch her even more intimately.

'You see, *cara*,' he whispered, 'this is how we communicate best. You want me—your body doesn't lie, see?' He parted her tenderly and slid his finger in deep, watching the way she arched and pushed against him. She was ready for him, hot and moist, and he was overwhelmed with the urge to tear off his clothes and take what she was offering. No woman had ever affected him the way Eden did, and he shifted uncomfortably, trying to ease the ache in his loins. Her perfume, a light, floral fragrance, assailed his senses and he buried his face in her neck, breathing her in. He wanted to push her back against the cushions and drag her long skirt aside to reveal those long, shapely limbs he remembered so well. He wanted to plunge into her and feel her muscles close around his shaft. Just the thought of it made him so hard that he was sure he would explode, but he was aware that he needed to take things slowly.

She was so responsive, such an innately sensual woman, that she must have had other lovers during the past four years. The idea made his body clench; she was his woman, *his*, and he was determined that she would never forget it. He would use all his skill and expertise to bind her to him. He knew how to please her and he felt a surge of primitive satisfaction as he moved his fingers inside her and felt her muscles contract. She was breathing hard, her whole body tense and trembling, and the speed of her climax took him by surprise. Perhaps there hadn't been many other lovers and suddenly he didn't care, from now on there would only be him. Her sobbing gasps of pleasure turned him on and he vowed that her cries would be heard for the rest of the night as he wrung every ounce of pleasure from her body.

Eden came back to earth to find that Rafe had eased her off his lap and she was lying on the sofa with the bodice of her dress down around her waist. For a moment she closed her mind to the voice that warned her she was on a path she was going to regret following. But how could she regret this? This was Rafe, the only man she had ever loved, and making love with him felt so right. Her body had waited patiently for him for four years but it wouldn't wait any longer; she needed him now.

'You don't know how often I've dreamed of you wrapping your long legs around me, *cara*,' he murmured, and his words shattered the spell. His hand slid up her uninjured leg and he hooked his fingers around the top of her stocking, intent on drawing the sheer hose down. She tensed, desire quickly replaced by panic. He was expecting to remove her stockings and reveal the slender, tanned legs he had so admired. She couldn't bear to watch the revulsion that would surely cross his face when he saw her scars.

'Rafe, no, I can't.' She pushed his hand away and sat up, frantically trying to adjust the straps of her dress.

For a second Rafe frowned, but then his expression cleared and he took her hand to draw her to her feet. 'I agree, *cara*. I don't want our first time together after all the years apart to be a hurried fumble on the sofa. I want to make love to you all night in the comfort of a double bed, before we fly to Portugal tomorrow.'

'Portugal!' Eden stared at him as if he'd suddenly grown another head. 'I'm not going to Portugal.'

Rafe was already tugging her towards his room, seemingly oblivious to the dismay in her eyes, and he sighed when she pulled her hand free.

'I know it's sudden but the next two races are back to back—Portugal and then the Italian Grand Prix at Monza. I'm sorry, *cara*, but there'll still be time for us, I promise you.' He tilted her chin and bestowed a brief, hard kiss on her mouth. His lips were warm and enticing and for a moment Eden closed her eyes and gave rein to the fantasy that involved walking into his bedroom and allowing passion to consume her in its fiery blaze.

'Rafe, I'm not going to Portugal or anywhere else, least of all your bedroom.' With a supreme effort she put some space between them and he dropped his hand to his side, his eyes suddenly hooded as the silence between them thrummed with tension.

'What do you mean, *cara*?' he asked, but she wasn't fooled by his deceptively quiet tone and shivered at the hardness in his eyes. 'You know I'm committed to compete for the remainder of this season. How can we maintain any kind of relationship if you refuse to travel with me, or do you expect me to fly back to England whenever I have the chance?'

'I don't expect you to do anything. Why do you expect that you can just walk back into my life and demand that I rearrange it around you?'

'Obviously I mistook your eager response as an indication that you wanted to give our relationship another chance,' Rafe said coldly. 'I didn't realise that you were looking for a one-night stand.'

'I wasn't looking for anything—you started it…' She broke off, miserably aware that even if she hadn't made the first move she'd practically screamed her eagerness from the rooftops.

'At least be honest, Eden,' he taunted. 'Sexual frustration is nothing to be ashamed of. If you just want to scratch an itch, that's fine with me.'

'So you want to give our relationship another chance, do you, Rafe?' Eden hissed. 'But how amazing. Nothing's changed. You still expect me to make all the compromises, to follow you around the world, flaunted in the papers as your blonde tart and held at the mercy of your father's contempt.'

'My father is a good man, a great man, and I won't have you sully his reputation with your spite,' Rafe threw at her, his black eyes burning with fury. 'We had something good, something more than just great sex,' he said more quietly, his nostrils flaring with the effort of controlling his temper. 'We could have it again, *cara*, but not while you maintain this hate campaign against the man I respect more than any other. I wouldn't be where I am today without him,' he told her, his voice ringing with emotion. 'I'm trying very hard to accept that I misjudged you four years ago, and that it was Gianni who lied to me, not you. But it's difficult,' he admitted rawly. 'I loved him, yet in the end I couldn't save him or make him happy enough to want to continue his life. Isn't it enough that you've made me doubt my own brother? Don't start on my father, too.'

'So what are you suggesting?' Eden queried tightly. 'That we pick up where we left off, our affair played out in every tabloid that sees us as easy pickings? What did we really have, anyways, other than an energetic love life?'

'We had more than that,' he insisted, and she shook her head sadly as memories crowded back.

'Did we? Most of the time I was bored and lonely. The focal point of my day was when you came back from the track, and I was so unsure of myself, of my place in your life, that I was desperate for your attention. I turned into someone I didn't like very much,' she whispered. 'I was clingy and pathetic, always looking over my shoulder to see who you might be planning to replace me with. I don't want to become that person again, Rafe, and despite what you think I don't want you.'

It would be eminently satisfying to make her eat those words, Rafe thought darkly, and he could, they both knew. Even now she couldn't disguise her quiver of awareness when he moved closer. It would be so easy to sweep her into his arms and carry her to his bed. Her physical resistance would be minimal, but mentally it would be a different matter, and when he made love to her he intended that there would be no barriers between them.

'In that case I'd better help you to your room,' he said coldly, fighting the urge to plunder that wide, sexy mouth with his, to force his tongue between her soft lips and to hell with the consequences.

'I can manage, thanks.'

'*Dio!* Do you have to argue about everything?' His cool was being sorely tested! He wanted to *shake* her until every stubborn, obstinate bone in her body rattled, and with a muttered oath he pulled her into his arms and strode into her bedroom. 'Dr Hillier said you have prescription painkillers, I suggest you take them,' he said shortly, concern replacing his frustration as he noted the shadows in her eyes and the purple smudges beneath them. She looked all in, infinitely fragile, and he wanted to wrap her in cotton wool, although he was sure he'd receive a physical assault if he tried.

'I don't need any pills. I'm just tired, that's all, and stressed,' she added pointedly.

'Make that an order rather than a suggestion. Where are they—in your handbag or the bathroom?'

He was the bitter end, Eden thought furiously, refusing to admit that she felt nauseous and faint with pain. How dare he accuse her of trying to blacken his father's name, when Fabrizzio had done his best to ruin her reputation and had actually labelled her a whore? The Santini blood ran thick, she conceded bleakly, and she was an outsider who could never come between father and son, brother and brother—she didn't even want to try.

'You have two minutes to get into bed while I get you a

glass of water,' he warned from the doorway. 'Any longer and I'll strip you myself, and who knows where that might lead, *cara mia*?'

She had already slipped off her shoes, and the sound of his mocking laughter goaded her into picking one up and hurling it across the room, her disappointment acute when it missed his head.

'When did you gain that temper?' he queried, amusement gleaming in his eyes, and she glared at him.

'The year I spent with you would have incited a saint to commit murder. You were an inspired tutor, Rafe.'

'I'm glad you think so, *cara*, although I think we may be referring to different subjects!'

She should have known that in a verbal sparring match she was no contest for his acerbic wit, she conceded as she struggled out of her dress and into her nightshirt, anxious to ensure she was safely under the covers before he returned.

'What happens now?' she asked huskily when she had swallowed the two tablets under his watchful gaze.

'I go to my bedroom and you go to sleep, with my assurance that I won't disturb your dreams.'

If only! He'd done so for the last four years, why should tonight be any different?

'I mean between us,' she qualified awkwardly. 'I meant what I said, Rafe, there's no future for us.' She wished she could read the expression in those unfathomable black depths, wished she knew what he was really thinking. 'I'll move out of the Dower House as soon as possible.'

His careless shrug screamed his indifference, and she felt a sharp pain in her chest. This really was the end. He'd run out of patience with her—hardly surprising when she'd led him on and then rejected him tonight—and the reality of seeing him walk out of her life for the second time caused tears to well in her eyes.

'There's no rush; I'll be away for the rest of the summer at least and there's a year's lease to run on the house. My driver will take you back to Wellworth when you're ready in the morning, but I have an early flight, so I'll try not to disturb you.'

She must need her head tested, Eden thought dismally as she stared at the proud tilt of his head. Rafe Santini, the man who was idolised by women the world over, had asked her to be his mistress and she had turned him down! Most women would jump at the chance to travel to exotic locations with a sexy, handsome millionaire lover, but she had tried it once and concluded that she wasn't like most women. She wasn't in- terested in the high-profile lifestyle and certainly wasn't in- terested in the money. She didn't want to spend her life shopping for clothes that she hoped would retain her lover's interest and prevent his eyes from straying to the countless wannabes who hung around the track. She just wanted the man, she conceded sadly. She wanted Rafe to love her as she loved him, but his arrogant assumption that he could click his fingers and she would jump to his bidding was proof that nothing had changed. He hadn't loved her four years ago. She doubted he had ever loved any woman. His first love was for racing, for speed and excitement, and the thrill of danger was his overriding mistress.

She needed him to leave her room now, before she did something stupid like throw herself into his arms and promise to become his lover for however long he wanted her. Pride was her only defence against his magnetic pull, and she lifted her chin, determined to hide the fact that she was on shaky ground. 'I guess this is goodbye,' she whispered, and was rewarded with an insolent smile.

'For now, *cara*, but not for long, I think,' he said, his accent very pronounced as he strolled towards the bed. 'How long will it take, I wonder, for you to grow bored with your lonely bed? You'll come back to me, Eden. I know you too well and that passionate nature of yours will make your life hell. I look forward to the day that you come crawling back, *cara mia*. You'll beg me to make you mine again because you belong to me.'

He leaned across the bed and her cry of outraged denial was muffled beneath the force of his lips as he initiated a kiss that was a flagrant assault of her senses. She *hated* him, hated every arrogant, cocksure bone in his body, but by the time she had recovered sufficiently to tell him, he had gone.

CHAPTER SEVEN

WALKING through the front door of the Dower House was like returning to an old friend, Eden thought as she stared up at the mellow, ivy-covered walls that she had so quickly grown to love. Her heart seemed destined to remain in pieces—she couldn't stay in the house and she couldn't have Rafe, although she would happily live in a shoebox if he showed any signs that he wanted more from a relationship with her than just sex.

She handed Nev her formal notice to leave the house, with the request that he keep her posted on any suitable properties she could rent, and after one look at her drawn features he wisely hid his curiosity. Fortunately, summer was a busy time in Wellworth and she spent the remainder of the week covering the vicarage fête, a veterans' cricket match and a scoop about bad drains at the local hospital. After three years reporting on drought and disaster in Africa, it was hard to drum up much enthusiasm for parochial life. Her career was important, she reminded herself. She'd given it up once, caught up in the heady excitement of her romance with Rafe, and she was determined not to sacrifice it again.

If she was honest, she couldn't drum up much enthusiasm for anything, and certainly not food. Her clothes were hanging off her and several friends had asked if she was ill. Only lovesick, she thought grimly—for the second time in four years. But the truth was she hadn't gotten over Rafe the first time and meeting him again had lacerated her already-wounded heart.

She was determined to avoid the television coverage of the Portuguese Grand Prix, and spent the whole of Sunday with Cliff and Jenny and their new baby. She was incredibly lucky, she told herself. She had wonderful friends and lived in one of the most beautiful villages in England. Life was good, and much simpler without Rafe in it, yet later that night she found herself flicking television channels from an amusing comedy to a programme showing highlights of the day's sporting events.

Rafe was in pole position for the start of the race and she experienced the familiar sick feeling in the pit of her stomach as she watched him streak out ahead of all the other cars. Unable to sit still, she wandered edgily between the living room and kitchen, the sudden shout of the commentator causing her to spill an entire carton of orange juice as she shot back to the screen.

'…Santini's off. Rafe Santini, five times World Champion, has crashed at the Portuguese Grand Prix, and I have to say that, from the pictures I'm getting from the scene, it would be a miracle if he emerges from the wreck of his car.'

'No, please, no,' Eden whispered. Where was Rafe? She couldn't see past the throng of track officials but, as the commentator said, it seemed impossible that he could have survived the crash that had left his car a twisted pile of metal.

The programme was showing the highlights, she suddenly remembered. The race had taken place hours before. Rafe could have been dead for hours and she hadn't even known!

'Rafe, get out of the car,' she begged, her heart pounding, and suddenly, incredibly, the crowd of track officials parted and the camera focused on him easing himself out of the protective pod that contained the driver's seat. As he was helped away from the track, the camera closed in on him and Eden sank to her knees in front of the screen. His face was hidden beneath his helmet, so all she could see were his eyes, but as she reached out and touched his image he seemed to stare straight at her and she felt as though she were drowning in those dark, unfathomable depths.

In an instant his image was gone. The programme covered the remainder of the race and then switched to a rugby match, but Eden saw nothing, heard nothing. Shock, fear and ultimately relief had left her so drained that she simply sat in front of the television, her hand resting on the screen as if she could somehow reach through it and touch him. Slowly, she uncurled her legs, wincing as cramps gripped her muscles, and she staggered upstairs, not to her bedroom but to the master suite Rafe had slept in for one night. The misery that she'd held in check all week broke over her in a wave and she cried until her chest hurt and her eyes were red-rimmed. So this was love, she thought bitterly. This agonising fear for his safety and a clawing desperation to jump on the next flight and follow him to whichever corner of the world he was in.

She couldn't live without him, she acknowledged wearily, but neither could she live with him. How could she even contemplate returning to life as his mistress, moving constantly from hotel to hotel and waiting, always waiting for him to finish a race, a Press interview or a function in his honour before she was able to grab his attention for a few brief hours? It seemed that she was forever destined to love a man who was out of her reach, because Rafe didn't love her; she doubted that he ever had. The question that kept her awake for the rest of he night was, could she settle for anything less?

The Italian Grand Prix was staged at Monza and the roads leading to the racetrack were heavily congested, despite the fact that the race wasn't due to start for several hours. Rafe's personal assistant, Petra—a woman who would one day surely be canonised in recognition of her patience—had listened to Eden's request for a ticket to the race without asking any difficult questions. Discretion was Petra's byword and no doubt a necessary part of her job as she tried to unravel Rafe's love life, Eden thought bleakly. But Petra had been one of her few allies during her time with the Santini team, and the following day a VIP ticket and flight details had arrived at the Dower House.

The rest was up to her, Eden acknowledged, and fear lurched sickly in the pit of her stomach. She must be mad, walking of her own accord into the lion's den, and quite possibly Rafe would reject her, but since she'd witnessed his accident she'd been forced to accept that her life without him was no life at all.

Her ticket included a champagne reception and she was whisked off to the VIP box by an official, her heart sinking at the bevy of beautiful women around her. Monza was a big event in Italy's social calendar and the room was full of high-ranking members of Italian society, plus the usual array of models and glamour girls that followed the Formula 1 scene. She couldn't compete, Eden thought bleakly, ready to turn tail and run. Some of the women were truly stunning, tall, tanned, with impossibly long legs and incredibly short skirts. Rafe liked women in skirts—he thought trousers were unfeminine—but Eden had had no option but to wear a trouser suit to hide her scars.

The ice-blue suit had been ruinously expensive but worth every penny for its superb cut, the trousers skimming her curves while the jacket emphasised her slender waist. She looked cool and elegant yet innately sensual with her lacy camisole just visible beneath the jacket, and her hair caught up in a loose chignon.

Compared to the skimpily dressed women in the VIP box, she looked like one of the vestal virgins, Eden decided, but pride forced her to hold her head high and she smiled as she recognised one of the mechanics from the Santini team.

Alonso spoke little English and she wasn't even sure he would remember her after all this time, but as she approached him he grinned and ran his eyes over her, his admiration clearly evident.

'I've come to see Rafe,' she began hesitantly, and he shrugged but picked up on the one word he understood.

'Rafe? You come. He's on the grid.'

Before the start of a race the grid was packed with track officials and celebrities mingling with the drivers. Monza was a big race for Rafe, before his home crowd. He was a legendary figure in Italy and thousands of fans flocked to see him win. Failing them wasn't an option and the sense of excited anticipation in the air emphasised to Eden the intense pressure he was under.

He was leaning against his car, dressed in a white race suit decorated with the logos of his many sponsors, a white cap jammed on his head. He looked bronzed and fit, his black hair just visible from beneath the cap, his eyes gleaming like polished jet as he laughed with the photographers. Around him was a group of stunning, bikini-clad girls, the sashes across their voluptuous bodies displaying the logo of the company they were advertising.

'OK, Rafe, if you could put your arm round Cindy's waist, and Cindy, snuggle up to him, sweetheart, that's it, put your hand on his chest. Great shot, and again.'

At the edge of the group was the one man Eden had hoped not to see, and her heart sank as she stared at Fabrizzio Santini. A Sicilian by birth, Fabrizzio was several inches shorter than his son, but with the same broad shoulders and strong jaw. The son of a peasant farmer made good. His rise to the top, and as the force behind the Santini car company, were well-documented, as was the fact that his marriage to a wealthy heiress had much to do with his success. Even now, with a billion-pound fortune to his name, he possessed a ruthless streak that business rivals feared. He took what he wanted from life, discarding anything he deemed not good enough, and Eden had been top of his junk pile.

'Hey, boss!' Alonso called cheerfully, and Rafe turned his head, his whole body stiffening as he stared at Eden. 'Signorina Eden's back.'

'Is that so?' Rafe crossed his arms over his chest and let his gaze trawl over Eden in a slow appraisal as if she were a particularly curious specimen in a jar. Around him the girls stopped chattering and the photographers fiddled with their cameras, the nuance in Rafe's voice warning them to be ready for what might be an interesting shot. 'This is a surprise,' he drawled. 'What do you want, Eden?'

Beneath his indolent stance he was tense, aggression emanating from every pore, his eyes cold and hard as he waited for her to speak.

'You,' Eden replied simply. She didn't know what else to say other than the truth.

She had the interest of everyone in the crowd now and the models giggled and moved closer to Rafe. The sun beat down mercilessly, forming a shimmering heat haze on the tarmac, and all around race marshals scurried like busy ants. There was no way she could come out of this with any vestige of pride intact, Eden acknowledged as she stared at Rafe and remembered his taunts that she would one day crawl back to him. There was no chink of softness in his expression; he was hard and unrelenting, bristling with injured male pride at the way she had rejected him, and she sighed. He wasn't going to make this easy but her pride had already suffered its last death throes, and abject humiliation before a crowd of gorgeous blondes wasn't going to make much difference now.

'You said you would enjoy seeing me beg for a chance to come back to you,' she reminded him steadily, her eyes focused only on him. 'Well, here I am, begging.'

The giggling grew bolder. A couple of photographers snapped shots of Eden, but she didn't spare them a glance and it was Rafe who moved impatiently, shrugging out of Cindy's hold while a nerve jumped in his cheek.

'No more photos,' he demanded, 'we've finished now.' He strode off, only pausing for a second to glare at Eden. 'Are you coming, or not?' he snapped, and hastily she stumbled after him, unable to decipher his reaction and unaware that Fabrizzio Santini's speculative gaze followed them both.

His trailer was far from luxurious. He might be a multi-millionaire, but there were no airs and graces to him, and he preferred to hang out with the other members of the team. Once inside he headed for the fridge, extracted a bottle of water and flipped the lid before taking a swig.

'Just what the hell are you playing at, Eden?' he growled as he leaned against a cupboard and surveyed her grimly. 'Two weeks ago you were adamant you wanted nothing more to do with me. Why the sudden change of heart?'

'I miss you,' she replied honestly. During the long, sleepless night after his crash, she'd finally concluded that life was too short and precarious. It was only the most incredible luck that had seen her escape with her life after the land-mine explosion, the same luck that meant he'd climbed out of the car unhurt in Portugal. What if one day their luck ran out? she wondered. Wasn't it time to follow her heart rather than her head?

Rafe gave a disbelieving snort and paced the trailer restlessly, pulling his cap from his head and raking his hand through his hair. 'Is that the truth?' he demanded, but beneath the arrogance she caught the faint note of uncertainty in his husky voice, and her heart turned over. He didn't do uncertain, he was the most self-assured man on the planet, yet, incredible though it seemed, her answer mattered to him. Despite the attentions of every gorgeous woman on the circuit, Rafe still wanted *her*.

'I'm not playing at anything,' she promised as she walked towards him. 'All I want is this.' Taking a deep breath, she reached up on tiptoe and drew his head down, her lips seeking his with an air of self-possession that hid her quaking nerves.

He smelled so good—warm and male—the exotic musk of his aftershave stirring her senses. For what seemed an eternity he made no response, his hands clenched by his sides, his mouth set in an inflexible line, and with a growing sense of desperation Eden deepened the kiss, her tongue exploring the contours of his lips before tentatively dipping between them. She'd misread the signs, came the agonising realisation. He didn't want her, and in a few seconds he would thrust her from him, crucify her with his contempt. But just as she was ready to admit defeat, he groaned low in his throat and his arms clamped round her, pulling her hard against him.

As his lips parted Eden felt almost faint with relief, and she sagged against him, allowing him to take control, and he kissed her with a hungry passion that demanded her response.

This was where she was meant to be, she thought with an almost fatalistic acceptance. She was Rafe's woman, and despite the years apart he was the only man she would ever want.

'This time there will be no going back, no changing your mind at the last minute,' Rafe warned when at last he lifted his head and she dragged oxygen into her lungs. 'I'm so desperate for you I could take you right now, in a trailer in the middle of the bloody Grand Prix, and to hell with whoever walks in on us.' He inhaled sharply, his nostrils flaring with the effort of enforcing control over his desire, and Eden reached up to stroke his jaw. 'There's no time, as usual,' he muttered. 'There was never any time for us.'

'We'll make time,' she promised. 'After the race, I'll be here, waiting for you.'

He muttered something in Italian before his mouth captured hers once more and he ran his hands over her body in a fevered exploration, unfastening her jacket to slip inside, and he growled his pleasure when he discovered the delicate camisole and the indubitable proof that she wasn't wearing a bra. '*Cara mia*, I want you so badly I will explode with it,' he muttered rawly, and Eden couldn't disguise her shiver of excitement when he stroked her nipples through the sheer silk of her camisole. She wanted more, wanted him to strip her and take her *now*, but a huge crowd of fans had gathered to see their nation's hero, and her time would come later.

'I'll be here,' she vowed once more, and the rap on the door of the trailer warned her that she would have to contain her impatience, although Rafe's muttered curse told her he was also struggling.

'Why have you really come?' he asked again as he jammed his cap on his head and pulled the peak low, hiding his eyes.

'I watched the Portuguese Grand Prix. You were the highlight of the day.' She closed her eyes briefly, reliving those terrifying moments before she had seen him climb out of the car.

'I wasn't hurt, *cara*, a few bruises, that's all.'

'I know—I spoke to Petra afterwards. But what if you hadn't survived, Rafe? All I would have is my pride. You said you wanted to give our relationship another chance, a fresh start.' She hesitated for a moment and then whispered, 'I want that, too. I'm tired of thinking about the past or worrying about the future, and I don't know how long it'll last between us, but quite frankly I don't care any more. I want you now, today,' she told him firmly, and his mouth curved into the slow, sexy smile she adored.

'I'm a little busy right now, *cara mia*. Can you wait until tonight?'

The Villa Mimosa was situated a half-hour drive away from Milan, in a small village on the shores of Lake Como. The master suite, at the front of the villa, afforded stunning views across the sparkling blue water of the lake, while the back looked over a fabulous private garden and pool. It was an oasis of tranquillity, yet surprisingly close to cosmopolitan Milan, which boasted designer shops and magnificent architecture.

Returning to the villa was like stepping back in time and as Eden glanced around the master suite she was assailed by memories. In this room, she had known heaven and hell! During the year she had spent with Rafe the villa had been home, although they had spent little time in it, but for a few precious weeks after the end of the racing season when she had revelled in the intimacy of sharing his bedroom. Rafe had no doubt employed top interior designers to decorate the villa, but the decor of his suite was unchanged, even to the collection of glass frogs on the dressing table, and Eden felt a curious pain in her chest as she picked one up. They were cheap and gaudy, made from green glass, but she had fallen in love with them in a marketplace in Spain and had been delighted when Rafe had bought them for her. Why had he kept them? she wondered. They looked painfully out of place in the elegant room, but for some reason he had them on prominent display, and she wondered if he ever thought of her when he looked at them.

She set the frog back in its place and studied her reflection in the dressing-table mirror. She had bought the sexy black negligee for one purpose only—seduction—and she had to admit that she looked the part of a sensual siren, but inside she was so nervous she felt sick. It had been midnight by the time they were able to leave the after-race party, and, as the winner of the Monza Grand Prix, Rafe had been in huge demand. Eden had attempted to keep out of the limelight, but he would have none of it and kept her clamped to his side all evening, arousing the curiosity of the Press photographers. Now, finally, they had some privacy, but as the car had swung onto the driveway of the villa she had been beset with nerves, and gladly accepted Rafe's suggestion of a shower.

'Did you find everything you required in the bathroom?'

The sound of his voice caused her to whirl away from the mirror, eyes wide, the pulse at the base of her throat setting up a frantic tattoo as she stared at him. 'Yes, thank you.' She had been stunned to discover her favourite range of toiletries set out in the bathroom, but had told herself it must be coincidence; Rafe was hardly likely to have remembered the fragrance she had used five years ago.

He strolled across the room to extract a bottle of champagne from the ice bucket, and her eyes were drawn to the width of his shoulders, his white silk shirt open at the throat to reveal an expanse of olive skin. If anything, he was even more devastatingly attractive than five years ago. His body was leaner, harder, and the bold expression in his eyes caused a familiar weakness to flood through her. His eyes were telling her that he would make love to her tonight, that there would be no reprieve, and the thought filled her with nervous anticipation, an excitement she could no longer deny.

Rafe's eyes narrowed as he released the champagne cork, noting the way Eden jumped liked a startled doe at the sound. She was not as self-assured as she would have him believe, but he liked that, liked the fact that she was nervous about their first time together after all the years apart. It mirrored his own tension. *Dio!* She was beautiful, he thought as he handed her a glass. He'd fantasised about her body all day, imagined the fullness of her breasts and her long, slender legs which were hidden beneath her trousers. The negligee left little to the imagination and his fingers itched to untie the ribbons that laced the bodice so that her breasts spilled from the black silk. The gown was floor-length, hiding her legs, but not for long, he acknowledged, his heart rate quickening as he mentally stripped her.

He intended to take it slow, to savour every delicious moment, but already he was so aroused that his trousers felt uncomfortably tight and he was filled with a primitive urge to rip the enticing scrap of black silk from her body and take her hard and fast, make her his in a way she would never forget.

'I think tonight calls for a toast,' he murmured, his eyes never leaving her face as he raised his glass. 'To us, Eden— for as long as it lasts.'

His words caused a sliver of ice to run down Eden's spine, but she took a sip of champagne before obediently agreeing.

'For as long as it lasts,' she said coolly, and anything else she might have said was lost beneath the pressure of his mouth. He tasted of champagne, and her already heightened senses went into overdrive as he forced his tongue between her lips in a fierce exploration that forewarned her of his hunger and his overriding need to possess her. She was on fire for him instantly. There was no slow build-up of passion, just a whoosh, like setting a flame to tinder, and she ran her hands over him, her fingers fumbling with his shirt buttons in her feverish desperation to touch his skin. Beneath her fingertips she could feel his heart pounding in his chest. He wasn't as in control as he made out, not quite the all-conquering master he portrayed, but a man enslaved by the burning passion that consumed them both.

'You fill my senses until I can think of nothing but you,' he muttered against her throat when at last he lifted his head and trailed his mouth down to the valley between her breasts. His fingers tugged impatiently at the ribbon that secured the bodice of her negligee, his hands cupping her breasts, moulding them and lifting them so that he could take first one throbbing peak, and then the other, into his mouth. 'I want you now, *cara*, I can't wait.'

The room spun as he lifted her and laid her on the bed and she watched through half-closed eyes as he shrugged out of his shirt before coming down on top of her. She wanted him, too, wanted him with an urgency that shook her, made her forget, but as she felt him tug the negligee over her hips her memory returned with a vengeance.

'I want to keep it on,' she whispered, and heard his low growl of laughter.

'Not a hope. I have spent the last four years fantasising about your body, the whiteness of your skin spread on black silk sheets, ready for me. I want to see all of you, *cara*, every beautiful inch of those long, sexy legs I remember so well.' With a final tug he discarded the negligee and let his gaze roam her body. *'Madre de Dio!'*

Eden squeezed her eyes closed. Hearing the shock in his voice was bad enough without witnessing the revulsion on his face. 'I warned you my leg wasn't a pretty sight,' she said thickly, striving for a light tone and failing miserably.

Still nothing. Rafe's silence was worse than any kind of verbal rejection, and in an agony of despair she opened her eyes to face the look of horror in his. 'You don't have to... I mean, I'll understand if the urge has gone,' she quipped huskily, and his eyes darkened.

'Why do you think I no longer desire you?' he asked, and she twisted restlessly, wanting to drag her nightgown back over her body to hide her scars. 'Do you really think these,' he traced his finger over the scars that criss-crossed her leg, 'would make any difference to my hunger for you?'

'They're horrible,' Eden whispered, blinking back her tears. It was pathetic to cry, especially when she had witnessed the bravery of people with far worse injuries, but she felt so vulnerable. Rafe could take his pick from the most beautiful women in the world, why on earth would he pick her, now? 'The surgeon said they'll fade a little in time, but my leg's a mess and you always were a leg man,' she finished, unable to disguise the wobble in her voice.

'I was always *your* man,' Rafe told her, so forcefully that she stared at him. 'Is this the reason you rejected me in London?' he asked as realisation dawned, and Eden nodded.

'I thought you would be disgusted and I couldn't bear the fact that you would find me ugly.' She sniffed inelegantly and scrubbed her eyes with the back of her hand. As a passion killer it worked wonders, she thought bleakly. She felt cold and devoid of anything but a need to hide herself away to metaphorically lick her wounds, and despite Rafe's protestations he didn't look like a man overwhelmed by passion, either. 'I'll sleep in the guest suite,' she told him, but as she went to sit up he pushed her back against the pillows.

'Neither of us will be sleeping anywhere, not if I can help it,' he informed her coolly, and she watched with wide eyes as he stood up and unzipped his trousers. He took his time. If it hadn't been such an incredible idea she would have said he was doing it deliberately, stripping in front of her with slow, steady intent, and her mouth ran dry when he slid his boxers over his hips and stood naked and magnificently aroused.

'Rafe, you don't have to...' Eden began and he gave a harsh laugh.

'I think it's rather obvious that I do, *cara*.' He knelt at the end of the bed, lowered his head and feathered a line of kisses along the deep scar that ran the length of her shin.

'Don't,' she pleaded, his touch making her flinch, and he stared into her eyes.

'Does it hurt when I touch them?'

'No,' she admitted, 'but they're hardly attractive.'

'They're part of you,' he said simply, 'and I want you,

all of you. If I looked shocked when I first saw your leg, it was not through disgust, it was…' He broke off, searching for the words. '…Compassion, pain, here inside.' He held his hand against his heart. 'I can't bear to think of you lying somewhere, bloodied and hurt. I wasn't there, I couldn't help you.'

He bent his head once more and this time she forced herself to relax as his lips anointed each scar in gentle benediction. By the time he reached the sensitive flesh of her inner thigh she was breathing hard, desire flooding through her so that she moved her hips restlessly and held her breath when he hooked his fingers around the waistband of her briefs.

'You will always be the most beautiful woman in the world to me, *cara*,' he told her, and even if she had not trusted the words, the burning intensity in his dark eyes revealed the depths of his passion. A mixture of relief and joy filled her, banishing the last of her inhibitions, and she lifted her hips, enabling him to draw her knickers down over her hips.

Her skin was creamy and satin-smooth, an erotic contrast to the black silk sheets, and Rafe surveyed her in silence for a moment, a tide of colour running along his cheekbones. 'Four years is a long time, *cara mia*. Have there been many others?' he queried, his voice such a deep, husky growl she could barely make out the words.

She wanted to say something glib, taunt him that her tally of lovers was hardly likely to match his, but there was a curious vulnerability about the way he refused to meet her gaze and she ran her fingers over his jaw. 'Does it matter?' she whispered, and he shook his head.

'No, you're in my bed now and that's all that matters.' He allowed her to guide his face down to hers, and she smiled against his lips.

'You're the only one, Rafe, the only man I've ever wanted.'

'The only man you'll ever know,' he corrected. 'Promise me you'll stay with me, Eden, for as long as I want you.'

Her reply was lost beneath the force of his lips. Her admission that he was her only lover had opened the floodgates and he claimed her mouth in a devastating assault while his hands roamed her body, down over her stomach to slip between her thighs. She was ready for him, slick and wet, and he pushed her legs apart, sliding his hands beneath her bottom to lift her. He entered her slowly, his body rigid with the effort, but by her own admission it had been a long time and he wanted to give her time to accommodate him. His intentions were good, but she was so tight, felt so good, that he was afraid he would explode, and he stilled and rested his forehead against hers, his brow beaded with sweat.

'I don't want to hurt you, *cara*,' he muttered and inhaled sharply as she wriggled experimentally beneath him.

'The only way you could hurt me is if you stop,' she assured him, and he snatched the remnants of his self-control and began to thrust, deep and slow, waiting for her to match his rhythm before he increased the pace.

Eden clung to his shoulders as he drove into her. It was so good—she had forgotten how good—and she twisted her head from side to side, her body arching as he took her higher and higher until her muscles clenched in a spasm of pleasure that ripped through her. 'Rafe,' she cried brokenly as wave after wave kept coming, each powerful thrust causing her to contract around him, and he groaned, his face a taut mask in the seconds before he shuddered with the force of his release.

'You made a promise to stay for as long as I want you.'

Eden tensed. She didn't know what she had expected his first words to be after they had shared such mind-blowing intimacy and she opened her eyes to stare at him uncertainly. Had it all been a power game after all, and, now that he had won, was he going to tell her that she had served her purpose and he no longer wanted her? 'Yes, I did,' she agreed huskily, and watched as his mouth curved into a sensual smile.

'I'll want you for a long, long time,' he warned her. 'Maybe forever.'

'Then that's how long I'll stay,' she said simply, and his smile faded, his eyes darkening as he captured her lips in a kiss that held tenderness as well as passion.

CHAPTER EIGHT

THE Villa Mimosa boasted a fabulous pool, and for the last few days Eden had found plenty of time to admire it. It was a beautiful Italian summer's day. Rafe's housekeeper, Sophia, was on hand to provide tempting delicacies and her paperback was reasonably entertaining. She had everything she could possibly want, she reminded herself, ignoring the voice in her head that pointed out she didn't have Rafe.

He was there at night, of course. She couldn't complain about his lack of attention in the bedroom, or his passion. He made love to her with single-minded dedication, as if he was determined to make up for the years they'd spent apart. In bed, nothing seemed as important as the way he made her feel, the touch of his hands and mouth on her skin, the way he took her to the very edge of ecstasy, prolonged her agony and then tipped her over. When he made love to her she became a mindless, wanton creature intent only on the giving and receiving of pleasure until she fell into a dreamless sleep in his arms.

Sometimes he woke her in the hour before dawn by the simple method of trailing his lips over her already-sensitised skin. Then she would smile sleepily, her body instantly ready to welcome his as he entered her with slow, deep thrusts that quickly fanned the flames of her desire, but when she stirred later the bed was always empty.

He had commitments; she knew that. The time between races was as crucial as the race itself as he worked closely with the designers and engineers to perfect the car's performance. Now he had the added pressure of heading the Santini business interests. He'd explained that his father had suffered a mild stroke, possibly brought on by the devastation of Gianni's suicide, and Fabrizzio was determined to hand over the reins of power to his remaining son and heir.

She understood all of that, so why did the demon in her head whisper that nothing had changed, that their relationship was based on sex, and nothing else? She was acting like a spoilt child, she told herself. Rafe had always lived his life at a furious pace, both on and off the track; she couldn't realistically have expected things to be any different. She hadn't been happy four years ago, but then she had lacked the confidence to tell him. If their relationship was to stand a chance, she would have to speak out and fight for the kind of life she wanted before her self-respect was eroded as it had been once before.

He arrived back at the villa in time for lunch, and as he strolled across the terrace her heart flipped. He looked utterly gorgeous in chinos and a cream shirt that was open at the throat to reveal an expanse of dark chest hair. With his designer shades and the chunky gold Rolex on his wrist he was every inch the millionaire playboy, not a man who would be content to settle for a life of domestic harmony, she conceded sadly.

'*Buon giorno, cara,*' he greeted, leaning down to capture her mouth in a fierce, hungry kiss that drove everything but him from her mind. 'What have you been doing this morning?'

'Swimming, reading…' She kept her tone deliberately light. 'The exercise and sunshine are good for my leg. The scars are definitely fading a bit.'

He settled on the edge of her sun lounger and ran his hand gently over her injured leg. 'Good, I'm glad for you, but I told you, if the scars upset you I'll arrange an appointment with the best plastic surgeon I can find.'

'Do you want me to have surgery?' she asked curiously. He told her endlessly that she was beautiful with or without her scars, but surely, if he was honest, he would prefer her to have the perfect, smooth limbs she'd once had.

He removed his sunglasses and trapped her gaze, a wealth of gentle emotion in his dark eyes. 'If I'm honest…no. Your scars are part of you, an important reminder of the brave and fearless woman you are. You are perfect to me, *cara*,' he murmured deeply, and tears burned behind her eyelids as he bent his head and trailed a line of kisses along each of the welts that criss-crossed her leg.

His lips moved on upwards over her thighs and she held her breath as he dipped his tongue into the sensitive hollow of her navel. The tenure of his caresses changed and she stirred restlessly on the lounger as he unhooked the clasp of her halter-neck bikini and drew the triangles of material down so that her breasts were exposed to his gaze.

'Sophia said she would bring lunch out onto the terrace,' Eden murmured distractedly, finding it hard to think when he cupped each breast in his hands, his olive-skinned fingers splayed in stark relief against the whiteness of her flesh.

'I told her to wait a while,' he said, his voice laced with amusement and a fierce sexual excitement she had only be-latedly recognised.

'But I'm hungry,' she reproached, not bothering to disguise the wicked gleam in her eyes, 'aren't you?'

'Starving, *cara*,' he groaned as he pushed her breasts together, his tongue drawing wet circles around each aureole before he took one hard nub into his mouth. 'Feed me!'

She was on fire for him, desperate for him to discard her bikini pants in the same way that he had done the top, but instead he sat up and ran his fingers down her body, stroking insistently against the clinging Lycra until molten heat flooded between her thighs.

'Rafe! Please…now.' She couldn't wait much longer. He hadn't even touched her intimately, yet she could feel the first delicious spasm of pleasure rip through her and the desire to feel him inside her had spiralled into a desperate, clawing need. Still he sat looking down at her, his eyes hooded as he watched the expression on her face, saw her desperation.

'Lift your hips,' he commanded, his voice as thick as treacle slowly trickling over her, and when she obeyed he pulled her briefs off with quiet intent and ran his hands over her thighs, parting them so that her ankles hung over either side of the lounger. He stood then and stripped, not hurrying, his eyes locked with hers, and she thought she would die with anticipation when he finally lowered himself onto her and entered her with a hard, deliberate thrust. He moved deep within her and then withdrew almost completely so that she gasped his name and dug her nails into his shoulders, urging him to fill her again and matching his steady rhythm. She was so turned on that her control stood no chance and she tipped her head back to stare up at the cloudless sky as sensation built, wave upon wave, her muscles contracting around him, her climax so intense that she sobbed his name and clung on for dear life. He paused momentarily, poised above her, his brow beaded with sweat as he fought for control, and when her first spasms eased he moved again, pumping into her, harder, faster, until he could no longer hold back and felt the glory of release as he spilled inside her.

The sound of his mobile phone shattered the exquisite peace and Eden held her breath as, for a few seconds, Rafe ignored it. He stared into her eyes, his frustration evident, and then muttered an oath and snatched it up.

'Papa.' Instantly he reverted to his native, voluble Italian that Eden couldn't understand, even if she was interested, which she was not. Most of Rafe's phone conversations were with his father and Fabrizzio demanded his son's attention at any hour of the day or, more usually, night. Eden could almost believe he was watching them, somehow spying on them, determined to intrude on the few precious hours they spent alone, and she knew with absolute certainty that Fabrizzio was far from happy about her place in Rafe's life.

She wriggled off the lounger, slid her arms into her robe and headed for the cool of the villa. A shower, something to eat and an afternoon doing…well, she'd think of something, she reassured herself. Rafe would no doubt go to the Santini offices at the behest of his father.

He was waiting in their bedroom when she padded through from the *ensuite*, her hair wrapped in a towel.

'I'm sorry about that. My father—'

'You don't have to explain, I know he's been ill and that you're busy.'

'Not usually this busy,' Rafe murmured, his frown deepening as he swung away from her to stare out of the window. She looked gorgeous, pink and soft, wrapped in a fluffy towel, and he would like nothing better than to unwrap her, inch by delectable inch, and tumble her onto the bed. Their loving would be slow and sensuous this time, but as he felt his body harden in eager anticipation he shut his eyes and willed his hormones into line. Fabrizzio wanted him in the office, ostensibly to go through some paperwork that had suddenly been elevated to urgent, although he couldn't understand the reason why.

For the first time in his life he resented the demands Fabrizzio made. If he was honest, he resented anything and anyone that took him away from Eden, and even the hours at the test track suddenly seemed a chore. At the back of his mind lurked the accusation Eden had made that his father had despised and insulted her. At first he'd angrily discounted her suggestion that Fabrizzio had actively sought to wreck their relationship and had even involved Gianni in his plans. She must have been mistaken, he assured himself. She had been young and shy; quite possibly she'd felt in awe of Fabrizzio's dominant personality and imagined his dislike. His father had always been courteous towards her, hadn't he? It was true he hadn't welcomed her with open arms, but then he'd never hidden his hope that his eldest son would marry an Italian girl. A girl like Valentina de Domenici!

'I have a few days clear before the Indianapolis Grand Prix,' he said as he watched her dress. 'I thought we could explore Venice.'

'Really?' Pleasure glowed in her eyes before her lashes swept down to conceal her emotions. 'Don't you have things to do? Your father…'

'Can manage without me for a few days. Four years ago I made the mistake of not spending enough time with you. I don't want to go down that route again, but I'm afraid I'll be out for the rest of today.'

'Luckily I have a good book,' she said cheerfully, as she anticipated the pleasure of a few whole days and nights of his exclusive company in Venice.

'You could go out,' he muttered, wishing he could stay with her and they could barricade themselves in against the rest of the world. 'You could go shopping. Milan is world-renowned for its exclusive boutiques and most women like to shop,' he finished on a note of frustration that she didn't fit the mould.

'You said you liked me because I'm different,' she reminded him with a smile. 'I'm not interested in your money, Rafe,' she told him softly as she linked her arms around his neck. 'I'm just interested in you.'

Venice had lived up to its reputation as one of the world's most romantic cites, Eden mused as she stretched beneath the tangled sheets and stared up at the ornate carvings that decorated the four-poster bed. She would have been content to remain at the villa, but Rafe was determined to honour a promise he'd made four years before and they'd spent a blissful few days exploring the network of canals that wound through the city.

While the days had been spent absorbing the rich history and culture of Venice, the nights had been no less energetic, and Eden's body ached pleasurably. Rafe's desire for her was like a bottomless well, but she wasn't complaining, and even though he had made love to her several times during the night she smiled at the memory of how he liked to spend his mornings. She rolled over, her smile fading when she discovered the bed empty.

A breeze lifted the voile curtain and she glimpsed him, sitting on one of the ornate chairs on the balcony where they ate breakfast each morning.

'You're up early,' she murmured, coming to stand behind him and sliding her arms over his shoulders.

He made no reply but caught hold of one of her hands and held it to his mouth, his lips warm against the pulse point at her wrist.

'I've been thinking,' he murmured at last, and she felt a *frisson* of apprehension run the length of her spine. Thinking had an ominous ring to it. 'About the past, you and Gianni,' he added quietly.

'I thought we'd agreed to live firmly in the present, but there never was a me and Gianni. I wasn't kissing him by the pool that night and I didn't have an affair with him.'

'I believe you, *cara*,' he said heavily. 'I should have known then that you would never lie. You're the most transparent person I've ever met. You don't keep secrets, not from me. Your mind is as clear as a crystal pool.'

She hoped it wasn't that clear: there was one secret she

could never reveal. Love didn't enter into their relationship and she refused to embarrass both of them with the declaration that he was the love of her life.

'I owe you an apology.' He stood and drew her into his arms, his hands gentle as he stroked her hair. 'I don't know why Gianni wanted to break us up, all I can think is that he wanted you for himself and his feelings were so strong that he was prepared to sacrifice his bond with me.' He paused and she felt his lips on her brow, trailing over her cheek to rest at the corner of her mouth. 'We lost four years. Because of him I threw away something that was very precious to me. You,' he told her when she could only stare at him in stunned silence. 'I trusted his word over yours, but I can't hate him for what he did. *Madre de Dio*, Eden, despite the hurt he caused us both, I still wish he was here and I still miss him.'

'I know,' she cried as she flung her arms round him and held him tight. 'I don't hate Gianni and I certainly don't expect you to. He was your brother. I saw how close the two of you were.'

'But why did he try so hard to wreck the thing that made me so happy—my relationship with you? He knew how I felt about you.'

'I don't know, but he must have had a good reason because he idolised you, Rafe.' Someone must have persuaded Gianni to lie, she thought silently, and she had a pretty good idea of who that someone was, but she could hardly voice her suspicions about Fabrizzio to Rafe again—he was already hurting enough. 'It's over now,' she murmured against his neck, 'and despite everything, we've found our way back to each other. I think we should let Gianni and his secrets rest in peace.'

He kissed her then, an evocative caress that stirred her soul with its tenderness, and she wound her arms round his neck as he lifted her and carried her through to the bedroom.

'I think your suggestion that we concentrate on the present rather than the past is an excellent idea,' he told her as he laid her on the sheets and untied the belt of her robe to part the material with deliberate intent. She said nothing, but her eyes darkened, her lips parting slightly as she watched him shrug out of his own robe and come down on the bed beside her.

'You're the only man I've ever wanted, Rafe,' she whispered, aware that she was in danger of revealing too much, but unable to stop herself. For a few moments she'd witnessed the utter devastation he felt at Gianni's death, a sadness that was now compounded by the realisation that his brother had lied to him, and she wanted to comfort him, show him she cared.

He stilled at her words and then ran his hands lightly over her body, gently nudging her legs apart, and she held her breath as he knelt beside her, feeling the warmth of his breath on the sensitive flesh of her inner thigh.

'Then I'd better make sure the situation stays that way, *cara mia*,' he teased, and proceeded to use his tongue with such devastating effect that she was lost to everything but the mastery of his touch.

Rafe dropped the bombshell as his private jet circled over Milan, preparing to land. He'd spent most of the flight with his mobile phone clamped to his ear and, although she'd been unable to understand much of his conversation, Eden gathered from the terseness of his voice that he wasn't happy. Their few blissful days together were over and reality was pounding on the door.

'I'm hosting a dinner party at the villa tonight, nothing too grand, just a handful of business associates.'

Eden stared at him, unable to hide her dismay. 'How big is a handful?'

He gave a careless shrug. 'Twenty or so guests.'

'Do you think you could have given me a little more notice?' she demanded, the surge of panic that swept through her making her snappy. 'How am I going to organise a dinner party in a couple of hours? You know I can't cook.'

'You don't have to do anything, *cara*. It's Sophia's job to deal with these things, and out of kindness to her I ask that you keep well away from the kitchen.'

'Thanks,' Eden said huffily. She might be a hopeless cook but he didn't have to emphasise the point. She felt hurt that he hadn't found it necessary to consult her. It brought home how unimportant she was in his life. He didn't need her, that much was obvious, especially when he had his unflappable housekeeper to deal with his domestic arrangements. She felt like a spare part, superfluous to requirements except in the bedroom, and he couldn't have shouted any louder that to him she was simply his mistress. 'I still think you might have warned me,' she muttered, and he sighed.

'I didn't know myself. My father only sprang it on me this morning that he'd arranged for the dinner to take place at the villa rather than his own home.'

Fabrizzio, again—Eden sniffed. 'Does he often do things like that, expect you to be constantly at his beck and call?'

Never before, was the truthful answer, and Rafe stared

moodily out of the window as the limousine whisked them back to the villa. 'My father's been ill, the heart scare last year shook him, and he's no longer a young man,' he told her shortly. 'It's understandable that he wants me to increase my involvement in the Santini business. I can't race forever and, now that Gianni's gone, I am the sole heir.'

His phone rang again, demanding his attention for the remainder of the journey, and he gave her a distracted glance when they arrived at the villa.

'You don't have to worry about a thing, *cara*. Everything's taken care of. Why don't you relax by the pool for a couple of hours until the guests arrive?'

'Next you'll be patting my bottom and telling me not to bother my pretty little head,' she snapped furiously. 'I know where I'm not wanted, Rafe. I'll just keep out of the way. Are you sure you can put up with my embarrassing presence at dinner, or would you rather send a bowl of gruel up to my room later?'

'*Dio!* You have developed the tongue of a viper,' he roared, his temper exploding like a volcanic eruption, his accent very pronounced as he rounded on her. 'Four years ago you would never have—'

'Answered back?' she suggested sweetly, and received a furious glare.

'I'm sorry I didn't let you know earlier about the dinner party,' he stated more quietly as he took a deep breath. 'But it's only for a few hours, and you're behaving like a spoilt child.'

'I know,' she yelled. She really didn't need him to point it out so she swung her back on him and marched out to the pool. As she passed him he made to stop her, but his phone rang again and, with a torrent of Italian words that she guessed she wouldn't find in the dictionary, he let her go.

It took twenty lengths of energetic swimming before Eden's temper dissipated, and she must have fallen asleep on the sun lounger, waking with a start to discover that it was six o'clock. Rafe's guests were arriving at seven, she remembered with a groan as she hurried up the steps of the villa. She needed to shower and do something with her hair. If she was going to be paraded in public as Rafe's mistress, she was determined, for the sake of her self-respect, to look as good as possible.

She flew across the marble hall, remembered she'd left her handbag in the sitting room and changed direction, coming to an abrupt halt just inside the door as four startled faces met her gaze.

'I'm so sorry.' Her cheeks flooded with colour and she edged backwards, vainly trying to hold her sarong in front of her to cover her tiny gold bikini.

Rafe had jumped to his feet while the other three men, Fabrizzio and two associates, stared at her expressionlessly. 'Eden, I thought you were upstairs, dressing for dinner.'

'Obviously not,' she quipped, trying to disguise her mortification with a smile. 'I must have fallen asleep by the pool.'

Fabrizzio Santini sat back in his chair and surveyed her clinically, as if she were a prize heifer in a cattle market. '*Buona sera*, Eden. Rafael mentioned you were staying at the villa for a while.' He paused fractionally and then murmured, 'I hope you are recovering well from your accident. I see you have been left terribly scarred.' The solicitude in his voice disguised the sting, but Eden felt it anyways and immediately tried to hide her injured leg behind the other one, lost her balance and would have fallen but for Rafe's biting grip as he caught hold of her arm.

Round one to you, Fabrizzio, she thought darkly, not taken in by his smile, and as soon as she had stepped through the door she shrugged free of Rafe's hold.

'What are you playing at? I thought you were getting ready,' he hissed, and she glared at him, her temper at boiling point.

'I told you. I fell asleep. I didn't get much last night, if you remember. There's still an hour until your guests arrive, apart from the early birds,' she added sarcastically. 'And was it really necessary for your father to mention my leg?'

'*Dio*, you are impossible sometimes. He was offering his sympathy, and no doubt trying to draw attention away from the fact that you were cavorting through the house half naked in front of the company's bankers,' said Rafe coldly. 'You'd better go and shower. And don't argue, you don't have time.'

Boiling him in oil would be too good for him, she thought bitterly half an hour later as she struggled with the zip of her dress. He was the most arrogant, annoying, chauvinistic male she'd ever met, and the tears that stung her eyes were from anger, not the loss of the closeness they'd shared in Venice.

To her amazement, dinner was not the ordeal she had dreaded. When she walked down the sweeping central staircase Rafe was waiting at the bottom for her and for a moment was unable to disguise the flare of hunger in his eyes as he took in her full-length, white halter-neck dress that displayed her curves and golden, tanned shoulders. Far from him wanting to hide her away, his voice rang with quiet pride when he introduced her to the array of business associates and their wives, and gradually Eden felt herself relax.

Fabrizzio was surprisingly courteous; indeed, it was he who insisted that everyone should speak in English rather than Italian, in deference to Eden, and Rafe felt his tension ease. Eden was wrong about his father. She'd obviously misunderstood his attitude towards her four years ago but she was older now and her new confidence meant she would be better equipped to deal with the strong-willed old man.

There had been no subterfuge between Fabrizzio and Gianni. No covert plan to rid her from his life. Gianni had lied; he had to accept that along with the fact that he would never know why. But his little brother had tried to make amends. He recalled a conversation between them months before Gianni had taken the overdose. In the throes of a deep depression, Gianni had suddenly taken great interest in his life and had questioned him on his future plans, what he would do when his racing days were over and the likelihood that he would marry and give Fabrizzio the grandchildren he longed for. Rafe had shrugged, his answer noncommittal, not daring to point out that Gianni had wrecked his relationship with the only woman who had ever been more to him than a brief diversion. Maybe his brother had understood more than he let on, he mused.

'Eden was always the girl you believed her to be.' Gianni's words still rang in his head, hardly an admission that he'd lied, but they had added weight to the decision he'd already made to find her, if only to bury the past and all its bitterness for good.

It was late when Rafe's guests departed, and Eden gave a

deep sigh of relief as she wandered into the sitting room and kicked her shoes off before collapsing onto the sofa. It had been a good evening, better than she'd hoped for, and she smiled as a slight movement from the terrace caught her attention.

'Rafe, what are you doing out there?'

'Rafael is taking a phone call in his office.' Fabrizzio Santini walked through the French doors and Eden's smile faded at the cold contempt in his eyes.

'I see,' she murmured quietly, and he gave a harsh laugh.

'I wonder if you do, Eden. Tell me, how long do you intend to act as my son's whore this time?'

'I don't need to listen to this.' Eden jumped up and headed for the door. Four years ago his patent dislike of her had unnerved her and she hadn't dared to stand up for herself, but a lot had changed since then. 'I don't know what you have against me, but out of respect for Rafe I think you should keep your feelings and your insults to yourself.'

She made to sweep past him but he gripped her wrist, so hard that she knew she would find bruises there later. 'I will not stand by and watch my son make a fool of himself over a cheap little nonentity,' he informed her in his gravelly, heavily accented voice. 'I thought I'd succeeded in getting rid of you four years ago, and I tell you now, Rafael will never marry you.'

Appealing to the swarthy Sicilian's softer side was a waste of time, Eden acknowledged. Fabrizzio wouldn't rest until he'd evicted her from Rafe's life once more and he was cunning enough to manipulate events in a way that wouldn't alert his son's suspicions. Attempting to convince Rafe of

Fabrizzio's hatred of her would be futile. Rafe adored and respected his father, the Santini blood ran thick and, although he had finally chosen to believe her over Gianni, his loyalties would be stretched to breaking point if she asked him to choose between her and Fabrizzio.

Fabrizzio's biggest fear, it seemed, was that Rafe would marry her. If only he knew how unlikely that was, she thought bleakly. There was no chance, and even less now that Fabrizzio had thrown down the gauntlet. Somehow she had to convince the older man that he had nothing to fear from her, that marriage to Rafe was the last thing she wanted. At least then he might leave them alone and wait for the affair to run its course.

'Actually, I have no intention of marrying your son,' she said coolly, and Fabrizzio gave her a disbelieving glare.

'I find it hard to believe that you don't want to get your claws into the Santini fortune.'

Eden shrugged. 'The price is too high. I don't want to live my life in a goldfish bowl, my every move reported in the tabloid Press. I'd be happy to settle for an English country house, a few acres of prime estate that I can cash in if necessary.'

Fabrizzio stared at her with his beady black eyes, as if he could see inside her head, and she shivered but held her ground, determined not to feel intimidated. 'And you think Rafael will buy you this house?'

'I'm working on it.'

'Perhaps I should warn my son that his English rose is a mercenary little bitch, available to the highest bidder.'

Nausea swept over her at his vile insinuations, but she lifted her head and met his gaze. 'Perhaps he already knows,' she suggested coolly. 'You have nothing to fear from me, Signor Santini. My relationship with your son is based on the most primitive of needs. To put it crudely, Rafe will slake his appetite and I will expect payment. I grew out of dewy-eyed romanticism a long time ago—four years ago, to be precise.'

Fabrizzio Santini had probably never been lost for words before, and Eden took pleasure in his momentary uncertainty. The expression on his face would be funny if she wasn't so close to tears.

'So for both of you it is a casual sexual liaison.' He assessed her with a speculative gleam in his eyes. 'Forgive me, but I'm not convinced. Four years ago you were in love with my son. What's changed?'

'I have, signor. I've grown up.'

She made her escape then before she broke down and spoilt the illusion that she had a heart of stone. A shower washed away her tears but it was harder to scrub Fabrizzio's contempt from her skin, and she wondered just what she'd done to make him despise her so much. The simple answer was that he was desperate for his remaining son to produce grandchildren with aristocratic Italian blood, and he'd seen her as a threat. Now that the threat, the fear that Rafe would choose her as his wife, was gone, perhaps he would leave them both alone.

There was no sign of Rafe when she slid into bed, and she guessed he was still working before they flew to Indianapolis for the next race of the season. She wished he would come to bed—she needed his solid strength and the reassurance of his touch—but eventually she fell asleep alone, and it was the early hours before he entered the bedroom to stare down at her with eyes that were as bleak as midwinter.

CHAPTER NINE

INDIANAPOLIS in August was hot and dusty. The car wasn't performing well; Rafe didn't make pole position on the grid, and, in an effort to lead the race, he pushed the engine too hard. Eden spent an agonising few minutes watching flames spew from the back of the car before he ground to a stand-still, relief overwhelming her when she saw him climb out and stride away from the track.

'You're lucky you didn't burn to death,' she told him when they returned to the hotel. The heat and tension made her feel snappy and Rafe's unconcerned attitude didn't help.

'No one burns to death in Formula 1—the safety measures are stringent,' he said coolly as he headed for the shower. 'I'm more at risk of being nagged to death.'

'That's not fair.' Determined to keep his attention, Eden followed him into the *ensuite*. 'You have no idea what it feels like to watch a car go up in smoke, knowing you're still inside, although why I care beats me.' She glared at him, hands on her hips, her anger dissolving as she watched him shower. His body was to die for, she conceded, her eyes drawn to the way the soapsuds slid over the powerful muscles of his abdomen and then lower, down his thighs. She felt a familiar heat pool inside her and hastily dragged her gaze back to his face, mortification scalding her at the amused glint in his eyes. He knew exactly what she was thinking.

'Do you care, *cara*? I didn't realise.' That hateful, mocking tone that he used whenever he spoke to her lately was back, and she bit her lip.

'I know you're in a foul mood because you lost the race, but actually you've been pretty unpleasant since we left Italy,' she accused miserably. She didn't understand the reason for his sudden coolness towards her, but the closeness they'd shared in Venice had vanished and, although she'd asked him countless times, he simply shrugged and denied anything was wrong.

Persuading him to confide in her was like banging her head against a brick wall. He'd perfected stubbornness to a fine art and she was reduced to racking her brains for anything she might have done to upset him. All she could think of was the dinner party he'd hosted at the villa. His guests had been top executives from the business world, bankers, lawyers, and members of the highest echelons of Italian society. Had she inadvertently embarrassed him? she wondered. Admittedly, she'd felt nervous to begin with, but she hadn't made any major *faux pas*, like using the wrong fork or drinking from the finger bowl.

Perhaps the sight of her in her chain-store dress and costume jewellery had brought it home to him that she didn't fit in his world. She remembered how he had tried to persuade her to wear the pair of exquisite pearl and diamond drop earrings he'd presented her with.

'I'd be terrified of losing one,' she had argued as she adamantly refused to try them on. 'If the sole reason you want me to attend this dinner party is to display the signs of your wealth then let's forget this relationship here and now.'

Being flaunted in public as his mistress was one thing, but she was determined to hang on to her self-respect, and she couldn't do that with speculation on just how she had earned such expensive gifts.

'Are you ashamed of me?' she demanded huskily now, and he frowned and reached for a towel.'

'Of course not. What a ridiculous thing to say,' he snapped. 'Why do you think I might be?'

'I don't wear haute couture or expensive jewellery like the wives of the executives who attended the dinner party.'

'You could have done. It was your choice not to wear the earrings I bought for you and you have several credit cards at your disposal to buy clothes.'

'I know, but I prefer to pay for my own things. I've told you I'm not interested in your money.'

'So you have,' he murmured, and she blinked at the barely leashed fury behind the words. 'Your parsimony is admirable, *cara*. Sometimes I wonder what you do hope to gain from our liaison—apart from sex, that is.'

'That's a foul thing to say.' She had followed him through to the bedroom and stopped dead, hurt beyond belief at the deliberate cruelty in his tone. It was as if he was intentionally trying to upset her, and doubts formed thick and fast in her head. Had he tired of her? Had she served her purpose and he was pushing her away, preparing her for the end of their affair? He hadn't made love to her since their trip to

Venice, and celibacy didn't agree with him, which could only mean one thing. 'Are you seeing someone else?'

'*Madre de Dio*, when would I have the time? You have an insatiable appetite, *cara*,' he murmured silkily, and she felt a tide of colour stain her cheeks. He made her sound like a nymphomaniac.

'Well, I'm sorry if I'm too much for you,' she said stiffly.

'Your eagerness to climb into my bed is flattering but sometimes I wonder if there's an ulterior motive behind it. Can you think of anything, Eden, anything you haven't told me?'

She shook her head in genuine confusion. 'You're talking in riddles, I don't know what you mean.'

He strolled across the room towards her and she couldn't drag her gaze from the minuscule towel around his hips that left little to the imagination.

'Perhaps it'll come to you,' he suggested blandly, 'and in the meantime I have no objection to satisfying your more primitive urges.'

There was something about this conversation that evoked vague memories, a hidden message in his mocking tone that she couldn't grasp.

'That's not a very nice thing to say,' she whispered, her eyes trapped by his dark, unfathomable gaze, and his slow smile sent ice slithering down her backbone.

'I don't feel very nice right now, *cara*.' His arm snaked out before she had time to react, his hand gripping her hair to yank her up against his chest. Droplets of water clung to his dark chest hair, heat and the exotic scent of the shower cream he had used assailing her senses, and to her abject shame she wanted to bury her face in him and breathe him in. 'Let's do something about those urges, shall we?' he breathed against her throat, but as she shook her head, murmuring a despairing protest, his fingers tightened in her hair.

'Don't even try to tell me you don't want this,' he hissed, his lips grazing her skin as he spoke. 'In this, at least, be honest, Eden. I watched you watching me in the shower and you're desperate, aren't you?' His mouth closed over hers in a kiss that warned of his absolute mastery, and pride demanded she resist, but her body had a will of its own and it was past caring about anything other than assuaging the driving need to feel him inside her.

He was breathing hard when he finally released her swollen lips, and his eyes travelled over her in a slow, assessing appraisal before he gripped the neckline of her dress and wrenched the material from her shoulders so that the buttons that fastened the front flew in all directions.

'Rafe! You didn't have to tear it.' His barely suppressed violence should have appalled her, yet to her shame she was filled with a fierce excitement. He would never hurt her, she knew that, but she recognised the urgency of his desire and it fanned the flames of her own.

'I'll buy you another,' he muttered as he dispensed with her bra, his eyes narrowing as he absorbed the rounded fullness of her breasts. 'Rest assured, I can afford you, *cara*.'

'I don't want your damned money,' Eden cried, desperately trying to cling to the edge of sanity while his hands cupped her breasts, and she drew a sharp breath as he lowered his head and lathered one nipple with his tongue before drawing it fully into his mouth.

'So you keep saying, which only leaves sex, because there's nothing else between us, is there?' His vicious taunts made her recoil and she tried frantically to pull away. In reply, he tugged a fistful of her hair until her back arched and he was able to torment her other breast, suckling hard so that she teetered on a fine line between pleasure and pain.

'Rafe, I don't want it to be like this,' she pleaded, 'not when you're angry and I don't even understand why.' He stiffened at her words but instead of releasing her, he scooped her into his arms and dropped her onto the bed. With one deft movement he stripped her of her knickers and pushed her legs apart with firm intent, before unwrapping the towel from his hips. He was all proud, arrogant male, fiercely aroused, and Eden closed her eyes in despair as the ache between her thighs throbbed unbearably.

'So stop me,' he challenged, his voice echoing the hardness in his eyes, and she swallowed.

'I can't,' she admitted on a sob of humiliation and misery at her own weakness, and he entered her with one powerful thrust.

Without the touch of his hands and mouth to arouse her, she was tight but no less ready for him and a groan was wrenched from him as her muscles closed around his shaft. He shouldn't have done that, shouldn't have taken possession of her so fiercely without any foreplay. Disgust at his own brutality made him attempt to withdraw, but she wrapped her long legs around him and held him fast.

'Don't stop,' she whispered, a husky sob leaving her when he continued to stare down at her, his body held still. 'What is it, Rafe—do you want to hear the words, do you want to hear me beg? All right,' she threw at him, her anger suddenly matching his, 'please don't stop, please make love to me…Rafe.' Her words were lost beneath his lips as with a muffled oath he initiated a kiss that drugged her senses, hot and passionate, demanding her response. She had no thought to deny him and kissed him back with a hunger that bordered on desperation, her body arching as he began to move within her, thrusting deeper and deeper, driving her to the edge, and she sobbed his name as he sent her hurtling over. He was right behind her, her name a savage imprecation torn from his throat as he slumped on top of her. But seconds later he rolled off the bed and marched into the *ensuite*, slamming the door behind him, and only then did she bury her head in the pillows, determined that he wouldn't hear her cry.

They had flown to Indianapolis on a chartered plane with the rest of the team rather than on his private jet, and on the journey home he avoided her, spending the time talking to the chief engineer. Eden was glad. They had nothing to say to one another, apart from goodbye, because he couldn't have demonstrated more clearly that their relationship was over.

As they were coming in to land he slid into the seat next to her and she instantly stiffened. He was invading her personal space and, worse still, the heat that emanated from his body and the clean, fresh scent of him made her want to bury her face against his chest.

'Are you all right?' he asked in a low, husky voice that even now did strange things to her insides. 'I behaved like an animal last night and I…' He hesitated and raked his hand through his hair. If he hadn't been so damned arrogant, she would have sworn he felt awkward. 'I should apologise.'

'Well, don't make a meal of it, I know how hard you find it to admit you're in the wrong.'

'I'm in the wrong?' He bristled with outraged pride, and heads turned at the sound of his raised voice. With a supreme effort he took a deep, calming breath and tried again. 'I'm trying to, how do you say, pour oil on the fire?'

'The expression is pour oil on troubled waters—pour oil onto a fire and it'll burn itself out, rather like our relationship, wouldn't you say?'

'We need to talk,' he muttered, and she gave a hollow laugh.

'We *needed* to talk,' she corrected. 'It's a bit late for that now. I don't know what terrible crime I've committed to make you so brutal, but I refuse to play mind games. You won't say what's bugging you, and after last night I really don't care any more.'

He visibly flinched at the word 'brutal,' his eyes dark and tortured, and she quickly looked away, fighting the compassion that was seeping through her. He'd always had a hot temper, her mind pointed out. He was a volatile Latin male and his mood swings were legendary, but although he hadn't hurt her physically last night, the mental wounds ran deep. She was his mistress, useful for only one thing, and she didn't think she could live that way for much longer.

At the airport they were whisked through Security but as they entered the main concourse she was blinded by flash bulbs as they were surrounded by a frenzied pack of Press reporters. It wasn't an unusual situation—Rafe was a national hero in Italy, and he only had to sneeze and it was headline news—but today the paparazzi's interest seemed to be focused on her.

Rafe hurled a stream of instructions to his bodyguards as he slung his arm around her shoulders and hauled her close, practically carrying her across the vast hall, but the reporters dogged them insistently, snapping at their heels like a pack of hyenas. This was a side of journalism she loathed, Eden thought as someone thrust a copy of that day's paper into her hands, and as she glanced at it the world tilted on its axis.

It would be hard to find a more unflattering photograph of her, she thought sickly as she studied the front page. It had been taken on the steps of the hotel in Indianapolis. Rafe looked every inch the playboy heartthrob in his dinner suit, and she was slightly behind him, hanging on to his arm and staring up at him with bleary eyes. She looked drunk, she noted disgustedly, although in fact she had been tired and miserable and had just tripped over a step.

Inside the front cover it got worse: pictures of her in her bikini that left little to the imagination and a horrific close-up of her scarred leg. But the photo that hurt most of all was the one taken in Venice. She was lying back in a gondola, seemingly smiling up at the camera, although in reality she'd been smiling at Rafe, and what had been one of the most romantic moments of their trip appeared tacky and distasteful. She looked like a hooker about to sell her wares.

'Oh, God!' she whispered, and Rafe snatched the paper out of her hands.

'Ignore it, it means nothing.'

'It means a lot to me—the pictures are *horrible*. I feel…*defiled*. I can't imagine how they got hold of them. It's as if someone was spying on us.'

'The paparazzi are everywhere,' he told her bluntly when

they finally reached the car and the chauffeur opened the door for them to bundle in. 'Their intrusion is just part of life.'

'Not my life,' she said quietly as she scanned the paper. She didn't speak much Italian but the written word was easier to follow and it was quite obvious that the article was a scurrilous, no-holds-barred account of their love life.

'Life in a goldfish bowl,' he murmured almost to himself, and she frowned, trying to remember where she'd heard the phrase before.

'They didn't get hold of this information by chance. Someone must have fed it to them, tipped them off about our trip to Venice. But who knew about it—only me and you?' She came to an abrupt halt, nausea churning in her stomach. For reasons she didn't understand he had been angry with her, but he wouldn't hurt her so cruelly, would he? 'Rafe, you didn't…?'

'*Madre de Dio!* That you could think even for one minute that I would do such a thing emphasises how little trust there is between us,' he said savagely.

'Then who, Rafe? Because someone has tried to humiliate me and they've damn well succeeded. Who else knew we were going to Venice?'

His father had known, whispered the insidious voice in Rafe's head, and he furiously blanked it. Not his father, no way. Fabrizzio might have disapproved of his relationship with Eden four years ago, but things were different now; he'd demonstrated that at the dinner party when he'd been so friendly towards her.

'Did you tell your father?' They arrived at the villa and she followed him up the front steps, her face a mask of misery that tugged at his heart even as he angrily refuted her suggestion.

'Leave my father out of this. Is it insecurity that makes you so jealous of my closeness to him, in the same way that you resented the bond I shared with Gianni?'

'No,' she denied furiously, 'but he doesn't like me. To him I'm just your whore. He told me that on the night of the dinner party,' she added shakily, quailing at the bitter contempt in Rafe's eyes.

'Was that during the conversation I overheard, in which you told him you were prepared to prostitute yourself for the sake of a house—I assume the Dower House?' he added silkily, and her legs buckled so that she collapsed in a heap on the marble floor of the hallway.

He made no move towards her, simply stared, his face a mask of arrogant indifference, and she bit back a sob. 'It wasn't what you think,' she whispered sadly. 'Fabrizzio's greatest fear is that you might choose to marry me rather than an upper-class Italian girl. I'm convinced he was behind Gianni's lies four years ago and I was certain he'd try to break us up again. I was trying to convince him that I'm not a threat.'

'You didn't need to go to such extraordinary lengths, *cara*,' he told her coldly. 'I could have told him that myself. You're the last woman on earth I'd choose for my wife.'

Eden sat at the kitchen table and cried until the tears ran dry and she was left with a pounding headache and red eyes. Rafe had disappeared into his office, the resounding slam of the door warning her she wouldn't be welcome, but she had no intention of trying to speak to him. It would be a waste of time. She didn't know exactly how much he had heard of her conversation with Fabrizzio, but obviously enough to condemn her without giving her the chance to explain how she really felt about him.

The bitter truth was that he wasn't interested and, even if she could find the evidence to prove Fabrizzio had been behind the Press tip-off, Rafe didn't want to know. He was a Santini and he would defend his family above all else. He adored his father and even now, when her heart was in pieces, she couldn't hurt him by forcing him to accept Fabrizzio's darker side.

'*Signorina.*' A tentative voice broke through her misery and she forced a watery smile as Sophia set down a cup of frothy cappuccino in front of her. She had established a firm friendship with Rafe's housekeeper but she was startled by the trace of tears on Sophia's cheeks. 'It is my fault,' Sophia sobbed, followed by a stream of Italian that Eden couldn't comprehend. 'The newspaper stories are so unkind and you are so upset, and it is my fault, I think,' Sophia managed to explain in her broken English.

'But how?' Eden queried gently. Sophia might have inadvertently revealed information about her life with Rafe to the media, but she would not have knowingly spoken to a reporter when she knew how much Rafe loathed the paparazzi.

'Signor Santini—we were talking, joking a little about how you were always too busy to eat the meals I prepared,' she confided with an embarrassed air. 'And he was interested to know when you were going to Venice.'

'Which Signor Santini?' Eden asked carefully. Rafe had

made the arrangements for the trip; he'd hardly have needed to discuss it with his housekeeper.

'Signor Fabrizzio,' Sophia whispered fearfully, glancing around the kitchen as she spoke, and Eden put a reassuring hand on her arm.

'Thank you for telling me. I promise you won't get into any trouble, Sophia.'

It only confirmed what she had already thought, she mused as she dragged herself upstairs and pulled her clothes out of the wardrobe. Fabrizzio had somehow been behind the newspaper article, but she would never convince Rafe of that. She spent the rest of the day alternating between misery and a growing anger that history was repeating itself. Fabrizzio had done his best to oust her from Rafe's life once before and she had let him do it without a fight, without defending herself. Against all the odds, Rafe had searched for her, he'd wanted to give their relationship another chance, and despite everything that had passed between them since she couldn't forget the closeness they'd shared in Venice.

He had been so tender, so *loving*, she recalled as a tiny flicker of hope burned in her chest once more. The exquisite attention he paid to making love to her and the softly spoken words he'd whispered in his native Italian were not the actions of a man who just wanted sex. Surely it had meant something special to him, as special as it had been to her, and she couldn't walk away from him again without one last attempt to bridge the chasm that had opened up between them.

As Eden took her place at the dinner table that evening, Sophia imparted the news that Rafe wouldn't be joining her. He'd left in a hurry an hour before, the housekeeper explained, and he'd given no indication of when he would be coming back. By midnight Eden had worked herself into a state of emotional meltdown, filled with a new determination to force Rafe to listen to her. His non-appearance stretched her already overwrought nerves and she paced the floor of the guest bedroom she had moved into, listening for the sound of his footsteps on the landing.

By one o'clock her imagination had clicked into overdrive as she pictured him with one of the gorgeous blondes who followed him avidly whenever he went out. He had to have found a bed somewhere, she reasoned, although it was debatable that he was sleeping in it. The thought of him making love to another woman made her feel physically sick and she hurried downstairs, wondering if he'd left a clue to his whereabouts in his study.

The sight of him sitting behind his desk knocked the air from her lungs as she stumbled to a halt in the doorway. But it was the haggard, almost shell-shocked expression on his face, and the emptiness in his black eyes, that made her gasp.

'Do you know what the time is? Where have you been?' Trepidation, mingled with relief that he was home, lent a sharp edge to her voice, and he stared at her, his eyes narrowing at the sight of her slender form.

'You sound like a nagging wife rather than an obedient mistress,' he murmured unpleasantly, and she flushed.

'Have you been drinking?'

He glanced at the half-empty bottle of whisky on his desk and poured a liberal amount into a glass before downing it in one gulp. 'I would say so, wouldn't you, *cara*?'

She should leave things until the morning, when they

might both be in a calmer frame of mind, but she'd been working herself up for a showdown all night and the temptation to fight her corner was too strong to deny.

'You have to listen to me,' she demanded, walking across the room to stand in front of his desk. 'I know it's not what you want to hear, but I can prove your father was behind the revolting articles in the papers. I know he set Gianni up to lie to you four years ago, and even persuaded him to kiss me in an effort to convince you to end our relationship.'

'He's obviously a busy man,' Rafe said with dangerous calm, and too late she recognised the burning fury in his eyes, her reactions too slow as he shot round the desk and gripped her shoulders. 'But not any more,' he continued, his temper barely constrained, and she winced as his fingers bit into her tender flesh as he shook her. 'My father suffered major heart failure late this afternoon. He's on a life-support machine and it's debatable whether he'll make it through the night.'

'Oh, God, I'm sorry.' She covered her trembling lips with her hand as the full horror of Rafe's words hit her. What if she had accused Fabrizzio unfairly? In her heart she knew she hadn't; he would have done anything to wreck her relationship with his son, and the clinical part of her brain noted that he'd even managed to suffer a heart attack at the right moment. Rafe would never listen to her now, and in all fairness she couldn't expect him to. All that mattered was that his father recovered, and, desperate to comfort him, she reached up and touched his face.

He recoiled as if she had struck him, and she shivered at the contempt in his eyes. 'Don't you dare offer meaningless words of sympathy when we both know how much you hate him. My father is dying and still you insist on trying to poison my mind against him,' he hissed, his teeth clenched as he sought to control his fury. 'But you're wasting your breath, Eden. I gave you the benefit of the doubt over Gianni—don't expect me to do it again.'

CHAPTER TEN

How could the sun still shine with its usual brilliance? Rafe thought as he stepped out onto the terrace. How could the bougainvillaea bloom with such fiery colour? His life was falling apart, yet the world looked on indifferently.

His parents' house had always been dark, but today it seemed like a mausoleum, and he was glad to escape its gloom, even though the sunshine affronted him. Children's voices, high-pitched with laughter, jarred the still air, followed by the hushed tones of their nanny as she tried to quell them. They were his cousin's two little boys—Marisa was in the house with his mother—and as he watched them playing he snatched a glimpse of the past. He saw two boys racing across the lawn on their bikes, each so determined to win that hurtling over the handlebars into the fishpond was a small price to pay for victory. He heard the booming laughter of the man who had urged them on, and the impish chuckles of his little brother.

'*Il Dio li benedice*—God bless you, Gianni,' he whispered huskily, past the boulder that had lodged in his throat. There was a curious pain in his gut—he felt as if he had been punched in the stomach—and his eyes were gritty and sore from the lack of sleep that was impossible while his father's life hung in the balance.

'Rafe!'

He tensed as a voice as cool and clear as a mountain stream slid over him, and for a moment he closed his eyes in despair. Eden! Wherever he turned she was there, quiet, gentle, bringing an air of calm to the huge, extended Santini family, who had gathered at his father's house to wait for news. Somehow, incredibly, since the night of Fabrizzio's heart attack a shaky truce had developed between them, down entirely to her steady insistence that she would not leave him while his father fought for life.

He wanted to shout and rave and tell her he didn't need her false pity, but, God help him, he needed her the way he needed oxygen to breathe and nothing, it seemed, could shake his intrinsic belief that she was the other half of his soul.

'The hospital just phoned with an update. No significant change,' she said softly, coming to stand beside him, and as he caught the drift of her perfume some of his tension drained away.

'You should go back to the villa,' he growled. 'It's a madhouse here.'

'I want to stay with you…I want to help.'

'I must go back in, my mother…'

'Is with the priest and her sisters. She wants you to go back to the villa for a few hours, Rafe. You need to eat and get some sleep.'

She was so beautiful, Rafe thought, so gentle in her compassion that his heart turned over. He had been unnecessarily cruel in Indianapolis, had behaved like a barbarian, and he closed his eyes, trying to shut out the knowledge that he must have hurt her, although even then she had been so responsive he ached at the memory.

'I need you.' The admission was wrenched from him. He was a strong man, proud and fearless—he had never needed anyone in his life until now—and Eden gave a low murmur, understanding his distress, as she wrapped her arms around him.

An hour later they returned to the Villa Mimosa to be greeted by Sophia's tear-stained face. Aware that Rafe had had enough, Eden took charge and steered Sophia to the kitchen with the request that she prepare something to tempt her master's appetite.

'I thought you'd agreed to a shower and a couple of hours' sleep?' she demanded as she caught Rafe heading for his study, where the phone rang constantly.

'There are people I need to speak to before the Monaco Grand Prix,' he argued.

'Petra has been your personal assistant for years, so she's perfectly capable of dealing with your calls, and you've been the head of the Santini group in all but name for months, ever since your father's first stroke. What's so important that you need to deal with it today?'

'Why do you care?' he asked huskily as he followed her up the stairs, and she stopped outside the master suite she no longer shared with him, staring at him with gentle compassion.

'I don't know,' she answered truthfully, remembering the hurt he'd inflicted. 'All I know is that I do.'

'I'll only go to bed if you come with me.'

The request shook her, the temptation to communicate in

the most basic, honest way tugging at her emotions, but she couldn't keep giving. He would drain her dry. 'You need to sleep,' she reminded him lightly, unable to hide the tremor in her voice. 'I'll come up and see you later.'

He slept for an hour and joined her for dinner, although he barely did justice to the meal Sophia had prepared before he returned to the hospital.

The next day followed a similar pattern until Eden received a phone call, Rafe's voice laced with pain as he explained that Fabrizzio had suffered another attack and was hanging on to life by the most tenuous of threads.

Eventually Eden went to bed. She had heard nothing more and dreaded the sound of the phone ringing, but sleep was vital if she was to be of any help to Rafe. She woke several hours later and fumbled for her watch to discover that it was three in the morning. Moonlight filtered through the shutters, slanting pale beams across the bed, and in its silver gleam she saw Rafe sitting, shoulders hunched, at the end of the mattress. The expression on his face, his silent agony, caused her heart to clench and her one thought was to comfort him as she moved to kneel behind him, sliding her arms around his neck.

'Is there any news on Fabrizzio's condition?' she asked fearfully, and he nodded.

'A slight improvement. He's from tough Sicilian stock and he won't give up his grip on life without a fight.' There was admiration in his voice, an affection he had never tried to hide, and she hoped with all her heart that, for his sake, Fabrizzio would make a full recovery.

'I'm glad,' she said simply, and he turned his head, his mouth searching for hers with an almost fevered desperation.

'I want to make love to you, *cara mia*. You have no idea how much I need the soft sweetness of your body right now.' His words were slurred with a mixture of exhaustion and pent-up emotions that were clamouring to be released, and she understood his need to find solace in the one place that provided sanctuary for both of them.

Perhaps it was a natural reaction, a reaffirmation of life, and she couldn't deny him when her own body was instantly on fire for him. He needed her and that was all that mattered.

He pulled her onto his lap and kissed her; long, slow kisses that drugged her senses and made her feel boneless and weak with longing.

'I hurt you in Indianapolis,' he muttered thickly against her throat. 'I was rough, brutal, and I am ashamed.' He lifted his head and she was shaken by the depth of emotion in his eyes, the self-loathing, and sought to reassure him.

'You didn't; I wanted you every bit as much as you wanted me. I think I rather proved that,' she added, her cheeks growing pink at the memory of her wild response to him.

'I'll be gentle this time,' he insisted as he scooped her up into his arms and strode into his bedroom. 'I have done things, said things to deliberately hurt you, yet you've shown me nothing but kindness while I pray for my father. Your compassion humbles me, *cara*. We need to talk.'

Eden reached up and laid her finger across his lips. 'Not now, Rafe; you once said that we communicate better without words and it's time to let our bodies speak.'

He shrugged out of his robe and untied the ribbons that fastened her silk negligee so that her breasts spilled into his hands while his lips found hers in a kiss that was full of ten-

derness, contrition and a plea for forgiveness. Passion overwhelmed her, stark and intense, desperate for fulfilment, and
she gasped as he moved lower to suckle her nipple with
gentle insistence until it was a hard, throbbing peak. When
he transferred his attention to the other she arched and dug
her nails into his shoulders as heat pooled between her thighs.

She wanted him now, her hunger white-hot, and she lifted
her hips in mute supplication, needing to feel him inside her.

'I won't rush it this time,' Rafe promised deeply. 'I will
make sure you are ready for me.'

'I am,' she muttered. She was in agony with wanting him
but he was determined to make amends for the last time,
when he had taken her with such selfish disregard for her
pleasure. Eden deliberately opened her legs and tilted her
hips, her heart thudding as she felt the rigid hardness of his
arousal against her thigh, but instead of entering her he caught
her two hands in one of his and lifted her arms above her
head.

'Patience,' he growled as he laved one throbbing peak and
then the other with his tongue while his hand slipped between
her legs and parted her, gently, delicately, before pushing
inside. His fingers explored her in an erotic dance and Eden
whimpered and tried to control the ripples of pleasure that
were building inexorably. She wanted to drag him up her
body so that he had no choice but to enter her, but her hands
were still pinioned behind her head and she twisted restlessly, almost sobbing his name as her climax neared its crescendo.

On the edge of ecstasy, he slipped his fingers out, the
weight of his chest a welcome burden as he drove into her,

slow, deep, filling her until she thought she would explode, and every thrust sent her higher and higher until restraint was smashed beneath the force of her contractions. Still he continued with his steady rhythm, although she was aware of the hoarseness of his breathing, his pace increasing, faster, deeper until he cried out her name and she clung to him while his body shuddered with the force of his release.

The aftermath was so sweet, she had never felt closer to him and knew she would never love anyone as much as she loved him. But did she have the courage to reveal how she felt, to tell him she had never stopped loving him throughout all the years apart, and was it really what he wanted to hear? She lay still, stroking his hair, and her heart missed a beat as she felt wetness against her neck, felt his shoulders heave as he finally gave in to the fear he felt for his father's life.

Over the next few days Fabrizzio stunned his doctors and family alike with the speed of his recovery. He still had a long way to go, but with his life no longer in imminent danger Rafe lost his look of haunted anxiety.

After the passionate night they had spent together, Eden had hoped their relationship would survive the traumas of the past few weeks, but Rafe seemed curiously reluctant to be alone with her. It was as if he regretted his display of emotion that night and hoped she hadn't read too much into it. He made no attempt to make love to her again or persuade her to move back into his bedroom, and her last vestige of pride meant that she refused to suggest it.

Pride made a lonely bedfellow, she conceded miserably after spending another night missing him so badly that she *ached*, not just for the pleasure he could give, but also for the feeling of oneness with the man who had captured her heart. He was polite and friendly but curiously distant, and in the run up to the Monaco Grand Prix she was forced to accept that they could never go back. Too much damage had been inflicted on a relationship that had been on shaky ground to start with.

On the day before they flew to the principality he received a visitor, a man she assumed to be a business associate, although Rafe never introduced her to him. After that his attitude towards her changed even more. He was excruciatingly polite and solicitous during the flight but the barrier he had erected between them seemed impossible to penetrate and she knew with a heavy heart that when the race was over it would be time to return to England to pick up the pieces of her life.

They arrived in Monaco to face a barrage of Press photographers as the world speculated on whether Fabrizzio Santini's close shave with death would affect his son's performance on the track. They needn't have worried, Eden thought bleakly as Rafe took the lead early on in the race and drove with a mixture of skill and sheer disregard for his safety. She only relaxed when he shot past the chequered flag, feeling as physically drained by nervous tension as if she had competed herself.

This was his life, she acknowledged as she watched him stand triumphant on the podium, spraying the crowd with champagne and grinning at the girls who flocked round him. He was a millionaire playboy with the world at his feet and, although she loved him more than life, she couldn't spend any more time chasing him round the world as his very public mistress, waiting for him to tire of her.

When they arrived back in Milan he escorted her over to the limousine but didn't slide in next to her.

'I'm going straight to the hospital,' he told her. 'Apparently Fabrizzio is sitting up in bed, demanding to take back control of the company.'

'Do you want me to come with you?' she asked, and he shook his head.

'Not this time; I want to see him alone. There are a few things we need to discuss,' he added, his expression suddenly grim. He didn't enlighten her further, but why would he? She wasn't part of his family, and now that Fabrizzio was recovering there was no need for her to hang around. His coolness towards her made that clear.

The villa was in darkness when Rafe's powerful sports car swung through the gates and roared up the driveway. No doubt Sophia would have retired to bed long ago, he thought grimly, a glance at his watch revealing that hours had passed since he had visited his father at the hospital.

What about Eden—would she have waited up for him? he wondered as he raced up the stairs. He should have phoned her but he'd been in shock, genuinely devastated by the conversation with Fabrizzio, and the only way he knew how to exorcise his demons was with speed. He must have covered hundreds of miles just racing up and down the motorways. Driving was second nature to him, the thing he did best, and while his attention was focused on the road he couldn't think about Eden and the way he had wronged her.

He didn't like guilt. It didn't sit comfortably on his shoulders, he conceded darkly as he pushed open the door of the guest bedroom that Eden had moved into. The bed was empty, stripped of its sheets, and a bolt of fear, greater even than when he'd heard of his father's heart attack, swept through him as he flung open the wardrobes and discovered they were bare. He had been preparing for the fact that she might decide to leave after he had spoken to her, after he'd revealed that he now knew the truth, but he hadn't expected to come home and find her gone.

Numbly he stumbled into the hall, his heart quickening as he saw the stream of light from beneath his bedroom door and he threw it open with such force that it creaked on its hinges. For a brief, joyous moment he thought she had moved back into the room they had once shared, but the suitcase lying open on the bed dashed his hopes.

'I wondered when you would turn up, or if you'd even bother,' she said coolly, carefully avoiding his gaze, but when he looked closely he noted the streaks of tears on her face and his heart turned over.

'Where did you think I'd gone, *cara*?' he asked gently, and she shrugged.

'I'm sure you have dozens of names in your phone book, you'd never be stuck for female company, Rafe.'

'The only company I want is yours,' he said forcefully.

'Oh, please! Let's not pretend that I'm anything other than a temporary diversion. I'm your mistress, nothing more, as you so clearly pointed out.'

'The night we arrived back from Indianapolis I was angry,' he began, but she shook her head wildly, and for the first time he noticed the perilous control she had over her emotions. She was practically breaking up before his eyes and he only had himself to blame.

'You were angry before, during and after Indianapolis,' she accused him furiously. 'I'm tired of always trying to pre-empt your moods, and nothing excuses your treatment of me. You blow hot and cold so fast I never know where I am with you,' she continued as weeks of hurt and frustration finally spilled over. 'While your father was ill I thought you actually needed me, but you don't need anyone, do you, Rafe? I provided a useful shoulder to cry on but since Fabrizzio has shown signs of recovery I'm no longer required. Your attitude towards me this last week is proof of that.'

It was proof that he had been left reeling from the information the private investigator had unearthed. He'd learned the day before they flew to Monaco that he had misjudged Eden so badly, he didn't stand a chance of winning her forgiveness. Not only that, but since he had demanded the truth from his father he now knew that he had misjudged her twice, the first time four years ago. The guilt he felt had been hard to handle; he didn't know how to approach her or where to start in begging for another chance, and his remorse had made him seem distant and aloof. Four years ago he had refused to listen to her, and he could hardly blame her for wanting to extract a bitter retribution.

'If you want proof of the way I feel about you, this is it,' he said calmly as he walked towards her, and she gasped as he pulled her into his arms and took her mouth in a devastating assault that left her trembling. 'This is all the proof we need,' he insisted when she stopped fighting and sagged weakly against his chest, but the tears in her eyes warned him the battle was far from won.

'The great sex was never in dispute,' she said quietly. 'But I want more than that, I deserve more. I don't want to be afraid to open a newspaper because there might be another picture or damning article about me. You didn't even defend my name, Rafe, you didn't care who was responsible for setting a photographer to spy on us in Venice. As your mistress I'm public property and I've decided to quit.'

'I know who set the paparazzi on us,' he told her urgently when she picked up her suitcase and headed for the door. 'And I have taken steps to ensure nothing like that will happen again. I would willingly protect you with my life, *cara mia*, and you will never suffer hurt like that again, I promise you.'

Eden studied him for several minutes, as if the blinkers had been removed and she was looking at him for the first time, and from her expression he guessed she didn't like what she saw. 'I don't believe you,' she replied with simple finality, 'and I want to go home.'

The sun was low in the late-September sky. It bathed the mellow stones of the Dower House in a golden glow and danced among the leaves that were beginning to turn russet in colour. She would miss the garden most, Eden thought as she wandered across the lawn and stepped through the French doors, before locking them for the last time. Nev would keep an eye on the house until the new owners moved in; he'd let slip that the sale had already gone through and, although he had assured her there was no rush for her to move out, it was time to go.

She watched the taxi turn into the drive with a sinking heart. Funny how she'd never really believed this day would come. She had clung to the pathetic daydream that Rafe would materialise and declare his undying love for her, but the reality was that he had spent the last month jetting around the globe in his bid for a sixth World Championship title. His decisive victory in Japan had sealed his place as one of the most successful Formula 1 drivers of all time and his picture had been on the front page of every newspaper, the obligatory blonde beauty at his side.

'Ready to go, love?' the taxi driver called cheerfully. 'I'll put your suitcase in the boot.'

'I'll just check I've locked the windows,' she murmured, furious with herself for giving in to the urge for one last look round. This had never been her home and it was ridiculous to feel so sentimental about it. It was a family house, a house that should be filled with children, but they wouldn't be hers and it was time to stop wishing for the moon.

She frowned when she came back downstairs to hear voices from the drive. Surely Nev would have told her if the new owners were arriving today? The bright red sports car caught her attention first—it was hard to miss—and her disbelieving gaze turned to find Rafe and the taxi driver practically coming to blows over her suitcase.

'Do you want me to stow it in the boot, or don't you?' the driver demanded belligerently.

'Yes!' Eden shouted as she stepped outside.

'No! Not yet,' Rafe qualified, and the driver let go of the handle in disgust.

'Well, when you've decided, perhaps you'll let me know,'

he snorted as he climbed into the car and turned the radio on. 'I'll just sit here and listen to the cricket while you make up your minds.'

'I've got a train to catch,' Eden warned, striving to sound cool and hide the fact that she was actually trembling. 'What do you want, Rafe?'

'Five minutes of your time,' he asked, with such serious intent in his eyes that she knew arguing with him would be pointless. 'I thought you loved this house,' he murmured as she led the way into the sitting room. 'I thought it was the reason you came back to me. That's what you told my father,' he reminded her, and she paled.

'You know why I said those things,' she whispered.

'To convince Fabrizzio that our relationship was a casual affair that meant nothing to either of us, rather than a prelude to marriage?'

'Yes.'

'Because you feared that if he saw you as a threat he would engineer a way of breaking us up, like he did four years ago? Only then, of course, he persuaded Gianni to help him,' Rafe said slowly, and she caught the note of pain in his voice.

'I honestly believe he did it because he thought it was best for you. He wanted you to marry an Italian heiress, not an English vicar's daughter with no social standing,' she replied hastily. Even now, after everything, she hated to see him hurt, and discovering that the father he idolised had betrayed him must be agonising.

'Actually the main reason he disapproved of my relationship with you was that he feared there was a high risk that any children we might have would be handicapped. He knew that your brother, Simon, was confined to a wheelchair, but not the reason for it,' Rafe added, his eyes never leaving her face. 'It doesn't excuse what he did, but it's an explanation of sorts.'

'Simon was hurt in an accident,' Eden said dazedly.

'I know and so does my father, now. He's also aware that, whatever the reason for Simon's condition, it would never have dissuaded me from wanting to marry you.'

'I see,' she murmured, still not really understanding why he was here. The real reason their relationship had foundered hadn't changed. He hadn't trusted her or believed in her and ultimately he didn't love her. Those things were a requisite of any relationship she embarked on from now on and she gave him a brisk smile, wishing that the sight of him didn't hurt so much. He was the sexiest man on the planet, she thought ruefully, but sadly she wasn't the only woman to find him so—the queue went twice around the block and she was tired of getting trampled on.

'I really have to go, so if that's all…'

'Of course it's not all.' The old Rafe exploded back on the scene, arrogant, demanding, his eyes flashing fire as he raked his hand through his hair and fought to contain his temper. 'I am trying to say I'm sorry,' he told her, faint outrage in his voice that she hadn't realised. 'I'm trying to make amends for the way I hurt you. Here,' he pulled an envelope from his jacket pocket and thrust it into her hands, 'this might explain things better.'

Eden stared at him and then slowly scanned the enclosed documents, her heart thudding in her chest as she carefully replaced them in the envelope and handed it back to him. 'It's a nice gesture,' she said huskily, her throat tight with suppressed tears, 'but no, thanks.'

'They are the deeds to the Dower House. I've bought it for you,' he yelled, as if raising his voice would make her understand.

'I know, and I can't accept it,' she replied with a calmness she didn't feel. 'You don't have to pay me off, Rafe, I came to you willingly, both times.'

'I'm not trying to pay you off. *Madre de Dio*, you are the most impossible woman I have ever met.' He glared at her, all powerful, dominant, angry male, and she tore her gaze from his mouth. She would not give in to the temptation to reach up and kiss him even though she yearned to with every fibre of her being. Loving him didn't mean it was right and his next sentence confirmed that.

'I haven't bought it for you alone—it's for us, for when I'm in England.'

It sounded worse and worse, he was planning to set her up as his resident mistress for when he happened to be passing through—a bit like a housekeeper with extracurricular duties, and the terrible thing was, she was tempted.

A glance at her watch revealed that time was getting on and she hoped the taxi driver wasn't charging her by the hour. 'I'm sorry, Rafe, but I'm not interested and if I miss my train I'll be late to check in at the airport.'

'I thought you were going to London. Your estate-agent friend told me you've got a job with a news agency,' he muttered as he followed her out of the front door.

'I have, but not in London.'

'So where—somewhere in Europe?'

'Sierra Leone,' she admitted. 'The news agency has asked me to write a series of special reports on the situation there.'

'Over my dead body, *cara*; it's too dangerous.'

'It will be over your dead body if you don't move out of the way of the taxi, and as for dangerous…' She broke off as words failed her. 'You're a racing driver, for heaven's sake! Don't talk to me about dangerous when I've stood at the trackside and watched you risk your life driving at ridiculous speeds for *entertainment.*'

'That's the other thing I came to tell you. I'm holding a Press conference tomorrow to announce my retirement from racing but I wanted you to be the first to know.'

He didn't know what he had expected her reaction to be— surprise, shock…he dared even hope for some indication that she was pleased, but instead she stared at him blankly as if he'd announced he was giving up eating chocolate. 'Well, I suppose you are getting on a bit,' she remarked finally, and the last vestiges of his patience went up in smoke.

'*Dio!* I can't do anything right. I buy the house you love and you throw it back in my face. I give up racing, the thing you hate most, and you act like you don't care.' He ran a shaky hand through his hair as Eden climbed into the waiting taxi. He needed some feedback here, some indication of her feelings, and adrenalin coursed through him as he tasted fear. This was the most important event in his life and losing wasn't an option.

'Tell me, *cara*, what do I have to do to make you come back to me?' He thrust his head through the open window of the car to glare at her, and Eden closed her eyes in despair. Another minute and she would be asking the driver to take her suitcase out of the boot again.

'You have to love me, like I love you,' she whispered, unable to hold back the tears as the car pulled away. 'It's all I ever wanted, Rafe, and the one thing you could never give me.'

She asked the man to drive away and was too busy scrubbing her eyes to take much notice of the passing scenery but the taxi driver suddenly braked sharply and muttered an oath.

'Road hog,' he shouted as he climbed out of the car. 'I recognise you now; you're that racing-driver bloke. Nice car,' he added with a sniff.

'Have it,' Rafe thrust the keys under the driver's nose as he slid behind the wheel of the taxi. 'I don't need it any more. I need a nice, safe, family car, isn't that right, *cara*?'

'I think you need to turn this car around and take me to the station,' Eden said shakily. 'What are you doing, Rafe?'

He made no reply but shot down the narrow country lanes so fast that she closed her eyes and when she opened them they were back outside the Dower House.

'Put me down,' she pleaded when he scooped her into his arms and carried her into the house. It was embarrassing enough that she had told him how she felt without him treating her like a rag doll, which was exactly how she felt right now.

'Of course I love you, you crazy woman,' he yelled, his temper at a simmering point as he headed for the stairs. 'My love for you was never in doubt.'

The look of stunned shock on her face told him she'd had plenty of doubts and still did, and his frustration disappeared, to be replaced with a rush of tenderness for the woman who was his very reason for living.

'*Ti amo, cara mia.* I see I'm going to have to work on your Italian,' he murmured gently. 'I've been telling you I love you for months, and in my dreams for years.'

Eden wriggled frantically in his arms, needing to escape him before she crumbled. 'You don't have to say it to make me feel better.'

'I'm saying it to make me feel better, *cara.* You are my life, my love and you have been since you fell through my hotel window and assured me that you were not a fan,' he told her softly and she swallowed at the depth of emotion evident in his dark eyes.

'But you didn't trust me, you believed I'd cheated on you with Gianni and you were so cruel. You broke my heart,' she accused huskily, and he lowered her to her feet, his arms around her holding her tight against his chest.

'If it's any consolation, I spent the next four years in purgatory. I missed you so much but Gianni had been horrifically injured and I couldn't leave him. It seemed wrong to search for happiness when he had none but I never forgot you, not for one day, and when I learned that you'd returned to Wellworth I knew I had to find you.'

'Have you really retired from racing?' Eden asked wonderingly. 'It's the most important thing in your life, Rafe, and I don't want you to make that kind of sacrifice for me.'

'You are my life, *cara.* Nothing else comes close. It's no sacrifice; I'm not giving up racing for you, but because I would rather be with you, in an English country house that we'll fill with our children.' His lips claimed hers in a kiss that touched her soul. Hungry, passionate yet filled with such tenderness that she knew with utter certainty that he was speaking the truth. Incredible as it seemed, this amazing, charismatic, infuriating man really loved her.

'Marry me?' he asked huskily as he trailed a line of kisses down her neck to the pulse that beat frantically at its base. She hesitated, the wariness back in her eyes. 'Your father...' she began, and he tilted her chin to stare down at her as if determined to blind her with his love.

'Knew that I wanted to marry you four years ago and that no other woman has ever come close. He also knows that his only chance of holding his grandchild is if I can persuade you to become my wife. Trust me, *cara*, he's hoping and praying you say yes.'

She had always loved this room, Eden thought as she glanced around the master bedroom that Rafe had used for the one night he'd spent at the Dower House. After he'd gone she had slept in his bed, desperate for some link with him, and she smiled as he laid her on the silk counterpane of the four-poster bed.

'Are you hoping I'll say yes?' she queried as he struggled with the buttons that fastened her blouse before impatience took over and he tugged so that the tiny pearls pinged across the room. He caught the remnants of uncertainty in her voice and sought to reassure her in the way he knew best, his lips caressing hers with tender passion until there was no room for doubt.

'Not hoping, *cara mia*, expecting,' he told her as his glorious arrogance bounced back. 'You are my other half, the keeper of my soul, and I love you with all my heart. You have to say yes because I will spend the rest of my life hounding you until you do and there are so many more pleasurable ways that we can spend our time.' He proceeded to demonstrate some of them and she linked her arms around his neck as he trailed his lips over her breasts.

'I won't waste time arguing, then,' she said breathlessly, lifting her hips obligingly so that he could dispense with her skirt. 'I love you, Rafe,' she whispered, and drowned in the emotion in his dark eyes as he made them one.

'And I love you, *cara mia*, always, for the rest of my life.'

THE MILLIONAIRE'S
SECRET MISTRESS

BY
KATHRYN ROSS

Kathryn Ross was born in Zambia, where her parents happened to live at that time. Educated in Ireland and England, she now lives in a village near Blackpool, Lancashire. Kathryn is a professional beauty therapist, but writing is her first love. As a child she wrote adventure stories and at thirteen was editor of her school magazine. Happily, ten writing years later, *Designed with Love* was accepted by Mills & Boon. A romantic Sagittarian, she loves travelling to exotic locations.

Don't miss Kathryn Ross's exciting new novel, *Italian Marriage: In Name Only*, available this month from Mills & Boon® Modern™.

To my editor Kate, with thanks.

CHAPTER ONE

'I BELIEVE you're going speed dating tonight?'

The casual question was asked just as Lucy was preparing to go into the boardroom to deliver what could possibly be one of the most important presentations of her career.

'How on earth do you know that?' she asked abstractedly, and hoped her cheeks weren't bright red with embarrassment.

'Mel in Accounts told me.' Carolyn seemed blithely unaware of her discomfort.

Not for the first time Lucy felt as if she was working in a giant goldfish bowl. 'Well, it's just a bit of fun.' She shot a look around the busy department to see if any curious eyes were flicking her way. But thankfully it was Friday afternoon and everyone was at the far end of the office, all eyes and ears on computer screens and telephones, so that they could make a fast exit at five-thirty.

'It's about time you started to have some fun,' Carolyn continued unabashed. 'You've been working too hard recently.'

'Well, I suppose we all have. This takeover by EC Cruises has made us all worry about our jobs.'

'You're not kidding. I've hardly slept since the announcement last month and I'm not even in management.'

'I'm sure we will all feel better next week when the new owners come in to talk with us. Maybe there won't be any redundancies and things will tick along the same as before.'

'That's not what they are saying on the grapevine,' Carolyn muttered. 'They say EC Cruises are ruthless; they gobble up their competition and tear them apart.'

Lucy had heard that too. She had read up on the company last month and the facts hadn't been pleasant. 'No use worrying about that now,' she said firmly, trying not to think about it. 'We have other things to concentrate on at the moment.'

She glanced up and noticed that the MD and some of the members of the board were making their way down the corridor towards the boardroom. Carolyn was right: she had been working relentlessly hard. She had put months of preparation into her report for this afternoon. She just hoped it all hadn't been a waste of time now that the company had been taken over.

'I wish I was able to block things out the way you can, Lucy. You are always so cool and confident in a crisis.'

'Do you think so?' Lucy shook her head. There had been times when she had felt anything but cool and confident.

'Definitely. For example every time I look at that rat of an ex-husband of yours, I marvel that you are able to stand seeing him here every day in the office.'

'I've just come to terms with it.'

'You were always too good for him,' Carolyn continued dryly.

'Thanks for the vote of confidence, Caro.' Lucy smiled at her friend and closed her briefcase. Would she ever get away from the spectre of her ex-husband? she wondered.

As she glanced up through the glass partition she saw the object of her thoughts heading down the corridor. Kris was six years older than her, thirty-five now, and still a good-looking man if you liked blue-eyed men with blond hair. Personally, Lucy was completely off that type...in fact she was completely off men at the moment.

It was only the fact that her friend Mel wouldn't take no for an answer that was making her go speed dating tonight.

'You only have to give each man three minutes,' she had said coaxingly. 'And if you don't like any of them you go home and you don't need to see them again.' It sounded good in theory. Three minutes was about all the time she wanted to give to any man anyway.

Kris wasn't on his own, she noticed now. Another man had walked down the corridor to join him. He was taller than Kris, and broader. Lucy had always thought Kris had a good physique, but next to this guy he looked a bit weedy. In fact next to this guy he seemed to almost pale into insignificance.

Who was he? she wondered. As she stared at him he turned and their eyes met through the glass partition. He was very attractive: dark intense eyes, dark hair and a square jaw. He looked Spanish or maybe Latin American. He smiled at her and she gave a brief smile back and then hastily looked away.

The one thing she didn't need was complications at work. She had enough of those.

As if to prove the point, Carolyn was still going on about her ex-husband and how he'd probably regret what he'd done one day.

'Carolyn!' Lucy cut across her swiftly. 'If you don't mind I really don't want to talk about this…especially in *here*.' Lucy shot another look around the room. Whoever had designed open-plan offices should be taken out and shot, she thought forcefully.

Carolyn followed her gaze and grimaced. 'Sorry.' She mouthed the word. 'I'll ring you later.'

'Yes, good idea.'

Lucy put the letter she had brought her onto a spike with more force than was necessary. Carolyn was a nice person and a good friend, but she did go on too much. And Lucy was tired of being the focus of gossip. Surely people should be getting tired of discussing her marriage breakup by now?

One thing was for sure: she would never, *ever* date anyone at work again. Not that Kris had worked here when she had started dating him. That was another galling fact. She had been the one who had helped him get a job here.

Concentrate on work, she told herself fiercely. Kris and his blonde bombshell were welcome to each other. Holding her head high, Lucy picked up her briefcase and headed for the boardroom.

She was wearing a pinstriped dark trouser suit with a plain white blouse. Her long dark straight hair was caught back from her face. A few men looked over at her with interest as she took her place at the polished table, but she was unaware of their admiring glances. She was too busy getting out papers, going over last-minute figures in her mind.

Kris stepped in through the door behind her. 'Ah, Lucy, there you are,' he said briskly, as if she had been hiding in some dark corner of the universe. 'Mr Connors, I'd like you to meet the head of our marketing department, Lucy Blake. Lucy, this is Mr Connors who is visiting us from the new company headquarters in Barbados.'

Getting to her feet, Lucy found herself face to face with the man who had smiled at her in the corridor and a very strange thing happened. Everything flew out of her mind and she found herself forgetting how annoying Kris was, forgetting even where she was…and instead drowning in the most incredibly sexy dark-eyed gaze she had ever met.

'Pleased to meet you, Mr Connors.' She hadn't imagined it earlier—this man was simply gorgeous. Lucy was quite tall and there weren't many men who could make her feel petite, but he was one. He had to be well over six feet. His hair was thick and dark with a slight wave and his features were somehow powerfully arresting.

He smiled back at her and she noticed that his lips seemed to have a dominant curve that hinted at a strong sensuality. What would it be like to be kissed by such a man? she wondered hazily. To be taken into his arms and…well, just taken? Her stomach gave a wild flip of emotion.

Horrified, she unhooked her eyes from his. Never in her life had such a strange frisson of awareness shot through her. Maybe she had been on her own for too long, she thought wildly. To make up for it she put on her best, brisk, businesslike tone. 'Welcome to the London office.' She held out her hand.

'Thank you.' He looked as if her crisp formality amused him. But he enveloped her hand in a firm grip. 'And please call me Rick.'

Lucy didn't allow her hand to rest in his for a minute longer than was absolutely necessary. Somehow the touch of his skin against hers was deeply unsettling. But she inclined her head and murmured, 'Rick,' in acquiescence. Even the sound of his name on her lips seemed dangerously provocative somehow.

There was a moment's silence as she just stared up at him.

'Mr Connors is here to evaluate the way things are run in London.' Kris cut into the silence. 'He'll be with us for about a week and during that time it would be appreciated if you would give him every assistance, by answering his questions and taking time to show him exactly how your department works and has contributed towards making us one of the most successful cruising lines in the business.'

Why did Kris sound as if he'd just swallowed one of her brochures? Lucy wondered irately. She glanced up at him and he gave her a warm look of approval. Totally false, of course, Lucy reminded herself.

'Certainly.' Lucy steeled herself to look at Rick Connors again.

He smiled at her. 'Well, that's the gist of things, but we can be a little less formal about it.'

Was he Spanish American? she wondered. With dark,

smouldering looks like that she would have thought so, yet his name wasn't Spanish and his deep attractive tone was more mid-Atlantic, making it hard to place where he was from.

The MD, John Layton, came over to speak to them. 'Good to see you again, Rick.' The two men shook hands. 'I see you've met Lucy. She is an invaluable member of the team…invaluable. And she is going to kick things off for us today with a presentation on this season's forthcoming cruises.'

'Yes, so I believe, and I'm looking forward to it,' Rick drawled. Something about the way he said that, the way he looked at her, made an extra flutter of nerves stir in her stomach.

As the men moved away to talk to other members of the board Lucy gave a last-minute flick through her papers. She had prepared thoroughly for this and it was going to be no problem, she told herself calmly.

'Who is that handsome man?' her secretary Gina whispered as she slipped into the seat beside her. Lucy followed her gaze and smiled.

'Mr Connors, over from the new company in Barbados to check us out,' she told her succinctly. 'A sort of spy, I gather, possibly wanting to make sure we are all doing our jobs properly before the new bosses arrive next week.'

'He can check me out any time!' Gina breathed shakily. 'Talk about drop-dead gorgeous!'

'Probably married with three children,' Lucy murmured dismissively.

'Probably…' Gina still sounded dreamy. 'Which reminds me, have you heard the gossip?'

'What about?' Lucy asked, flicking through the slides she was going to show. 'Did you get me that file I asked for?'

'Yes, sorry it took me a while. I got sidetracked. I met

someone down the corridor who told me a bit of startling news.'

Lucy glanced at the papers she had passed over. 'What news?'

Her secretary hesitated.

The meeting was being called to order.

'For heaven's sake, Gina, spit it out,' Lucy murmured.

Her secretary leaned a little closer. 'Apparently your ex-husband's girlfriend is pregnant. Someone saw her; she's at least seven months.'

Lucy felt suddenly sick inside. It was crazy to feel like this, she told herself fiercely. Her marriage was over. She didn't care.

The MD was speaking. Then suddenly a hush had fallen over the room.

'Lucy?'

She was vaguely aware that everyone was looking at her, waiting for her to start her presentation.

Hastily she got to her feet. For a second her mind went completely blank. She glanced down the table and her eyes met with Kris's.

The sick feeling intensified inside her.

Kris seemed to be watching her very closely, possibly thinking that she was going to make a complete mess of this. The thought made her very quickly pull herself together.

'I am putting before you the proposed cruises for the forthcoming season...' She glanced down at her notes and then up again as she launched into the details. Her voice was clear and confident, her manner very businesslike.

Watching her, Rick was impressed. He liked the way she held the room spellbound. He liked her efficiency, her calm delivery. She had certainly done her homework. He watched as she flicked through the PowerPoint slides. The husky softness of her voice filled the darkened room.

There was something about her that really intrigued him. Maybe it was that flicker of vulnerability beneath the crisp confidence of her tone...or maybe it was just the fact that there was a very sexy body hiding beneath that crisp, businesslike suit.

The lights went back on and she was now inviting questions from the room. She glanced around the table and for a moment their eyes met, then quickly she looked away.

A couple of people asked her in-depth questions on cost analysis. She answered without hesitation.

Then the meeting moved on to wider aspects. John Layton spoke, and one of the accountants. Finally it was all over. As people packed their papers away and filed out of the room, Rick made his way towards her.

She glanced up at him and he noticed again that flicker of vulnerability in her eyes.

'Great presentation,' he said easily.

'Thanks.' She smiled briefly at him and then continued putting papers away.

'There was just one thing I wanted to ask you.'

'Yes?'

She looked up again and he watched the way she tucked a stray strand of hair behind her ear. He could almost see her mind ticking over, going through the facts and figures of her work.

'Would you like to have dinner with me tonight?'

He could see that he had definitely taken her by surprise.

Then quickly she looked away from him. 'Sorry, I can't tonight. I'm busy.'

Her tone was brisk.

'How about tomorrow, then?' Rick wasn't one for giving up easily.

'I can't tomorrow either.' She finished putting her papers away and snapped her briefcase shut before looking back up at him. 'Thank you for the invitation,' she said politely.

'But I never mix pleasure with business. It's a bad combination.'

Rick watched as she walked away and a smile touched his lips. It was years since he'd been turned down with such brisk resolve and he found it a very refreshing challenge. He liked her spirit—it intrigued him.

CHAPTER TWO

RICK glanced up from his newspaper as a waitress put down his drink.

'Bourbon on the rocks, Mr Connors,' she said with a smile.

'Thank you, Stacie,' he said, reading her name badge.

She smiled again and walked away. Rick folded his copy of the *Financial Times* and lifted his drink. His gaze drifted around the comfortable lounge with its pale gold flock sofas, down towards the hotel foyer. There was no doubt about it, Cleary's was a very stylish hotel, well deserving its five stars. He liked the high ceilings with their elaborate covings and chandeliers. He liked the polished wooden floors and the pale Egyptian rugs and the fact that real fires burned in the period fireplaces. Of all the hotels he owned around the world, this was undoubtedly one of his favourites. The place had a timeless elegance.

His gaze moved from the warmth of the interior out towards the window. Kensington looked bleak; rain was slanting almost sideways as bitter gusts of wind swept down the dark streets. He'd forgotten how much he disliked London in January. The place was abysmal. The sooner he got his business transactions completed and headed back to his house in Barbados, the better.

A black taxi pulled up outside and the hotel doorman stepped out to open the passenger door. Two women emerged. Rick sipped his drink and watched as the wind swooped on them, making one hold onto her black beret whilst her blonde hair swirled around her face. The other held onto her beige coat as it ruffled up showing a little glimpse of long, shapely legs in sheer stockings. They were both laughing breathlessly as they hurried towards the door.

'Whose mad idea was this?' the blonde asked as they stepped into the foyer. She took off her coat revealing a black dress that did little to disguise a curvaceous figure. But it was the brunette who held Rick's attention. He'd recognised her as soon as she had stepped out of the taxi. There was no mistaking that glorious tumbling dark hair and pale skin. What was Lucy doing at Cleary's? he wondered, intrigued.

'Actually, it was your mad idea,' she said, laughing over at her friend. 'And I don't know why I let you talk me into it. Any sane, sensible person would be tucked up at home with a bottle of wine and a roaring fire.'

'Yes, well, since when have you been sane and sensible? Come on, let's go get a glass of wine and eye up the talent.'

'Talent! Gosh, you're optimistic.'

'You may mock, but George Clooney could be waiting for me just at the other end of this corridor.'

'I think the only male likely to be out on a night like this is Donald Duck.'

They both laughed again.

Rick smiled to himself as he watched them walk down past the reception. Their voices and their laughter faded and silence descended again, a silence that seemed somehow less tranquil than before, somehow rather dull, in fact. Rick finished his drink and got up as curiosity got the better of him.

His feet sank into the luxurious rugs as he crossed towards the reception area.

'Evening, Mr Connors.' The head receptionist smiled at him as he wandered past.

'Evening.' He noticed a sign with an arrow pointing towards one of the banqueting suites that said, 'Speed dating located in the Mayfair Suite.'

'Speed dating?' One dark eyebrow lifted wryly as he looked back at the receptionist. 'Since when have we hosted speed dating events?'

'This is the first one.'

'Really—and whose idea was that?'

'That would be Julie Banks, our functions manager. Shall I get her for you? She is still on duty.'

'No, that won't be necessary, thank you.' Rick moved away from the reception and followed the arrows for the Mayfair Suite, down the long corridors.

The double doors to the suite were open. There were a lot of people milling around and tables and chairs had been set out on the ballroom floor. Rick's eyes flicked around the room and then spied Lucy sitting on one of the bar stools at the far end of the room.

Her coat had been dispensed with and she was wearing a pale blue Angora sweater with a sweetheart neckline, teamed with a pale blue skirt. As she swivelled sideways on the chair to glance around the room his gaze flicked downwards over her shapely legs to her high heels in two-tone blue and beige. There was something very classy about Lucy Blake, almost preppy, he thought.

The woman organising the event was standing a few yards away giving instructions to a member of staff. She was middle-aged, wearing dark-rimmed glasses and a smart black suit that sat rather awkwardly on her very thin frame. However, there was nothing awkward about her manner, which was brisk and efficient, and there was no doubting who was in charge.

As Rick made to go across to her the functions manager hurtled in through the door behind him and waylaid him. 'Mr Connors, they told me you were looking for me at Reception,' she said breathlessly and thrust out her hand. 'I'm Julie Banks, Functions Manager. Is there anything wrong? Can I help you?'

'Not at all, Julie, I'm just being nosy.' He smiled reassuringly at the harassed-looking blonde. 'I just wondered what kind of response you'd had to this speed-dating idea.'

She visibly seemed to relax. 'Well, as you can see we've had a big response. I thought we'd just try it out—we've been thinking of ways to fill up the third function suite at off-peak periods. We had an arts and crafts seminar last week and that was successful as well, but—'

'If you'll excuse me, Julie, I just want to speak to the lady organising things for a moment.'

'Oh, but she isn't employed by the hotel, she just runs these speed-dating events at different places—'

'Yes, that's fine, Julie.' Rick moved purposefully away from the woman, but she trailed after him, an anxious look stretched across her young face.

The organiser was ruffling through pages of paper on a clipboard as Rick approached.

'Yes, your name, please?' she asked abruptly without looking up.

'Rick Connors.'

'C…for Connors…you don't seem to be down here. Have you paid your fee, Mr Connors?' Still she didn't look up.

Julie Banks started to edge in nervously. 'Em…you don't quite understand, Ms Sullivan. Er, Mr Connors is—'

'It doesn't matter who he is, Ms Banks. If his name isn't on the list he can't take part in the speed dating.' She darted a rather frosty glance at the functions manager.

'*Mr Connors* doesn't want to take part.' Julie sounded horrified. 'You don't understand… I should introduce you properly. Mr Connors is the owner of this hotel and—'

'I just want to take part fleetingly.' Rick cut in smoothly and was amused momentarily by the fact that Julie's mouth had dropped open. 'Five minutes at the end of proceedings will do me. I just want to speak to one particular woman.'

'But that's not how it works, Mr Connors.' For the first

time Ms Sullivan looked at Rick and her voice altered immediately to a softer more encouraging tone. 'You see, the idea is that you spend a few minutes with each person and that way you can gauge which woman you'd like to see again. Then you tick her name in the box on your sheet and if she also ticks your name, you have a match.'

'Yes, but I already know which woman I'd like to see again. So I'd like to skip the preliminaries.' Rick reached into his inside pocket and took out a wallet. 'And I'm willing to pay, of course.'

Ms Sullivan looked flustered now. 'Well, this is highly irregular.'

Rick smiled at her. 'I know. But I thought it might be a bit of fun. So perhaps you'd be kind enough to bend the rules just this once…'

Ms Sullivan pushed her glasses further up her nose. 'Well, I…suppose I could.'

'This is really very kind of you, Ms Sullivan. Most appreciated.'

'I told you there would be a lot of people here,' Mel said smugly.

'Yes, you were right,' Lucy remarked, but her attention was on her new shoes. She should never have worn them tonight; they were too high and her feet were killing her already.

'This is the modern way to meet people. It's just perfect for busy career girls like us. One night and approximately thirty dates—what more could a girl ask for?'

'Hmm…' Lucy took another sip of her drink. 'Let me see now. Hot bath? Good book? Both sound like heaven to me.'

'Oh, that's rubbish! You're just scared of getting involved with someone again.'

For some reason a picture of Rick Connors asking her out to dinner flashed in her mind. If he hadn't been involved with the company she knew she would have been tempted to go out with him. 'I'm not scared of anything!' Lucy said hotly. 'And I have been out on a few dates since Kris and I divorced, so you can't accuse me of living life like a nun.'

'A few dates that led to you being back in your flat and tucked up in your bed by ten with a mug of cocoa,' Mel said scathingly.

'Well, I didn't really fancy any of them.' Lucy scowled at her. 'And I couldn't get involved with someone if I really didn't fancy them…if there was no spark.'

'So what about that Ryan guy? He was very good-looking. Why didn't you fancy him?' Mel persisted.

Lucy shrugged. 'Well, for a start he lied to me, told me he'd never been married, then halfway through dinner he admitted that he was divorced and that he'd left his wife. It put me off him.'

'For heaven's sake, Luce, if you're looking for the perfect man then you're never going to find him. Such a creature doesn't exist.'

'Yes, but you know how I feel about lies. I had a bellyful of them when I was married to Kris. I don't want a man who can't be truthful.'

'Maybe he was just too upset to talk about his divorce.'

'Maybe,' Lucy conceded.

'Anyway, I think you are approaching this man thing with the wrong mindset.'

'How do you mean?' Lucy took a sip of her wine.

'Well, you don't want to get married again just yet, do you?'

'No!' Lucy shook her head.

'Or live with anyone?'

'I want my independence,' Lucy said firmly. 'It will be a long time before I do anything like that again…if ever.' But for a moment she thought about the fact that she had wanted a baby… She hadn't told Mel about Kris's girlfriend being pregnant. Somehow it hurt too much to talk about.

She swallowed hard and tried not to think about it.

'You need to view relationships and men in a different light—follow a whole different set of criteria,' Mel continued.

'Yes, you're right.'

'You're looking for a man who sets your pulses on fire—nothing else. It doesn't matter if he's not the settling-down type. Because all you want is a no-strings, sophisticated affair. And, believe me, there is *nothing* as exciting as one of those. You tumble into bed and have wild, passionate sex and meet for secret assignations…and real life never has to cloud things. Then when the novelty wears off you move on to the next conquest.'

'I don't think I'm ready for that, Mel,' Lucy said lightly. To be honest she didn't know if she would ever be ready for that. It all sounded a bit too modern for her. 'I don't think it's quite my thing.'

'Listen; after all you've been through you need a little light fun,' Mel insisted firmly.

'Yes, I agree with that. But just a little light flirtation will do for now.' Lucy swirled her wine around in her glass and tried to work up some enthusiasm for the evening. 'So what's the talent like out there?' She took another sip of her wine. 'Have you seen George Clooney yet?'

'Actually, there's an absolutely gorgeous man talking to the woman who is organising things. Move over, George. I can't wait to have my three minutes with him, I can tell you.'

Lucy swivelled around in her chair and searched the crowd. 'Where? I can't see him.'

'He was there a moment ago.' Mel frowned. 'Damn. Well, anyway, just remember I bagged him first.'

'Okay, I'll remember.' Lucy grinned.

The organiser was calling everyone to the tables and chairs on the dance floor so there was no further time for conversation.

Immediately Lucy sat down, a man sat opposite her and the dating game began. Surprisingly, after the first few men Lucy started to relax and enjoy herself. It was quite good fun being chatted up by someone new every few minutes; there wasn't time to feel awkward, and on the whole she had a laugh with each person who sat opposite. In fact time seemed to fly past.

None of the men set her pulses racing, though there was one, a Mark Kirkland, who was semi interesting and not bad-looking. She made a note of him on the form she had been given and ticked his name in the box.

'So what's a nice girl like you doing in a place like this?' A deep sexy voice interrupted her writing.

'That's not a very original line, if I may say so...' She glanced up with a smile and met Rick Connors' dark, steady gaze.

CHAPTER THREE

'WHAT on earth are you doing here?' A wave of surprise rippled through Lucy's entire body...along with some other inexplicable emotion that was very disturbing.

'You just told me that was a very unoriginal question,' Rick reminded her with a grin.

'Yes...but...' Her brain seemed to have gone into free fall, along with her stomach. '*Really*, what are you doing here?' she repeated distractedly.

'Actually, I'm staying here at this hotel.'

'The company have put you up at Cleary's!'

He watched the incredulous expression on her face with a grin. 'You find that hard to believe?'

'Well...yes. It must cost a fortune to stay here. EC Cruises must be very generous with their staff.'

'They try to look after them.' He grinned.

'Well, that's good news,' Lucy said lightly. 'Maybe they'll do something about the drinks machine at the office.'

'Is it bad?'

Lucy raised an eyebrow. 'Have you tasted the coffee from it, and seen how much they charge us for it?'

Rick grinned. 'No, but thanks for the warning. I'll put it on my list of recommended changes.'

She wanted to ask him if that was his job in the company, recommending changes, but maybe this wasn't the time or the place. 'So have the company really installed you here for the whole week?' she asked lightly instead.

For a moment Rick hesitated and contemplated telling her the truth: that he wasn't an employee of EC Cruises, that he owned the company and Cleary's was one of a family

22

of hotels also owned by him. He opened his mouth and then as he met the candid green beauty of her eyes closed it again. He liked the way Lucy acted around him, liked the fact that unlike other people she didn't fawn over his every word. Her naturalness was a refreshing change in a world where everyone was impressed by his power and wealth. And, besides, he was in London to inspect his new acquisition from the grass roots up. He didn't want anyone at the office knowing who he was yet; it would make it harder to really assess things. The only person to know his true identity was John Layton.

'Well, actually EC Cruises own this hotel,' he said instead with a shrug. 'So they've found me a broom cupboard for the week.'

'That figures.' Lucy smiled at him. 'So have you tried speed dating before?'

'No, this is all new to me. As a matter of fact I saw you arrive and just followed you through.' He grinned. 'I was curious as to why you turned my dinner invitation down.'

'My secret is out.' Lucy smiled. 'I had a previous engagement with thirty men.'

'Do you go speed dating often?'

'No.' Lucy shook her head. 'To be honest I've been dragged here by a friend. It's a whole new experience.'

'And what do you think of it?'

Her eyes drifted over him. What she was thinking at the moment was how exceptionally handsome he was. She noticed how expensive his suit looked, how easily it sat on his broad shoulders, how his crisp white shirt was open at the neck revealing a healthy tan. His dark hair seemed to glint under the overhead chandeliers and he really had the most incredibly sexy eyes, eyes that seemed to be burning into hers.

Realising he was waiting for her to answer him, she hurriedly gathered her senses. 'I think it's been good fun.'

'Well, I'm certainly glad I wandered in,' he murmured. There was a seductive tone to his voice now that, teamed with the way he was watching her, made her feel even hotter inside. 'And it's given me a real insight into the London office.'

Lucy was relieved that he had lightened his tone, was glad to be able to joke back. 'Well, if this is all part of your work assessment for the company, then I think you might be going above and beyond the call of duty.'

'I'm getting a generous overtime rate, so what the heck?' He shrugged and his lips twisted in a ruggedly attractive smile. 'So tell me, have you ticked many names on that form yet?' He nodded at the piece of paper in front of her.

Lucy hesitated and then decided to play along. 'Just one. What about you?'

'Just one.' His eyes held hers.

With difficulty she wrenched her gaze away. 'Actually I can't see your name on this list,' she told him quickly as she looked back down at the form in front of her.

'That's because it's not there. I was too late a contender, but don't worry, the indomitable Ms Sullivan said it was all right. You can just pencil me in at the bottom of the page.' He grinned at her wryly. 'Or better still, we could dispense with the formalities. How about joining me for a drink in the bar?'

The suddenly serious question took her by surprise. 'Well…when were you thinking?'

'Now.' He grinned at her. 'After all, there's no time like the present. And I bet you're thirsty after all the talking you've been doing.'

Danger signals started to course through her in thunderous waves. This man was just too attractive…and he was having too weird an effect on her senses. Suddenly it felt safer to start backing away from the situation. 'Thanks for the offer, Rick. But I don't think it's a good idea.'

'Why not?' He didn't seem in the least thrown by her refusal.

'I told you earlier; I've made it a rule never to get involved with anyone at work.'

'Very sensible.' He nodded his head. 'But I don't think I count as someone at work. After all, I'm only going to be in the country for a week.'

'Yes, but even so, we will be working together on Monday, so—'

'All the more reason to get better acquainted before then.' He cut across her and leaned his elbows on the table, watching her with great amusement. 'I'm only suggesting we have a drink—jumping into bed together is optional.' He watched the flare of colour in her cheeks and his grin stretched wider. 'Sorry, am I embarrassing you?'

Embarrassment was far too light a word for what he was doing to her. For some reason her blood pressure seemed to have rocketed just at the mention of going to bed with him. 'No, of course not, and, I assure you, jumping into bed with you was the last thing on my mind.' With a supreme effort she managed to sound composed.

'Now, that's a shame,' he drawled, still with that note of warm enjoyment in his tone.

Lucy glanced away from him and noticed with relief that the speed dating had finished and that most people had stood up and were milling around chatting. She spied Mel standing a little further away, talking to the organiser.

'Well, I think things have come to an end here,' she said, pushing her chair back from the table. 'And I've arranged to share a cab back home with my friend, so I really should go.'

Rick also rose to his feet. She noticed again how tall he was, how petite he made her feel.

'Anyway, Rick, nice talking to you,' she said in what she hoped was a dismissive tone.

Before she could turn and walk away, however, Mel arrived beside them.

'Hi.' She flashed a brilliant smile at Rick, batting her wide blue eyes and tossing back her long blonde mane of hair. 'I think something went terribly wrong with the organisation on this event, because we didn't get to meet up. I'm Melanie Roberts.'

'Hi, Melanie.' Rick bestowed a very warm smile on her and took the hand that she offered. 'I'm Rick Connors. Lucy and I know each other from work.'

'Oh, I see! I work in the accounts office but I haven't seen you around.' Melanie darted a look of surprise over at Lucy, a look that clearly said: How come you haven't told me about this man?

'Rick is from the new head office in Barbados, here to assess operations,' Lucy explained. 'He only arrived today.'

'I haven't got around all the departments yet,' Rick said easily.

'Oh, I see.'

Mel was starting to sound like a parrot, Lucy thought with irritation. And did she have to look up at Rick with such adoring eyes? It was no wonder the guy was so coolly confident.

'I was just suggesting to Lucy that we head off for a drink in the bar. But she tells me that you are both dashing for a taxi,' Rick informed her lightly.

Mel darted a look at Lucy that said very clearly she thought she was mad. 'We don't have to dash off straight away, Lucy,' she said with scolding emphasis. 'I'm sure we've got time for one drink.'

Before Lucy could say anything to this Rick was taking control. 'Well, that's settled, then. Let's head for the bar, shall we?'

'Great idea.' Mel pointedly ignored the fact that Lucy was

glaring at her and linked her arm with Rick. 'So how long are you here for, Rick?' she asked jovially.

'Just a week.'

'And then it's back to Barbados, is it?'

'That's right.'

A member of staff came around collecting their forms. 'If you have a match you will be contacted via your e-mail or contact number,' Ms Sullivan informed everyone loudly.

Lucy handed hers in and then, faced with no other alternative, found herself trailing along beside Rick towards the bar.

'I'd love to go to Barbados.' Mel glanced across Rick's chest at Lucy. 'Luce would as well, wouldn't you, Luce?'

'Well, I—'

'In fact Lucy was only saying the other day how much she could do with some sunshine,' Mel continued merrily.

'You should take one of the cruises that you sell so well,' Rick said, looking over at Lucy.

'I fly out to Miami occasionally to inspect new ships.' Lucy shrugged. 'But there's never time to sit in the sun.'

Rick looked at her with a raised eyebrow. 'Now that is a definite oversight on the part of the company. How can you sell something when you have never tried it?'

'I have all the necessary details about the cruises at my fingertips,' Lucy said with another shrug. 'That's all I need.'

'Well, I'll grant that you certainly know your job,' Rick said easily. 'That much was very clear during your presentation today.'

The bar lounge had filled up, but they managed to find some seats in an alcove. Rick glanced around for a waitress, then decided he'd probably get served quicker at the bar. 'What can I get you to drink?' he asked them. 'How about a cocktail?'

They both ordered a Margarita.

'He's very handsome,' Mel said dreamily as they watched him weave his way through the crowds towards the bar.

'I suppose he is,' Lucy conceded. 'A bit pushy, though. I'd turned down the offer of a drink.'

'Yes, and it's a good job I was here to rescue the situation. Honestly, Luce, you don't turn down someone like him.'

'He's from work, and you know I have rules about that.'

'Then it's about time you threw that rule book of yours away,' Mel said firmly. 'But if you don't want him…well, hey, I had my eye on him first anyway.'

'Is he the guy you saw earlier?'

'Of course he is. How many men like him can you see floating around?' Mel grinned over at her. 'I'd say I'd fight you for him, but unfortunately he only seems to have eyes for you so I think I'd lose the battle.'

'Rubbish. He's over here on business and just at a loose end, that's all.'

'Maybe so, but he still fancies you. I can read the signs, which is why I'm going to make an excuse and leave in a few minutes.'

'Mel! You are to do no such thing!' Lucy said in alarm. Somehow the thought of being left alone with Rick Connors made her heart race with very peculiar panic.

'You *do* like him, don't you?' Mel's grin stretched wider. 'Well, good. It's about time you took a dive into a little romantic water. This could be just what you need to get you back in the flow.'

'Mel, you are not to leave…' Lucy insisted urgently, but there wasn't time to say anything else because Rick arrived back.

'So what shall we drink to?' he asked with a grin as he took a seat opposite Lucy and put the drinks on the table.

'How about speed dating?' Mel suggested.

'Speed dating it is,' Rick said as he raised his glass.

A waitress stopped by their table. 'Can I get you anything, Mr Connors?'

'No, we're fine, thanks.' Rick smiled up at her easily.

The woman smiled back at him warmly and fluttered her eyelashes a little. 'Well, anything else you need, don't hesitate to call me over.'

'The staff are very attentive in here, aren't they?' Mel murmured as the woman left them. 'And she remembered your name!'

'Yes, they certainly train their staff well. The personal touch is very important, don't you think?' Rick murmured.

Although she agreed with him, Lucy couldn't help but think that probably every woman with a pulse would remember Rick's name. And any woman who fell for Rick Connors would be asking for big trouble. He had heartbreaker written all over him in capital letters. She wondered if he had a wife or a girlfriend waiting patiently for him back in Barbados.

He looked across and met her eyes and smiled.

Silly question, she thought hazily. Some woman would definitely be waiting for him.

'That's my phone,' Mel said suddenly as she took her mobile out of her bag.

'I didn't hear anything.' Lucy looked over at her suspiciously.

'Well, it was. I've had a message.' Mel peered at the screen. 'Oh, dear, I'm afraid I'm going to have to leave. It's from my mother. I completely forgot that I said I'd call in on the way home and she's waiting patiently for me.' Mel popped the phone back in her bag. 'I am sorry about this.' She carefully avoided looking at Lucy, who was frowning at her, and smiled instead at Rick. 'It was lovely meeting you, Rick. Maybe we'll meet again before you return to Head Office.'

'I hope so, Mel.' He grinned at her. 'And it was good meeting you too.'

'And don't let this one—' she pointed at Lucy '—dash off home too early. Contrary to what she thinks, her clothes will not turn to rags when the clock strikes twelve.'

'Very funny, Mel,' Lucy said dryly.

With a mischievous grin Mel picked up her bag and walked away.

'So, alone at last,' Rick said with a smile as she looked across and met his dark steady gaze.

The teasing tone and the way he looked at her caused another flurry of disquiet inside Lucy. 'I don't know where Mel is dashing off to in such a hurry,' she murmured distractedly. 'Her mother moved to live in the South of France over a year ago.'

Rick laughed at that. 'Well, maybe she's suddenly remembered a hot date.'

'Maybe,' Lucy murmured. 'Or maybe she has the wrong impression about us…imagined that she was playing gooseberry or something stupid like that.'

Rick's gaze swept slowly over her. There was no doubt about it; Lucy was an extremely attractive woman. And the fact that every aspect of her body language was telling him clearly to keep his distance, from the tips of her beautifully shod feet to the way she held her head high, her chin angled up slightly, intrigued him immensely.

'Now, I wonder where she could have got a ludicrous idea like that from,' he said softly, a gleam of sardonic humour in his voice.

'Lord alone knows.' Lucy crossed her long legs and leaned back in her chair. 'I did try to tell her that we are just work colleagues, but I don't think she believed me.'

Rick's gaze was distracted for a moment by the way she crossed her legs, by the sensuous curves of her body held so ramrod straight in her chair.

Then as their eyes met again he noted that she was very aware of his scrutiny, and for a second there was a flicker of warmth in the wide beauty of her eyes that told very clearly she wasn't immune to him.

He smiled at her and watched the slight flush of colour in the smooth, high cheeks. Hastily she looked away from him.

'So, Rick, what are your impressions about our London office?' she asked as she took a sip of her drink.

He noted how swiftly she brought the subject of conversation round to work like a hastily erected barrier with a sign that stated very clearly that trespassers onto private property would be prosecuted. It wasn't the kind of reaction he was used to from a woman, and it amused him, aroused a feeling of challenge inside him.

'I think the London office has some very strong possibilities,' he drawled slowly.

'Possibilities?' She looked confused. 'How do you mean?'

'I mean there is room for development.'

'Is that a polite way of saying there is room for improvement?'

He laughed at that. 'Maybe. Isn't there always room for improvement with everything?'

'I suppose so. But John Layton runs a pretty tight ship, if you'll pardon the pun.'

Rick smiled. 'Yes, so I've been told. I've also been told that you have helped him a great deal. That in fact it was your marketing skills that facilitated a turn-around in the company's fortunes last year.'

'I wouldn't go that far,' Lucy said firmly. 'As you probably know, there was a slump in profits for a while last year, but things have picked up again and it's not just down to me. There has been an upswing in the economy, which has helped, plus we have good teamwork at the London office.'

'Modest as well as talented,' Rick remarked with a grin and watched the glow of colour in her cheeks. 'But I know how much your input has helped. I've read numerous reports on the upswing of the company's profit margins. And your name has cropped up several times when I've been talking to John.'

Lucy felt a little uncomfortable with the praise. 'Well, as I said before I have a good team working with me.' Her eyes narrowed on him for a moment as she noticed suddenly his easy use of the MD's first name.

'So what exactly is your job?' she asked curiously. 'How come you are reading past financial records? Are you employed by EC Cruises as a kind of troubleshooter?'

Rick thought about that for a moment. 'Yes, I suppose I am a troubleshooter of sorts. I look for ways of getting the best out of a business, of maximising profits.'

'And do you do that by cutting staff?' She probably shouldn't have asked that question, but she had read the reports about the company he worked for and she wasn't overly impressed.

'Not always, no,' he answered calmly. 'I make an assessment of every aspect of the business and I take it from there.'

Lucy nodded. She supposed he was just following orders, and doing his job. She couldn't dislike him for that.

'So you're an accountant?' She lifted her glass and took a sip.

'I trained as an economist and then branched out a little from there.'

For some reason she was glad that he wasn't an accountant. Kris was an accountant and she didn't want him to have anything in common with her ex. As the thought crossed her mind she frowned. It didn't matter what Rick did for a living because it was of no significance to her, and anyway wasn't there a bit of a fine line between accountant and economist?

'What about you? Have you always worked in marketing?'

Lucy shook her thoughts away from any comparisons with Kris. 'I've been with the company for four years, before that I worked for Galaxino, they're a big—'

'Advertising company,' he finished for her. 'Yes, I've heard of them.'

Lucy nodded. 'I got a bit bored with them, used to spend a lot of my days thinking up new ways to sell shampoo…'

'So are you happy working where you are?'

'Yes, I suppose I'm happy for now.' Lucy tried not to think about the gossip she would have to endure once it became public knowledge about Kris becoming a father. 'I'll have to wait and see what changes are made now we've been taken over,' she added briskly.

'There will be meetings next week to discuss all that.'

'Yes, I gather the big boss is coming.' Lucy swirled her drink around the glass. 'Do you know him well?'

'You could say that.' Rick smiled.

'Everyone has been very on edge about this takeover, you know.'

Rick nodded. 'It's a difficult time. But they have no need to be.'

'We'll have to wait and see, I suppose.' She looked over at him directly then. 'You'll have been involved in a lot of EC takeovers, I suppose.'

'A fair few over the years,' he agreed.

'Do you enjoy your job?'

'Yes, I do. I get to do a lot of travelling. We have offices in Miami and New York as well as Barbados and London.'

'And you live in Barbados?'

He nodded. 'What about you? Have you always lived in London?'

She looked over at him and smiled. 'No, I was brought up in Devon.'

'You're a country girl, then?'

She smiled. 'In my heart anyway.'

'You don't have an accent.'

'No…well, I moved to London when I was thirteen.' She took another sip of her drink. 'You don't have an accent either.'

'I moved around a lot when I was growing up. My father was Irish and my mother from Buenos Aires. My real name is Enrique, but everyone has always just called me Rick.'

That explained his Latin good looks, she thought idly, her gaze moving over the darkness of his hair and eyes. 'Do you speak Spanish?'

To her surprise he answered her in the language. It sounded warmly sensual and it had a perturbing effect on her senses. 'What does that mean?' she asked hesitantly.

'It means I'm very glad that we bumped into each other this evening.' He smiled and it had an even more disturbing effect.

'Would you like another drink?' he asked as the waitress passed close to their table.

'Actually, I'd better not have any more,' she said quickly. 'I don't really drink a lot and I've already had wine tonight.'

He didn't press her.

The bar was starting to empty now, Lucy noticed. She glanced at her watch and noticed it was almost eleven-thirty. 'Actually I didn't realise how late it was.' She looked over at him. 'I really ought to be going.'

It surprised her how much she regretted saying that; there was a part of her that could have sat on here and talked to him all night. She would have liked to know more about him.

Rick Connors was very interesting, she decided. She liked the warmth of his gaze, the humour in his tone…the way her body went hot all over when he looked at her in a certain way… The thought crept in surreptitiously catching her by surprise and sending a wave of renewed heat through her. It was a long time since a man had had that effect on her and it was truly disconcerting. Hastily she reached for her coat.

'Your clothes won't really turn to rags at midnight, you know,' Rick teased lightly.

'No, but my transport might disappear and that would be much worse. It can be hard getting a taxi when the weather is so bad.' She smiled back at him and as their eyes met she felt a shiver of sexual awareness slice straight through her. Hurriedly she turned away from him and stood up.

'I'll see you home,' Rick said, rising to his feet with her.

'Oh, no, really, there's no need.' She looked up at him, flustered by the offer. 'I'll just take a taxi from outside.'

'Well, I'll come and see you safely into your taxi, then.'

Lucy tried to protest, but he had hold of her arm and was walking with her towards the front entrance.

'It's still raining,' Lucy noticed as they neared the glass doors and saw the rain slanting down onto the road in diagonal sheets. 'Don't come outside, Rick.'

But he ignored her and as the doorman opened the ornate door for them he stepped out under the awning into the bitter cold air with her.

'Good night, Mr Connors.' The doorman touched his hat.

'How does he know your name?' Lucy asked, perplexed.

'I was talking to him earlier.' Rick glanced along the pavement. They weren't the only ones standing under the hotel's wide awning waiting for a taxi; there was a crowd of people in front of them. 'You know, it might be quicker to go back inside and ring for a taxi…in fact, this hotel has a fleet of limousines. We could ring for one of them.'

'Are you joking?' Lucy looked up at him in astonishment. 'That would cost a fortune.'

'Would it?' Rick shrugged. 'I could always put it on expenses,' he suggested with a grin.

She laughed at that. 'Yes, I suppose you could if you don't mind losing your job.'

For a moment Rick contemplated telling her the truth: that it wouldn't cost him anything, that he owned the hotel and the limousines and the phenomenally high expense account was his to do with as he pleased. But then she might start acting differently around him…and, well…this was fun. So instead he said lightly, 'At least come back inside so I can ring for a taxi. This weather is horrendous.'

Lucy watched the way the rain was bouncing off the pavements. 'I won't melt. I'm made of tougher stuff. Actually there's a tube station not far from here, I might head up there… Oh, hold on.' She broke off as a red double-decker bus rounded the corner. 'I can catch this. It goes right to the bottom of my road.'

'A bus! Hang on, Lucy, you'd be better getting a taxi at this time of night.'

'No need, honestly. I'll be fine.' She was pulling up the collar on her coat as she spoke. 'Thanks for the drink, Rick.'

The next moment she was gone, darting out into the rain and dashing towards the bus stop.

Rick hesitated for just a second and then set off after her.

CHAPTER FOUR

LUCY only just caught the bus and was slightly out of breath as she got on board. Downstairs was packed so she climbed the stairs and found herself alone up there.

She sat down and stared out of the dark, rain-streaked windows as the bus rattled off down the road again, and for a moment she thought back on the evening and the peculiar effect Rick had on her senses. There had been a part of her that had been glad to run away from him…and another that couldn't help regretting the fact that he hadn't kissed her. If she'd hung around would that have happened? And what would it have felt like? Maybe she had been imagining it, but there had seemed to be a very strong chemistry between them.

Someone slid into the seat beside her and she looked round in alarm, wondering why anyone would sit so close when there were so many empty seats. She didn't know if she was relieved or not as she met Rick's dark gaze because her heart seemed to do an almost violent somersault. 'What on earth are you doing here?'

'That's the second time you've asked me that tonight.' He looked amused. 'The fact is, I couldn't let you travel home alone at night on a bus. I mean, anything could happen to you.'

For a moment her lips curved in a wry smile. 'This is London, Rick. Not Miami.'

'Actually Miami is pretty safe these days,' Rick countered. 'But, call me old-fashioned, I just wanted to see you safely to your front door.'

There was something about the sincerity of his tone that

touched her. Since Kris had left she'd had to get used to looking out for herself. No one had worried about whether she got home safely in a very long time.

'That's very kind of you…but there was no need,' she added hastily. 'Actually I have a black belt in karate, so I can look after myself, you know.'

'Really?' He watched as she pushed her wet hair back from her face, noticing how small and slender her wrists were. She didn't look as if she could fend off a fly, never mind a strong attacker.

'Yes, really.' Her green eyes glittered with a sudden boldness and she angled her chin up defiantly. 'Don't you believe me?'

Her slender femininity gave him a cause not to, yet the determination in her eyes, in her demeanour, made him think again. 'Yes, I believe you,' he said with a grin.

'Good.' She grinned back at him. 'I'd have hated it if I'd had to throw you to the ground just to prove my point.'

One dark eyebrow rose slightly. 'Oh, I don't know…' he murmured with teasing seductiveness. 'I might have liked falling at your feet. It sounds kind of promising.'

For some reason the tone of his voice, the gleam of his eye made her pulses race, made her blush.

She looked away from him. 'Anyway, it is very gallant of you to see me home. I'll have to buy you a coffee in the office as a thank-you.'

'Okay, I'll hold you to that,' he said firmly. 'But after what you've told me about the coffee in the office I'm going to insist we go out.'

'If we have time,' Lucy countered. 'It can be pretty hectic in that office on a Monday.'

'Don't worry, we'll find some time to play truant,' he assured her solemnly.

'I thought you were being employed by the company to

try and make things better in the office, not worse,' she said with a smile.

'I've been given a pretty wide remit,' he assured her. 'Lunch can go under the heading of getting to know the staff and their requirements.'

'Lunch! We were talking about coffee.' She laughed and then said jokingly, 'And it had better be all above board, because I'm very conscientious, you know. And you can pass that message on to the new boss.'

'Don't worry, I will.' He smiled at her. 'You have some very admirable qualities, Ms Blake.'

His voice had a husky, very sexy quality and he seemed to be looking very deeply into her eyes. She noticed how dark his eyes were, noticed the golden flecks in their depths. His skin was a smooth olive colour and there was the beginning of a dark shadow along the square lines of his jaw. For a moment her eyes lingered on the sensual curve of his lips and she felt her heart starting to pound against her chest with the painful awareness that she would give anything for him to kiss her. He was just too...gorgeous.

Realising suddenly that they were just sitting there staring at each other, she pulled her gaze away and glanced out of the window. 'I think we're nearing my stop.' Her voice wobbled peculiarly and she frowned, hating herself for allowing her emotions to take over from common sense. He was a work colleague, she told herself fiercely, and her number one rule was not to get involved with anyone from work. 'Yes, it is my stop,' she added with relief. 'We need to get off here.'

Rick slid out from the seat and preceded her down the stairs. Then as she stepped off the bus he held out his hand to help her.

'Thanks.' Her hand rested in his for a moment and then hastily she pulled away.

The rain had abated a little, but it was still drizzling and cold. Lucy huddled further into her coat and glanced up at Rick. 'How are you planning to get back to the hotel?' she asked suddenly.

'I'll think about that when I've seen you to your front door. Which way is it?'

She was going to argue that there was no need for him to come any further, but it seemed churlish as he had already come this far. 'It's just around the corner.'

They set off walking. It was very quiet, just an occasional car swishing along the waterlogged roads past them. As they turned into the elegant Georgian square where Lucy had her apartment the rain started to come down in earnest.

'Maybe you should turn back now.' Lucy gasped as the icy water lashed against them.

'As you said earlier, I won't melt.' Rick reached out and caught hold of her hand. 'Come on, we'd better hurry.'

After a moment's hesitation she was running along beside him, jumping over puddles on the pavement. This was the second time tonight he had taken hold of her hand and she liked it, liked the fact that they were both laughing breathlessly by the time they arrived outside her house.

'Nice area,' Rick remarked as he let go of her and looked up at the buildings that curved so gracefully around the small park in the centre.

'Yes, I like it. Let's get out of this rain.' Lucy led the way up the steps so that they could stand in the shelter of the vestibule.

'It was very kind of you to see me home.' She turned to look up at him.

'It was no problem.' He stepped a little closer and for some reason her heart started to thump wildly against her chest. This was crazy, but she felt like a teenager on a first date.

She looked past him back at the street. 'The rain seems to be easing a bit now. There's a tube station on the road where the bus dropped us. Just turn left up there.' She waved airily back in the direction they had come from. 'It might be quicker than waiting for a bus or a taxi.'

He nodded.

Her eyes drifted over his broad shouldered frame. He wasn't wearing a coat and the expensive suit shimmered with raindrops in the light that slanted out from the hallway. 'Perhaps you had better come in and dry off before heading back?' The words were out of her mouth before she could stop them.

He didn't answer immediately.

'Unless you'd rather not.' Hurriedly she tried to back-track. 'I suppose it is rather late.'

'Not that late.' He smiled at her. 'And I'd love to come in, thanks.'

His smile did funny things to her pulse rate, made it skip unevenly. Nervously she searched in her bag for her front-door key.

Lucy was very aware of his eyes on her as she walked in front of him across the wide hallway and up the graceful curving staircase. 'I live up on the second floor so it's quite a climb, I'm afraid.'

'That must be what keeps you so beautifully slim,' he remarked.

It was just a light-hearted remark, but it caused the butterflies in her stomach to flutter even more.

Lucy fitted the key in her front-door lock and wondered suddenly if she had left the place tidy. She had been in such a rush trying to get ready to go out that she hadn't had time to do much in the way of housework. And she had certainly never imagined in her wildest dreams that she would bring anyone home with her.

It was a relief to find the place didn't look too bad. The cushions on the settee were a bit higgledy-piggledy and there were a few newspapers and magazines on the glass coffee-table, but it could have been worse.

'Sorry about the mess,' she said as she took off her coat and hastily rearranged the cushions and gathered up the papers.

Rick watched her, a gleam of amusement in his dark eyes. 'I think you are a bit of a perfectionist, Lucy.'

'No, not really. To be honest I've been so busy at work recently that I haven't had a lot of time for housework.'

His gaze moved around the room. It had a comfortable elegance with its maple floor and the wide bay windows that no doubt would look out over the park. Her décor was pleasing on the eye. Everything was plain; the only colour was the vibrant pictures on the walls and the books that were crammed into bookshelves along one side of the room.

Lucy moved to light the fire. 'I bet you're missing the heat of Barbados.'

'You're not kidding. I'd forgotten how cold London can be.'

'At least the gale-force wind has dropped. When Mel and I arrived at Cleary's tonight we were nearly blown away.'

'I know. I saw you.' Rick grinned.

Lucy looked over at him in surprise.

'I was sitting in the front lounge.' Rick moved to look at some of the pictures on the walls. 'These are lovely,' he said, admiring a seascape.

'It used to be a hobby of mine, but I don't get much time for it any more.'

'You painted them?' He sounded genuinely impressed.

She nodded. 'There was a time…long ago…when I wanted to be an artist. But my careers advisor informed me that trying to make a living as a painter is not so easy. So it was either starve in a garret somewhere, or get a real job.'

Rick shook his head wryly. 'Many a great talent has been

squashed like that. You should have paid no attention and followed your heart.'

She grinned. 'And maybe I'd be broke now.'

'And maybe you'd be rich beyond your wildest dreams.'

She met the gleam of amusement in his dark eyes and laughed. 'Thank you for the compliment, but I don't think so. So what about you, Rick? Have you got any secret regrets? Would you have liked to have become a biologist instead of an economist?'

'I can honestly say that is an idea that never crossed my mind,' he said with a grin. 'And I never waste time with regrets. I tend to go out and get what I want in life.'

'And do you always get what you want?' Lucy asked curiously.

'Nearly always.' As their eyes met Lucy felt a strange frisson of awareness. There was a strength about him that said very clearly that this was probably true, and for some reason it unnerved her.

'Lucky you,' she said quietly.

He shrugged. 'I've had my fair share of disappointments.'

Somehow that was harder to believe. Her eyes moved over the solidly handsome physique, the dark, purposeful gleam in his oh, so attractive, sexy eyes. 'What kind of disappointments?'

'Oh, the usual kind…relationships that haven't worked out, that sort of thing.'

'Someone managed to break your heart at school?' she asked impishly.

He laughed at that. 'Well, now you come to mention it, yes, they did actually. Marion Woods.' He shook his head. 'I was seven. She was the love of my life.'

Lucy laughed in turn. 'So what happened?'

'She dumped me for a guy a year older whose parents owned a sweet shop.' He shook his head wryly. 'Just think, if my parents had only owned that sweet shop instead of

their restaurant, we probably would have been married...'
There was a gleam of teasing amusement in his eyes. 'Now
I think about it, it's probably the reason I've grown into the
commitment-phobic, confirmed bachelor you see before you
today.'

'So much for having no regrets,' Lucy laughed. 'That's
a really sad story.'

'Tragic.'

'And are you? A confirmed bachelor, I mean?' Before
she could stop herself Lucy was asking the question.

Rick inclined his head and for a moment his dark eyes
were serious. 'Well, I'm thirty-eight and I've never been
married, so I must be. What about you, Lucy? Has anyone
ever broken your heart?' He looked over at her steadily and
suddenly the mood between them seemed to change away
from the light-hearted.

She wondered how they had managed to skate so abruptly
onto such disturbingly personal ground.

Rick watched the conflicting emotions in her eyes and
knew then that the answer to that was a definite yes. But
then she looked away from him for a moment and when she
glanced back the shadows were successfully hidden. 'Well,
I suppose there was Steve Donnelly when I was in year
three.'

'Childhood has a lot to answer for,' Rick said steadily.

'Can leave you scarred for life,' she agreed.

'So, are you a confirmed bachelor as well?' he asked
lightly.

'I am now. But I had to get married first, just so I could
discover how much that institution didn't suit me.'

'You're divorced?'

Lucy nodded. 'Married for three years, divorced for one.'
She wondered why she had told him that. The strange thing
was he was disturbingly easy to talk to.

'Anyway.' She moved away from the fire. 'You'd better stand here and try and dry off. I'll make us a coffee.'

He smiled at her and as their eyes met her heart seemed to miss a beat.

Hastily she wrenched her eyes away from him and hurried into the small kitchen.

He is a work colleague, she told herself firmly as she flicked on the kettle. And she really didn't need any more complications at work.

Then she caught a glimpse of her reflection in the mirror beside the door and cringed. Her hair was sticking to her head and her face looked unbelievably pale. 'I'm just going to dry my hair, I won't be a minute,' she called, going through to her bedroom.

She was only gone a few minutes, but when she came back she found Rick in the kitchen making the coffee. It seemed strange to see him in there. He had taken off his jacket and the white shirt seemed to emphasise the breadth of his shoulders, the darkness of his hair. Lucy wondered suddenly what it would be like to have a Latin lover. The thought caught her by surprise…shocked her.

He turned to find her watching him from the doorway and grinned. 'I thought I'd make myself at home. Hope you don't mind?'

'No.' She shook her head, but it crossed her mind that the last man who had been in her kitchen making her a drink had been Kris, and that had been just before he'd told her he was leaving her.

'Do you take milk and sugar?' He turned and looked at her again and then frowned. 'Are you okay?'

'Yes, fine.' She smiled brightly, annoyed with herself for letting any memories of Kris into her mind. That man had hurt her more than she had ever been hurt in her life, and she just wanted to forget all about him.

Rick left the cups on the sideboard and walked towards her. 'You looked sad for a moment.'

'Did I?' She shook her head, wishing he would just drop the subject. 'Well, I don't feel sad.'

'Sure?' He reached out and tipped her chin up so that she was forced to meet his eyes.

The impact of his hand against her skin sent wild floods of pure adrenalin pumping through her veins. 'Absolutely sure,' she breathed. And it was true. At this moment she felt anything but upset. What she felt was a wild surge of excitement and desire as her eyes moved over the handsome contours of his face. She wanted him to kiss her, wanted it so badly that she leaned closer. 'Rick.' She whispered his name.

'That's me.' He stroked the silky strands of her mahogany hair back from her face and the next moment his lips were on hers. Lucy had never known anything like the explosion of passion that followed, had never experienced a kiss like it in her life. His lips possessed hers totally and they set such a fire raging inside her that all she could do was lean closer, wind her arms around his neck and surrender to it.

She felt his hands on her waist and his touch seemed to burn through the thin material of her top, making her long for them to move beneath and touch her more intimately. Pressing herself closer, she opened her mouth to the masterful persuasion of his. The sensuality of his tongue against the softness of her lips made her heart beat wildly against her chest, and her senses clamour with dizzy need.

'That was some kiss!' He was the one to pull back; his tone was velvet-smooth with a relaxed, lazy seductiveness.

'Yes.' She stared up at him feeling dazed. 'It was… slightly unreal.'

'Do you think we should try it again?' He murmured the words softly, almost playfully, his eyes on her lips. 'Just to test that it wasn't a figment of our imagination?'

'I think that would be a very good idea,' she agreed and leaned closer to meet his caress. Again as soon as their lips met it was like some explosion inside her. At first the kiss was slow and gently probing. Lucy could feel its effect winding its way insidiously right the way through her body and she felt with each second that passed as if she were falling deeper and deeper into a complete whirlpool of desire until suddenly she couldn't get enough of him…as if he were some kind of drug and she were now totally hooked. Just when she felt she might explode with need, he deepened the kiss.

She was aware that he was the one dictating the pace. He was very much in control and obviously he was a very experienced lover, probably knew all kinds of tricks to turn a woman on. But suddenly nothing else mattered in the world except the desire that had taken complete control of her senses.

Lucy wound her arms around his neck, wanting more, and their kisses entered a new stage, one that was frenzied and wild and totally mind-blowing. She felt his hands on her body, moving more intimately over her now, his hand sliding from her slender waist to the thrust of her breast and every inch of her ached for him to undress her and quench the thirst of her desire.

Then suddenly he stopped and pulled back. She stared up at him breathlessly, her eyes wide with questions—with need.

'Well, I think we've proved one thing beyond doubt…' His voice was husky with emotion. 'We definitely weren't imagining it. The sexual chemistry between us is wild. So much so that I think we'd better stop now because if we carry on I'm going to want to make love to you right here in the kitchen.'

'You're right…' Desperately she tried to pull herself together. But her senses were raging at the interruption and her body was aching with unfulfilled, insistent need.

His gaze flicked over her, taking in the way her body was struggling to get a breath, the way her eyes were clouded with longing and her softly parted lips still swollen with desire. 'There is no doubt about it, believe me. If I kiss you again I'm going to want to take you right here…right now.' For a moment there was naked hunger in his voice.

'And that would be so wrong.' Her voice trembled slightly.

His lips twisted wryly. 'Well, I suppose it depends how you look at it. We are both single…'

'Yes, but it would still be wrong.' She took a deep breath. 'After all, why make love in here when I've got a perfectly comfortable double bed in the next room?'

Even as she said the words she couldn't believe she was saying them. This was the sort of thing her friend Mel might say, but not her.

'Why indeed…?' he drawled, and stroked a hand softly along the side of her face. The touch of his skin against hers made her burn inside with need.

What on earth was wrong with her? she wondered frantically. She had always shied away from transitory affairs and this could be nothing more than that. And she was breaking all her rules about getting involved with a work colleague.

The thought should have brought her back to some semblance of sanity, but strangely it didn't. The trouble was that right at this moment she didn't care about any of that. She wanted him. In fact she couldn't remember ever wanting any man this badly.

So what if he was a work colleague and probably a philanderer…what the heck? she thought as she stood on tiptoe to kiss him again. He would be going back to Barbados in a week.

Just how many complications could one man stir up in a week?

CHAPTER FIVE

LUCY had left the bedside lamp on when she was drying her hair; she wished now that she hadn't. She would rather have had the comforting veil of darkness to hide behind. As soon as she stepped into the bedroom she felt awkward, shy even.

The gold covers on the bed and the gold and damson satin cushions gleamed softly in the subdued light. It was a stylish bedroom filled with period pieces. A Louis XV chair sat in the window and the dressing table held her silver-backed hairbrush and mirror.

Rick pulled her into his arms and there was a look of purpose in his dark eyes that set her heart thundering in her breast. 'Now...where were we?' he murmured.

'I think we were just about here.' She reached up and kissed him softly. For a moment they just stood entwined in each other's arms, then she felt his hand on the buttons of her skirt. 'Shall I turn the light off?' She pulled back from him nervously and made to reach towards the lamp by the side of the bed.

'No, leave it.' He pulled her back and peppered little kisses along her neck. 'I want to see you.' He murmured the words seductively against her ear. 'Want to explore every inch of you.'

Her heart skipped several beats, and the tension inside her spiralled. She wished now she hadn't asked him, had just plunged the room into darkness. He was obviously very experienced and, apart from a boyfriend when she had been at university, she had only ever been with one man—then they had married, and look how that had turned out.

Rick felt her stiffen in his arms. 'Are you okay?'

'Yes…'

He stopped kissing her and tipped her chin up so that he could look deeply into her eyes. There were shadows in their dark green beautiful depths.

'We don't need to go ahead with this if you've changed your mind.' His voice was velvet-soft, so gentle, so infinitely tender that it made her heart turn over with a renewed wave of longing.

'I haven't changed my mind,' she whispered.

He didn't answer her immediately; he still seemed to be studying her very closely.

'Have you got something?' she asked. 'Protection, I mean?'

He smiled. 'Yes…' Tenderly he brushed her hair back from her face. 'Is that what was worrying you?'

She hesitated for just a moment. She didn't want to tell him what had really been going through her mind—didn't want to spoil things by even mentioning Kris's name. That man had ruined enough of her life. So she just nodded.

He kissed the side of her neck. The sensation was overwhelmingly erotic, sending tingles of pleasure all the way through her. Then he kissed the side of her face across her cheekbones before finally capturing her lips. At the same time his hands were moving beneath her jumper, finding the lace of her bra and unhooking it with adept speed.

It was at that point that the last rational thoughts left her mind and sensible thoughts were discarded along with nerves. Suddenly nothing else mattered except the fact that she wanted this man, wanted him urgently—now.

His hands moved possessively over the generous curves of her body and she closed her eyes, giving herself up to the pleasure of his caresses. He pulled her jumper up further and she helped him pull it over her head, her hair falling in glossy wild abandon around her bare shoulders.

Then they were undressing each other. She was unbuttoning his shirt and at the same time she felt his hands unfastening the buttons of her skirt and drawing the zip down. It slithered to the floor leaving her standing before him in just her pants and lace-top stockings.

'You are so beautiful, Lucy,' he murmured, his fingers tracing along the curves of her firm up-tilted breasts. He bent his head and his lips followed the trail of his hands, dusting kisses across her body. The next moment he had swept her up off her feet and was laying her down against the satin cushions of the bed. He kicked off his shoes and joined her on the deep comfort of the double bed.

He had a fabulous physique, she thought as she looked up at him. And suddenly she was very glad that they had left the light on as she drank in the broad power of his shoulders that tapered to a lean waist and lithe hips. She reached up and let her fingers stroke down his chest, touching the hard flat muscles of his stomach. He was in perfect shape. Lucy felt her stomach contract with little darts of excitement and apprehension as he started to unbuckle the belt on his trousers.

'Hurry…' She whispered the word half playfully, and he laughed. Then he reached down and kissed her, with such a seductive kiss that it set her heart racing with pure adrenalin.

His kisses moved across her face and nuzzled in beside her ear as he whispered something to her in Spanish.

'What does that mean?' she murmured, her voice almost incoherent with need.

'It means, patience, my beautiful one. Have patience.' His fingers stroked slowly over her bare breasts, finding the sensitised peaks and toying with them, caressing her until she felt crazy with longing. Then he bent his head and the warmth of his mouth replaced his hands. She felt her body rack with shudders of pure pleasure and she took deep breaths trying to steady herself. Her hands raked through the dark thickness of his hair, loving the smooth texture of it, and then moved down his back, drawing him closer. She felt as if she could never, ever get close enough to this man.

It was early the next morning when Lucy woke. She was cradled gently in Rick's arms and she felt warm and comfortable and somehow filled with a wonderful sense of well-being. It was odd: she didn't really know this man at all, he was a virtual stranger, and yet lying in his arms she felt safe and protected and more secure than she had ever done in her life.

It was just an illusion, she told herself quickly, but for now it was a very wonderful illusion, and she lay still and revelled in the warm cocoon, her thoughts drifting hazily back to the night before and the incredible passion they had shared.

Rick was a fabulous lover. He had taken her to heights of pleasure again and again and they were heights she had never even known existed until last night.

She remembered Mel telling her that it was about time she took a dive into a little romantic water and that it could be just what she needed to get her back in the flow. Well, last night she had felt as if she had taken more than a little dip—it felt as if some almighty tidal wave had swept her away. The thought unnerved her slightly. When Kris had walked out she had sworn that no one would ever get the opportunity to hurt her like that again and she had meant it. She still meant it.

She turned restlessly and looked up at Rick, studying his features. Some people looked vulnerable as they slept, but Rick still had that air of strength about him. Maybe it was just the fact that he was so powerfully good-looking. Her eyes moved from the thick dark length of his lashes to the sensual curve of his lips, and her stomach tightened suddenly with renewed longing as she remembered how his lips had felt against the softness of her skin and how wildly he had stirred her senses. Kris had never made her lose control like that…had never swept her away on such a wild ride of exhilaration.

All in your imagination, Lucy, she told herself swiftly. And anyway, maybe she had just blocked out how Kris had made her feel. It wasn't something she wanted to think about.

Last night had been wonderful, but it wasn't anything too special, she told herself firmly. She had to get with the modern programme and start thinking like Mel. It had been just a bit of fun, that was all. And it had probably felt so good because she hadn't done it in such a long time…yes, that could be it. The thought reassured her, made her relax again.

Rick opened his eyes suddenly and she smiled. 'Good morning, lazybones. I was wondering if you were ever going to wake up.'

'Were you now?' His voice was languidly amused. 'Well, you see, the problem was that some young hussy kept me awake well into the small hours.'

'Really?' Lucy grinned and snuggled closer. 'Some people have no scruples.'

'I'm very glad to say that you're right.' He breathed the words huskily and bent to nibble on her ear. It sent a flood of sweet sensations racing through her.

She trailed her hand along the breadth of his shoulders, feeling the strength of his muscles rippling as he rolled her over so that she lay trapped beneath him.

'Last night was fabulous.' He said the words softly as he looked into the beauty of her eyes.

'Yes, it was.' She smiled.

He bent his head and kissed her lips, slowly, possessively. Lucy kissed him back, loving the sensation. And then suddenly they were making love again, only this was nothing like last night. There was none of the wild urgency that had driven them almost senseless…this was different. This was slow and leisurely and tender and somehow much more deeply intimate. Rick looked into her eyes as he entered her, watching her, and then devouring her, tasting the shuddering ecstasy of her lips, taking charge of all of her senses. This was being taken completely…in every sense of the word.

Afterwards she lay in his arms, deeply sated, a feeling of wonderment flooding through her. So much for last night being sensational because she hadn't done it in a long time. She could get used to having Rick in her bed—in her life.

With the thought came the first real sensation of deep unease.

Swiftly she forced herself to pull away from him.

'Where are you going?' he asked, rolling onto his side and watching her as she got out of bed.

'I thought I'd make us a cup of tea.' She picked her silk dressing gown up from a chair and, extremely conscious of his eyes on her naked body, she hurriedly put it on, belting it tightly around her slender waist.

'Actually I prefer coffee in the morning.'

'Do you?' She glanced over at him and it occurred to her again that she knew nothing about this man with whom she had just shared such intimate hours.

'Black, no sugar,' he told her.

'Okay.' It was something of a relief to get out of the room. She couldn't think straight around him. He was too handsome, too disturbingly sensual.

The coffee-cups still sat on the sideboard where he had left them last night. For a moment a vivid replay of how she had invited him into her bed flicked through her mind, making her go hot all over.

It was just sex, she told herself forcefully, no big deal. Okay, she had broken her rules about not getting involved with someone at work, but he would be gone at the end of the week. And as for those weird thoughts about how she could get used to having Rick in her life…well, they were just crazy, passion-induced illusions. Rick was a stranger to her and that was the way she wanted it to stay.

She felt a bit better after the pep talk, stronger, more in control.

She opened cupboard doors searching for some ground coffee, couldn't find any and just settled for instant.

Then the door opened behind her and Rick stood there. He was naked except for a white towel strung low around his waist and obviously he had just had a quick shower because his hair was wet and his broad chest still gleamed with droplets of water. 'How's the coffee coming?'

'Er…fine, all done.' Her heart seemed to be booming in her ears. This was all slightly unreal. Who was this gorgeous man draped just in a towel standing in her kitchen, making himself so much at home?

He strolled over and she hurriedly picked up his cup and handed it to him. 'Thanks.' He took a sip. 'That's good.' He grinned at her. 'Just what I needed after an exhausting night.'

She felt her skin heat up with embarrassing warmth and he laughed. 'I'm just teasing you, Lucy.'

'I know.'

He put his coffee down and caught hold of her before she could move away again. 'We can exhaust each other some more…if you'd like.'

She felt the heat of his arousal through the flimsy material between them and, despite the fact that she tried to hold herself back from him, she felt herself weaken instantly.

She swallowed on a knot in her throat, panic-stricken suddenly by the fact that she wanted this man all over again.

He bent and kissed her, teasingly, tantalizingly, and she responded.

Then suddenly they were kissing passionately and Lucy's

pulses were racing madly and all sensible thoughts had flown out the window.

She felt him untying the belt of her dressing gown, felt his hands moving over her body, and then the next moment he was lifting her up and carrying her back to the bedroom.

It was much later before Lucy could muster up enough energy to think straight. She lay curled up in his arms, wondering breathlessly how their lovemaking could keep getting better.

Her mobile phone buzzed and sleepily she reached out and lifted it. 'I've got a text message,' she murmured, flicking up the screen and peering at it. 'It's from the agency.'

'What agency?' Rick rolled over onto his side and propped himself up on his elbow so that he could look down at her.

'The speed-dating agency.' Lucy pulled up the sheet to cover her breast. It was crazy, Rick had sampled and seen every last inch of her, yet she still felt shy around him. 'Apparently I've got one match.'

'Yes, I know. You're in bed with him.' Rick grinned.

'No…actually this match is with someone called Mark Kirkland,' Lucy said as she scrolled down the message. 'They've sent me his mobile number.' She glanced teasingly up at Rick. 'He must have ticked my box…something you forgot to do.'

'On the contrary, I think I ticked your box several times,' Rick murmured, trailing a hand playfully over the top of the sheet. 'So you'll have to tell Mark that he's just too late. In fact…' he reached and took the phone out of her hand '…you're too busy to tell him anything.'

'Hey! Give me my phone.' She laughed and stretched to get it back, but he held it out of her reach.

'No, you're incommunicado for the morning.'

'Am I indeed?' Lucy looked up at him archly. 'How do you know I don't have a million plans for this morning?'

'And have you?'

'Well…' She felt herself blush. 'I was going to catch up on some housework and I've brought some files home that I need to go through—'

'Lucy!' He grinned at her. 'The housework and the files will have to wait. Because I'm going to ravish you sense-less.' Slowly he bent his head and kissed her teasingly on the lips. Then he drew her down in the bed and took full possession of her mouth, kissing her with mind-altering pas-sion.

The phone dropped to the floor as they both forgot about it.

'You know this is just sex…don't you.' Lucy murmured incoherently when he finally released her.

Rick pulled back from her, one dark eyebrow lifted wryly. 'Well, I didn't think we were playing cards, if that's what you mean. What are you talking about, Lucy?'

'I…' She felt her skin flushing wildly. The words had been playing in her head and she hadn't realised she had spoken them out loud. 'Sorry, that came out all wrong…' she murmured breathlessly. 'It's just that it's a long time since I've done this.'

Rick frowned. 'Done what?'

'This…' He watched as she moistened her lips nervously. 'It's a long time since I went to bed with a man.'

'Oh, I see.' For a moment his dark eyes were watchful. Then he stroked her hair back from her face and the whis-per-soft caress made all her senses tingle. 'How long?'

'I don't know.' Lucy looked away from him, suddenly wishing she hadn't started this conversation.

'Yes, you do. You know exactly.' His voice was quiet.

She tried to pull away from him, but he wouldn't let her go.

'Anyway, the point is that I have this rule about not getting involved with anyone at work.' Hurriedly she tried to move the subject along.

'I know, you told me.' He sounded amused now. 'Looks like you've just broken that rule, doesn't it?'

'No! Not really.' She frowned up at him. 'Because you don't really count, do you? As you said yourself, you'll be leaving at the end of the week.'

'Possibly.'

'What do you mean, "possibly"?' She pulled away from him and sat up, holding the sheet very tightly across her now. 'You told me you were only going to be in the office for a week and then you were going back to Barbados.'

He lay back against the pillows and noted the way her breathing had speeded up, the sudden wariness in her beautiful eyes. 'And I probably am. It just depends how long it takes me to make my final assessments at the office. What are you so afraid of, Lucy?' he asked suddenly.

'I'm not afraid of anything.' She swallowed hard and tried to force herself to sound relaxed. But the truth was that she *was* afraid—afraid of the way he made her feel. She didn't want any man getting under her skin again, and she needed to know in her heart that he was going away soon—that this was just a fling. 'I just…I just don't want what has happened between us to compromise our working relationship. That's all,' she finished carefully.

'You are *so* conscientious,' he murmured with a grin.

She tried to ignore his warmly teasing tone. 'And I don't want us to feel embarrassed around each other on Monday morning.'

'I promise I won't feel embarrassed.' He put one hand on his heart.

She met his eye and had to grin. 'Yes, okay, Rick, you're not the type to get embarrassed by such things. I should have realised that.'

'Yes, you should.' He pulled her down in the bed again, a gleam of purpose in his eyes.

'So, we are clear about our boundaries, then?' She forced herself to say the words even though a molten heat was starting to weaken her resolve.

Rick pulled back for a moment and fixed her with a quizzical gaze. 'What boundaries?'

'Well, for one, that we don't take this into the office.'

'I'm not so sure about that.' He sounded lazily amused for a moment. 'Because, you know, I was kind of looking forward to having sex on the photocopier.'

He watched the way her skin flushed with crimson heat and trailed a cooling hand over her cheekbones. 'Relax, Lucy. I never mix business with pleasure.' For just a second the bantering undertone had gone, replaced with a steely seriousness. 'Work always comes first with me.'

'Well, good.' She nodded. 'It seems we've got something in common, then.'

'So it does.' He trailed a hand over the side of her face. 'You know, you're the first woman I have ever met who is pleased about the fact I put my work first.'

'Good.' She smiled up at him. 'I like to be different.'

'You are different.' He looked into her eyes, liking the spirited way she held his gaze. 'But, you know, the most interesting thing we have in common is this.' He bent and kissed her softly on the lips and instantly a wild passion flared between them.

When he lifted his mouth she was breathless with longing.

'Now, I'm going to make love to you again, and it will have nothing to do with our relationship in the office. The two are entirely separate issues.'

'You're right,' she whispered huskily. 'But don't go reading anything into the fact that I'm letting you stay here in my bed a bit longer,' she added more firmly, and her eyes shimmered with vivid emphasis. 'It doesn't mean anything. Like I said before, this is just sex.'

'Yes, Lucy, it's just sex.' He smiled down at her. 'And it's the first time I've ever had to reassure a woman in this way.'

'I've turned the tables on you, have I? Well, that's good news. I'm all for girl power.' She grinned impishly at him.

'So am I.' He kissed her softly again and she wound her arms around his neck.

A few more hours wouldn't hurt. What were a few hours in the grand scheme of things? And then next week he would be gone.

CHAPTER SIX

LUCY went into the office early on Monday morning. She had slept badly the night before, had tossed and turned wondering how she was going to face Rick at work.

It was all very well trying to act oh, so casual when they were in bed together, telling him that what they had shared was just sex, but in truth she wasn't nearly so blasé. And as soon as he had left her apartment on Saturday afternoon reality had hit her. For one thing she couldn't believe that she had broken all her rules about getting involved with someone at work! What on earth had happened to make her lose her senses like that? She just couldn't understand it.

So here she was at eight-fifteen, calmly trying to arrange her diary. To the outward world she probably looked the personification of calm competence. But inside she felt a complete mess.

Don't be ridiculous, Lucy, she told herself firmly. It was just sex, as Mel would say, no big deal. All she had done was join the modern world.

'Hi, Lucy!' Carolyn put her head around the partition on her way down the corridor. 'How was your weekend?'

'It was fine.' Lucy smiled at her. 'How was yours?'

'Oh, it was lovely. Carl took his first step.'

'Carolyn! It happened when you were home! How wonderful!' Lucy smiled at her friend; pleased for her because she knew she had been worried she might miss that precious first moment with her baby.

'Yes, we were both there.' Carolyn's eyes shimmered with happiness. 'And we got a photo!'

'That's great.'

'And how was the speed dating?' Carolyn asked, suddenly changing the subject.

'It was okay…a bit of fun.'

'Did you meet anybody special?'

'Not really,' Lucy murmured, trying to ignore the strange little flutters of distress. She wasn't lying, she told herself firmly. Rick was very sexy, very nice, but not special to her. The fact that somehow she had spent a whole night and morning in bed with him, and he'd made her feel…well, she didn't want to think about the way he'd made her feel. It wasn't relevant. He wasn't special.

Why couldn't her life be uncomplicated like Carolyn's? she wondered suddenly. She had thought when she'd married Kris that it would be. That they would settle down and live happily ever after with two lovely children and that the weekend would be dedicated to family times… Fiercely she switched her mind away from that. Her marriage hadn't worked. She had tried…heavens, how she had tried…but in the end she had had to just say that she had made a mistake. Married the wrong man. It happened.

'So you didn't meet anyone who made your heart beat even a little bit faster?' Carolyn persisted.

'You are such a romantic, Caro.' Lucy laughed.

'You used to be a romantic too,' Carolyn said softly.

'Maybe.' Lucy shrugged. 'But that seems like a very long time ago.' She was a different person now, she told herself firmly. No one would ever get to her the way Kris had.

But for a moment she remembered how wonderful it felt lying entwined in Rick's arms, giggling, messing about. Abruptly she closed the memory. Rick had kissed her good-bye with a slow, lingering intensity and that, she told herself firmly now, was the end of that. She just hoped it wouldn't interfere with their professional relationship. The big boss was arriving this week and she desperately needed to have her wits about her. She needed this job.

Trying very hard to ignore all the little harbingers of doom, she hit the button on her answer machine to check her messages.

'Hello, Lucy.' A man's deep voice filtered out. 'This is Mark Kirkland. We met Friday night, remember? I hope you don't mind my phoning you on this number, but I haven't been able to get through to you on your mobile and the agency gave me this number as well. I was wondering if you'd like to have dinner with me, either tonight or tomorrow. Give me a ring, will you? My number is...'

'So you did meet somebody!' Carolyn smiled. 'You dark horse, Lucy! I can see I'm going to have to collar Mel for all the juicy details.'

'There are no juicy details!' Lucy said in consternation. But Carolyn wasn't listening. She just smiled as she headed off towards her own desk.

Cringing, Lucy switched off the machine. That message was all she needed to add to her discomfort.

She hoped to high heaven Mel wouldn't say anything about Rick if asked about Friday night. The thought made little butterflies do a clog dance in her stomach.

Trying to forget about that, she rang Mark Kirkland and told him she wouldn't be able to meet him after all and that she was very sorry. It was one less complication in her life, she told herself firmly as she replaced the receiver.

The rest of the staff started to arrive, and Lucy switched her mind to the morning's work.

It wasn't long before computers were on and the usual hustle and bustle of Monday got under way. One of the staff had problems with a crashed program and Lucy went to help her sort it out. She felt immediately better. She could deal with this; she could deal with a thousand problems in the office; and she could deal with seeing Rick Connors...could forget what had happened between them.

Then as she turned around she saw Rick standing watching her, and her calm confidence immediately wavered.

'Morning, Lucy.' He smiled at her.

'Good morning, Mr Connors.' She tried very hard to sound breezily indifferent to him.

He was wearing a dark suit that sat with continental stylishness on his broad shoulders, and he looked incredibly handsome, so much so that Lucy could feel her senses starting to take a dive. Her heart rate increased dramatically as their eyes met and held.

His dark eyes were steady and intense. What was he thinking? Did he find it amusing that she was now calling him Mr Connors? Was he remembering the ease with which he had taken her to bed, the wild passion? Abruptly she tried to switch her mind away from all that as her skin started to heat up.

He smiled, and then his gaze swept over her and she didn't know if it was her imagination, but in a moment he seemed to take in everything about her, from her high heels to the knee-length grey pencil skirt, and pale pink top she wore, to the way she had pinned her long hair back from her face. Then his gaze locked with hers again. 'Did you have a good weekend?'

He was one cool customer, she thought shakily. Far, far too relaxed. She remembered how he had assured her that he wouldn't feel embarrassed today and a sudden thought occurred to her. Maybe he had lied about not mixing business with pleasure. Maybe he was used to it.

She raised her chin a little, determined to be equally sanguine about the situation. 'It was okay.' She forced herself not to flinch away from his scrutiny and noted a flicker of amusement in his eyes.

'Have you been having some problems with the computers?' He stepped nearer.

'Nothing I couldn't fix,' she said quickly.

'Yes, so I noticed. You seem very capable on all levels, Lucy.'

What was that supposed to mean? A few of the staff were flicking interested glances over in Rick's direction now.

'So what can I do for you this morning, Mr Connors?' she said, raising her voice and trying her best to sound very businesslike. She really was going to have to dismiss Friday night from her mind, she told herself very firmly.

'Well, Ms Blake, I'd like it very much if you'd give me a tour of your department and introduce me to your staff,' he said, matching her tone.

She glanced over and saw the flicker of amusement in his dark eyes again. Did he think this was just one big joke? Of course, it was all right for him. He was going back to Barbados soon; she was the one who would be left dealing with the gossip if any of this got out.

Carefully she avoided looking at him and nodded. 'Of course, no problem,' she said lightly, but inside she felt a bit annoyed that her department should be the first to come under scrutiny today.

Linda Fellows' desk was the nearest, so Lucy introduced her first. Lucy was amused to see that she wasn't the only one mesmerised by Rick's good looks. Linda was practically swooning on the spot as Rick spoke to her.

Lucy hoped fervently that her reaction to the man wasn't so obvious.

As each of the women in the room fell like skittles the moment he smiled at them Lucy's manner became more and more efficient. She was very glad that she had caught herself up this morning before she became one more adoring female fan. No man's ego deserved that much stroking, she thought irately.

Rick finished talking to the last of the staff, then turned his attention to the filing systems and the computer programs they were using.

'Perhaps you'd talk me through these.' He glanced over at her as he flicked through different screens.

'Certainly.' She had to go closer to him to use the keyboard. She could smell the tang of his cologne; it brought back intense memories from the weekend…memories of lying in his arms, of feeling his hands moving over her with such sure, sweet sensuality. Her stomach flipped wildly. She tried to move away from him, but it was impossible in front of such a small screen.

As she reached for the mouse her hand collided with his and she felt a shot of electricity flood through her body. Sharply she pulled away.

'Is this the system you usually use?' Rick asked nonchalantly. He seemed totally unaware of the effect he was having on her; in fact he was leaning closer to look at the screen, and for a moment his shoulder rested against hers. She could feel his touch burning through to her very skin.

'Yes. That's about it.' She stepped away from him. 'If you'll excuse me, I've just remembered I have an important phone call to make. Linda will go through the rest of the programs with you.' Lucy smiled over at her colleague and Linda seemed only too pleased to come over to relieve her.

It was a relief to get back to her desk. Lucy wasted some time flicking through her diary, trying to get her heart rate under some kind of control. What on earth was wrong with her? she wondered frantically.

She slanted a surreptitious glance over at Rick as she picked up the phone to make her bogus phone call. He hadn't seemed to mind her leaving him with Linda. She was fluttering around him now, explaining the filing system they used.

Rick smiled at the other woman, thanking her, charm just oozing from him.

Lucy dialled Mel's number.

'Mel Roberts here.' Her friend's helpful tone was an immediate balm.

'Hi, it's me,' Lucy murmured, turning her swivel chair away from the source of her agitation. 'I made a big, big mistake on Friday night.'

'No, you didn't,' Mel said swiftly. 'He was gorgeous.'

'Yes, and now he's running an assessment on my department,' she hissed. 'And I feel totally out of my depth.'

Mel laughed. 'I bet he was good in bed.'

'Mel! Please! I'm feeling bad enough.'

'Maybe you just need second helpings.'

'That's something I definitely don't need. Listen, if Carolyn asks you about Friday night, don't for heaven's sake tell her anything.'

'Of course not. I know you value your privacy, Lucy. I would never say anything.'

Lucy felt awful now for doubting her friend.

Out of the corner of her eye Lucy saw Rick heading towards her. 'So I want the advert to run from tomorrow until the following Tuesday,' she said, switching her tone to a brisk business one.

'Got company?' Mel guessed.

'Yes, that's right.'

'Everything all right, Lucy?' Rick asked nonchalantly and, much to Lucy's consternation, he perched himself on the side of her desk next to her.

'I won't be a moment, Rick,' she said calmly. 'I've just got to place a few adverts before the time deadline.'

'Fine.'

To her consternation he didn't move away, just sat there watching her.

'So have you got that, Ms Barry?' Lucy improvised wildly. 'We want the advert to run for five consecutive weeknights.'

Mel laughed. 'Shall we meet for a drink after work?'

'I think the budget might just stretch to that.'

'Great. Usual place, six-thirty.' Mel put the phone down.

'Sorry about that.' She summoned her best impersonal kind of smile as she turned her attention back to Rick.

Rick smiled. 'I think we need to have an in-depth talk, Lucy,' he said easily.

'Do we?' Her heart jumped nervously against her chest. 'What about?'

'About your advertising budget for next month and the various itineraries that you are promoting at the moment.'

'Oh, I see.' She hoped she wasn't blushing. She had mistakenly thought he was talking on a personal basis. 'Well, yes, of course.'

'Good.' His dark eyes held with hers. 'We'll talk over lunch; shall we say one-thirty?'

Now Lucy was totally wrong-footed. Was this a business lunch or something else? She remembered he had mentioned something about lunch when they had been on the bus together on Friday. Hard to believe now that this man had ever sat with her on a bus...or nibbled her ear so provocatively. Hastily she switched her mind away from all of that.

'Is this a business lunch?' She forced herself to ask the question.

'Absolutely.' He smiled at her.

The smile was the same warm smile that had done dizzying things to her emotions over the weekend.

'That's okay, then.' She tried to sound firmly in control, but in reality she was anything but.

It was almost a relief when Kris walked in.

'Morning, Kris.' Her smile was warmer than usual as she looked up at him. How bad is that? she thought wryly. Any distraction was welcome...even her ex!

'Hi.' He smiled back and for a moment he seemed distracted as he gazed at her. Then swiftly he turned his attention to Rick. 'I have the files ready that you requested. They are waiting for you in Accounts.'

'Great.' Rick stood up from the desk. Lucy noticed how he seemed to tower over her ex.

'If you'd like a more detailed breakdown of each itinerary including cost analysis, I'd be happy to run through things now,' Kris said briskly.

'Thanks, Kris, but I haven't got time,' Rick said easily. He glanced at his watch. 'I have a meeting scheduled. We'll do it later this afternoon.'

'Fine.' Kris nodded.

'See you later, Lucy.' Rick smiled at her.

For a second Lucy smiled back, and then she caught herself up and returned briskly back to her work. No man had a right to have a smile like that, she thought distractedly. It should come with a health-warning sign.

As Rick turned to leave Kris lingered by her desk.

'Was there something else?' Lucy asked him, wishing he would move away and leave her in peace.

'Well, actually, yes. I was wondering if I could have a word.' Kris paused and then to her consternation perched himself on the edge of her desk where Rick had been sitting just a moment ago.

'I'm a bit busy, Kris,' Lucy murmured uncomfortably. She flashed a wary look up at him. 'What's it about?'

'Well, if you're busy maybe it can wait,' he said.

'Okay, see you later,' she said quickly.

He hesitated and she could feel his eyes moving over her.

What on earth was going on in his mind? Since their divorce they had carefully avoided each other whenever possible, always acting with polite civility when they had to speak. Kris had never tried to cross that line before and she was very glad about it. The situation was difficult enough.

Maybe he wanted to tell her about the baby? The thought made her stiffen. She sat up straighter in her chair.

'You know you're looking very well recently, Lucy,' he said suddenly. 'Radiant, almost.'

'Thanks.' Her tone was dismissive. She desperately needed him to go now.

'I am glad we can still be friends, you know.'

'Are you?'

'Yes, of course I am.' He frowned and for a moment there was a flicker of genuine concern in his blue eyes. 'I've always cared about you, Lucy,' he said, lowering his tone to almost a whisper.

It was on the tip of Lucy's tongue to tell him he had a funny way of showing it, but she reined back the sarcasm. 'I really need to get on with work now, Kris,' she said abruptly instead. 'I'm behind with things this morning as it is.'

He nodded, but still didn't move away. 'Maybe we could have a coffee some time?'

She didn't answer him, just turned to her computer and started to tap in some figures.

'You know, I am sorry I hurt you, Lucy.' He whispered the words softly. 'Really I am.'

'It's all in the past, Kris, and maybe it was all for the best. Let's not rake over it.' She didn't take her eyes away from the screen of her computer.

Kris seemed about to say something else, then he shot a look around the office to see if anyone was looking in their direction. A few people hurriedly glanced back at their screens. 'We can't talk in here. Maybe we could meet at lunchtime?'

'I can't.'

'Why not?'

'I'm meeting Rick Connors to go over my advertising budget with him.'

Kris frowned. 'You seem…different around him.'

'Different?' She looked up at him. 'How do you mean?'

He shrugged. 'I can't explain it, but I sense something between you when he looks at you. A frisson of something.'

'Rubbish!' Lucy's heart was thundering against her breast now.

'It's not rubbish. Don't forget, I know you, Lucy…'

'Look, is this leading anywhere? Because I really am busy.' She continued tapping the figures in, but her fingers were hitting the wrong keys now.

'No. I just…never mind.' Kris leaned closer and whispered loudly, 'Look, Lucy, if you want a word of advice then it's this: tread carefully around Rick Connors; I think he's well up in this new company. They say he's a very powerful, very influential man.'

For a second a picture of Rick undressing her flashed into her mind, followed by even more intimate memories of how wildly and how uninhibitedly she had given herself to him. That advice was just a little too late, she thought uncomfortably.

'I'm having a working lunch with him, Kris. Thank you for the advice, but I don't need it.'

'Just trying to be helpful.' To her relief he stood up. 'Okay, well, I'll see you later.'

What on earth was that all about? Lucy wondered as she watched him walk away. That had to be the most she had spoken to Kris in nearly a year.

I sense something between you when he looks at you. A frisson of something. The words played uncomfortably through her mind.

Rubbish, she told herself firmly. Absolute rubbish. And why was Kris suddenly so concerned?

The phone rang next to her and she snapped it up. 'Lucy Blake, how may I help you?'

'Hi, Lucy, it's Rick.'

She felt a sudden rush of disquiet as she heard his smoothly confident tone.

'Lucy, are you there?'

She could hear traffic noises in the background; obviously he was out somewhere and calling her from his mobile.

'Yes, I'm here.'

'I'm stuck in traffic, which means I'm going to be late for my next meeting. So we'll have to reschedule lunch for later. Shall we say two-fifteen?'

'I can't make that,' Lucy told him bluntly. 'I have a few meetings scheduled myself.' She glanced down at the blank pages of her diary and hastily picked up a pencil to scribble in some bogus names. She didn't want to have lunch with Rick Connors. In fact she wanted to run as far as she could in the opposite direction from him.

'Cancel them.' There was no doubting the fact that she had just been issued with an order. Who the hell did he think he was? Lucy wondered angrily.

'That's not so easy—'

'Yes, it is. Just pick up the phone and do it.' Rick's tone brooked no argument. 'I'll send a car for you, be down in the foyer at ten past two.'

The line went dead.

Lucy put the receiver down with a resounding crash and a few people glanced over at her. The nerve of the guy, she thought furiously. Sending a car for her indeed!

CHAPTER SEVEN

SOMEHOW Lucy managed to put in a few hours' work, but her mind kept wandering. First she was thinking about Rick, and the strange effect he had on her. Then she was thinking about Kris and how weird their conversation had been.

She had first met Kris when she was twenty-two. They been attending a two-day seminar; Lucy had been sent by her office, Kris by his. Lucy had to admit the attraction had been instantaneous. He had looked very handsome and trendy and he had made her laugh. They had agreed to meet up when the course was over.

She remembered that first date very clearly. He had picked her up in his bright yellow convertible sports car and had driven her out into the country and they had enjoyed lunch at a picturesque pub sitting by the banks of the River Thames. It had been spring and everything had seemed vibrant and fresh and filled with possibilities.

Kris had reached out and caught hold of her hand across the table and told her how lovely she looked.

He had always known the right things to say, she thought now. She remembered when she had brought him home and introduced him to her parents he had charmed them too.

They had dated for a few years before getting engaged. Then there had been the big white wedding.

She remembered how when they had danced together at their reception he had told her he felt he was the luckiest man in the world, and she had looked up into his eyes and had been so much in love…

A wave of anger flooded through her. Why was she thinking about this now? She had been a fool, an absolute fool.

And, yes, he had seemed so sincere, but it had been an act. As soon as they had been married he had changed.

At first she had put it down to stress. They had taken out a big mortgage to buy the flat and three months later Kris had lost his job. Lucy had remained positive and motivated. After all, Kris was well qualified; she had known he'd get something else. But after six weeks of job-hunting Kris had sunk into a bit of a depression. Nothing he'd been offered had been as good as his old job. Then an opening had come up here, and Lucy had pounced on it for him, had got the forms and, if she was honest, pulled a few strings to get him in.

Things had been better after that, or so she had thought. She remembered how on the day he got the job she had cooked him a special meal and they had opened a bottle of champagne. They had cuddled up in bed later that night and talked about starting a family.

'I love you, Lucy,' he whispered. 'And we'll definitely start thinking about a family some time soon.'

'What about now?' She kissed him playfully.

'Let's just enjoy ourselves for a little while, Lucy. We're not ready yet. And also I think we should get some capital behind us first.'

He knew she wanted a baby but he kept putting her off. It wasn't the right time; work was at a delicate stage; maybe next year when he was more settled...maybe they should wait until he got promoted.

Kris was quite obsessed with the notion of getting further up the company ladder. He worked long hours and gave everything towards getting that promotion but it didn't happen. At the last moment he was bypassed for someone else. Thinking back, that affected their relationship. He was so angry about it, almost as if he blamed her, yet it was nothing to do with her. After that, the subject of a baby was never mentioned again.

There were some people who said that Kris was jealous of her successful career; wasn't able to handle the fact that she was higher up the ladder than him. They said that was why he left her...maybe they were right. Lucy didn't know, although she thought it was probably more to do with the fact that his new partner was a twenty-three-year-old blonde with legs that seemed to go on for ever.

Lucy didn't have a clue about the affair. Yes, he was late home some nights. But he said he was at the gym and she believed him. She wasn't the clinging, suspicious type; she trusted him. Even when he told her he was going away for a week golfing with some friends, she believed him.

It was such a shock when she found out the truth. She felt so stupid, so naïve, so desperately hurt. Even now, when she thought about it, the rawness could strike straight into her heart like a cancer.

Don't think about it, she told herself fiercely. She had made a mistake with Kris; there was no point beating herself up about it.

The buzzer on her phone went. 'Lucy, there is someone waiting for you in Reception,' a voice told her.

She glanced at her watch and got a shock. She was late for her lunch appointment with Rick. 'I'll be right down.'

Hastily she gathered the files that Rick wanted to discuss and, snatching her coat from the stand, hurried downstairs.

Lucy was a bit taken aback when she saw the chauffeur standing in the foyer waiting for her. When Rick had said he'd send someone to collect her she had assumed it would be a taxi.

Followed by some curious glances from the girls on the reception desk, Lucy left the building and slid into the back seat of the stretched limo.

'Mr Connors says if you'd like a drink, then help yourself.' The chauffeur pointed to the drinks bar facing her.

'Er…no, thanks, this is a working lunch,' Lucy told him politely.

The door closed and then he was driving her through the busy streets.

Lucy busied herself sorting through her files and tried not to think about being alone with Rick for lunch. The restaurant would probably be busy and they would just be talking about work. It would be no big deal, she told herself firmly. But every now and then a glimmer of apprehension stirred and she glanced up, wondering where the driver was taking her. She was just about to lean forward to ask him, when to her surprise he turned and pulled up outside Cleary's hotel.

'Here we are, ma'am.' He got out and opened the door for her. 'Mr Connors will be waiting for you inside.'

'Thank you.' Lucy smiled at him and stepped out of the car.

It was one of those days that looked lovely when viewed from inside. There was a bright blue sky and the sun was dazzling, but the air was bitingly cold. Lucy was glad to step into the luxurious warmth of the hotel foyer. She supposed it made sense that their business lunch was here— after all the company owned the hotel—but, even so, it felt strange revisiting the place so soon and she couldn't help but remember what had happened after her last meeting here with Rick. Swiftly she shut that thought away.

'Lucy. Over here.'

She looked over and saw Rick leaning nonchalantly against the reception desk, talking on his mobile phone. He waved to her and she walked towards him.

'I'd like you to get onto that straight away.' He continued with his conversation, but mouthed to her that he wouldn't be long.

She put her heavy files down on the desk and stood patiently waiting. The foyer was busy; there were people checking in and bellboys bringing luggage over towards the lifts. Probably the restaurant would be packed out, she told herself, and the thought comforted her.

'Yes, all right. But make sure it's sorted by Wednesday at the latest.' Lucy noticed he used the same tone he had used with her earlier. It sounded as if he was used to giving orders.

'Sorry about that.' He put his phone away and his eyes moved to the stack of files beside him on the counter. 'I see you've come prepared.' He grinned.

'I brought this year's figures as well as last, so you can compare the logistics.'

'Good thinking.' He smiled at her and picked them up. 'But maybe we'll need an extra-long lunch hour to get through all this.'

'That won't be possible,' Lucy told him quickly. 'I have a meeting in just over an hour and a half.'

'I told you to cancel all your meetings.' His voice was brisk.

'I thought you just meant the ones over lunch!'

Rick shook his head. 'Never mind. If necessary you can ring and cancel from here.'

Lucy wanted to argue with that. Cancelling meetings at the last minute was hardly professional…but as, in reality, she had no meetings and his manner was so authoritative, she closed her mouth again and said nothing.

Instead of following the signs for the restaurant, Rick headed towards a lift on the far side of the room.

'Where are we going?' Lucy watched with mounting concern as he inserted a security card into a slot.

'The company have a suite on the top floor. It will be more private.'

The lift doors swished open.

'I don't see why we need to closet ourselves away up there. Surely the restaurant would be fine—'

'It's too busy, Lucy. We wouldn't be able to concentrate on work in there.' He stepped in and she had no option other than to follow him. The alternative was to make a fuss, draw attention to the fact that her mind was not fully on work, but preoccupied by more personal matters, and she would never admit to that. It was far too embarrassing.

They travelled upwards in silence, Lucy trying her best to avoid eye contact with him.

Rick noticed the way she held herself so straight. His eyes moved over her, taking in the stunning contrast between her creamy skin and the dark luxurious hair. The long dark eyelashes were lowered, the softness of her lips parted. She was an extremely sensuous woman.

'Tell me, Lucy…'

Her eyes flicked up towards him and he noticed the wariness in their green depths.

'Is there any Irish blood in your veins?'

He saw the surprise in her expression and he wondered what she had thought he was going to ask.

'Not to my knowledge, no.' She shrugged. 'Why do you ask?'

'You have the same colouring as my father. His hair was maybe a little darker, but his skin was like yours, pale as alabaster.'

'You're talking about him in the past tense. Is he dead?'

Rick shook his head. 'No, but he's extremely ill. I don't think he'll last the year out.'

'I'm sorry.' She held his gaze for a moment. Lucy was close to her father and she didn't even want to begin to imagine how awful it would be to lose him.

'It's been a pretty rough time. Made worse, I suppose, by the fact that we hadn't spoken for a year before he was diagnosed.'

'How awful!' Lucy frowned. 'Why weren't you speaking?'

'Long story of boring family politics.' Rick shrugged. 'But to cut it short, he wanted me to be married and to produce a son and heir.'

'A bit of old-fashioned thinking,' Lucy murmured.

'Yes, well, he is a bit old-fashioned. I lived with a woman for a few years and it was assumed we would marry. When we didn't he was bitterly disappointed.'

Lucy wondered what had happened, and why he had split up from the woman. Had he walked out on the relationship when the word 'commitment' was raised? She would have liked to ask, but Rick's expression was grim for a second and the subject seemed too intensely personal somehow, so instead she said lightly, 'Marriage is not something you can foist on a person.'

'Yes, and I think you know deep inside when something will work and when it won't,' Rick said seriously.

'Sometimes.' Lucy shrugged and looked away from him again. When she had married Kris she hadn't had any doubts. She hadn't realised what a huge mistake she had made until the last moments of their marriage. 'But sometimes your instincts can be fooled,' she added quietly.

The lift doors swished open and Lucy was distracted from their conversation by the view that greeted her. The ultra-modern lounge they stepped out into was vast and there was a wall of glass looking out over a breathtaking panorama of London.

'Gosh, you can see everything from up here, can't you?' Lucy moved across the highly polished wood floor to look out. She could see the London Eye and the Houses of Parliament in the distance, and the River Thames snaking its way through the heart of the city looked as blue as the sky.

'Yes, it's a good view.' Rick put her files down on the chrome and glass side table. 'Would you like a drink?'

'Just a mineral water, please.' She turned and watched as he went to a bar area and got a bottle from the fridge.

'What does the company use this place for?' she asked curiously as she looked around at the white leather settees, the black rugs, and the very expensive abstract paintings.

'Business trips to the City.' Rick handed her drink over and then picked up the files. 'Come on, I'll show you around.'

She followed him, curious to see what was up here.

From the lounge there was a corridor, and through the first door there was a state-of-the-art office complete with flat-screened computers, printers, fax machines. It was probably big enough to accommodate five staff.

'Does the boss bring his own personal team of workers with him when he travels?' Lucy asked.

'Sometimes.' Rick went in and put her files down on one of the desks.

'And what's down here?' Lucy wandered further along the corridor. Next door there was a huge boardroom with a table that would probably have seated thirty people.

'Have you attended many meetings here?' Lucy asked as he joined her by the door.

'A fair few.'

'He likes his gadgets, doesn't he?' Lucy remarked dryly as she noticed the large motorised screen that would probably slide from the ceiling with the touch of a button.

'I suppose he does. That's for watching films of new businesses—'

'And after the film you all sit around and discuss how many jobs should go.'

'Not always.'

Lucy looked up at him in disbelief.

Rick met her eyes steadily. 'Why do I get the feeling you don't approve of your new boss very much?' he drawled.

'Maybe I don't.' Lucy shrugged. 'Let's face it, Rick,

nearly every business that has been taken over by EC Cruises has been divided up. I suppose the word asset-stripper comes to mind.'

'He's a businessman,' Rick said nonchalantly.

'Yes, a cold-blooded, ruthless one.' The words were out before she could stop them.

'I didn't realise you felt so strongly.' His voice was quiet, almost deathly quiet.

'Yes, well, maybe I don't…maybe I'm just concerned about the way things are going to go at the office.' She quickly tried to backtrack. It probably wasn't a good idea to start criticising her new boss; after all, she didn't know how close Rick was to him. What was it Kris had said? *Tread carefully around Rick Connors…he's a very powerful, very influential man.*

Rick smiled. 'Don't try and wriggle away from the truth, Lucy. You don't like EC Cruises.'

'I didn't say that.' Lucy looked up and met the wry expression in Rick's eyes. 'I just…well, I suppose I think they are more interested in profit than people.'

'If a company is to survive it has to be interested in profit; otherwise nobody would have a job.'

'Yes, but it doesn't have to be ruthless,' she said firmly. 'It doesn't have to go out to totally annihilate.'

'And that's what you think we do?'

The quietly asked question made her shift uncomfortably. 'I don't think that of you personally. You're just doing your job.'

'Thanks for the endorsement.' Rick's lips twisted wryly.

She shrugged. 'It's just that I've read a few business reports—'

'You can't always believe what you read.' Rick cut across her swiftly. 'And I suggest you give your new boss a chance to take over properly before you start criticising him.'

'I suppose you're right,' she agreed warily.

'No supposing about it, I am right.' Rick reached out a hand and caught hold of her chin, forcing her to look up and meet his eyes. 'You should definitely give him a chance.'

Although his voice was firm almost to the point of authoritative, the hand on her skin was gentle and it sent immediate shock waves racing through her.

Their eyes held for a moment and she could feel her heart beating painfully against her chest. Then suddenly, instead of thinking about her new boss, she was remembering all the things she shouldn't…like how good it had felt in Rick's arms. Hastily she stepped back from him. 'Well, maybe I'm wrong and I'll give him a chance,' she murmured lightly. 'You know him, after all, and I don't.'

'You could say that.'

'And you like him.'

Rick's lips twisted wryly. 'Let's say he's a man who knows what he wants, and is not afraid to go after it.'

'And do you think there will be redundancies?' She forced herself to concentrate on work and not think about the way he was looking at her.

'I think he will try to avoid them at all costs. But there can be no guarantees, Lucy. Just as there can be no guarantees anywhere in life.'

Lucy nodded, but couldn't help herself from adding dryly, 'I still don't think I like the sound of him.'

'Well, I suppose, we all can't afford your high principles.' Rick held her gaze unwaveringly. 'And maybe there is something you should know—'

The shrill ring of a telephone suddenly cut through the tense atmosphere between them.

Rick hesitated, and then he moved away from her. 'Excuse me. I won't be a moment.'

She watched as he walked away and disappeared back into the office. What had he been about to say? She wandered further along the corridor away from the boardroom and tried not to think about the strange kind of tension that had been spiralling between them. There had been part of her that hadn't wanted to talk about the business or about the new boss, but had just wanted him to take her into his arms again. It was probably what had driven her to be deliberately inflammatory about the new company...it had been a cloak to hide behind. Had she gone too far? she wondered now. Rick hadn't looked amused.

She pushed open a door and found herself looking into a most magnificent bedroom. Obviously no expense had been spared in its décor. The bed was enormous; the floors were polished mahogany. The windows covered the wall and had the same panoramic vista of London as the lounge.

Lucy wandered further inside and looked around the corner at the white marble bathroom with gold taps. She put her glass of water down on the bedside table, and then sat for a moment on the bed. It was a waterbed and it moved seductively under her weight. What kind of a man was her boss? she wondered.

'Lucy.'

Rick's voice from the doorway made her jump. She looked over at him, feeling guilty at being caught snooping.

'Sorry.' She stood up quickly. 'I was being nosy. We should get back to work.'

'I suppose we should.' He moved further into the room and something about the way he was looking at her made her heart miss several beats.

'This is some bedroom.' She tried to sound nonchalant. 'I've never slept on a waterbed.'

'Haven't you?' He moved closer. 'Would you like to sleep on one?' The husky question made her body temperature soar.

She looked over at him uncertainly. 'I hope you're not

suggesting anything improper!' Her shocked tones seemed
to echo around the huge room.

He smiled. 'Would I do something like that?'

The teasing gleam in his eye did nothing to allay the wild
turmoil flooding through her. 'Probably.'

'You know, you can be very serious, Lucy. And, anyway,
weren't you the one who told me it was just sex, no big
deal?' He watched the way her cheeks flooded with colour.

'Look, I think maybe you got the wrong idea about me
on Friday night,' she said briskly.

'Did I?'

'Yes.' She tried to meet his eyes firmly. 'I don't go in
for casual sex. It was a moment of madness.'

'Several moments of madness,' he murmured with a grin.

She glared at him, her eyes sparkling with fire. 'If you
were any kind of a gentleman you wouldn't mention that.'

'Wouldn't I?' Rick shook his head. 'Then maybe I'm not
any kind of a gentleman.'

'No, you're not.' She put her hand on her hip. 'Look, if
it's all the same to you, I just want to forget about what
happened between us at the weekend. I wasn't thinking
straight. I was upset.' She added the words desperately.

'Were you?' His eyes were serious now the smile had
gone. 'Why were you upset?' he asked gently.

'I just was.' She said the words firmly, and hoped that
would be the end of the discussion, but Rick still stood
between her and the door, watching her, waiting.

'I'd heard some news about my ex-husband, okay?' she
said at length, hoping that would suffice.

'And that upset you?'

She nodded. But the awful thing, the really appalling
thing, was that deep down she knew she was lying. Okay,
she had been upset when she had heard Kris's partner was
pregnant, but it had had nothing to do with the way she had
fallen into Rick's arms on Friday night. Absolutely nothing.

She had slept with Rick because she had wanted to, because she found him wildly exciting. And probably if he were to touch her now, kiss her…she would fall into his arms and it would happen all over again. The realisation made her heart thump painfully against her chest.

'So what was the news?' Rick asked calmly.

'That's really none of your business.'

'I thought it became my business when you used me for solace.'

'I didn't use you!' She looked over at him, horrified by the suggestion, and he grinned.

'Hey, I'm not complaining. I enjoyed myself.'

Her cheeks glowed bright pink at those words. 'Can we just forget about it now and get back to work?'

'Sure,' he agreed easily.

'Thanks.' Lucy gave him a shadowy smile. She supposed it was no big deal for him; he was probably used to transitory affairs. He obviously just found her attitude towards it highly amusing. That much was clear from the way he was able to joke about it.

'I asked the restaurant to set a table for us in the lounge.' Rick glanced at his watch. 'It should be waiting for us now. Let's go through.'

'Well, I am on a bit of a tight schedule, Rick…' She didn't feel in the least bit hungry. In fact she felt food would probably just stick in her throat. She wanted to keep busy around Rick Connors…needed to keep busy. 'Shall I run through a few items as we eat?'

'By all means.'

He stood back and allowed her to precede him through the door and for just a second his hand rested against her shoulder. She was acutely aware of that fleeting touch; acutely aware that, for all her firm words of protestation, just forgetting about Friday was proving much harder than she had hoped.

CHAPTER EIGHT

IT WAS Thursday afternoon. Only one more day of work and then Rick Connors would be gone. The thought flicked through Lucy's mind as she finished up some letters. She wondered if they would ever see each other again. If they did, it probably wouldn't be for a very long time. Rick's time was probably strictly metered out. She knew EC Cruises had offices in Miami and New York as well as London and Barbados. Well, good, she told herself firmly. All week she'd been trying to avoid him, with little success. Every time she looked up he seemed to be in her line of vision. Talking to someone, laughing with someone… breathing down her department's neck, asking for files, suggesting changes. She'd be glad when he was gone.

Lucy corrected a mistake in the letter and printed it, then sat staring at the blank screen. Would she really be happy when he'd gone? The question sneaked in on her unexpectedly. For a moment she remembered the heat of his kisses, the way he had held her. Then she remembered their lunch together in the hotel suite. Surprisingly it had been quite a relaxed affair. Rick had been businesslike and courteous. They had combed through the files she had brought, and he had asked questions, listening carefully to her replies. They had talked about the general running of the office, Rick asking for her views on things. There had been no reference to their earlier, more embarrassing conversation.

As far as Rick was concerned it was probably all forgotten. And a good job too, she thought fiercely. The new boss was arriving today, and a meeting had been called for four o'clock. The atmosphere throughout the office was tense. There was enough to worry about.

'He's arrived.' Carolyn put her head around the office door to make the dramatic announcement.

There was an instant buzz of conversation. 'What's he like?' Linda Fellows asked curiously.

'About fifty, grey-haired…distinguished.'

'Well, I suppose he would be distinguished. He's a millionaire, isn't he?' Linda murmured. 'I thought he was older than fifty. Someone told me that he was in his late sixties.'

'Yes, I heard that as well…' someone else piped up.

'So where is he now?' Linda asked.

'Closeted in the boardroom with the MD, Rick Connors and a few of the accountants,' Carolyn replied. 'Mr Connors is probably bringing him up to speed with the place, passing on the individual reports he's made on members of staff.'

'I didn't know he was doing individual reports. I thought he was just assessing departments.' Lucy looked up now.

'That's not what I've heard.' Carolyn pulled a face. 'Some staff are going to lose their jobs. Let's face it, it's inevitable in cases like this.'

For a moment Lucy remembered the questions Rick had asked her over lunch about some members of the staff. She had thought it was just a light-hearted, informal chat, but had he been pumping her for information to put in his reports? She frowned and was glad now that she'd been circumspect in her replies.

'Let's not speculate until we've heard what our new boss has to say,' Lucy cut in hurriedly as there was another rumble of panic around the office. But deep down she was a bit worried herself. If Rick was drawing up individual reports, what would he put in hers? Would he mention the negative things she had said about their new boss? As soon as that thought crossed her mind she dismissed it. Rick wouldn't be that petty. And, anyway, all the new company would be concerned about was whether she was doing her job well. And she was, so there was no cause for concern.

Carolyn disappeared back to her own desk. Lucy finished the letter she was working on and passed it over onto her secretary's desk. As usual Gina wasn't there. Probably flirting or gossiping down by the water fountain, Lucy thought wryly.

She came in a few minutes later. 'Have you heard the new boss is here?' she said as she flung herself down in her chair. 'He's in the boardroom.'

'Yes, we've all heard,' Lucy murmured.

'Oh, and Kris says can you spare him a few moments? He's down by the coffee machine.'

Lucy frowned. 'What does he want?'

'Don't know; he didn't say.'

Lucy glanced down at her watch. The staff meeting was in fifteen minutes. 'All right,' she said, getting to her feet.

She didn't know what had got into Kris lately. He had taken to popping into the office to ask her if she was okay. In fact, he seemed to be under her feet every time she moved.

Kris smiled as he saw her heading down the corridor. 'Thanks for coming.'

'That's okay. What do you want, Kris?'

'There's something I think you should know before we go into the staff meeting.'

'And what's that?' Lucy glanced at her watch. 'We'd better be quick. People will be starting to go through in a minute.'

'All isn't as it seems, Lucy.'

'Isn't it?' Lucy frowned.

'No.' Kris took a few steps closer to her and lowered his voice. 'We've all been…I suppose you could say hoodwinked, this week.'

The cryptic tone started to annoy Lucy, or maybe it was

the over-friendly way he was resting his arm around her shoulder as he spoke.

'Just spit it out, Kris. I don't know what you're talking about.' She tried to move away from him, but he held her tightly against him.

'You've spent a fair bit of time with Rick Connors this week, haven't you?'

'No more than anyone else,' she said hastily, and hoped her skin wasn't going red.

Kris looked at her with a raised eyebrow. 'Anyway, I've just come from the boardroom. I had to deliver some papers for the new financial director. And something was said that gave me a hell of a shock. I thought maybe I should run it by you.'

'What was said?' Lucy was really getting tired of this now.

'It was about the new boss. The thing is, he's—'

The boardroom door opened further down the hall and some men stepped out into the corridor. One of them was Rick Connors; Lucy didn't recognise the others.

Rick glanced down towards them, noticing how close Kris was standing to her.

'Kris, did you get the rest of those figures I asked you for?' he asked impatiently.

'Er, not yet.' Kris moved back from Lucy hastily. 'I was just on my way when I got…sidetracked.'

'There isn't time to be sidetracked.' Rick glanced at his gold wrist-watch. 'I suggest you go and get them. And, Lucy, perhaps you'd be good enough to rally your department and get everyone through into the main office ready for our meeting.'

'Yes, of course,' Lucy said smoothly and met his gaze steadily. She wasn't about to be intimidated by him, no matter how cool his gaze, or abrupt his manner.

Kris shot back down the corridor towards his office, but Lucy didn't hurry away.

Rick smiled then, as if her defiant manner amused him somewhat. The gleam of amusement in his eyes irritated her...and so did the fact that her heart seemed to miss a beat as he walked closer.

She glanced at the two men with him, wondering who they were. They were both in their late twenties with dark hair. So neither of them was the boss. One of them smiled at her and his eyes flicked over her slender figure admiringly. She smiled back and was about to return to her desk when Rick halted her.

'Actually, Lucy, could I have a quick word?'

She turned slowly and watched as the two men walked on, leaving them alone.

'After the staff meeting I'd like you to come up to the MD's office.'

'Oh!' Lucy tried very hard not to sound rattled. 'Why is that?'

'Because I want to talk to you about things privately.' Rick glanced at his watch. 'Actually I've been wanting to have a private word with you for the last couple of days but things have just been too hectic.'

'Is this anything to do with the individual reports you've been drawing up?'

Rick looked up at her and smiled. 'Why do you think that?'

'I was just wondering.' She shrugged and then met his eyes directly. 'Have you been drawing up a report on me?'

Rick grinned. 'Actually your report has turned into more of a...tome. I started off with three paragraphs and I'm onto my second notepad now.'

'Very funny, Rick.' Her eyes glinted dangerously green for a second. 'What have you written about me?'

One dark eyebrow lifted sardonically. 'Lucy, I couldn't possibly tell you that.' He smiled. 'It's confidential.'

'And so were some of the things I've told you over the last few days,' she said quickly. 'You seem to find this all very amusing, Rick, but I won't be amused if you have written down any of the things I said about the new boss.'

'Ah, I see…' Rick murmured wryly.

'What do you mean, "Ah, I see"?' She glared at him. 'I mean it, Rick. I don't think it would be fair of you to include my personal observations. And that goes for any comments I've made about staff as well.'

'You've never made any derogatory comments about staff,' Rick countered. 'In fact I've noticed you've gone out of your way to be very fair and very generous in your praise of co-workers. It's a pity the same couldn't be said of your attitude towards the new management.'

'I'm entitled to a personal opinion,' Lucy muttered uncomfortably.

'Yes, you are. And don't worry, I haven't written any of that down on paper…just made a mental note of it up here.' He tapped his head.

Lucy didn't know if that made her feel better or worse.

He watched the flickering light of consternation in her eyes. 'Lucy,' he said firmly. 'There's something—'

They were interrupted as the door of the boardroom opened again. 'Ah, there you are, Mr Connors.' One of the secretaries looked around. 'There is a phone call for you.'

'Can you tell whoever it is I'll ring them back?' Rick said abruptly.

'It's New York and they said it was important.'

A flicker of annoyance passed over Rick's face. 'Okay, I'm coming.' He looked back at Lucy. 'We'll finish this discussion later. Make sure you come straight up to the office after the meeting.'

'Yes, okay.' She turned away from him. 'Yes, sir,' she

muttered sarcastically under her breath, 'Certainly, sir. Three bags damn well full, sir.' Honestly there was something very irritating about that man, she thought as she marched back to her desk. He obviously thought it was very funny to hold the sword of Damocles over her head regarding her comments on the boss. But perhaps the most irritating thing of all was the fact that even as he was giving his orders and winding her up she still was very aware of that undercurrent between them. It was hard to put into coherent words. But there was something…some feeling twisting inside her when he looked at her, when he smiled, when he even raised one eyebrow in that vaguely sardonic way of his.

But she wasn't going to think about that, she told herself crossly, because Rick Connors was trouble with a capital T. He was too close to the new boss and…he'd somehow managed to get too close to her. Way, way too close.

It wasn't until Lucy was filing in with everyone else for the staff meeting that she wondered what Kris had been going to say to her earlier. She saw him briefly at the far side of the room, but the place was so packed with people that it would have been an impossible struggle to get across to him. It had probably been about something and nothing anyway, she thought with a sigh. Kris always had liked to be dramatic.

Mel was over on that side of the room as well; she caught sight of Lucy and waved.

There were no seats left so Lucy found herself jammed back against the wall. The place was hot and airless and filled with the babble of different conversations. But as soon as Rick Connors and his entourage walked in, a hush fell over everything.

They made their way towards the top of the room. There were five of them in all. The two dark-haired younger men, a man with grey hair wearing a silver grey suit who had to be the boss, John Layton, and of course Rick Connors.

It was John Layton who kick-started the meeting off by welcoming everyone and thanking them for their support during the takeover of the business. Lucy wondered if he would stay on as MD or if the new company would want him to retire. She hoped he would stay. He was a decent man and he had always cared a lot about the business. Her eyes flicked along the group towards Rick. He was at least a head taller than the rest of the men. Her eyes drifted over him, noticing how his dark suit was perfectly tailored over the powerful breadth of his shoulders. There was no doubt about it: he was an extremely handsome man and she quite liked being able to feast her eyes on him without anyone noticing. In fact she could have gazed at him all day, and it wasn't just because he was handsome, she thought hazily. There was something powerful about him, something that held her captivated and then pulled at her as if she were a fish at the end of a hook. Rick glanced in her direction and for a moment their eyes met across the crowds. And for just a second it was as if they were alone. The MD's voice seemed to blur into the distance, as did the crowds. And Rick's dark sexy eyes seemed to burn into hers. Maybe she would be sorry when he'd gone, she thought fuzzily. Maybe she'd be extremely sorry…because she was attracted to him, and she would have liked to make love with him again.

The thought sizzled through her.

'And so, ladies and gentlemen, without further ado, I would like to introduce you to the new owner of the company…'

Lucy wrenched her gaze away from Rick, appalled by her thoughts. Firmly she tried to concentrate on what was going on. Her attention winged towards the grey-haired man, waiting for him to step forward. But that man made no attempt to move; instead he was looking around at someone else.

Lucy followed his gaze and skipped over the two younger men. Neither of them was moving either. Then she watched in shocked disbelief as Rick Connors stepped forward.

'...Mr Rick Connors.' John Layton smiled at the other man and they shook hands briefly before Rick turned to look at the crowd.

Lucy wasn't the only one to feel shock; she could sense it rippling around the audience in waves.

'I'd just like to say thank you to John for making this transition period run so smoothly,' Rick said with a smile. 'I've enjoyed my first week here and I've enjoyed meeting all of you and seeing exactly how each department runs. I have to say I've been very impressed with my findings.'

Maybe she had missed something, Lucy thought anxiously. Maybe John Layton hadn't been introducing the new boss...she hadn't really been listening, had been too busy having foolish thoughts about Rick. He wasn't the new boss. He couldn't be. He would have told her...

'And I'd like to apologise if any of you are upset about the fact that I didn't tell you who I was. I always find it breaks the ice and makes things much more relaxed if I can get to know a business from behind the scenes, so to speak.'

Lucy felt slightly sick inside as the realisation dawned. She hadn't made a mistake. Rick Connors was her new boss. She'd slept with her new boss last Friday night, and a moment ago had been fantasising about sleeping with him again!

Suddenly she was frantically flicking through all their conversations in her mind. How she'd told him she didn't like him, that he was ruthless and cold-hearted.

She pictured the way he had looked at her a few moments ago in the corridor. *Don't worry, I haven't written any of that down on paper...just made a mental note...* And, more worryingly: *We'll finish this discussion later. Make sure you come straight up to the office after the meeting.*

Was he going to give her the sack? She wouldn't be surprised. For a second she thought about all the bills she had to pay. When she and Kris had divorced she had bought out his share of the flat, and she had stretched herself to do it. She could probably survive there a couple of months without a job...but no longer. It would have to go on the market.

Lucy felt her hands clenching into tight fists at her side. Through the feeling of sickness, anger was spiralling upwards. She was in this mess because once again she had trusted the wrong man. Rick had lied to her about who he was, probably tried to use her to get inside information about staff...and right at this moment she hated the man, hated him even more than she had once hated Kris. Kris was weak. Rick was...well, she had been right about the new boss all along. He was a ruthless, cold-blooded rat.

'I'm hoping that there will be very few redundancies.' Lucy pricked up her ears and tried to tune into Rick's speech. 'And to that end I have decided to run English Caribbean Cruises as a separate business to EC Cruises. The two will not merge but will be separate in every way. The head office, however, will be based in Barbados, which will mean I will need key members of staff to move over there.'

There was a wild buzz of excited conversation around the room.

'That does not mean that the offices here will close,' Rick cut across the babble in a loudly reassuring tone. 'Now, has anyone any questions?'

A few dozen hands shot up.

'How many people will be transferred to Barbados?' a woman at the front asked.

'That's still to be decided.'

'And what happens if someone is asked to transfer but doesn't want to go?' someone else asked.

'Well, we will try and find key members of staff who do

want to go,' Rick said smoothly. 'Help will be given with the relocation costs.'

Several people were trying to ask questions at the same time now and order was starting to break. Rick held up his hand and people started to hush down again.

'I suggest we leave things there for today, ladies and gentlemen. Thank you for your time.'

There was no arguing with that tone of voice. It was the same commanding tone Lucy had heard him use before. He was a man used to being obeyed. She couldn't believe how stupid she had been, how blind not to see what was staring her in the face. EC Cruises…Enrique Connors Cruises! And then there was that air of powerful authority that sat so easily on his shoulders. She felt so foolish, she didn't know whether to cry or rail against the sheer, infuriating injustice of the fact that if there was a wrong man to get involved with, she sure as hell could pick him.

People were starting to head out of the room and the crowd swept Lucy along with them. She felt so numb inside that she barely noticed Mel waiting for her outside the door.

'What do you think of that?' her friend asked excitedly, drawing her to one side.

'I think I've been a damn fool,' Lucy said furiously.

'Had he not even hinted to you who he was?'

Lucy looked at Mel deprecatingly. 'Do you think if I'd had an idea who he was I would have let last Friday night happen?'

Mel shrugged. 'It wouldn't have made any difference to me. Let's face it, Lucy, he's loaded as well as gorgeous.'

Lucy bit down on her lip.

'Are you okay? You look a bit pale.' Mel looked at her anxiously.

'I'm fine. But I've got to go and face the lion in his den now.' Lucy glanced around and saw Kris heading in her direction. 'Oh, no, he's all I need right now,' she murmured to her friend.

'Lucy…Lucy!' Kris caught up with her before she could disappear into the stream of people still filing past. 'Turn-up for the book or what?' He looked at her pale face and shook his head. 'I tried to tell you earlier, but—'

'But the boss got in the way?' Lucy murmured dryly.

'Did you have any idea Rick Connors was the boss?'

'No, Kris, no idea at all.' Why did everyone think she should know? she wondered angrily.

'Well, I put two and two together as soon as I stepped into the boardroom earlier. That grey-haired man is the financial director, and the two younger men are both lawyers who work for the firm.'

'I see.' Having two lawyers on his team spoke volumes, Lucy thought dryly. Rick Connors probably had everything sorted out to the last letter and there would certainly be no comeback if he sacked her.

'Are you okay? You look a bit pale,' Kris asked anxiously, leaning closer.

'I'm fine.' Why did everyone keep asking her that? She glanced up and saw Rick Connors coming out of the room now, followed by his associates. He glanced over at her and indicated that she should follow him upstairs.

Lucy felt her stomach twisting. She felt as if she were being summoned to the headmaster's study.

'Okay, I'll see you two later.' With a brief smile at Kris and Mel, she headed after him, but by the time she reached the lifts he had already gone up.

Lucy waited patiently for the next lift and then stepped in with the crowd. Everyone was talking about Rick Connors. Who would go to Barbados? How many people would lose their jobs?

At each floor a group stepped out and then she was alone travelling up to the MD's office on the top floor. Would

John Layton be there? God, she hoped so. Lucy glanced at her reflection in the lift mirrors. No wonder everyone had kept asking her if she was okay. She looked terrible. Her skin was white, her eyes shadowed. Come to think about it, she felt physically sick.

Probably nerves. She opened her handbag and hastily reapplied some lipstick, then fluffed up her hair. If she was to maintain some semblance of confidence it was important to look her best.

The lift doors swished open and she stepped out. Lucy could count the number of times she had been up here on one hand. Once for an interview when she had first started to work for the company, once when the company was in dire straits and John Layton had called her up to discuss some of her proposals, and once just after Kris had left her, when she had been going to give her notice in and John Layton had talked her out of it.

She remembered how adamant the MD had been. 'I won't hear of you leaving us, Lucy, it's craziness. We need you here. You enjoy working here, don't you? You have lots of friends here who think the world of you.'

'Yes, but my ex-husband is here and it's…difficult,' she said carefully.

'I understand that and I understand the need for a new start. You've had a shock, Lucy, but they do say that after a shock you shouldn't do anything rash. You should wait at least a year before doing anything that changes your life radically because you might not be thinking straight.'

'I think that would only apply to someone who's been widowed, John,' she said softly.

'Please think about this carefully, Lucy. Wait a while, just a year, and then see how you feel.'

Ironic that just over a year later she should be facing the sack. Lucy stopped outside the door and ran a smoothing hand over her black trouser suit. Maybe she was blowing this out of proportion; maybe Rick wasn't going to sack her. But if not, why had he summoned her up here?

She took a deep breath and knocked on the door.

'Come.'

The authoritative tone from within increased the feeling of anger and tension inside her. It made her wish she hadn't knocked, had just barged in.

'Come in!' the voice called again and hastily she stepped into the room.

Rick was alone, seated behind John Layton's massive desk. In front of him were piles of documents and files. He was flicking through them and at the same time talking to someone on his cell phone. His voice seemed to echo slightly in the cavernous room.

'Yes, the lawyers have been over them and I got the okay this morning. No, I've sent copies to the New York office. So I don't know why we've got a problem.' He glanced up at Lucy and indicated that she should take the seat opposite. Then he continued to rummage through the paperwork in front of him. 'No, Cindy is off with personal problems so I'm minus my PA at the moment.'

Lucy made no attempt to sit down on the chair he had indicated, she just continued to stand at the other side of the table watching him. How had she been so stupid? she asked herself angrily. How had she missed that air of power that sat so easily on his shoulders? The expensive suits, the stylish haircut…everything about him screamed success and money.

She remembered the way he had laughingly told her that, although he was staying at Cleary's, his room was little better than a broom cupboard.

And she had believed him!

How he must have laughed about that as he'd showed her around his penthouse suite the other day. In fact she had probably just been one big joke to him all along.

'Lucy, are you going to sit down or are you going to stand there glaring at me all day?' he asked as he put the phone down.

His calm demeanour only served to make her angrier. She fixed him with a steady, blazing gaze. 'That depends. Is it worth my sitting down or are you just going to fire me?' she asked tightly.

'Fire you?' He leaned back in his chair and once more there was that dark glint of amusement in his eyes that really irritated her. 'Why would I fire you?'

The question should have helped calm her nerves, but she was too angry to feel any sense of relief.

'Because I told you I don't like you, or the way you do business.'

Rick shrugged. 'I thought we'd agreed that you were going to give your new boss a chance before you passed judgement.'

'That was before I knew who he was,' Lucy murmured. Her eyes narrowed on him. 'You told me a pack of lies.'

'That's a slight exaggeration, Lucy,' he said easily. 'I just didn't tell you the whole truth.'

'In my book, that's lying.' She rested one hand on the desk and leaned closer. 'If you went to bed with someone and casually didn't mention the fact you'd got a wife and three children, would that not be lying either?'

'No, of course that would be lying.' He frowned. 'But I haven't got a wife or three children.'

She looked away from him, wishing for some reason she hadn't said that. She didn't want him to get the wrong idea and think she cared on any deep emotional level about his lies.

'Well, I don't much care for your behaviour,' she said quickly, her tone calm and icy cool. 'You knew I had reservations about sleeping with you because of the fact that I was working with you this week. So you should have stopped to think how much more uncomfortable I'd feel when I found out I'd slept with my boss.'

'I wasn't your boss at the weekend, Lucy,' he said quietly. 'I think we transcended beyond what job titles we have. We were ourselves and it felt special.'

She stared at him and for a moment her heart beat rapidly and painfully against her chest. She remembered the way he had held her, the way he had kissed her…the way he had made her feel alive and cherished. Then hastily she blanked out the memory. 'It was just a roll in the sack,' she said carefully. 'We both know that. So you can cut the charm, Rick. I didn't want or expect anything from you. But it would have been nice if you'd been honest with me.'

For a fleeting second Rick glimpsed a raw vulnerability in her, then it was gone, replaced by a flush of heat on her high cheekbones, a blaze of fire in her green eyes.

'Anyway…' she looked away from him, cross with herself for mentioning what had happened between them '…I'm sure you haven't summoned me up here to rake over all that, and I certainly want to forget it—'

'Lucy, sit down.' He cut across her gently. 'I'm sorry you feel hurt by the fact that I didn't tell you who I was—'

'Not hurt, cross,' she interrupted him firmly, and he smiled.

'Believe it or not, I did intend to have a word with you before the meeting today, but it's just been hectic.' As if to prove his point, his phone rang again. Impatiently he reached to pick it up.

Lucy listened as he had a brusque conversation with someone who should have received some vital papers and hadn't. She supposed she shouldn't have allowed herself to lose her temper, not if she wanted to keep her job. And as for mentioning the fact that they'd slept together—that was a big mistake. That should all be forgotten. Rick Connors certainly wasn't wasting any energy thinking about it; why should she?

She sat down in the chair beside her.

'Sorry about that.' Rick put the phone down. 'Now, where were we? Oh, yes. I didn't tell you who I was straight away because I wanted complete confidentiality to assess this office, and also...I liked the way you acted so naturally around me, said exactly what you thought.' He watched the way her eyebrows rose and grinned. 'Yes, even when I didn't agree with you.'

'You were picking my brains, using me as a kind of spy. That's why you were asking me my thoughts on the running of the office—'

'Lucy.' He cut across her firmly. 'I was asking your opinion because I want you to go out to Barbados for a year and help set up the new offices.'

Lucy stared at him blankly.

'That's why I asked you to come up here. So we can discuss it.' He glanced at his watch. 'But unfortunately I'm running out of time.'

The phone rang again and he shook his head and picked it up. 'Yes...just forget about it. I'll fly back via the New York office today and sort it out myself.' He slammed the receiver back down again and stared at Lucy. 'So what do you think?' he asked as if they hadn't been interrupted.

'Well...' Lucy shrugged. In the space of just a few minutes she had gone from thinking she was being sacked to being offered what sounded like a promotion. 'I'm not sure.'

'I'll tell you what.' Rick glanced at his watch again. 'I'll get my secretary to organise some tickets for you. You can fly out...' He reached for a calendar and flicked over the pages. 'I'm going to be stuck in New York for at least a week...so say the beginning of next month?' He glanced back at her. 'In fact, that should be good timing. We're organising a three-day cruise launch party for the managers and hierarchy in the company to mark the takeover of this London office. You can join me for it and lend a hand with some of the last-minute organisation details.'

Join him on a three-day cruise! As their eyes locked across the table she felt a shiver run through her that was half apprehension, half exhilaration. Was this strictly business? If it wasn't, maybe she shouldn't go. She was already out of her depth. 'Rick, I—'

'Then you can stay out there a week and look over the new offices, see what you think,' he continued firmly. It didn't sound as if he was asking her...he was telling her.

Before she could say anything the buzzer on his desk rang. 'Honey, I'm down in Reception waiting for you,' a huskily attractive woman's voice cut into the silence.

Rick grinned and reached to press the button to reply. 'I'll be right down, Karina.'

Now, who was that? By the sounds of it, whoever it was was close...very close. And to think she had worried—imagined—that Rick might have been asking her to join him on that cruise for reasons other than business! Really, sometimes she was incredibly naïve. Rick had taken her to bed; he was onto his next conquest now.

'I'll have to go, Lucy.' Rick looked across at her steadily. 'I'm leaving London late tonight.'

'Well, I hope you have a pleasant flight,' Lucy told him coolly.

He smiled as if her coolness amused him. 'I'll see you in Barbados,' he said firmly.

For just a second she hesitated and then she nodded. What had she got to lose? It was a possible promotion, or at worst ten days in the Tropics. 'I'll see you in Barbados.' She slid the chair back and walked from the room without a backward glance.

CHAPTER NINE

THE plane was circling. Beneath her Lucy could see the vivid turquoise of the Caribbean Sea and her senses soared. Despite all her initial misgivings, she was glad she had come. This had to beat sitting in the cold grey surroundings of the miserable English climate, and it was only for ten days. She could handle seeing Rick again for ten days. Her stomach skipped at the thought as the plane banked and started its final descent.

It was three and a half weeks since she had last seen Rick. She knew he had been in New York for two of those weeks, because he had phoned her at the office to check she had got her tickets and to run through a few of the details for the trip.

It had been really strange picking up the phone and hearing his voice again, especially as she had been sitting at her desk thinking about him at the time, wondering where he was, what he was doing. Not that she cared, of course. She was just curious.

Their conversation had been very businesslike. It was only when they had finished discussing work that he had asked her how she was. 'I'm fine,' she answered airily. 'How are you?'

'Cold. It's snowing here. I'm looking forward to getting back to Barbados.'

'It's a tough life,' she said, idly drawing circles on a blank piece of paper. 'And I suppose the company have installed you in another broom closet.' She hadn't been able to resist the mischievous jibe.

105

He laughed at that. 'Afraid so, and it's worse than the last.'

'That bad?' Lucy grinned. 'I just hope they aren't going to install me anywhere as grim as that in Barbados...which reminds me. I haven't had any hotel vouchers or reservation details.'

'That's because you're not staying in a hotel. I figured you may as well stay on board the *Contessa*. You'll be on there for three nights anyway and it will be docked near the offices so it will be handy.'

'Okay.' Lucy was quite happy with that. She knew the *Contessa* was a first-class ship. Even the staff quarters were luxurious, so ten days on board would be no hardship. 'I'll take a taxi down there when I arrive.'

'No, I'll send someone to collect you,' Rick said firmly. 'You'll need a security pass for the docks.'

The plane bounced down onto the runway.

'Welcome to Barbados,' the air hostess said as people started to gather their belongings. 'The local time is four-fifteen and the outside temperature is thirty degrees.'

Lucy smiled to herself and put the jacket she had worn on the way to Heathrow into her hand luggage. It didn't sound as if she would need it again for ten whole days.

The heat hit her as soon she stepped out of the aircraft; the sky was clear blue and even the breeze that ruffled her hair was warm. She was glad now that she had changed out of her jeans and into a lightweight dress.

It didn't take long to clear Immigration, and because her luggage was going to be transferred directly to the cruise ship she headed straight out into the arrivals hall and scanned the name boards held up by people waiting for passengers. Her name was nowhere in sight and she was just about to head towards an information desk when she turned and saw Rick walking towards her. She felt a jolt of surprise and also something else, something far more disturbing—a twist of excitement and longing that made her insides wrench.

Trying very hard to ignore the feeling, she put a bright smile on her face. 'Hello, this is a surprise. I didn't expect to see you here.'

'Hello, Lucy.' To her consternation he bent and kissed her on the cheek. The familiar scent of his cologne and the touch of his lips against her skin brought back a rush of memories from their night together, and made her heart race unsteadily against her chest.

'Did you have a good journey?' He reached to take her hand luggage from her.

'Yes, it was pleasant. I managed to sleep for a few hours.' She was very conscious now of the way he was looking at her, and she was really glad that she had spent time freshening and tidying her appearance before landing. At least her hair and make-up were passable.

As always he looked incredibly good. She had never seen him dressed so casually; he was wearing a lightweight pair of beige trousers and a short-sleeved shirt in the same colour. He looked tall and bronzed and powerfully handsome. She tried very hard not to notice the effect he had on her.

'Come on, then, I'm just parked outside.' He strode away from her, leading the way out into the brightness of the sunshine.

'Wow, it's hot,' she murmured as they stopped next to his bright red Porsche.

'Is that a complaint?' He stowed her bag away in the boot and grinned over at her.

'After the weather I've left, certainly not.' She got into the car, settling herself in the deep leather seats appreciatively. 'So what brings you all the way out here to collect me?' she asked lightly as he got behind the driving wheel. 'Got no chauffeur today?'

Rick glanced across at her. 'Nowhere is very far away on Barbados. And I was heading down to the ship anyway.'

'Well, it's very good of you, thanks,' she said quickly, not wanting to sound ungrateful.

'But you'd rather I'd sent the chauffeur,' Rick said wryly as he started the engine. 'Do I intimidate you, Lucy?'

'No, of course not.' She looked over at him with a frown.

'I didn't think so,' he said with a smile. 'So why do you jump a mile every time I come close?'

The casually asked question took her by surprise. 'I wasn't aware I did.'

He glanced across at her with a raised brow and she felt herself blush to the roots of her hair. 'Okay, maybe I do.' She shrugged. 'I don't know why. Nobody else makes me do that. Maybe it's just you...you have a weird effect on me.'

His lips twisted wryly for a moment. 'You have a bit of an unsettling effect on me, too. You irritate the hell out of me sometimes, you're so infuriating, and sometimes...' The engine started with a powerful roar, cutting off his words so that she wasn't sure if he'd finished that sentence or not.

'And sometimes?' She looked over at him curiously. 'I didn't hear what you said.'

'Didn't you?' He grinned and then slipped the car into gear. 'Maybe it's just as well. We do have to work together after all.'

Lucy glanced out of the window, tried to concentrate on the passing scenery and not on his words...but she was fighting a losing battle. She was consumed with curiosity. 'So, in what way do you find me infuriating, exactly?' she probed.

'Hard to put a finger on it...exactly.' He glanced over at her and his eyes gleamed with amusement. 'I'll tell you next time it happens.'

'Well, gee, thanks,' she muttered sarcastically. 'I suppose you don't like the fact that I tend to say what I think.'

'No, I told you, on the whole I like that about you. It's very refreshing.' He grinned. 'Except of course for the times when you are being less than complimentary about your boss.'

'Yes, well. I'm sorry about that.' She cringed a little at the reference. Would she ever live down those remarks? she wondered uncomfortably. 'It seems I was wrong about you.'

'Were you?' He glanced over at her.

'Well, you haven't dissected the company and sacked half the workforce, have you? At least, not yet. So I must have been wrong.'

He smiled. 'That's a very wary apology, if I may say so.'

'Is it?' She shrugged. 'Well, don't take it personally. Maybe I'm just a wary person.'

'Yes…' He looked at her, and for a moment his eyes were serious. 'I think perhaps you are. Obviously a person has to work at gaining your trust.'

'Maybe.' She conceded the point. 'And we didn't exactly get off to a good start, did we?'

'Didn't we?'

She wished she hadn't looked over at him just then because as their eyes met she felt herself blush wildly. 'I was referring to the fact that you lied about who you were,' she said stiffly, trying very hard not to remember their time together in bed.

'Ah. I see.' He nodded. 'Well, I'm sorry about that. Maybe we are both similar characters…both quite wary.' He changed down a gear and the car slowed as it approached a town. 'So, in this new light of reconciliation, shall we bury the past and start again?'

She shrugged. 'Yes, of course. I think it's important that we have a good working relationship.'

'Me too.' He smiled at her.

Something about the way he looked at her made something stir inside her, some kind of longing that was wildly preposterous. Hastily she looked away from him. He was her boss. They had turned a corner away from all of that, she told herself firmly.

'So where are we now?' she asked, changing the subject.

'This is Bridgetown, the island's capital.'

With the suddenness of the Tropics it had started to go dark now. Lucy had an impression of quite a small town with old colonial-type buildings. Fairy lights twinkled along their roofs and on trees in the park.

'In case you're wondering, they still have some of their Christmas decorations up,' Rick said with a grin as she noticed a reindeer lit up on a roof. 'They don't have the same sense of urgency about taking them down within twelve days as they do in England. In fact they don't tend to have a sense of urgency about anything, really. It's all very laid-back here.'

'That's nice.' Lucy smiled. 'Wish I could be that laid-back, but I'm very superstitious. If I didn't take down my decorations in time I'd worry that I was storing up bad luck for the rest of the year.'

'Really?' Rick looked over at her. 'I didn't have you pegged as the superstitious type.'

'Oh, yes. I always throw salt over my shoulder if I spill some.'

He laughed. 'But, Lucy, all those things are just based on practicalities. Salt used to be expensive; that's why it was bad luck to spill it.'

'I know all that.' She shook her head. 'But I don't want to tempt fate so I have all sorts of little idiosyncrasies.'

Rick grinned. 'That sounds interesting. You'll have to tell me more over dinner.'

'Dinner?' She looked over at him sharply.

'You know, that meal you eat with a knife and fork, taking care not to spill any salt.' He smiled at her.

'I'm a bit tired, Rick,' she said cautiously.

He nodded. 'I'm sure you are, it's a long flight. But you should eat something. The *Contessa* is fully staffed and stocked up...and tonight we'll be the only passengers on board so we should take advantage of the situation and relax.'

'We'll be the only passengers?' She looked over at him in surprise and felt a momentary tingle of alarm. 'I didn't know you were staying on board the ship? I thought you would be staying at your own house.'

'I thought I might as well stay on board this evening. I've got a lot of last minute work to do down here in the morning and then in the afternoon the managerial staff and VIPs will be arriving for the three-day cruise.'

Rick stopped at a security checkpoint for the piers and flashed a pass at the man on the gate.

'Evening, Mr Connors.' The man smiled and the electric barrier immediately lifted to allow them through.

As they drove down towards the berth Lucy had her first glimpse of the *Contessa* lit up against the night sky. She was a magnificent-looking ship, small by cruising standards; she carried more crew than passengers and was aimed at the luxury end of the market.

Rick parked the car down by the end of the quay and Lucy stepped out into the night air. It was a soft, sultry evening and the breeze that ruffled in over the calm dark water of the Caribbean did nothing to alleviate the stickiness of the temperature.

Lucy couldn't get over how quiet it was. When she had visited ships in Miami the docks had always been bustling with people; here there was just one member of staff waiting for them by the end of the gangplank. They walked up and into the cool, air-conditioned interior and stepped straight into the main foyer, a vast space with a gold staircase that branched off into two and circled the upstairs gallery. There were shops and a reception desk and a row of glass-fronted lifts.

Rick led the way into one of the lifts and pushed the button for the top floor.

'Have you been on board the *Contessa* before?'

She shook her head. 'No, but I did an assessment of her last year for the new brochure, so I feel I know her very well. She's an Italian ship, isn't she?'

Rick nodded. 'Yes, and finished with a lot of style. I think the management will enjoy their party cruise.'

'I'm sure they will. And I believe there is another party to launch the takeover of the company for the rest of the London staff at Cleary's next month?'

Rick grinned over at her. 'Well, you know how I like to keep my staff happy.'

'And of course it's all tax deductible,' Lucy said with a wry smile, in case he thought that she was fooled into thinking he was completely altruistic.

'Ah…rumbled again.' Rick laughed. 'It's very hard trying to shake off my ruthless image with someone like you around, Lucy. Let's hope I have better luck with the journalists I've invited along.'

Lucy met his eyes and smiled. It had been her idea to invite some members of the press; she had thought it would be a good move because hopefully they'd get some favourable write-ups in the travel columns. 'Knowing how charming you can be, I'm sure it will be quite a PR triumph.'

'Do you know, I think that's the nicest thing you've ever said to me,' he said teasingly. The lift doors swished open and Rick led the way down the corridor and then inserted a card into a door and swung it open to reveal a very large and elegant suite.

'This is lovely.' Lucy wandered across the lounge area to

look out of French windows that opened onto a private balcony.

'Your room is through here.' Rick opened a door to her left and she could see a large cabin decorated in shades of rose and cream with a double bed and another door out towards the balcony and one towards the corridor.

'This is very luxurious. I expected to be in staff quarters.'

'Now, what kind of a boss do you think I am?' Rick asked. 'No, I want you here where I can keep an eye on you. We've got lots of work to do.'

'And where will you be staying?' Lucy asked guardedly.

Rick opened the door on the other side of the lounge to reveal an identical cabin to hers, only at one side of the room there was a desk piled up with papers.

'I see.' She felt a flicker of apprehension at working in such close proximity to him, but the thing that worried her most was her own will-power and ability to keep things businesslike. She was sure he would have no problems with it, after all he was a businessman and she knew he had the ability to put work in front of all else. He had probably dismissed anything on a personal level between them long ago, right to the back of his mind. So why couldn't she?

Why was it that as soon as she was in his company common sense seemed to fade into the background? For some reason he only had to look at her to play complete havoc with her emotions.

No other man had ever had this effect on her before and she really hated herself for it. But, being fair, she supposed most women would feel the same. Rick was just too attractive. She was sure those dark eyes alone could melt any woman's resistance in seconds.

There was a knock at the door. 'That will be your luggage,' Rick said as he went to answer it.

A porter brought in her case and placed it in her bedroom.

Rick glanced at his watch. 'I've got some business to

attend to up on the bridge, so I'll leave you to settle in and I'll see you on deck five for dinner. Shall we say in about an hour?'

She nodded, and he smiled at her in that warm, disarming way of his. It had an immediate and strong effect on her pulse rate and as soon as the door closed behind him she had to sink down into one of the comfortable armchairs. Given the way Rick made her feel, it was probably a very bad idea having dinner alone with him. But what else could she do? It wasn't like a date that you could turn down; it was dinner with the boss. She had to go.

Lucy leaned her head back and closed her eyes. Who was she kidding? she asked herself crossly. She wanted to have dinner with him. Every little fibre of her soul seemed to zing with a curious feeling of excitement just at the thought of being in his company.

Her eyes flew open. Every time he smiled at her, she wanted him; every time his hand so much as brushed against hers it sent tremors of awareness racing through her. A sudden feeling of sickness twisted inside her. It was nerves, she supposed; nerves because she knew how foolish she was being. Rick was off limits; he was her boss…and anyway he wasn't interested in her. He had moved on to other pastures.

Lucy stood up and went through to her cabin to unpack. She was furious with herself for allowing such weak feelings of desire to flood through her. Rick had lied to her about who he was, for heaven's sake. How could she have any feelings for a man like that? She couldn't trust him…

She unpacked haphazardly, throwing things into drawers and cupboards, then went into the *en suite* bathroom to shower.

'And he's probably an incorrigible womaniser,' she told herself as she lifted her head to the powerful jet of water. Probably had more women than she'd had cups of tea. With his looks and money they were in all probability throwing themselves at him all the time. She remembered the huskily sexy voice of the woman who had spoken to him at the office. What was her name…Karina? Not for the first time, she wondered who she was. Not that she cared, of course, because one thing was for sure, she wasn't going to be another one of his harem. She had far too much pride and common sense for that.

A little while later, wearing a buttercup-yellow summer dress and a matching pair of high heels, Lucy made her way up to the fifth deck to have dinner with Rick. She stepped out of the lift, her head held high, a defiant gleam in her green eyes. She wasn't going to be swayed towards dark feelings of desire for Rick ever again. That was an end to it. She was going to be sensible and from now on become immune to him.

There was a member of staff standing outside the lift. 'Good evening, Ms Blake. Mr Connors is waiting for you in the restaurant, if you'd like to follow me.'

'Thank you.' She followed the man towards some doors, which he held open for her, and then she stepped out onto the deck and found herself in the open-air restaurant at the back of the ship. The heat of the tropical night was soft against her skin and pleasant after the cool of the air-conditioning.

Candlelight flickered on the fresh white tablecloths and music played gently in the background. Rick was sitting at a table by some open rails and behind him the lights of Barbados twinkled invitingly. He stood up as he saw her walking towards him and she noticed he had changed into a dark suit with a white shirt. He looked very handsome— in fact, so handsome that she could feel all her firm intentions wavering dangerously.

He smiled at her as she reached his side and she could

almost feel his eyes as they swept appraisingly over her. 'You look lovely, Lucy.'

'Thank you.' She sat down in the chair that one of the waiters pulled out for her. 'This is very unexpected. I thought we would be having a quick snack in the pizzeria on the other side.'

'I thought this would be a little more relaxing.' Rick took his seat opposite her again. 'After a long, tiring flight it's good to sit back and be pampered.' He passed a menu across to her. 'Now, what can I get you to drink?' he asked solicitously. 'Would you like white wine or would you prefer something else?'

Lucy glanced over at his glass and noticed he was drinking white wine. 'I'll have the same as you.'

She watched as he lifted the bottle from the cool-bucket next to him and poured her a glass.

'So did you see to all your business on the bridge?' she asked briskly, trying very hard to steer the mood of the evening towards sensible and away from seductive, but it felt like an uphill task against the candlelight and the soft music and the gentle swish of the sea against the ship.

'Yes, all done. We are all ready to take our passengers onboard tomorrow.'

'The ship seems eerily quiet.' She sipped her wine and looked around at the deserted restaurant. 'It's a bit like being on the *Marie Celeste*.'

'Do you think so?' His lips twisted in a wry smile. 'If no waiter comes to take our order I'll start to worry. But I thought it was rather pleasant myself, like the calm before the storm. Because at approximately three o'clock tomorrow afternoon, over one hundred members of the management team will be descending on us.'

'Should be fun.'

Rick shrugged. 'I hope so. I'm just glad you're here to

help, especially as my personal assistant is off work at the moment.'

'What exactly do you want me to do?' Lucy asked, taking a sip of her wine.

'Just meet and greet all of the passengers, and generally act as hostess for the trip.'

'Oh?' Lucy looked over at him in surprise. 'I would have thought that was a job for your girlfriend.'

Rick laughed at that. 'Well, I was kind of hoping that you'd act as a bit of a go-between. You know all of the top management from your side of the company very well, Lucy. So you'll be able to prompt me if I forget a name and help me with the introductions between them and the EC Cruises crowd.'

'That's no problem.' She nodded.

'And I could also do with some help sorting through my paperwork, ready for some discussions I will be having later. My desk is in a bit of disorder at the moment.'

Lucy laughed. 'If that's the desk I glimpsed through the open door of your cabin, then I think chaotic would be a better description.'

'I was hoping you hadn't spotted that.' He grinned.

A waiter arrived to take their order and Lucy hastily glanced at the menu. There was a large choice, but after all the travelling she only wanted something light so she selected a simple starter of melon with Parma ham and steak with a green salad.

'So how were things at the office when you left?' Rick asked once they were on their own again.

'Ticking along nicely. Everyone has been in better spirits since learning you're not closing the London office.'

'And what about Kris Bradshaw? Is he in better spirits these days?'

The quietly asked question took her by surprise. 'Kris?'

She shrugged and tried to look impassive. 'I don't know. I suppose so. Why do you ask?'

'I guess I'm just curious. I noticed that he seemed to be around you a lot in the office. And then someone informed me that he was your ex-husband.'

'Who told you that?' Lucy could feel herself growing hot inside. She didn't want to talk about Kris; it was too personal.

'Does it matter who told me?' Rick murmured quietly. 'The thing is, you didn't tell me.'

'I didn't think it was relevant. Yes, he's my ex-husband, but it doesn't interfere with my work in any way, so there's not much else to say.'

Rick seemed to be watching her very intently. 'But will it interfere with your decision on whether or not you take the job here in Barbados?'

'No, of course not!' Lucy was taken aback by the question. 'He's my *ex*-husband, Rick. He left me for another woman and we have nothing to do with each other any more.'

'But you still love him.'

Lucy stared at him, unsure if that quietly worded sentence was a statement or a question. 'No, of course not!' Her heart bounced unsteadily against her chest. 'I'd have to be crazy to still love Kris after the way he walked out. I don't know why you would even think such a thing!'

Rick watched the shadows flicker across her face, the way her eyes darkened to deepest jade. He had definitely hit a raw nerve.

'I'm just repeating the gossip that was flying around the office, Lucy.'

'I didn't have you pegged as the type of person who'd listen to gossip.' She glared at him.

'It was hard to avoid, and I suppose my ears pricked up

when I heard people mentioning the fact that you had gone speed dating.'

'People were talking about that?' Her skin blanched. 'They don't know about…what happened between us, do they?'

Rick shook his head. 'No, they were discussing the fact that you met someone and he invited you to dinner, but you turned him down.'

'That was Mark Kirkland.' Some colour returned to her cheeks. 'Thank heavens the gossips don't know about…us. They'd have had a field day.'

'It would be a nine-day wonder at most,' Rick said easily. 'Mark Kirkland? Was he the guy at the speed dating who ticked your box?'

For a moment she was transported back to that morning in bed with Rick when she'd received that text from the agency and they had giggled and wrestled over her mobile phone before succumbing to more tender emotions…

She looked across and met his eyes and tried very hard to shut her mind to those memories. 'Why are you asking all these questions, Rick?'

'Because I'm interested,' Rick said nonchalantly, holding her eyes steadily with his. 'So you didn't go out with him?'

'No, I didn't, and just for the record that wasn't because I'm still hankering after my ex-husband. The simple truth is that I've been too busy and too tired to go out on a date with him.'

'And you always put work first,' Rick remarked wryly. 'I noticed that when I was in London. You're first into the office in the morning and last to leave. Have you always been like that or is it just since your divorce?'

'Shall I lie down on a couch so you can analyse me properly?' she countered wryly.

He laughed at that. 'You can if you want, Lucy, but I can't promise I won't get sidetracked.'

She blushed wildly at the husky inflexion behind his words and he smiled. 'Sorry. I shouldn't tease you, should I?'

'No. After what's happened between us I don't think it's appropriate,' she murmured. Then quickly she tried to move the conversation along. 'I can't believe people are still gossiping about my private life. It's been over a year now since my divorce and they still seem fixated by it.'

'Maybe because you and your ex still look as if you are an item.'

'No, we don't! We have to work together, so Kris talks to me and we are civilised about things, but we are definitely not an item.' Lucy's eyes sparkled angrily. 'In fact, I think his girlfriend is pregnant...and before you jump to the conclusion that he's confiding in me, he's not. That was just another little thing I heard on the gossip grapevine recently. In fact I'm surprised that juicy little titbit hasn't reached your ears as well.'

'No, I hadn't heard that.' Rick picked up the bottle of wine and leaned across to top up her glass. 'Was that the news that upset you the night that you met me at Cleary's?'

Lucy flushed hotly. She had forgotten that, in a moment of weakness, she had used that as an excuse for what had happened between them. For a moment she considered lying, saying no, that was some different news...but then she shrugged. What was the point? 'Yes, okay, that was the news. But it didn't upset me in the way you think,' she murmured and darted a defiant glance across the table at him.

'So, in what way did it upset you?'

'It just made me angry, that's all.' Why was he persisting with this, she wondered angrily. 'But that doesn't mean I'm still in love with Kris.' She flashed him a very eloquent look from her emerald-green eyes. 'In fact, I don't even know if I believe in that emotion any more.'

Rick held her gaze steadily and there was silence between them for a heartbeat.

'I've rebuilt my life since Kris walked out. I'm enjoying my work and my life and, contrary to popular belief, I am certainly not pining away for him, or falling apart at the seams.' She raised her head in that determinedly proud way he was starting to recognise. 'And what's more,' she continued firmly, 'I'm stronger since my divorce and I know that no one will ever make me feel the way Kris did ever again.'

Before he could answer her she pushed her chair back from the table. 'Now, if you'll excuse me, I've lost my appetite and I'm very tired, so I think I'll turn in.'

'Lucy—'

She heard him call her name as she walked away across the restaurant, but she didn't look back. Her heart was drumming in her ears and she was furious with herself for losing her cool like that. But she couldn't have sat opposite him for one more minute, or she might have burst into tears.

She had only just reached the sanctuary of her cabin when Rick knocked on the door behind her.

'Lucy?'

'Just go away, Rick. I'll talk to you in the morning.'

'I want to talk to you now,' he said firmly.

Lucy raked a hand through her hair. She was nervous about opening the door because for some reason she felt very emotional. Maybe she was just overtired…

'Lucy, please open the door.'

The gentle tone of his voice was her undoing. Cautiously she moved to do as he asked.

'Hi.' He smiled at her and his eyes moved over the pallor of her skin with concern. 'I'm sorry. I really didn't mean to upset you like that.'

'I think I'm just tired.' She shrugged self-consciously.

'And I get so fed up and angry because the gossip-mongers never seem to leave me alone.'

'I can understand that.' He reached out and stroked a stray strand of her hair back from her face. The gesture was curiously tender and the touch of his hand made her heart flip wildly.

'All I can say, Lucy, is that your ex-husband must be a complete fool.'

'Why would you think that?' She frowned.

'Because he left you.' Rick said the words gently and something about the way he was looking at her, about the tone of his voice, made her ache inside with a strange kind of emotion.

She looked away from him and swallowed the feeling down. Rick was being kind; that was all. 'Thanks, for the vote of confidence.' She smiled and then flicked a look of amusement over at him. 'But he's not that stupid. Sandra is a very beautiful twenty-three-year-old blonde with a figure to die for.'

'But she's not *you*, is she?' Rick said with a shrug.

'I think that was the attraction.' Lucy laughed shakily.

Rick smiled back at her. 'I still think the guy is a fool. And just for the record...' he lowered his voice huskily '...she can't possibly have a lovelier figure than you.'

He's just being charming, she told herself firmly. Don't let it affect you...and definitely don't believe him!

'Rick, don't,' she whispered softly.

'Don't what?' He stepped a little closer.

'Don't try and bamboozle me. All that Latin charisma probably works on every other woman, but it doesn't work on me.' Even as she was speaking she knew she was lying. His charm definitely was working and as she looked into the intense darkness of his eyes she could feel desire twisting inside her like a serpent.

'I'm not trying to bamboozle you.' He smiled as if she

were the most amusing person. 'I admire you and respect you too much for that.'

'Rick, really...don't...' She swallowed down a feeling of complete panic as she felt her resistance starting to fade.

'I mean it, Lucy. I wouldn't hurt you for the world. In fact I'd like to punch anyone who tried to hurt you into the middle of next week, and that includes Kris Bradshaw.'

She smiled shakily at that.

'That's better. You have a beautiful smile, you know.'

'You're doing it again, Rick,' she whispered. 'Don't try and smooth-talk me, because I'm not going to be taken in by it...'

'Didn't anyone ever tell you that you should accept a compliment gracefully?' he said light-heartedly.

'My mother, I think.' She shrugged and then grinned shakily at him. 'But she also said to beware of wolves in sheep's clothing.'

'Your mother is a very wise woman, by the sounds of it.' Rick smiled. 'But I promise I'm not a wolf.'

'Oh, yes, you are,' Lucy murmured.

'Lucy, just accept it...you are a very beautiful, utterly beguiling woman. In fact...' he traced a finger down the side of her face and then tipped her chin upwards so that she was forced to look at him '...ever since we made love I've wanted to do it again.' He reached closer and his lips found hers in a gently provocative kiss. 'And again, and again...'

Each word was punctuated by the most blissfully mind-blowing kiss. And suddenly she was swaying closer and allowing him to do exactly what he wanted.

CHAPTER TEN

SHE'D let it happen again!

As soon as Lucy opened her eyes the thought whipped through her mind with sickening clarity. After all her strong words, all her resolve…here she was again. She turned her head and looked across at the man sleeping next to her.

How had this happened? How was it that Rick only had to lay a hand on her and she was his? For a moment she remembered the sure touch of his hands against her naked skin, the heat of his kisses and the weakness of her body as she had given herself up to the sheer pleasure of his love-making. She remembered the way she had allowed him to undress her and the powerful feeling of arousal and the need that had almost consumed her.

What on earth was the matter with her? He was her boss, for heaven's sake!

Suddenly he opened his eyes and she found herself held by his dark, sexy gaze as they lay looking across the pillow at each other. 'Good morning.' He smiled sleepily at her.

She smiled back, but it was a shadowy smile at best.

'How did you sleep?' he asked with a yawn.

'Okay.' A picture of their naked bodies entwined as Rick brought her very skilfully to climax rushed through her mind. He had sated her and exhausted her completely so that afterwards she had fallen immediately into a deep sleep and she hadn't woken or stirred all night.

He leaned up on his elbow and looked down at her, taking in the luxuriant gloss of her dark hair and the pale luminosity of her skin. 'You look very lovely first thing in the morning, do you know that?' He trailed a hand down the side of her face and the butterfly-light caress made her tingle all over.

'You are one smooth operator, Rick Connors,' she murmured, pulling away from him. 'You know, I told myself that I wasn't going to sleep with you again. I can't believe that I've let myself fall back into bed with you.'

'Well, I'm glad you did.' He leaned a little closer and kissed her on the tip of her nose. 'Very glad, in fact.'

His closeness unnerved her because it sent all sorts of conflicting emotions racing through her. Part of her wanted to carry on where they had left off last night, cuddle close, kiss him and just surrender to the power he had over her senses. The other part of her wanted to run as far away from him as it was possible to get.

Her eyes shimmered over-bright as she looked up at him. 'Yes, but it was a mistake. A big, big mistake,' she told him emphatically.

'Why?'

The calmness of his tone made her blood race angrily. 'Because you're my boss, of course!'

Rick glanced at his wrist-watch. 'Lucy, it's six-thirty in the morning. I'm only your boss during office hours. So relax. I won't ask you to, er, take anything down after eight-thirty, okay?'

The gently teasing tone did nothing to diminish the tension inside her. 'No, it's not okay, Rick. We have to work together. I shouldn't have slept with you. I was weak…overtired. It won't happen again.' She said the words firmly and made to pull away from him, but he caught her before she could move an inch and pulled her gently back.

'But it will happen again, Lucy,' he murmured. 'Because there is a certain chemistry between us. You know it and so do I.'

As if to demonstrate the point, his hand stroked lightly

up over the smooth curve of her waist and instantly she felt her body respond to his touch with a fiery thrust of need.

'So what are you saying?' she murmured huskily. 'That we should just give in to this…this chemistry, or whatever it is?'

'Yes, I suppose I am saying that.' He leaned closer and kissed the side of her face, then nuzzled kisses down her neck. The feeling he generated inside her was one of shivery sweet pleasure. 'We should let this run its course…not think too deeply…just feel the pleasure and enjoy each other…'

For a moment she gave herself up to the blissfully sensuous feelings and allowed herself to turn and meet his lips in a kiss that was explosively passionate.

'See?' He raised his head and looked down into her eyes. 'It's just chemistry. We can make it a no-strings affair—nothing to worry about, nothing to run away from.'

For a second she wanted to agree with him. Maybe he was right; they could have an affair. No big deal; she shouldn't be so old-fashioned. This was just sex. Then as she looked into his eyes she felt a jolt of pure panic as common sense seemed to kick in. She could get badly burnt here.

'No, Rick, this is craziness.' She pulled firmly away from him. 'I don't want any complications in my life and an affair with my boss is one hell of a complication. Last night was a one-off.'

'Can't have been.' He grinned at her wryly. 'Because we've done it before.'

'Don't get smart with me, Rick…' she warned him shakily.

He laughed and reached down and kissed her firmly and possessively on the lips. 'Okay, if it makes you happy, it was a one-off…until next time.'

She frowned. 'There won't be a next time.' She watched as he swung himself out of the bed and her eyes flicked down over his naked body. He really did have a tremendous physique…those broad shoulders tapering down to a taut, powerfully muscled stomach…

Rick glanced over and caught her watching him. He smiled and swiftly she tore her eyes away from him, blushing wildly.

'It will never, ever happen again,' she reiterated fiercely.

Rick laughed and picked up his clothes from the floor. 'Stop fighting it, Lucy. I'll meet you up on deck for breakfast in about thirty minutes, okay? And we'll talk.'

When she didn't answer him immediately he leaned down and planted another swift kiss on her lips. 'Don't be late…'

The door closed behind him. Her heart was thundering against her chest, her blood was zinging through her veins and all kinds of emotions were running wild. Sleeping with him had definitely been a mistake, she told herself angrily, because for one thing the guy was far too sure of himself, far too arrogantly confident. *Good in bed, though…* The thought crept in unwanted. He was extremely passionate and tender. She liked the way he whispered things to her in the darkness, things about how good she felt, how much he wanted her… Just remembering made her stomach flip. Maybe he was right; maybe they should just give into this. The chemistry between them was strong; maybe they should just let it run its course and after a short time it would burn itself out.

Feeling totally confused, she swung her legs out of bed and headed off to have a shower. A relationship just based on sex didn't seem right somehow. She wasn't sure she could handle it.

It was as she turned on the hot water in the shower that she felt suddenly sick. The nausea was accompanied by a severe feeling of debilitation and all she could do was lean against the washbasin taking deep steadying breaths. She didn't know if she was going to be sick or whether she was going to pass out. It was a horrible feeling and she couldn't move for several moments, then thankfully, as suddenly as the illness came, it seemed to pass.

What on earth had caused that? she wondered, staring at herself in the mirror. She looked very pale and drawn. Maybe it was the heat in here; her reflection was starting to steam up now. Hastily she flicked on the cold water and rinsed her face. Then she turned down the heat of the shower and stepped beneath a cooling jet. The sensation was refreshing and by the time she had dressed in a pair of light-weight white linen trousers and a black and white T-shirt she was looking remarkably well again.

It was probably nothing, she told herself as she headed towards the lifts. More worrying was what she should say to Rick over breakfast—how she should handle things between them.

Considering the fact that it was so early in the morning, the heat out on deck was incredible. There was a dazzling blue sky and the sea was a clear turquoise. There was no sign of Rick in the restaurant, but the table they had sat at last night was set up for breakfast under the shade of a giant green parasol. A waiter appeared, pulled out a chair for her and handed her a menu, and a few minutes later Rick sauntered in from the opposite direction.

He was wearing a pair of khaki-coloured trousers and a beige T-shirt. His hair was still damp from a shower. He looked fresh and vital and intensely attractive.

'Sorry, I got held up on the phone.' To her surprise he leaned down and kissed her on the cheek. The scent of his cologne was delicious, as was the brief moment of intimacy, much to her consternation. She flicked a glance around the restaurant to see if any of the staff had witnessed the kiss.

'Relax, Lucy.' Rick grinned at her as he took his seat opposite. 'There's nobody here and I assure you no member of the paparazzi is going to pop up from behind a potted plant.'

'Very funny, Rick, but if word of us gets back to the office I'll never hear the end of it.'

Rick nodded. 'I understand your concerns. And, to be honest, I'm wary mixing business with pleasure myself.'

Did that mean he had changed his mind about wanting to take her to bed again? She felt a momentary pang of disappointment and was immediately annoyed with herself. 'So we're both agreed, then, that the best thing would be if we could try to forget all about this,' she said firmly.

'And do you think that if you say it in a determined enough voice we'll just be able to do that?'

The sardonic tone made her blush.

'Lucy, as I said to you this morning, the chemistry is there; we may as well just face it. And just because you were my mistress, it wouldn't mean we couldn't have a good working relationship. Both of us are business orientated. Neither of us is looking for a long-term commitment; we both know the score.'

'I see.' Lucy felt her heart thump against her chest. 'You sound as if you've got this all worked out.'

'I wouldn't go that far.' He smiled at her. 'But, yes, I'd like you to take the job here in Barbados. I reckon it will take the best part of a year to get the office established. And during that time we could have some fun together.'

'And during that year the chemistry between us will have subsided.' She looked across at him, hardly able to believe that they were having this conversation. 'Is that what you're thinking?'

'I think we should just take things a day at a time,' Rick said gently.

'Well, I suppose that's easy for you to say,' Lucy said pointedly. 'When the affair ends you won't be the one worrying about your job.'

'You think if we stop sleeping together that I'll fire you?' Rick's tone was sharp for a moment. 'I thought we'd progressed past the point where you thought I was a ruthless bastard.'

'We have,' Lucy murmured awkwardly. 'I don't think that about you.' She looked across at him and their eyes met. 'But I can't help wondering now if you've offered me the job out here because you want me in your bed.'

'Lucy, I'm a businessman first and foremost.' Rick shook his head. 'There is no way I'd have offered you such a responsible job if I didn't think you were the best person for it. There is a lot of money riding on this new venture of mine and it's too important for me to jeopardise it in any way.'

She felt rather foolish now for asking the question. The waiter arrived and asked if they'd like tea or coffee. They both asked for coffee and watched silently as he poured them a cup then put the pot down on the table between them.

'Are you ready to order now?' the waiter asked as he stepped back.

'I'll just have some toast, please,' Lucy said without looking at the menu.

'Is that all you want?' Rick frowned across at her. 'You didn't eat anything last night. You must be hungry.'

'Really, I'm fine with just toast. I don't normally eat any breakfast.' She smiled at the waiter and handed him the menu back.

Rick ordered some maple syrup pancakes. Lucy's stomach protested just at the thought. In fact, even the smell of the coffee was upsetting her somewhat. Maybe it was the heat; maybe nerves from their discussion. She pushed the cup away and reached to pour herself a glass of water.

'Are you okay?' Rick asked her as the waiter left them. 'You look a bit pale.'

'That's the effect of the English climate.' She smiled

across at him. 'Hopefully I'll look a bit better by the end of the day.'

'You always look beautiful,' Rick said softly. He glanced across at her and met her eyes steadily. 'So what do you say—shall we give an affair a whirl? See where it leads us?'

The words were so casual, yet the way he was looking at her was anything but. She felt her heart thump painfully against her chest. There was a part of her that wanted to throw caution to the wind and just say yes. In one way it sounded exciting...in another it sounded dangerous.

'I'll think about it, Rick,' she murmured. 'Apart from anything else, I haven't decided yet whether or not I'm going to take the job you've offered me out here. And I suppose one thing is dependent on the other. I can't very well be your mistress if I'm in London and you're here.' She tried very hard to sound as casual about things as he did.

'Fair enough.' He nodded. 'But just one thing: even if you decide you don't want to continue with our relationship, I still want you to consider the job here.'

'Don't worry. Like you, I always put work first.' She took a sip of her water, and then glanced across at him wryly. What made him tick? she wondered. What drove him?

Business was obviously his main concern, the most important mistress in his life. She supposed he hadn't got where he was without being single-minded in his dealings. The business reports she had read on EC Cruises had all confirmed that.

'You are looking at me very pensively,' Rick said suddenly.

'Am I?' She blushed. 'I was just thinking how little I know about you. And yet here we are sitting over breakfast talking very casually about having an affair.'

'You know that sexually we are very compatible,' he said huskily.

She tried very hard not to look embarrassed. 'And that

your heart was broken at the age of seven by Marion Woods,' she said lightly.

He laughed at that. 'You see, you know more about me than most women. I don't think I've ever told anyone about Marion Woods before.'

The waiter arrived with their food. Lucy wondered if she should leave the conversation there. She sensed that Rick was a very private person, that he didn't really like it when she asked him too many in-depth questions.

But as they were left alone again she realised she didn't want to leave the conversation. She wanted to know more about him.

'Did you grow up in Buenos Aires?' she asked curiously.

'I was there until the age of seven, and then I was sent to boarding-school in England.'

'It must have been tough leaving your parents at such a young age.'

'It was okay. The tough part was four years later when they got divorced. All hell seemed to break loose. My father moved to live in London, my mother went with her new boyfriend to live in Miami. So holidays had to be split between the two.'

'That must have been difficult,' Lucy said sympathetically. 'Did you have any brothers or sisters?'

'I have a stepsister, from my mother's second marriage. And yes, it was a difficult time. My parents' divorce was very acrimonious and some twelve years later the fallout was still ongoing. The family business, which had been a very successful chain of restaurants, almost went into receivership because of it.' Rick reached to pour himself another coffee. 'My first job after leaving university was to go in to try and salvage things. You could say I was thrown in at the deep end.'

'And did you salvage it?' Lucy glanced across at Rick, watching the way the warm breeze ruffled his dark hair.

'Eventually, but it took a few years.' He glanced across at her and smiled. 'You ask a lot of questions.'

'Not as many as you asked me last night,' she said pointedly.

He laughed at that. *'Touché.'*

'And anyway,' she continued resolutely, 'if I'm going to become your mistress I need to know a little more about you.'

'I see.' Rick smiled over at her. It was an indulgent kind of smile and for some reason it made her heart rate speed up, made her almost forget what she was saying.

'Well, go ahead, then,' he encouraged her with a grin.

'So…how did you go from there to owning a chain of hotels and EC Cruises?'

'Once the restaurants were on their feet I split them up, sold half and turned the rest into franchises. From there we bought other businesses; some I split and sold off in smaller pieces, some I kept.'

'So you were an asset-stripper,' Lucy said dryly.

'I did what had to be done to turn a profit.' Rick shrugged. For a moment she had a glimpse of steely determination in his eyes. 'My father asked me to turn his company around for him and that's what I did. Along the way I made money for myself as well as him. I'm a businessman.'

'And are you still working with your father?'

'Since he told me about his health problems last year I've stepped in from time to time to try and keep an eye on things for him. But I'm pretty much tied up with my own company. So I'm trying to arrange for one of my managers, Karina Stockwell, to go in to oversee things for him.'

'Karina?' Lucy glanced across at him as the name resonated inside her. Was that the woman who had been waiting for Rick at the London office, the woman with the husky, sexy voice? She hardly liked to ask that question.

'Have I told you about Karina before?' Rick frowned.

'Was she in London just before you flew to New York?'

Rick nodded. 'Karina and I go way back. We lived together for a few years.'

'She's the woman your father wanted you to marry?'

'Yes, that's right. My father was very fond of Karina. Still is. But I think that's just his business head talking.'

'So what happened between you two?' Lucy tried to sound casual.

'It just didn't work out. We cared about each other—still do, and we are still good friends. But the relationship had run its course.'

'Who decided to call it a day?' She probably shouldn't have asked that question, but she couldn't help herself. There was a heartbeat of a second before he answered her.

'It was a mutual decision.' Rick looked across at her wryly. 'I'm not pretending that I've been an angel where women are concerned, Lucy. I know I haven't been. I've had a lot of girlfriends, probably broken a few hearts... unintentionally, of course.' He met her eyes firmly.

'But of course.' She echoed his words sardonically. 'Because you didn't really mean to stand them up, it was just that there was an important office meeting, or there was a crisis on the factory floor, et cetera, et cetera.'

'Okay.' Rick shrugged. 'Work has always come first. But I've always tried to be honest with people and told them that up front.'

'And did you tell Karina that up front or was she different?'

There was a moment's silence. 'Yes, Karina was different.' He leaned back in his chair and for just a moment she wondered if she glimpsed a flicker of regret in his eyes. 'And I was serious about her. But I knew marriage wouldn't work for us.'

'She wanted a family man, not a workaholic,' Lucy guessed.

'It wasn't quite that black and white,' Rick said curtly.

'Sorry.' She glanced away from him. 'I shouldn't have said that. It was far too personal.'

'Karina and I have managed to remain good friends. And she's married now. So, you see, some things happen for a reason. They are meant to be.'

'I suppose they are.'

She wondered suddenly if his aversion towards marriage was based on his experience of his parents' divorce.

Their eyes met across the table and there was a moment's silence.

'So, is the interview terminated?' He asked the question flippantly.

'Just about.' She smiled.

'And do I pass?' His voice was still laced with amusement.

'Just about.'

'Good, because I think we've done enough talking.' He reached across the table and took hold of her hand. 'We've got until three this afternoon before everyone arrives for the cruise. So how about I show you around the new offices…and take you out to the place I've earmarked especially for you?'

'Earmarked?' The touch of his fingers stroking against hers was sending bizarre little electrical impulses shooting through her. The feeling made her hot inside; made her want to move closer, feel his hands more intimately on her body. 'Earmarked for what?'

'For you to live, of course.'

'Oh. You've already found somewhere?'

'Yes.' He let go of her and stood up from the table. 'Come on, I'll show you.'

As Lucy sat beside him in his car she thought that she

would always remember this day in her mind. Everything looked so clear and freshly vital, the intense blue of the sky, the beauty of Barbados with its green fields and white beaches fringed with turquoise water.

Rick put the top down on his car and they roared along narrow lanes through the centre of the island, past whispering fields of sugar cane and small churches that looked as if they had been transported straight from a Devon English village into a tropical setting of palm trees and bougainvillea.

At the crest of a hill Rick slowed the car and below them Lucy could see a spectacular coastline where the Atlantic crashed in against deserted white beaches fringed by palm trees and fields of sugar cane.

'Beautiful, isn't it?' he said, looking over at her with a smile.

She nodded. 'It's breathtaking.'

'My house is just over there.' He pointed to a road leading off to the left and she could just make out a large manor-type house almost hidden by trees. 'You can't see it very well from here.' He put the car in gear and set off down the road again and a few minutes later turned through some high gateposts to pull up outside a quaint wooden house on stilts with a wraparound veranda. It was painted a pretty primrose-yellow and was surrounded by a riot of tropical greenery, lemon and banana trees, avocado and papaya.

'Here we are.' He turned the engine off. 'I thought you would like it here.'

Lucy glanced up at the house, totally charmed by it. 'This is for me?'

'If you like it.' Rick opened the car door and stepped out. 'Come on, I'll show you around.'

Hesitantly Lucy followed him. How anyone could not like this house, she didn't know. The property was like something from a tropical painting by Gauguin, delightfully proportioned and full of character. The first thing that struck her was the view from the veranda down towards the sea and the delicious warm breeze that rustled through the trees. There was no sound except the waves breaking on the beach and the occasional bird call.

Rick unlocked the front door and they walked straight into a living room with polished wooden floors and windows that folded back to allow the breeze to circulate through the building. It was furnished with the most exquisite taste. Polished mahogany tables and a desk positioned to look out towards the sea, a sofa and chairs in the palest of yellow damask.

Rick opened the door off it and there was a dining room with a large hardwood table and six carving chairs. Patio doors led out to the veranda.

Next to that was a large white kitchen with black granite counters and every modern convenience.

Lucy wandered silently from room to room.

Rick opened one of the doors and she found herself in a room with floor-to-ceiling windows that looked down towards the sea.

'I always think this room would make a good artist's studio,' Rick said nonchalantly. 'If you moved here maybe you'd take up your painting again?'

Lucy smiled at him. 'And maybe turn into the new Picasso?'

Rick laughed at that. She liked the sound of his laugh; it sounded warm and enticing. She wondered what it would be like to live in this house...and how often Rick would visit her. The question made strange little butterflies dance in her stomach. Hastily she stepped away from him out into the corridor again.

The room next door was the master bedroom. It held an enormous four-poster bed that was swathed in white nets and it looked tropically inviting...very seductive. Lucy tried to quickly step back out of the room, but Rick was behind her now in the open doorway.

'So what do you think?' he asked quietly. 'Do you like the house?'

'It would be hard not to like it.' She pretended to be absorbed in looking out of the windows at the sea. 'Does it belong to you?'

'Yes. It's the gatehouse. I live about a fifteen-minute walk away.'

'I see.' Her heart thumped crazily against her chest. So it wasn't far for him to visit.

'I know you are very independent and also that you're concerned about people gossiping about us, so I thought if you had this house it might just waylay a few of your concerns.'

'So I'd be your secret mistress?' She tried to make a joke, but her voice wavered unsteadily. She felt completely out of her depth. Rick took hold of her arm and pulled her around to face him.

'That's up to you,' he said quietly and his eyes held hers with a penetrating intensity that made her go hot inside. 'Personally I'd like everyone to know that your nights belong to me.' He reached out and traced a whisper soft caress over the side of her face. 'That you belong to me...'

A shiver of desire stirred powerfully inside her.

His eyes were on her lips now and she felt herself starting to sway closer to him. Drawn, trapped by an irresistible force that was telling her she needed to belong to him...that she would willingly give herself, do anything, just to be his.

Rick's lips touched hers with a commanding force that seemed to shake her inside. She rested her arms against him and kissed him back. For a while all confusion was lost in a whirl of pleasure and passion.

She felt his hand moving under her T-shirt, stroking her breast through the lace of her bra. Immediately her body responded to him and an ache of need opened wide inside her.

'I want you, Lucy.' He whispered the words against her ear and her heart slammed unsteadily against her chest. 'I want you right here, right now and on a very…very regular basis…'

The slam of a door somewhere in the house broke the sensual spell and hastily she pulled back from him, rearranging her T-shirt with fumbling hands, her face burning with embarrassment.

'Hello, Mr Connors,' a cheerful voice called from the lounge. 'Only me.'

'Relax, Lucy.' Rick smiled wryly. 'It's Mrs Lawson, my cleaner. I asked her to make the place ready for you, for when you return from the cruise.' Rick moved towards the door. 'I'll ask her to come back later.'

'No!' Lucy stopped him quickly. 'Don't, Rick.'

He turned and looked at her with questioning eyes.

'I don't want to fall into bed with you here. I need more time to think about things.' She said the words huskily. 'This is all moving too fast.'

'On the contrary, I don't think it's moving fast enough.' Rick smiled wryly. 'But then, patience never was one of my virtues. When I make my mind up about something I don't usually like waiting around.'

'Well, you'll have to wait, Rick,' she said firmly, and there was a determined gleam in her eyes as she looked over at him now. 'Obviously you've had time to give this…situation some thought, but don't forget you've only just sprung the idea on me. And maybe other women in your life have been quick to fall in with your plans at a moment's notice, but I'm different.'

'Oh, I realise that, Lucy,' he said and his smile broadened, his eyes gleaming with amusement. 'I got the drift of that the moment I first set eyes on you.'

'Good.' Her voice was calm and decisive. 'Then you should realise that the best thing you can do now is give me space and time to think about this. In fact I don't think you should...kiss me, or...or come near me until I've made my mind up about things, because it will only confuse matters.'

'You think?' Rick's voice was dry and the amusement still flickered in the depths of his dark eyes.

'Yes, I do.' She held his gaze resolutely, but as she looked across at him she knew that he was all too aware of the fact that all he had to do was walk across, take her into his arms and all her cool, logical resolutions would be thrown to the wind.

For a few seconds there was silence, then to her relief he inclined his head in agreement.

'Okay, Lucy, we'll play things your way...for now.'

CHAPTER ELEVEN

THE ship was preparing to pull out of the harbour. Lucy stood out on deck and watched the activity on the quay below. The last of the ropes were being released and the engines were stirring the water up into a white froth as the *Contessa* slipped her moorings and pushed away from the land.

With that suddenness of the Tropics the sun was sinking and the sky was streaked with orange and purple light. It reflected over the darkness of the water and lit the island of Barbados in the purple misty haze of twilight.

A few people on the dockside waved and Lucy waved back. Then the ship gave two loud blasts on its horn and turned for the open sea leaving a wake of white froth. Lucy was the only person out on the deck. She guessed that everyone was down in their cabins getting ready for the captain's cocktail party before dinner and she didn't know where Rick was. She hadn't seen him since his guests had arrived this afternoon.

Lucy had got ready early. She was wearing a long black dress with shoestring straps and her long hair was carefully swept upwards and held in place with some diamanté clips. With time to spare she watched as the sun disappeared completely and the lights on Barbados twinkled in the darkness.

Her mind played back over the day. After taking her to the gatehouse, Rick had called briefly at his own house to pick up his luggage. She had drunk a glass of ice tea in one of the formal reception rooms as she had waited for him, and had wandered around admiring the style and grandeur of his house. Until then she hadn't really thought a great deal about how wealthy Rick was. But that house must have been worth a fortune. It was palatial, with its numerous rooms and terraces and two large swimming pools. Lucy thought that her flat would probably have fitted into just one of the downstairs rooms and the furnishings alone must have cost a fortune.

It made her realise how different she was from Rick—how in fact they inhabited different worlds altogether. She was just an ordinary career girl with overheads that she sometimes worried about. Rick lived in a mansion with a team of staff and was used to the best of everything. Not that she was overly impressed with all that luxury—in fact, of the two houses today she probably would have chosen the gatehouse as a home anyway, not Rick's mansion—and as for the staff, she was probably too independent for all that help.

Barbados was fading into the distance now and the bright blanket of stars overhead and just the faintest twinkle of light from the coast were all that lit the tropical night.

Lucy wondered what it would be like to live on that island. Having a mansion and lots of money wouldn't excite her, but having Rick—lying in his arms…now, that set her senses reeling with a very different kind of excitement. She imagined her belongings in the gatehouse; imagined sitting out on the terrace in the heat of the evening, having a drink with him. Imagined him taking her by the hand and leading her into that cool white bedroom…

Swiftly she turned her mind away from that. Okay, she knew that they were sexually compatible, but there were more important things to think about than that.

After Rick had taken her to his house they had gone to visit the new offices down by the docks. They were large and modern and just a few minutes' walk from the capital. In practical terms she thought she would enjoy working there and would relish the new challenge of setting the business up.

So why was she hesitating about saying yes to Rick? she wondered in confusion.

She wanted him—heavens, she wanted him so much she could feel her stomach twisting with an ache of longing— and yet she was scared.

What she was scared of, she had no idea...maybe of being hurt again?

But Rick couldn't hurt her, she told herself firmly, not in the way Kris had hurt her anyway, because she didn't love him. She would never, ever let her heart be captured and broken like that again.

Lucy turned and looked along the deserted deck. Through the windows of the cocktail bar she could see the band were setting up for their evening performance. In a little while everyone would be arriving and she would have to be by Rick's side to help with some of the introductions. She was about to head back down to her cabin to pick up her handbag and have a last-minute check through the guest-list when she saw Rick walking into the bar.

He looked magnificent in his dark dress suit. Tall and handsome, he made her heart skip wildly. In fact she was so immersed in him that she didn't notice for a moment the woman on his arm. It was only when she reached up and whispered something close to his ear that Lucy's attention transferred to her. Rick laughed and as Lucy watched he put a hand under her chin and tipped her face up to look into her eyes.

For a moment the picture seemed to freeze in Lucy's mind. They made a very attractive couple. The woman was wearing a long red dress and was tall and willowy with short blonde hair. Lucy couldn't see her features properly, but from a distance she was stunning, like a supermodel.

Rick said something to her, then they went to sit down

in an alcove by the bar. Who was that woman? And was it her imagination or was there something intensely personal about the moment she had just witnessed? Obviously the two had arranged to meet early, before the crowds descended.

Lucy frowned as a sudden thought struck her. Was that Karina? She knew the other woman was a manager and most of the upper echelons of management were on board. So it stood to sense that she would be here. She wished she could go down and check on her list, but Rick had only given her the names from her side of the company.

Annoyed with herself for caring, she made her way back down to her cabin. So what if it was Karina? The two were good friends; they were probably just catching up with each other.

Lucy sat at the dressing table in her cabin and reapplied some gloss to her lips. Then she brushed some more blusher over her cheeks. Despite the sunshine today, she still looked pale.

The downside of being Rick's mistress would be that she would never be sure of him. The thought crept into her consciousness. There would always be other women in the background waiting, watching. With his looks and money it was inevitable.

Could she live like that? She knew Mel would tell her not to be so serious, to get with the modern programme. She could almost hear her friend's voice. 'Well, if he goes out with someone else, so can you. Just enjoy yourself.'

But Lucy didn't want to go out with anybody else and she certainly didn't like to think of Rick doing so. Even the thought of him being upstairs alone with his ex was eating into her. She remembered the way he had looked at the other woman, touched her, and something twisted inside her like a snake. She was jealous!

Lucy slammed the make-up brush down and glared at

herself in the mirror. Now she was being pathetic! Of course she wasn't jealous. She didn't care.

But the words rang hollowly inside her. She did care…in fact, she cared more than she could ever remember caring about anyone before. She was in love with Rick Connors.

The knowledge rushed in from nowhere and ricocheted painfully inside her, and for a moment she sat there in total shock. It couldn't be true, it just couldn't. She hardly knew the man, she told herself fiercely. And he wasn't even trustworthy…look how he had even lied to her about who he was! Desperately she searched around for all the reasons why her heart shouldn't get involved with him. He was probably a womaniser; he was too rich and probably too ambitious in business… But no matter what excuses she dragged up, her heart still thumped painfully with the realisation that it didn't matter how many sensible words she threw at herself. Her heart had made its decision. It had chosen Rick.

She had never felt this strongly about any man before, she realised shakily. Not even Kris, and look how he had hurt her! If Kris could hurt her like that, what could Rick do to her?

For a moment Lucy felt sick, she was so appalled…so frightened. After all her strong words about not getting involved with someone again, she had chosen a total heartbreaker and given her emotions to him on a plate.

But it wasn't too late, she told herself shakily. She would have to be strong and back away from the situation, say no to his proposition. Because she couldn't be his mistress, not now, knowing what she did. It would destroy her emotionally.

She would get over this. She was strong, and she would prove it by giving Rick her decision this very evening. And she would turn down his job here as well. She couldn't risk being near him.

Snatching up her handbag, she headed out of her cabin into the lounge and walked straight into Rick on the other side of the door.

'Hey, where are you tearing off to in such a hurry?' He put a steadying hand on her shoulder.

'I...I just didn't want to be late.' The light touch of his hand against her bare skin triggered an immediate response from her body and made her acutely conscious once more of just how easily he could stir desire in her. Quickly she took a step back.

'Well, you don't need to dash around like that. There's plenty of time.' He smiled at her. And even his smile set her senses reeling.

How blind she had been, she thought hazily. She had fallen for him almost from the first moment their eyes had met. And she had been so busy fighting it and making excuses for it that she hadn't seen the danger she was in, until now. And now it felt far, far too late. How could she end things feeling as she did? How could she tell him she never wanted to see him again? The very thought was like a knife in her heart. Suddenly all her strong resolutions were hanging precariously by a thread.

'We've got a few minutes to spare,' he said gently.

A few minutes for what? she wondered, and felt her temperature starting to increase as she noticed the way his eyes swept over her appreciatively.

'You look extremely beautiful,' he told her huskily.

Her emotions turned over. 'Thank you.' She whispered the words.

'I like your hair up like that. It makes you look very sophisticated.' His eyes moved from her hairstyle down over her naked shoulder and the low sweep of her dress over creamy skin.

She wished he wouldn't look at her so closely. She could

feel herself starting to tingle all over. 'Well, I'm glad I pass the test.' She tried to make light of the compliment.

'Oh, you definitely pass the test,' he said with a grin. 'You passed that a while ago. There's just one thing missing...'

'What's that?' She watched as he reached into the top pocket of his jacket and brought out a long narrow box.

'A little something I bought for you in New York.'

She leaned closer to see, but he waved her away. 'It's a necklace. Turn around and I'll put it on for you.'

Taken aback, she did as he asked. 'You really shouldn't be buying me things,' she told him shakily. She closed her eyes as she felt the light touch of his hands against her skin and it set all sorts of fires racing through her body.

'Why shouldn't I buy you something?' he murmured quietly as he deftly fastened the clasp. 'There...let me look at you.'

She turned and his eyes swept over her appraisingly. 'Now that is the perfect finishing touch.'

She should tell him that she couldn't accept the gift, that the affair was over. The words burned inside her, but she couldn't say them. Lucy fingered the heavy necklace tensely and then stepped across to glance at her reflection in the mirror.

The piece of jewellery was fabulous. It was beaten luminous silver with snake-like tentacles curling from a fine filigree band. She noticed as she leaned closer that some of the silver strands had what looked like Aztec writing down the sides. 'This is beautiful, Rick. It's so unusual. But you shouldn't have...'

'Stop saying that, Lucy, I'm just glad you like it. I saw it as I was walking along Fifth Avenue and I immediately thought it would look good on you.' He smiled. 'It's a limited edition copy of a necklace worn by an Aztec princess. Apparently it was given to her by her lover, and the scrolls down along some of the silver tentacles have secret meanings.'

Lucy was intrigued. 'What kind of secret meanings?'

Rick smiled. 'Maybe I should whisper that to you at some later date?' His voice lowered huskily, and he reached out to stroke one hand over her shoulder, tracing the line of the necklace with a casual yet intensely sensual caress.

Lucy wanted to move closer...wanted him to tell her: *now*. She looked up and met the dark, intense look in his eyes and was lost. She couldn't end it. She just couldn't.

Looking down at her, Rick saw the shadows in her eyes. The brief conflict in her was all too apparent. Her exhusband had certainly done a job of breaking her heart, he thought angrily. Sometimes the wariness he saw in those beautiful eyes made him so angry he wanted to punch the guy. 'Lucy, I'm not going to rush you about things so you don't need to worry.'

'I know...' She shook her head, the gentleness in his tone making her resistance melt further.

'Good.' He smiled at her. 'Well, I suppose we should get up on deck and meet our guests. Did you look over the list I gave you?'

The swift change of tone towards business made her senses whirl with confusion. 'Yes, I looked at it earlier.'

'Okay, well, let's get this show on the road.' He put a guiding hand at her back and together they left the room.

The captain and a few first officers were in the cocktail lounge. Rick introduced her and for a while they stood around making light conversation. Captain Michaels told her that they were due to dock in Grenada, the Spice Island, at six-thirty tomorrow morning.

There was a very convivial atmosphere. The band was playing a medley of swing numbers and waiters were circulating with champagne and canapés. Then the rest of the guests started to arrive and the time seemed to fly by as

Lucy concentrated on social niceties and making sure that everything ran smoothly.

By the time she had shaken hands with the hundredth guest through the doors, and smiled and said the right things to the right people, Lucy could almost have forgotten the fact that she had fallen in love with the one man she shouldn't have, could almost have persuaded herself that the emotions earlier were just a figment of her imagination—and then the doors opened and the woman Lucy had seen earlier walked in.

'Karina, hi.' Rick placed a hand on her arm and kissed her on both cheeks with the laid-back confidence of someone very much at ease.

'Hi again.' She smiled up at him with warmth and sincerity, and even reached up and very proprietorially brushed a stray strand of his hair away from his face.

And suddenly from nowhere all those horrible feelings of jealousy were twisting inside Lucy again.

'Lucy, I'd like you to meet Karina Stockwell. She's my right-hand woman in the day-to-day running of several businesses, and also a very good friend.'

Lucy smiled at the woman and reached to shake her hand. It was utterly ridiculous to be jealous of her, she told herself firmly. Jealousy was an ugly and destructive emotion and she would not give in to it. And, besides, Karina and Rick's close relationship was in the past—the woman was married now.

'Rick's told me all about you,' Karina said cheerily. 'I believe he's hoping you'll front up the new offices in Barbados.'

'That's right.' Lucy felt her smile slipping just a little. Somehow the thought that Rick had been discussing her made her feel uncomfortable. Exactly what had he been saying? She was tempted to say, *Rick's told me about you as well*, but she held her tongue.

A waiter arrived with a tray of drinks. Lucy helped herself to one and looked around towards Rick, but he was talking to someone else now.

'So, are you going to take the job?' Karina asked as she helped herself to a glass.

'I haven't made up my mind yet.' Lucy shrugged.

'Well, speaking from experience, working closely with Rick can be wonderful fun.' Karina took a sip of her champagne. 'Of course, he's a businessman to his fingertips.'

Lucy laughed. 'Yes, I noticed.'

Karina smiled back at her. 'I wish you luck, Lucy.'

Meaning what? Lucy wondered. That she would need it? Before she could answer, the crowds were swirling in around them and the conversation moved on. Then it was time for everyone to move through to the dining room for dinner.

The food was delicious, but Lucy couldn't help wishing that it were just her and Rick sitting out on deck under the stars like last night…only this time she wouldn't waste time talking about her ex-husband.

By contrast tonight they were in the more formal surroundings of the main dining room. Lucy was sitting at a large table opposite Rick. On his left sat Karina, on his right John Layton's wife. There were a few other managers around the table as well and Lucy was between John Layton and the ship's doctor, a rather pleasant middle-aged Scottish man.

The conversation flowed and Rick in particular was extremely entertaining.

Good-looking, amusing, intelligent…the list was endless, she thought as she glanced across the table at him. But she would still have to turn him down, she told herself firmly, because she could get badly burnt here, just like Karina Stockwell.

It was noticeable that Karina hadn't brought her husband

with her on this trip. Most of the other members of staff were accompanied by their partners. Lucy couldn't help wondering if the other woman still held a torch for Rick. She seemed to pay a lot of attention to him, to look very deeply into his eyes when he said anything to her.

John Layton leaned across towards her cutting into her thoughts. 'Before I forget, Lucy, Kris asked me to pass on a message to you.'

'Oh?' She looked around at him in surprise.

'He wants you to ring him.'

Lucy frowned. 'Did he say what it was about?'

John shook his head. 'But he did say it was rather urgent.'

'That's strange.' Lucy shook her head. 'But knowing Kris's sense of the dramatic, it's probably nothing.'

'Maybe he's going to try and tap you up for a job out here,' John suggested with a grin.

'I don't think so.' Lucy smiled at him. 'But you never know. Tell you what, I'll make him sweat for a few days and ring him when I get back to Barbados.'

'Good idea.' John said. 'And whatever it is he wants, Lucy, you tread with care around that man. I wouldn't like to see you hurt again.'

Lucy smiled at John, touched by the sincerity in his tone. 'Don't worry, John, that's not going to happen.'

Lucy glanced across the table. Karina was flirting with Rick now, laughing over some incident that had happened in the office years ago. Her wide blue eyes were trained on him, and one manicured hand rested on his shoulder. Lucy glanced away again and tried to pretend she didn't notice. But suddenly she was remembering another office party years ago, when Kris had sat opposite her and flirted like crazy with a woman who had been working as a temp on the reception. Lucy hadn't let it bother her; she had just told herself that it was a Christmas party and Kris had had too much to drink.

It had been much later in the evening when she had over-heard some colleagues having a discussion in the Ladies' about whether she suspected anything or not.

She could still remember that conversation as clearly as if it had happened yesterday. 'Kris really was sailing close to the wind tonight. Do you think she suspects he's having an affair? If she doesn't, she must be blind... And she is always so considerate to him, isn't she, so understanding? Letting him just go on that holiday and believing it was with the boys! Someone should say something to her. He's really taking her for a fool.'

Everyone had known...everyone except her. The memory of that humiliation was still there, buried somewhere deep down inside.

Lucy closed her eyes for just a moment. Why was she thinking about that? she wondered angrily. It was in the past and should be forgotten. When she glanced upwards she found that Rick was watching her.

Their eyes met and he smiled at her and suddenly it was as if everyone else in the restaurant disappeared and there were just the two of them.

Lucy could feel her heart thumping painfully against her ribs. She didn't know what to think where Rick was concerned. One minute she felt she could trust him totally, to the ends of the earth; the next she just wasn't sure if she was being naïve in the extreme. He'd asked her to be his mistress, nothing more.

Hastily she looked away.

The meal was drawing to an end. Lucy refused coffee and as a few people excused themselves from the table she took the opportunity to escape.

Most people were heading through to one of the main lounges to listen to a concert. But Lucy slipped out onto the deck. She felt she needed some fresh air to clear her mind.

The night was warm and balmy and Lucy walked around

towards the front of the ship watching the way she cut through the darkness of the sea. There was a full moon up in the sky and it reflected over the water, lighting it in patches as bright as the necklace Rick had placed around her neck.

Lucy leaned against the balustrade and breathed in the salt air.

'There you are.' Rick's voice from behind her made her turn. 'What are you doing out here?'

'Just admiring the view, and getting some fresh air.'

'It's warmer out here than it is inside.'

'Yes, that takes a bit of getting used to.' She laughed. 'But it's beautiful, isn't it?'

'Yes, it is,' he agreed, coming to stand beside her at the rail.

For a while they stood in silence, watching the ship ploughing steadily through the silky blackness of the sea. It was calm and peaceful, the only sound the gentle surge of water against the bow. 'When you live in the city you forget how beautiful the sky is at night,' Lucy murmured, looking upwards at the myriad stars.

'You can certainly see the stars better out here.' Rick placed a light arm around her shoulder. 'There are the Three Sisters.' He pointed out the constellation. 'And the Plough…'

Lucy could smell the scent of his cologne; it was warm and provocative and made her senses reel in disorder. She allowed herself to lean her head against his shoulder as she looked up. 'Do you think the stars really control our destiny?' she asked him suddenly.

He laughed. 'I think we control our own destiny.'

'Ah, there is an arrogant man talking,' she said with a smile. 'I think there is a far higher power that holds and controls us all.'

'Maybe.' Rick shrugged.

'What star sign are you?' she asked him suddenly.

'Leo.'

'Figures.'

'Now what do you mean by that?' he asked with amusement.

'Bossy, likes to be in charge.'

'Oh, really? So what star sign are you?' He laughed.

'Libra.'

'Now, let me take a guess. Stubborn, likes to do things her way, rather infuriating?'

'Well balanced, actually,' she said with a grin. 'But likes to weigh things up carefully.'

'I definitely noticed that.' Rick turned her around so that she was looking up at him instead of the stars. 'So tell me, how do Leo and Libra get along?'

'I'm not sure.' Her heart started to thump unevenly. 'I think that depends on the alignment of the planets when they were born. And I reckon you were born under the proverbial wandering star.'

'I like travelling, so maybe you have something there. And what about you?' he asked, suddenly serious. 'Do you like travelling to far-flung places or are you a home bird?'

'Depends who I'm with,' she said softly. 'I think people are more important than places.'

'So if you moved to Barbados you'd miss your friends?'

'I suppose so.'

'Would you miss seeing your ex-husband?'

Lucy frowned. 'Why do you keep asking me about him?'

'Because I know you think about him a lot. You were thinking about him tonight, weren't you?'

Rick noticed the way she blushed.

'Only because John Layton mentioned him to me,' she murmured defensively.

'Yes, I heard.' Rick's voice was dry.

'Really?' Lucy was surprised. 'I thought you were too

busy hanging on Karina's every word to hear anything John was saying.' As soon as she said the words she could have bitten her tongue out.

'Hanging on Karina's words?' Rick sounded surprised and amused. 'Lucy, are you jealous?'

'Certainly not. I couldn't care less who you flirt with.' She pulled away from him, angry with him and with herself.

'I wasn't flirting with her.'

'No?' She shrugged. 'Well, as I said, I really couldn't care.'

'Karina is just a friend now, Lucy.'

'Fine.' Lucy nodded and stared straight ahead. 'She still seems very fond of you.' She added the words as an afterthought in case she sounded too abrupt.

'Well, I'm fond of her.'

'It's nice when a relationship can end in a civilised manner.'

'You and Kris seem pretty civilised about things,' Rick said quietly.

'It's a veneer for work.' Lucy shrugged. 'I didn't feel civilised when he left. I wanted to throw all his clothes out of the window and get John Layton to sack him.'

Rick laughed at that. 'I can't imagine you doing anything like that. Are you sure you're not a fire sign?'

Lucy smiled. 'Well, I didn't do anything like that,' she added hurriedly. 'I just felt like it.'

'Understandable under the circumstances.'

'Doesn't make you feel good about yourself, though.' Lucy shrugged. 'Dark thoughts like that can destroy you.'

'That's what almost destroyed my father,' Rick said grimly. 'He was very bitter and quite twisted for a number of years after his divorce.'

Lucy shivered. 'I'm glad I didn't go there.'

'So you don't want me to sack Kris, then?' Rick smiled.

'No.' Lucy flicked an amused glance up at him, unsure if he was joking or not. 'But thanks for the offer.'

'Are you going to phone him?'

'Eventually.' She shrugged. 'Maybe when I get back to Barbados.'

'I think he wants you back.'

'Back in London?' She frowned.

'Back in his life.'

The quiet observation made her laugh. 'You must be joking. Really, I assure you, Rick, he's happy. He's probably much more suited to Sandra than he ever was to me. John is right, it's more likely to be the job out here that he's after.'

'Yes, well, he's definitely not having that,' Rick said firmly. 'So what about you and me? Do you want to give it a whirl?'

The conversation's sudden change in direction took her by surprise. 'I thought you weren't going to rush me?' she hedged.

'I didn't think I was.' His lips twisted wryly. 'But as I told you, I am not the most patient of men. And I want you back in my bed.' He added the words huskily and the way he said them, the way he looked at her, made her body catch fire.

Maybe she should just throw caution away, Lucy thought hazily as she looked up into his eyes. She wanted him so much, and could she get any more hurt than she would be right at this moment if she threw everything away?

'Rick, I—'

A couple walking around the deck interrupted them. It was John Layton and his wife, and they came over to stand beside them. 'Isn't it beautiful out here?' John said with a smile.

'Absolutely,' Lucy agreed. She wasn't sure if she was

glad of the interruption or sorry, because she had been going to say yes to Rick…

'I'm going to get John to take me on a fourteen-day cruise as soon as he retires,' his wife said dreamily. 'It's so romantic.'

'Well, we'll leave you two in peace.' John put his arm through his wife's and tried to lead her away, but she was in full flow of conversation.

'At first when John told me he was retiring, I was very taken aback and not pleased at all. But now I'm coming around to the idea, I'm feeling better about it.'

'I didn't know you were retiring, John?' Lucy said in surprise.

John shrugged. 'Nothing lasts for ever. You've got to embrace change.'

The words echoed peculiarly inside Lucy and before she could make any kind of a reply the couple were moving away on their amble around the deck.

'I didn't know John was leaving.' Lucy looked over at Rick. 'Are you forcing him out?'

'What makes you say that?' Rick's voice was suddenly terse.

'Because he didn't sound too pleased to be going.' Lucy stared at him. 'You are, aren't you? You're letting him go!' Suddenly Lucy could feel blood thundering through her veins in fury. 'How could you do that? He's a really decent man!'

'I'm not arguing with that,' Rick said calmly.

'But you've still pushed him out of the company!' Lucy's voice shook.

'I didn't get rid of him, Lucy,' he said quietly. 'And you're very quick to jump to all the wrong conclusions. I've noticed that a few times about you. It's as if you feel it's safer to think badly of me.'

Lucy swallowed down a feeling of panic. There was an

element of truth in those words and the fact that he had hit on it so concisely made her extremely nervous. 'Well, if I jumped to the wrong conclusion I'm sorry.' She murmured the words huskily.

'So why do you do it?' Rick asked coolly.

'Do what?'

'Put up these barriers, usually hastily erected barriers, when we hit anything emotional.'

She glanced up at him uncertainly. 'I don't do that.'

'Yes, you do.'

She shook her head helplessly. She didn't want him to press her like this. 'Well, maybe it just feels safer, okay?' She glared at him.

'Safer?' He frowned.

'Safer than being disappointed in someone later…let down.' She shrugged. 'I don't know, Rick. I just know that in every relationship it's best to keep your eyes open, better to face reality than be a fool.'

'He really did a job on you, didn't he?' Rick replied gruffly.

'Who?' Lucy looked over at him and shook her head. 'This has nothing to do with my ex-husband.'

'Lucy, it has everything to do with him.' Rick's voice was quiet. 'He is the reason why you can't say yes to me, isn't he?'

'No! He's not.' She glared at him.

'Our relationship would be nothing like the one you had with Kris.' Rick said the words softly.

'I know that! I was married to Kris, we made promises…till death do us part, that kind of thing.' Her voice trembled slightly. 'And I took them seriously.'

'I know.' Rick moved closer to her. 'And I know how much he hurt you. But you are going to have to start trusting people again. Not every man is like Kris Bradshaw.'

The words lingered between them.

'I know.' She looked up at him and her eyes shimmered in the moonlight. 'And I'm sorry I jumped to the wrong conclusions...about John.'

'So you should be.' Rick smiled. 'He's decided himself that he wants early retirement; he says he wants to spend more time on the golf course and with his grandchildren.'

Lucy nodded. 'It was just a shock, that's all.'

'So shall we kiss and make up, or is that against the rules?' Rick asked with a grin.

'Maybe rules are meant to be broken,' Lucy whispered tremulously.

Rick smiled and then gently his lips found hers. It was the sweetest kiss and she stretched her arms up and around his neck, welcoming his touch.

The kiss deepened and inflamed her senses. Nobody had ever turned her on like this with just a kiss.

She loved him so much...too much... The words thundered through her.

Hastily she pulled away. 'We should go inside.'

'Just what I was thinking.' Rick grinned.

'No, Rick, I meant we should circulate. You are supposed to be with your guests.'

'My guests can wait. Besides, half of them are watching a concert.'

Lucy smiled at him. 'And half of them aren't. And that was just a making-up kiss—my old rules still apply.'

'I thought you said rules were meant to be broken.'

'That was under duress. It was a moment of weakness.'

'You know, I think I've met my match with you,' he said with a grin.

'I know you have.' She reached out and took hold of his hand. 'Come on, let's go back inside.'

'Okay...but I want you back in my bed, Lucy. I'll only be patient for so long.'

Lucy smiled. It was taking every ounce of self-control to

keep him at bay. But she felt she needed to take things slowly.

Music was drifting out from one of the lounges and they followed the sound.

Karina was standing at the bar with a group of people, but as soon as she saw Rick she detached herself and came towards them.

'Before I forget, Rick. We must get together tomorrow to discuss a few details about your father's business. I'm going to fly back to London next month to visit his head office so we need to go over a few things.'

'Yes, we must do that,' Rick said easily. 'I think it will have to be later tomorrow evening, though. My schedule tomorrow is pretty full.'

'That's fine.'

A few people were taking to the dance floor as the band played a romantic ballad.

'Would you like to dance, Lucy?' Rick smiled over at her and she nodded.

Being in Rick's arms had to be the best feeling in the world, she thought dreamily as they danced close together on the crowded floor.

The light touch of his hand against her skin made her tremble inside with need, made her senses soar.

'Do you know what I'm thinking right now?' Rick whispered against her ear.

'End-of-year accounts?' Lucy smiled tremulously up at him.

He laughed. 'That is what I should be thinking of.' His arms tightened around her. 'But instead I'm thinking of all the things I'd like to do to you in bed.'

'You are a terrible tease, Mr Connors.' She smiled and leaned her head against his chest.

'I'm a man with an appetite, Ms Blake.'

The music finished abruptly and reluctantly Lucy broke away from him.

As they walked back to the bar they were engulfed in the crowds. And for the next hour or so they were pitched into conversation with different people.

After a while the buzz of conversation and the smell of alcohol suddenly seemed to make Lucy feel a bit queasy.

Rick glanced across at her. 'You look pale suddenly.'

'I'm fine, just a bit tired. I think I'll turn in.'

Rick nodded and reached to kiss her on the cheek.

Then he watched as she made her way out of the lounge, and it took all his self-control not to follow her. But he sensed if he didn't take this slowly he would lose her.

As Lucy lay in bed she could feel the ship moving gently up and down. It was a bit like being lulled to sleep on a hammock. She closed her eyes and thought back over the day.

There was a part of her that wished she had invited Rick back to her bed. But she was right to take this slowly, she told herself, trying very hard to be sensible. She agreed that it was time she learned to trust again. However she had already made one mistake in the past, thinking she knew Kris when really she hadn't. And if you didn't learn from the mistakes of the past there wasn't much hope for the future. No man would ever make a fool of her again.

It was strange how exhausted she felt, she thought, rolling over onto her side. And that feeling of sickness—that was strange too, but she supposed that could be down to the movement of the ship. She closed her eyes and fell into a deep sleep.

Lucy woke up several hours later. The room was still pitch black and through the window she could see the moon reflecting on the water. She felt incredibly thirsty. Sleepily she reached for her dressing gown and wandered through to the lounge to get a glass of water from the mini bar.

As she brought her drink back to bed she noticed that the door to Rick's cabin was ajar and the light was on in there. It swung open a little wider as the ship moved. And she had a clear view of Rick's bed. It was empty and still perfectly made.

Lucy frowned and glanced at her watch. It was two-thirty.

But then that was probably early on a ship. In all likelihood he was in the casino or talking with friends in the bar.

As she headed back to bed she suddenly felt a bit queasy again. The feeling was really quite odd. She had never suffered from travel sickness of any form in her life.

She finished the glass of water and lay down.

The next thing Lucy knew, sunlight was dazzling in through the window. She blinked and rubbed her eyes. A tropical island shimmered on the blue horizon. The hills were green and lush and palm trees fringed a white beach. It looked so beautiful that for a moment she just lay there drinking it in.

She felt okay this morning, so she must just have been overtired last night. Reaching for her dressing gown, she headed to have a shower.

It was as she walked towards the bathroom that the sickness struck again without warning. And this time it was so vicious that she had to run the last few steps, slamming the door behind her.

What on earth was wrong with her? As with yesterday morning, it took a while for the feeling to pass, but when it did she felt absolutely fine again.

She showered and changed into a pale blue dress that was summery and yet stylish. And after a few moments' attention on her hair and make-up, she looked almost radiant. She even felt hungry. So whatever it was that was wrong with her, it couldn't be serious.

When she stepped out into the lounge she was surprised to see the doors onto the balcony were open and Rick was sitting outside at a table laid for two, drinking a cup of coffee.

'Morning.' He stood up as soon as he saw her. 'How did you sleep?'

'Very well, thank you.' She smiled at him, feeling suddenly shy as she remembered some of their conversation last night, and the way he had held her on the dance floor.

She took the seat opposite and lifted up the menu on the table. 'What about you?'

'Well, eventually I slept...' She caught the gleam of amusement in his eye. 'I had a nightcap out on deck and it helped.'

'So what are the plans for today?' she asked briskly, thinking it was probably safer to focus on work, not on anything personal.

'Well, Grenada is beckoning. So at some point we should go ashore—'

'Yes, but don't forget you've got to give some interviews today to the journalists you've invited. They are scheduled for...' Lucy reached for her bag and got out her diary. 'Ah, yes, one-thirty. Then we're supposed to be meeting James Donaldson to discuss the Miami marketing plan...'

'What would I do without you, Lucy?' Rick grinned. 'You really are very efficient.'

'That's why you've brought me out here,' she said lightly, then glanced over at him with a frown. 'And are you being facetious?' she asked as an afterthought.

'No, Lucy.' He laughed. 'I was actually being serious. Although I have to say that your efficiency isn't the only reason I want you out here...' He murmured the words and she felt herself go hot all over in response.

Not wanting to give him the pleasure of seeing how easily he could embarrass her, she pretended to be deeply engrossed in the notes she had made at the back of her diary. 'Oh, and there's the presentation at twelve for the head of the sales team in Miami as well.'

He didn't answer her immediately and she flicked a curious glance across at him.

'Presentation at twelve.' He nodded seriously, but she could still see a hint of humour in his dark eyes.

He really could be quite infuriating, she thought. But he was also extremely attractive. She flicked another look across at him. He was dressed in a short-sleeved khaki shirt and lightweight trousers. She couldn't help noticing the strength of the muscles in his arms, the breadth of his shoulders.

Speedily she wrenched her gaze away from him as a steward arrived to ask if she'd like to order something for breakfast.

'Yes, please. I'll have the grapefruit, followed by cream cheese and smoked salmon bagels, and some orange juice, and can I have a glass of water? Thank you.'

She looked over to find Rick regarding her with some amusement. 'For a woman who said she doesn't eat breakfast, you're doing okay today.'

'Yes, it's pretty weird, actually.' She smiled, somewhat surprised herself. 'Especially as I felt a little bit seasick this morning.'

'Seasick!' Rick sounded amused.

'What's so funny about that?'

'Nothing.' He grinned at her. 'It's just that the sea is as calm as a millpond and apart from that there are enough stabilisers on this ship to make a force-ten storm feel tranquil.'

'Well, I must just be the sensitive type,' she said with a shrug.

'Yes, you must.'

'Anyway.' Lucy picked up her diary again and wished she hadn't told him that. She didn't want him to think she was weak; on the contrary, she wanted him to know that she was strong and capable. Firmly she concentrated on the day ahead. 'So, as I was saying, you have quite a busy schedule today.'

'Yes, I know.' Rick reached for the coffee pot. 'Would you like a cup?'

Lucy shook her head, her stomach protesting suddenly at the very thought of coffee.

'Oh, and I was also wondering if I should organise a leaving present for John Layton. We should mark the event in some way,' she said briskly.

'That is a good idea. But maybe we should do that back in London with the other staff. He's leaving the ship early tomorrow morning, because he and his wife are having a week's holiday on Antigua.'

Lucy nodded. 'Okay, I'll arrange it when I get home.'

The steward brought in the food she had ordered and there was silence for a while.

'So what should we do?' Rick asked as they were left alone again.

'I suppose we could get him a watch, although it's not very original.'

'Not about John Layton, about us,' Rick said quietly.

'Oh!' She looked across at him in surprise and as she met the darkness of his eyes her body seemed to pulse with adrenalin. How easy it would be to just say: yes, I want to come to Barbados; I want you to take me back to bed. It was what she wanted to say. But then the sensible side of her was saying: don't rush...be careful...

'I don't know, Rick,' she murmured. 'I need more time.'

'I thought a good night's sleep might have sufficed.'

Lucy shook her head. Then in an attempt to change the subject she glanced out over the sea towards the island. 'I take it that's Grenada?'

'Yes. If you close your eyes and take a deep breath you can smell the spices from here.'

Lucy did as he asked. She could smell the salt in the air but also a hint of warm spice. 'Nutmeg and cinnamon,' she guessed.

Rick watched her, watched the way the sun gleamed over

her hair highlighting the gold and bronze lights in it. She was incredibly beautiful.

'Lucy, I—'

'Oh, and before I forget,' she cut across him quickly. 'You have two meetings scheduled with someone called Brian Dawn. I came across some of the notes as I was flicking through those papers you gave me—'

'Lucy.' He cut across her firmly. 'Let's forget work for a moment, shall we?'

Lucy looked across and met his eyes. 'Let's not, Rick,' she answered with equal firmness. 'Today is Monday and as far as I'm concerned it's business as usual.'

Rick didn't look amused.

He liked business on his terms, she realised suddenly. He liked to dictate the pace. Well, he was going to have to just step back because, like it or not, she was going to dictate the pace with this.

There was a knock on the door and Karina walked in. She looked very attractive in a short skirt and clinging white top, almost as if she were off to play a game of tennis. 'Good morning.' She smiled at them both.

'Come and join us.' Rick pulled out a chair.

'Have you recovered yet?' Karina asked him and he grinned.

'Recovered from what?' Lucy asked.

'Oh, hasn't he told you?' Karina laughed. 'He was sitting out on deck with me last night, drinking.'

'Just one drink.' Rick smiled. 'And as I recall it was you who downed the rest of that champagne.'

'Yes, I have to admit, my head is pounding. I could do with some sunglasses, actually. You don't have a pair I could borrow, do you, Rick? I can't find mine.'

'I think I have a spare pair.' Lucy stood up. 'I'll go and have a look.'

When she returned Karina was leaning across the table smiling at Rick in an openly flirtatious way.

Lucy sat back down and handed her the glasses. 'Thank you, Lucy.' The woman smiled at her. 'Well, I'll run along…and I'll see you later, Rick.'

Then she was gone.

'I thought she was going to stay and have coffee,' Lucy said casually.

'She's booked on a trip around the island. I think it leaves at nine-thirty.'

Lucy nodded. 'Well I suppose I should get on myself,' she said briskly, not wanting to dwell on Karina Stockwell. Maybe the woman did still fancy Rick, but the relationship was finished and she was married, Lucy told herself firmly. 'I need to start going through those papers on your desk.'

Rick caught hold of her hand as she made to turn away. 'How about we have dinner together on Grenada tonight?' he asked softly. 'I know a nice little restaurant that is very secluded with wonderful views of the bay.'

Lucy hesitated and then smiled at him. 'Sounds wonderful.'

As the day wore on Lucy organised and sorted through a number of marketing plans. She chatted to the journalists and organised coffee and snacks to be served in the cabin whilst they were interviewing Rick. And then later she went up on deck to see how the entertainment on board was going.

A steel band was playing by the pool and a few people were lying on sunbeds, some sitting in the shade. There was a relaxed lazy atmosphere and the heat was intense.

'I think you've done enough for one day,' Rick said as he came through and saw her sitting in the shade for a moment. 'When I said I wanted you to help me with things, I didn't mean for you to work this hard. You haven't stopped all day.'

'I'm fine.'

'Take some time off,' Rick said firmly. 'Take a dip in the pool.'

Lucy looked over towards the water. It did look inviting. 'Maybe I will.'

He reached out and stroked a hand across her cheek. The gesture was so exquisitely tender that it made her heart turn over.

'Okay, I'll see you later.' He smiled at her and walked away.

Lucy leaned back against the sun lounger and closed her eyes. Love was such a strange emotion, she thought wryly. Such small gestures could bring such intense highs...

'Afternoon, Lucy.' She opened one eye and saw Karina standing over her.

'Hi, how's the hangover?' Lucy asked with a smile.

'It's much better. I've brought your sunglasses back for you.' Karina put them down beside her and then pulled out a chair at the table and beckoned to a passing waiter. 'Would you like a drink, Lucy?'

'Yes, okay, I'll have an orange juice.'

'Very virtuous.' Karina smiled. 'I'll have a vodka and tonic,' she told the waiter.

'Hair of the dog?' Lucy said with a smile.

'Something like that.'

'It's a pity your partner couldn't make this trip,' Lucy said casually, stretching her legs out into the sun. 'Is he working?'

'Yes. He's always working.' Karina shrugged.

Lucy frowned and wondered why she felt as if she had just stepped on a minefield. 'How did you enjoy the island tour?' she asked, changing the subject.'

'It was interesting,' Karina said with a nod.

The waiter brought their drinks.

Lucy searched around for some more light conversation, but nothing much presented itself.

'So what is Rick doing this afternoon?' Karina asked suddenly.

'He's got a meeting with James Donaldson.'

'Ah, yes.' Karina sipped her drink. 'You are very capable, Lucy,' she added wryly. 'Everyone says that about you.'

'Do they?' Lucy shrugged. 'Well, I enjoy my job.'

'Yes. Which makes you very much Rick's type. He loves intelligent, beautiful women who are an asset to his business.'

'Well, I'll take that as a compliment, Karina, thanks.'

Karina nodded and stood up. 'Just be very careful not to read too much into it,' she said softly. 'Because, believe me, getting serious about Rick is a big mistake. That's the moment when he cuts the ties.'

Lucy sat up and looked at the other woman. 'Thanks for the advice,' she said coolly. 'But I don't really need it.'

'No, of course not.' The other woman gave her a brittle smile. 'Well, I'll see you later.'

Lucy's blood was pounding through her veins as she leaned back against the chair again. How dared the woman say that to her? She had a real nerve... And what would she know about her relationship with Rick? Maybe he'd be different with her from how he'd been with Karina.

And maybe she was kidding herself. The words crept in, unwelcome, unwanted.

Lucy stood up. She didn't feel like a swim now. Instead she took her drink and returned to her cabin.

It was cool and pleasant inside. Lucy finished her drink and then wandered through and did some more paperwork at Rick's desk. Keeping her mind occupied helped. She didn't want to think about Karina's words; they were too upsetting, especially as she knew deep down that they were probably true.

Falling in love with Rick was doubtless a big mistake. A leopard didn't change his spots. And she could get badly hurt. But on the other hand maybe it would work out. If she didn't at least give it a go, wouldn't she always wonder what might have been?

The shrill ring of the phone coming from her cabin made her jump. Hurriedly she went to answer it. She half expected it to be Rick asking her why she wasn't lazing by the pool. Instead she was surprised and delighted to hear Mel's cheerful tones.

'Hi there, I thought I'd ring you from cold, rainy, miserable London and ask how things are.'

'Things are fine.' Lucy took the phone and sat down on her bed. 'It's so lovely to hear your voice.'

'Really? Things mustn't be *that* good, then. Listen, I won't stay on too long because this will cost me a fortune. But I just wanted to tell you a bit of gossip that's all over the office.'

'What's that?' Lucy asked curiously.

'Kris and his girlfriend have split.'

'Split!' Lucy was astounded. 'No, you've got that wrong. They're having a baby, Mel.'

'No, Sandra is having a baby…but it's not Kris's.'

For a moment Lucy was so dumbfounded she couldn't speak. 'Poor Kris,' she said eventually.

'Serves him right, you mean!' Mel spluttered.

Lucy shook her head. The strange thing was that she did feel sorry for Kris and, considering how angry and upset she had felt regarding that baby, her reaction surprised her. She wondered if it meant that finally she had left the past behind her and had moved on.

'Anyway, I had to tell you,' Mel continued cheerfully. 'Now I'd better go. Hope all is hot and steamy with you?'

'It is certainly hot.'

'Lucky thing, but hope it's steamy too. Just remember you are young, free and single—enjoy yourself!'

Lucy was still smiling as she put the phone down. Mel was such a breath of fresh air.

And she was right. Life was for living. She would take a chance on Rick, see where it led. She'd say yes to him tonight.

The door into the cabin opened and Rick walked in. 'Hello, I didn't expect to see you down here.'

'I thought I'd finish that paperwork, and then have a shower, ready for tonight.'

Rick's eyes moved to the telephone in her hand. 'Been phoning someone?'

Lucy shook her head. 'No.'

'Good.' He murmured the word in an absent fashion as he walked over towards his desk. 'You haven't seen that file that I earmarked for Miami, have you?'

'It's in the third drawer down.' She watched as he opened the drawer and found the document.

'Thanks.' He shot a glance over at her. 'What would I do without you?' he said with a grin. 'I'll see you later. I've got to get back; people are waiting for me.'

Lucy nodded.

When he left she walked back to the desk and tried to continue with her work.

What would I do without you? That was the second time today that Rick had joked like that.

But of course the truth was that he would do very well without her. Rick didn't need anyone.

She would just have to make herself even more indispensable, then, she thought firmly. And make him fall in love with her.

Her mind filled with Rick and their relationship, Lucy picked up her bag. She intended to fill a few dates in her diary from some lists Rick had left her. But as she flicked through the pages a red star caught her eye. She usually marked the first day of her period in her diary with a red star. The date was the fifth of January. There were no other red stars after it.

Lucy stared at the pages and then frantically started to count.

CHAPTER THIRTEEN

LUCY watched a moth fluttering around the candle on the table. It was tiny, but it keep determinedly fluttering and diving towards the flame.

It was a bit like her, Lucy thought. One moment full of bravado, the next almost giving up, then back for another try…

'Would you like a cognac with your coffee?' Rick asked her. She glanced across at him distractedly.

They were in an old-world restaurant up in the Grenada rainforest, and it was probably the most romantic place Lucy had ever visited. Its floors were uneven; the windows had no glass, just blue shutters opened wide to reveal a spectacular view down towards the bay of St George where their ship was moored. Now darkness had fallen and the lights below twinkled invitingly. The *Contessa* looked like a toy ship, its light reflecting like molten gold over the water.

But Lucy couldn't enjoy anything: not the surroundings, not the fabulous food, not even her handsome companion across the table from her. Because she was too busy trying not to think about what could be causing her bouts of illness.

'No, I'll just have coffee, thank you.' She smiled across at him.

Was she pregnant? With the thought her mind ricocheted back for the umpteenth time to that first night they had shared together in London.

She and Rick had taken precautions that night…so she couldn't be!

But there had been an accident. She hadn't thought anything about it at the time. It wasn't as if it had happened at an absolutely crucial moment...but then all it needed was one slip, one moment.

Lucy swallowed down a feeling of absolute disbelief. This was all in her imagination. Okay, her period was late...very late. But that could just be down to a glitch with her body clock.

'You've been very quiet tonight,' Rick said casually. 'And you haven't touched your wine.'

'I think the heat is getting to me.' She smiled over at him. 'But I shouldn't complain, should I? Not when it's raining and cold in London.'

'How do you know that it's raining and cold in London?'

Rick's eyes flicked over her and he noticed how the colour on her creamy skin heightened immediately.

'Isn't it always?' she said lightly. Lucy didn't want to start talking about Mel's phone call because that would only lead to talking about Kris. And frankly she was tired of that subject. She wasn't even going to phone him. Whatever he wanted, it would have to wait until she was back home.

The waitress brought their coffee and Lucy tried to relax back into the ambiance of the place.

'It's been a lovely evening, Rick. Thank you.'

Rick's gaze seemed very intense. 'I'm glad you enjoyed it.'

What should she say if he asked her for a decision? she wondered in panic. She could hardly say yes now.

Rick had made it very clear that he only wanted an affair with her. He wasn't a man who wanted to settle down and make a commitment, and wasn't a baby the biggest commitment of all?

She cleared her throat nervously. This was all hypothetical, because she didn't even know for certain if she was pregnant. But there was a way to find out, she thought suddenly. There was a doctor on board the ship. She had sat next to him last night at dinner.

'What time do we sail tonight?' she asked Rick.

'Nine-thirty.'

She pushed her coffee away from her slightly. The freshly ground smell, which she had once adored, seemed to be cloying and heavy, and she really didn't want it.

'Shall we go?' Rick asked her quietly and she nodded.

Rick put a hand up and the waitress brought the bill.

The drive in the taxi back down to the ship was made almost in silence. Rick put an arm around her and she allowed herself to lean her head against his shoulder. The breeze through the open windows was laced with cinnamon. She would always remember the Spice Island as the place where she thought she was pregnant. Lucy closed her eyes and allowed herself to dream that it was true and she was expecting a baby. A flutter of excitement stirred inside her. She imagined telling Rick…imagined that he was pleased. And a thrill of happiness swept through her.

But deep down she knew she was deluding herself. Rick wouldn't be pleased.

What was it Karina had said? *Getting serious about Rick is a big mistake. That's the moment when he cuts the ties.*

The taxi pulled up at the dockside and they got out. 'I almost forgot. I bought you something,' Rick said suddenly as they walked hand in hand towards the gangplank. He let go of her and reached into his pocket to bring out a small purple wristband.

'What is it?' she asked curiously.

'You wear it on your wrist and it's supposed to cure sea-sickness.'

Lucy laughed. 'I'll give it a try. Thank you.'

Rick took hold of her hand and gently he put it on for her. 'There.' The touch of his hands against her skin sent little darts of awareness racing through her. He looked into her eyes. 'I hope it helps. Because I don't want anything upsetting you, Lucy…' He reached out and traced a hand down over the side of her face.

Suddenly she wanted to cry. He was so sweet and so kind and she wanted more than anything to just go into his arms and tell him she was his…but she couldn't do that. She couldn't, because if she was pregnant, the relationship would be over.

Lucy pulled away from him. 'Better get back on board,' she said brightly.

'Yes.' He took hold of her hand again and they walked up towards the security check. 'We are in Antigua tomorrow. And as all the work is done we can relax and just enjoy ourselves. I'll take you to Nelson's Dockyard. It's worth a visit.'

Lucy tried to concentrate on what he was saying, but all she could think was that she needed to find out for certain one way or another if she was pregnant, and she needed to find out tonight.

'Shall we have a drink up on deck?' Rick asked her.

'Yes, good idea…but you go on ahead. I just want to change out of this dress.'

'What's wrong with your dress?' Rick asked in amusement, his eyes sweeping over the stylish black number. 'You look beautiful.'

'I just thought I'd put something else on.' She moved away from him towards the lifts. 'I won't be long. I'll see you up on deck.'

She knew the medical centre was at the back of the ship down on a lower floor. But it took her a while to find it and when she did it seemed to be deserted. Her heart plummeted. Lucy was just turning back when a nurse put her head out from an office door. 'Can I help you?'

'I hope so.' Lucy smiled at her. 'Can I come in?'

It was early morning and the ship was docking in Antigua. Lucy sat by the window in her cabin and looked out. Her bags were packed and on the dressing table there was a note for Rick. A note that apologised for leaving without telling him or saying goodbye, and thanking him for his offer of a job in Barbados—an offer she could not take. She hadn't given him any reasons.

Lucy bit down on her lip. She couldn't tell him that she was pregnant. It would be naïve in the extreme to think he would want the baby. And the thing was, *she* did. In fact she wanted this baby with all of her heart.

After the doctor had told her that the test was positive she had spent the whole night thinking about her situation.

If she decided to go ahead with the pregnancy she would not only lose Rick, but also her job in London. There was no way she could stay on there. Everyone would talk and the news would get back to Rick and he would do his sums and he would know that he was the father…

Knowing Rick, he would probably try and do the honourable thing by her, which in his case would mean money, not commitment or involvement.

She didn't want that. It was too painful. She'd rather be independent. And she was sure she would manage on her own. The thought of her baby was what spurred her on. She wanted a child so much that the momentous decision she had made at midnight to give up her job, sell her flat and move away to the country hadn't been that difficult. The money from her flat would be enough to pay for somewhere small and buy her some time to find another job.

But in the meantime her priority was to get away from here—from Rick—because if she saw him it would break her heart. Better to just leave a note and concentrate on practicalities, on things she could fix, not on things she couldn't have. She loved Rick so much that it hurt, but she had to be realistic.

From outside in the corridor she could hear the announcement that the ship had docked and the gangplanks were down for anyone who wanted to disembark.

There was a tap on the outer door that led direct from her cabin to the corridor. It would be the porter for her luggage.

CHAPTER FOURTEEN

LONDON was grey and cold and it seemed to match her mood. Lucy was exhausted both physically and emotionally.

Because she would have had to hang around the airport in Antigua for ten hours before she could get on a direct flight to London, Lucy had opted for a flight to Barbados that left immediately and had spare seats. This had then been linked immediately with a direct flight back to London. It had got her home quicker than waiting around in Antigua but she felt as if she had been travelling for ever, and although she was tired she hadn't been able to sleep on the plane. Her mind had been going over and over things.

What would Rick think when he got her note? Would he be angry? Or would he just shrug and forget about her?

The taxi pulled up outside her flat.

It was starting to rain now and the streets were misty and dark. She found her front-door key and stepped out of the car. The driver lifted her bag out of the boot and with a wave he drove away.

'What took you so long?'

The familiar voice made her whirl around.

It was a shock to see Rick stepping out from a car parked behind her. For a moment she thought she was imagining things, hallucinating. Maybe she wanted to see him so badly that her mind was playing tricks.

He walked closer towards her. It wasn't a dream—he really was here. Her heart lurched with joy and fear and a mixture of emotions so sharp and poignant she couldn't think straight. 'What are you doing here?' she whispered huskily.

'I was going to ask you the same question.'

He sounded cool and calm.

'Did you get my note?' Her voice wavered slightly.

It was raining harder now. Rick watched as it slanted over her, soaking her long hair. 'Let's discuss this inside, Lucy.' Calmly he reached out and picked up her suitcase for her.

Lucy hesitated. She supposed she had to let him in, and he did deserve some kind of explanation for her disappearance, but she didn't know what to say to him. She hadn't expected this. She felt unprepared, out of her depth...

Rick took her front-door key from her and with a grim look of determination he preceded her into the house.

Everything in her flat looked exactly the same and yet it felt different to her. She felt different, as if she had left as one person and arrived back as someone else. It was a weird feeling.

Rick took his jacket off and bent to light the fire. And suddenly it was as if nothing had changed, and she was transported back to that night after the speed dating when she had invited him in. The night she had slept with him...the night that had changed the whole course of her life.

She took off her coat and hung it behind the door. Her hands were trembling.

'So why did you run away?' Rick turned to face her.

'I didn't run away.' She raised her head in that determined way that Rick recognised so well, but he could see the shadows in her eyes.

'That's exactly what you did, Lucy,' he said softly. 'Was it because of Kris?'

'Kris?' She frowned.

'Come on, Lucy. I know he rang you when you were on board the ship in Grenada—'

'He didn't!'

'Yes, he did, and he told you his relationship was at an

end and that he wanted you back. That's the reason you were so quiet when we went out to dinner...the reason you retired to your cabin and told me you were tired. The reason you ran back here.'

'No!' Her voice broke slightly. 'You've got it all wrong!'

Rick shook his head. 'No, I haven't. You still love him, don't you?'

She shook her head.

'You're a fool if you go back to him, Lucy,' Rick continued firmly and he took another few steps closer. 'He'll hurt you again. You can't trust him.'

He looked down into her eyes and noticed how brightly they shimmered. 'Please don't go back to him, Lucy...'

The soft, husky words tore into her and she had to swallow down on a knot of tears in her throat. 'I'm not going to go back to him.'

Rick held her gaze steadily. 'So you'll come back to Barbados with me?' The question was put quite firmly.

She shook her head.

'Why not?'

She bit down on her lip. 'I just can't...' She whispered the words unsteadily.

'That's not good enough, Lucy. I want a reason.'

The silence stretched between them.

'I want you...' he said softly.

Her heart was thundering against her chest now. This was just too much for her to bear. She loved him so much, wanted him so much...

'It just wouldn't work out, Rick.' She forced herself to say the words, but a tear trickled down her face.

'Yes, it would. I'll make it work.' He said the words firmly. Then he reached and wiped her tears away with a gentle hand. 'Because I love you, Lucy. I love you with all my heart.'

Lucy looked up at him, astonished. She could hardly believe he had said those words to her. Her heart missed several beats.

'Don't say that, Rick.' She whispered the words unsteadily, and then she shook her head. 'You just want me to fill the space in your bed, but you don't really love me…'

'Yes, I want you to fill the space in my bed.' He said the words gently. 'But I also want you to fill the space in my life, because without you my life is empty. I love you more than I can tell you.'

Tears started to pour down her cheeks now.

'Please don't cry.' He wiped the tears away soothingly. 'I know you're scared of making a mistake, Lucy, and I know you still have feelings for Kris—'

'I *don't* have any feelings for Kris.' She said the words sternly but her voice was raw with tears. 'You've got it all wrong. I didn't speak to him on the phone. I haven't given him more than a passing thought in ages.'

'So why did you run away?'

'I just couldn't stay.'

'But we were getting on well together. I feel we belong together…can't you feel it?'

She shook her head helplessly.

'Lucy…' He tipped her face upwards and then he kissed her. It was such a tender, loving kiss that it took her breath away; it made her dizzy with need…it made her sway closer and kiss him back, pouring all her heart into that caress.

'There. Can't you feel how right this is?' Rick murmured the words huskily as he lifted his head. 'I knew it the first moment I kissed you…' He stroked her hair back from her face. 'The first moment I held you. And I've tried not to rush things, tried not to scare you away. I thought if I could just get you to Barbados and take things slowly from there, that one day you would start to trust me. That one day you might agree to become my wife.'

Lucy pulled back slightly from him. 'Now I know I'm

hallucinating.' She whispered the words in a dazed tone. 'Aren't you the man who is commitment phobic, the man who puts business first and wants no ties?'

'I used to be that man, before I met you.' Rick smiled at her. 'But I realise now that I was like that because I just hadn't met the right woman. I needed to be sure and there were always doubts with every other woman. It was easy to put business first and dedicate myself to my career. But now…' He stroked her hair back from her face and pulled her closer. 'Now I want so much more. I know without any doubt that you are the right woman, and I want you so much it hurts.'

Lucy smiled up at him tremulously. She felt as if this were some kind of a dream and she would wake at any moment and find that she was still on that plane circling over London. 'I think you might get more than you bargained for with me,' she murmured.

'Oh, I know that.' He smiled. 'That's one of the things I love about you.'

Lucy moved back from him. 'So, let me get this right…when you asked me to be your mistress you really wanted me as your wife?'

Rick nodded. 'I thought if I told you exactly what was in my heart you'd run a mile. But you seem to have run a few miles anyway.' His lips twisted wryly. 'So much for Plan A.'

'So this is Plan B, is it?' She smiled at him. 'Follow me back to London and put your cards on the table?'

He nodded. 'I'm not going to take no for an answer, Lucy. If you don't want to live in Barbados, then I'll just have to move to London.'

'You'd do that for me?'

'I'd do anything for you,' he said softly.

'Then maybe I'd better put my cards on the table as well.' Lucy took a deep breath. 'Rick, the reason I came home so abruptly was that I discovered I was pregnant. I'm going to have your baby.'

The words fell into a deep silence. She could see the shock on his face. He was totally dumbfounded.

'I know this changes things.' She said the words unsteadily. 'And don't worry, I don't expect anything from you,' she added hastily. 'Just because you say you love me doesn't mean I'm going to hold you to anything—'

'You're pregnant?' He was still staring at her blankly.

She nodded. 'I only found out yesterday.'

'And you weren't going to tell me?' His eyes narrowed on her.

'I didn't think you were serious about me.' Her voice sounded raw now. 'And I didn't want you to feel obligated in any way... I knew you weren't into commitment, so—'

'So you thought you'd just run away and not tell me.' He sounded angry now.

Lucy swallowed hard. 'It wasn't what I wanted to do. But I didn't think I had a choice...you never said anything about loving me...' Her eyes suddenly filled with tears.

'Oh, God, Lucy, don't cry.' He took hold of her and then led her over towards the sofa. 'Come on, sit down...you shouldn't be getting upset, not in your condition, and you shouldn't be in those wet clothes either.'

'Rick, stop fussing,' she murmured.

'Someone needs to fuss over you.' Rick headed into the bathroom and came back with a towel. 'You've just flown halfway around the world, you look exhausted and you need to take care of yourself.' He sat down beside her. 'I need to take care of you.' He amended the words firmly.

She glanced across at him sharply. 'No, you don't. I can manage on my own.'

Rick looked at her with a raised eyebrow. 'You are not on your own, Lucy,' he said softly. 'So you don't have to *manage*, as you put it. You do want this baby, don't you?' he asked suddenly.

She noticed how pale and tense he looked as he waited for her reply.

'Yes, of course I want it,' she said huskily.

He raked a hand through the darkness of his hair and the look of relief on his face was very evident. 'Thank heavens for that.'

She looked over at him hesitantly. 'So you don't mind that I'm pregnant?'

'Mind?' He shook his head. 'No, I don't mind. I'm just overwhelmed.'

'You don't have to stay with me just because I'm pregnant.' She put the towel down.

'Lucy, have you been listening to anything I've said?' he murmured quietly, his eyes holding steadily with hers. 'I love you.'

'I know what you said…' Her voice trembled. 'But a baby changes things.'

'Yes, a baby makes this even more special.' He pulled her around and reached to kiss her.

She kissed him back, her lips trembling beneath his.

'I love you so much, Lucy.' He put a hand on her stomach. 'And I'll love our baby very much. And I want to look after you and protect you and be with you for ever more.'

She started to cry again. 'Sorry, it must be my hormones or something.' She wiped the tears away. 'I love you too, Rick.'

'You do!' Rick sat back from her and looked into her eyes.

'Yes, of course I do. I've just been trying to fight it, that's all.'

'Really?' He sounded so amazed, so pleased that she laughed. He pulled her into his arms and held her tightly, then he kissed her again passionately, seductively. 'Tell me that again,' he demanded in a low growl next to her ear.

'I love you, Rick,' she told him steadily. 'I love you more than I've ever loved anyone before.' She glanced up at him. 'Even Kris,' she said firmly.

Rick watched her and smiled. 'And you trust me, then?'

She nodded.

'Enough to give marriage one last chance?'

She swallowed hard. 'Yes. Enough to give marriage one final chance.'

He looked at her adoringly. 'And this time it will be for ever,' he promised.

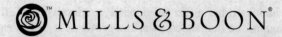